A CHÂTEAU FOR SALE

CARRIE PARKER

ACORN

TABLE OF CONTENTS

PROLOGUE

Spain. June, the year after next.

Dennis stretched out on the sun lounger and looked at his watch. Only ten in the morning and already the Spanish sun was high in the sky and he could feel the skin on his chest starting to tingle. He sat up, reaching for the sunscreen. It was maybe about time they thought about going back to Fromac for a couple of months. The Costa was wonderful most of the time, but summer could be a bit too much of a good thing. He'd have a word with Mother. But first he'd better check the newspapers. The new owners should be in the château by now and he wasn't sure it'd be a good thing to go back to the area if there was any chance of the police snooping around, however careful they'd been.

As if on cue, Maria came waddling across the terrace towards the pool, clutching an armful of newspapers.

"Here you are, Señor Dennis," she said, in heavily accented English. "Manuel has got you the French *Dépêches*, the *Sud Ouest* and the English small papers. All todays. Nothing in Spanish papers or on news. And Pedro has checked the Twitter and Facebook."

"Thanks, Maria. They're called 'red tops'."

Maria looked at him questioningly. Dennis laughed.

"Never mind," he said. "Is Mother up yet?"

"Señora is having breakfast," Maria replied. "She on top terrace."

"OK, I'll be up to join her. Another cuppa'd be nice too."

Maria nodded and made her way back towards the villa. Dennis watched her go. She and Manuel and their four sons had worked for his father and Uncle Jake for as long as he could remember. And now they worked for him. If anything was going on, they'd know about it before anyone else. And they were loyal to the family. Loyalty was important.

Dennis scanned the papers. Nothing. Good. He got up and strolled across the terrace where he stood looking down at the jumble of white villas below and the bright blue of the sea beyond. He smiled. Turning back towards the villa he paused for a moment, still smiling as he took in the fluted white columns of the massive structure under the red tiled roof. He could see Pedro, Maria's youngest son, adjusting the CCTV by the big iron gate. It was good to be prepared.

He made his way round the pool, up the wide flight of stairs and into the marble-floored lounge through the open French windows. Stopping to pick up his phone, he carried on across the hall and up the curving staircase. Out on the terrace he could see Mother sitting at the table under the large yellow parasol, pouring herself a cup of tea.

"Morning, Ma," Dennis bent to kiss her flabby cheek.

"Morning, Son. Anything to report? Sal was asking if we're going back to France for August. She fancies a trip down to Fromac."

"Perfect. Text her we'll be up there next week, if you're OK with that. It all seems pretty quiet."

"I hear the new people moved into St Geniès a couple of months ago. Apparently they're going to turn it into a hotel and restaurant."

"Yeah? Well, we'll have to go down there and see what it's like when they open, won't we? See if there's any sign of Frank, or those two women!"

Dora giggled and raised her tea cup. "Here's to Frank – he was useful, wasn't he, Den?"

"Too right, Ma. Too right!"

Kent, England. November, this year.

For sale: South West France

Superb château dating from the fifteenth and eighteenth centuries, located amidst beautiful countryside. Completely renovated. Kitchen with original massive stone fireplace, salon giving onto a huge terrace with magnificent views towards the lake. Ten bedrooms, all en suite. Coach house and several barns and outbuildings. Thirty hectares of gardens and woods. Euros 3.5 million.

Agence Sainte Croix, Cahors, France.

Joanne stared in disbelief at the photograph in the advertisement. There was no doubt about it. It was the Château de Saint Geniès-Lafontaine. It was her château! She reached for the phone.

"Alastair? This is Joanne. Can you come over? Yes, now. It's very important."

Alastair sighed and swung his feet down from the desk. What was the matter now, he wondered. He looked out of the study window. The last leaves of autumn clung forlornly to the branches of the apple and pear trees in the small orchard. Beyond it the kitchen garden lay sad, muddy and neglected. He really needed to spend time clearing it up. But since Kate had gone he hadn't had the heart to spend much time out there. He stood up now, involuntarily squaring his shoulders slightly and, crossing the brick floor of the old cottage, grabbed a jacket from the row of wooden pegs in the hall and closed the heavy front door behind him as he stepped out into the narrow lane.

He walked briskly in the cold, damp air. A tall man, in his early forties, sandy hair a bit thinner now than it used to be, with a few touches of grey at the temples. His thin face was gaunt and drawn, the deep blue eyes seeming out of place, as if still belonging to the happier man he used to be. A few minutes down the lane, he turned into the driveway that led to Joanne's house, glancing back at his own cottage, just visible through the trees. Despite their proximity, there could not have been a greater contrast between the two houses, nor between their occupants. Alastair's home had been a pair of farm labourers' cottages, tied to the estate. Joanne lived in the manor house and owned most of the land of the former estate. More than ten years earlier the last lord of the manor had died, leaving huge debts to an unfortunate heir who had no desire to spend his life in a decaying, medieval house in rural Kent. The estate had been put up for sale in lots when Alastair and Kate, then newly-weds, had been looking for their first home together. Like most things on the estate, the two tiny cottages had not been touched for years. They stood at the end of a narrow lane that rose quite steeply from the quiet road that led to the village. Twisting uphill through the beech woods, the lane emerged into open fields sloping gently away into the distance and petered out into a bridle path running along the edge of the cottage gardens. The only other house for miles was the manor, set back from the lane up its own long, gravelled drive. The cottages were just what they had been looking for. The original brick floors and open fireplaces were still there, both cottages had wooden, turning staircases to the first floor where the broad wooden floorboards sloped crazily. From the leaded dormer windows you could peep out under the tiled eaves and see across the weald of Kent, almost to the sea. The cottages came with a small orchard and two acres of meadow and gardens filled with herbs and old-fashioned roses, struggling against the weeds. There was no electricity, and no drains, the brick floors were so damp that moss was growing in the living room, the bathroom was a tap in the scullery. But they were entranced, out-bidding everyone else at the auction and the cottages were theirs.

Gradually, over the years, they knocked down walls, restored fireplaces and floors, installed modern comforts and decorated their dream home, acquiring furniture and artefacts from local junk shops, but keeping the cottages light and bright without the chintzy, cluttered look that Kate remembered only too well from her mother's house only a few miles away. Alastair worked hard as a surveyor, first with a local firm, then later in London, to earn them enough so that Kate could stay at home and work on the cottage and the garden. She had an empathy with nature and seemed to know instinctively what would grow well here and which vegetables would produce best there. Together Kate and Alastair created their country idyll, a haven of peace and happiness. That was, until their new neighbours arrived.

It was well over two years since Joanne and Nick Carslow had bought the manor house and a large part of the estate lands that surrounded it and Kate and Alastair's cottage. The house was a magnificent, timber-framed medieval hall house with an adjacent tithe barn, both of which Joanne and Nick had had restored by experts. The house sat in a clearing in the beech woods which in spring were carpeted with bluebells and wood anemones. A stream ran through the woods and Alastair had often glimpsed the bright turquoise-blue flash of a kingfisher as he walked through the woods with Kate. Today, however, the greyness of late November clung to the trees and there seemed to be no life in the woods as Alastair turned down the drive towards the manor.

It was mid-morning, but the house was lit up against the darkness of the dull day. Alastair climbed the shallow, worn, stone steps to the studded oak door and rang the bell. Mrs Fletcher opened the door immediately, duster in hand. She smiled at Alastair.

"Go through, m'dear. The missus is waiting for you."

She nodded in the direction of Joanne's study. She watched Alastair cross the hall, shaking her head slightly. Such a nice man, didn't deserve it. The tongues had nearly stopped wagging now in the village shop, but it had been the best scandal most of them had ever known. She wondered what was up now, but hesitated only briefly outside the study door, which stood ajar, before heading for the kitchen.

Alastair gave a cursory tap on the door.

"Hello, Jo."

"Alastair, Alastair! Have you seen this?" Joanne was waving a glossy magazine at him in agitation. "What on earth is going on now?"

She thrust the magazine into his hand.

"Look. See, there. At the top of the page."

Alastair took the magazine from her. It was open at the property section. His heart sank as he recognised the château in the advertisement immediately. The château for sale was the beautiful building in south west France that Joanne had bought and that Kate, Alastair's wife, was now living in.

"What is she up to? She can't sell it! It's not hers!"

Joanne was beside herself. Alastair stood stock-still. For several minutes, he couldn't think logically. His mind was in turmoil. Then suddenly it all became clear. He guessed what must have happened. The almost unthinkable! But what should he do? His thoughts raced. If he told Joanne the truth, Kate would be homeless and penniless, and he would have to admit the dark secrets that he'd kept for Kate's sake. If he didn't tell her, Joanne would be cheated out of hundreds of thousands of pounds – by Alastair's own wife. Alastair sighed. Cheated again. Of all of them, Joanne had been the innocent party.

Alastair was aware that Joanne was staring at him hard. His knees almost gave way beneath him and he sat down rather quickly on the leather sofa.

"Alastair?" Joanne said quietly. "What's the matter?"

Joanne had recovered her own composure now and called to Mrs Fletcher for coffee – strong and black. She walked over to the carved oak sideboard and poured a large measure of brandy from the crystal decanter. She handed the glass to Alastair and sat down opposite him.

"So there is more, isn't there?" she asked in a low voice. "And I'm still the one in the dark?"

Alastair gulped the brandy down. It burned his throat and he almost choked. He knew there was nothing for it. He had to tell Joanne the whole story. He should have done so from the start. He glanced around the cosy room. Everything was of the best quality. Real antique furniture, Persian carpets, original oil paintings on the walls. Joanne had it all, and all by her own efforts. He looked across at her and almost smiled as, once again, he registered the contrast with Kate. In her mid-thirties, Joanne owned a fitness and leisure empire, with a chain of health farms, leisure centres and gyms across Europe. She looked the part too, slim and fit with short, expertly-cut blonde hair framing a small, heart-shaped face. Not exactly beautiful, but very attractive, intelligent and sharp. A successful business woman with a reputation for fairness, but without a trace of sentiment. Alastair still hesitated. If he told the truth now, he laid his wife at Joanne's mercy. He knew Joanne could be ruthless. But if he didn't…….. It was too late anyway. Joanne knew now that he was keeping something from her. He knew he had to tell her.

Joanne had shifted her gaze from Alastair's ashen face to the fire burning in the inglenook. She didn't know how much more of this she could take. The last year had been a nightmare, a terrible series of events that had left her emotionally shattered and had made her cling to her work and her financial success as the only stable things left in her life. And now, just as she was coming to terms with the way things were, when she thought she knew the details of the whole unhappy story, now this. Alastair's reaction told her there was something that she still didn't know about. It was Alastair who had had to break the news to her the last time. What was he holding back on now? Joanne shivered despite the warmth from the fire.

The arrival of Mrs Fletcher with a tray of coffee broke the spell. Alastair visibly straightened and managed a smile as he took his cup. He had made his decision. He still loved Kate, he always would. But his loyalty had been tested so much that now he felt he owed it to Joanne to tell the truth. Loyalty. Again he almost smiled at the irony. Loyalty was what had started the whole chain of events last year. But after all she'd had to suffer, he couldn't let Joanne lose her château because of a secret that he shared with Kate.

Alastair took a deep breath. He glanced again at the magazine advert. The photograph showed the lake below the château. His blood ran cold again at the memory of what had happened there only a few months ago.

"Joanne," he began, and stopped.

He tried again. "Joanne, you're right. There is something I have to tell you. Something must have happened to make Kate do this and I think I know what. But there's something much more important that you should know. Something awful that I should have told you before. But I couldn't. Something that's haunted me since I came back from France in August."

Alastair looked into the fire. The look of complete anguish on his face shocked Joanne.

"You remember what happened – it's getting on for two years ago that it all started, you know."

Joanne nodded.

"I'm hardly likely to forget," she said with a hard little smile, reluctantly casting her mind back.

PART 1

The previous year

1

Kent, England. April.

The countryside of Kent is at its best in the late spring, thought Alastair. The narrow lanes were lined with the white froth of cow parsley, a few primroses still bloomed in the banks and the orchards were a sea of pink and white blossom. Kate's garden was crammed with colour, herbs and flowers growing in profusion up to the door of the picturesque cottage. The recreation of a romantic Victorian country cottage garden had been accomplished with skill, and a great deal of money, Alastair reflected ruefully as he pedalled down the lane towards his home. His wife Kate would be waiting for him, with the evening meal ready in the oven, flowers from the garden on the table, perhaps a bottle of elderflower wine chilling in the fridge. Kate herself would be wearing a long, floating skirt and probably a large, floppy-brimmed hat with pastel scarves tied around it. Her shoulder-length dark auburn hair would be loose, and she would be wearing the long, silver filigree earrings that he had bought her for her last birthday. Her pale skin would smell slightly of lemons, her hair of rosemary. She would have spent the day in the garden, or in their conservatory. She may have cycled to the village shop, and she may have walked along their lane to the neighbouring manor house to advise the new owners on the design of their garden. But she would not have gone to town, nor driven the car, nor bought a newspaper, or given a thought to the outside world. She wouldn't have been to the hairdresser, or to the gym, or to buy clothes. Her other-worldliness sometimes worried Alastair: what would happen if he were not there to shield her from the twenty-first century?

His cottage came into view, white-painted weatherboards gleaming in the early evening sun. As he cycled in through the gate, the two lilac-furred cats stretched lazily on the roof of the garage and jumped down, tails high and curled in greeting. He stooped to caress the solid little bodies, calling to Kate as he did so. There was no sign of her in the garden, nor in the kitchen, where there was no sign of his supper either. A crunching on the gravel outside announced not Kate's presence, but the arrival of Richard.

Alastair and Richard had been close friends for several years. They had met at university and, for some reason, they'd formed a strong bond. Maybe it was because others had shunned Richard that Alastair had made an effort to draw him out. Without doubt, Richard was not an ordinary character. His white-blond hair and pale eyes gave him a slightly unusual appearance, but the real problem was much deeper than that. As time went on and Richard began to trust Alastair, the full story of his problems came out. Damaged by growing up in a dysfunctional family where violence was normal had led to drug abuse from an early age. A spell in a young offenders' institution for attacking his stepfather had been the shock that he'd needed. Somehow he'd managed to turn his life around and made it to university, where he'd met Alastair. Alastair had somehow become part of Richard's therapy and gradually he got his anger under control. It had taken a long time for Richard to get used to Kate, but Alastair was pleased to see that now he seemed to be more relaxed in her presence. Kate, for her part, was wary of Richard but now even occasionally displayed affection for him. She had not objected when Alastair had suggested that Richard should help her maintain the large garden and orchard and had even suggested that he be given responsibility for creating a walled kitchen garden where now peach and fig trees produced their delicious fruit under Richard's tender care.

As Richard was unloading his tools from the back of his ancient pick-up truck, Kate appeared in the lane. Slightly flushed, turquoise-green eyes sparkling, she rushed up to Alastair, full of apologies.

"I'm so sorry, Alastair. I was at the manor and I quite forgot the time," she exclaimed. "You should see what they've done with the tithe barn. It's beautiful!" she rushed on. "They're restoring the whole thing, just as it was. They've got experts in for most of it, but Nick is carving the beams himself. We've been invited to dinner there next week."

Kate being excited at the prospect of a dinner invitation was rare, but Alastair was pleased that their new neighbours were taking such care with their splendid hall house and was happy at the prospect of Kate making friends with Nick and Joanne Carslow. It worried Alastair sometimes that Kate seemed to have no need of friends, although it did not seem to worry Kate. She had no one to confide in, with no sisters and both parents dead, and, Alastair reflected, she rarely confided in him. Although well known in the village, she did not seem interested in developing friendships. She was always polite and friendly, but somehow – what ? Distant? Reserved? Alastair thought guiltily of the rebuffs that Kate had given to some of their acquaintances. Perhaps, he thought, Joanne Carslow would turn out to be the friend that he felt Kate needed!

Kate hurried to the kitchen, humming to herself, to begin the preparations for the evening meal. It occurred fleetingly to Alastair that she must have spent most of the afternoon at the manor.

There was something different in Kate's behaviour that Richard sensed as he joined them for supper that evening. He felt uneasy with this new Kate and fearful for his friend Alastair. He thought that he understood Kate much better than her husband did, and in Richard's view, her animation and enthusiasm for the restoration of the manor was suspicious. He wondered what Nick Carslow was like.

****

The land surrounding the manor was still divided by thick hedges into small meadows, one of the few estates in England that still looked as it had when it was first described in the

Domesday Book. Nick took a final look across the gently sloping fields then made his way back to the house for breakfast. He had been lucky in life. Born into a wealthy, land-owning family, he'd breezed through university, getting the most out of Cambridge. Then a couple of years in a city bank before back to the family seat to oversee the estate. There he'd learnt a lot and was passionate about looking after his heritage. He took delight in describing himself as a 'gentleman farmer'. When he and Joanne had moved to Kent, he'd bought a few rare-breed sheep that he kept in the ancient meadows. Now he was turning his attention to the garden. He had been delighted when he had discovered that his neighbour had such a knowledge of plants. He also admitted to himself that she was very pretty in an ethereal sort of way and her gentle dreaminess made her much more relaxing company than Joanne.

In the old kitchen, he sat down at the big oak table and poured himself a cup of strong coffee. As he sat there, contentedly savouring the coffee, Joanne came in, dressed for her office. As usual, she looked great. He remembered when he'd first met her, just after his seventeenth birthday. She'd left school at sixteen and started her career teaching keep fit to overweight ladies in the village hall. He'd glanced in as he was passing one evening. The sight of Joanne's lycra-clad body bending and stretching was almost too much for him. Used to getting what he wanted, he'd followed her back to the council houses on the edge of the village. He'd been surprised when she'd laughed in his face and even more surprised when she'd thrown a bucket of water over him and told him to come back when he'd grown up. He smiled to himself, reflecting on his next meeting with her on the yacht in Cannes harbour, more than ten years later.

"And what is so amusing?"

Joanne sounded irritated. He knew how hard she worked, and how important her success was to her. But he also knew that her success was tainted by a huge disappointment. She desperately wanted to have her own children. It was an all too familiar story and she'd been insisting recently that he must take tests and more tests. He hadn't seemed to find the time but now at least he'd made an appointment with his doctor, so he thought she'd get off his case. They could have adopted a child, there seemed to be plenty of unwanted kids, except she wouldn't have it. It must be his fault, she was physically perfect: her business, her world were based on this premise.

"I am going to start on the walled garden. I was talking to Mrs Black yesterday. I thought I would go round and ask her for advice – hers is a picture."

Joanne snorted derisively.

"Well, enjoy your day. Don't drink too much dandelion tea. I expect I will be late back."

Nick heard the car door slam and the gravel crunch as she turned the Porsche into the lane and headed towards the station. He finished his coffee and, whistling quietly, set off down the lane towards Kate's cottage. As he approached the cottage, Nick saw the Blacks' gardener in the meadow. He called out a cheerful greeting, but the only response was a barely perceptible nod. Nick shrugged to himself. There was definitely something odd about the man.

As Nick entered the cottage garden, Richard straightened and watched as Kate came out of the house to meet him and the pair of them went back into the kitchen, her laughter reaching Richard's ears. The sun grew quite hot on his back as he bent to his work, and when he eventually looked at his watch, it was almost lunchtime. His sandwiches and flask of tea were in his pick-up, parked near the cottage. Passing the kitchen window, he glanced sideways into the room. He could see Kate and Nick, sitting together at the kitchen table, with a pile of papers and catalogues in front of them. Kate was bending over the table, drawing a sketch on the large sheet of paper spread out between them. Nick, however, was not looking at the sketch. He was gazing at Kate. Richard paused, an angry flush coming to his pallid face. In a flash, he saw Kate's impending, inevitable, infidelity to Alastair. He felt a surge of anger. He owed Alastair so much – his loyalty to Alastair was absolute. No one was going to hurt Alastair, least of all Kate. He must keep watch on her. And Nick. He had a good excuse to be around the cottage. It was the busiest time of the year in the garden. So he could keep an eye on both of them. He could follow them if necessary so that he could stop Kate before it was too late.

****

Inside the cottage, the sunlight fell in golden showers across the sweep of Kate's hair as she bent over the plan of the walled garden. She was sketching the outline of her ideas with a soft charcoal pencil that squeaked slightly in the silence of the room. She worked carefully, her cheeks still flushed from the emotions she had felt when, that morning, as he rose to leave, Nick had slipped his arm round her shoulders. As they had walked to the cottage door, she felt the warmth of his fingers slipping slowly down her back until, at the door, he released her and smiled into her eyes.

"Until tomorrow then, Mrs Black!"

She had closed the door, and leaned against it. Her knees felt weak, she wanted those warm fingers to caress her whole body. She felt elated, alive.

2

Kent, England. August.

It had been a beautiful, drowsy, August day. Kate sank onto the wooden seat beneath the canopy of white roses, still humming with bees and drifting clouds of perfume into the still air. The sun was slipping down towards the horizon, but was still warm on her skin, glowing pale-gold against her thin white shirt. The summer sun had lightened her thick hair, which she now pushed back off her face and twisted into a knot behind her head. She wore no make-up, her crystalline eyes reflecting the blue and green tones of her long, muslin skirt which she now hitched up over her thighs, stretching her legs to catch the last of the sun's rays. She lay back with eyes closed, her arms stretched out along the back of the seat.

Nick came quietly into the garden, looking for Kate. He stopped behind the seat as he caught sight of her, taking in every detail of her relaxed, voluptuous body. He stepped forward quickly and slid his hands over her shoulders, under the thin cotton of her shirt. Her head dropped back, her mouth seeking his, hungry for the touch of his lips and tongue.

****

Richard was almost at the end of the lane when he remembered that he had left his thermos flask in the small shed in Kate's garden where most of the gardening tools were kept. Today he had come to work on his bike and, cursing under his breath, he turned and rode back to the cottage. Leaving the cycle in the hedge, he walked down the side path towards the shed. He moved quietly, hoping he wouldn't meet Kate. Sometimes she seemed to want to talk and Richard didn't want to have to speak to her. He was still suspicious of her, ever since a few months ago he'd seen her in the kitchen with the new neighbour. He'd been keeping an eye out since then. She had been up at the manor a lot, but Richard knew there were a lot of workmen around. Nick had been round at the cottage a lot too, but Richard had always made sure he could see them, and they could see him. He was beginning to relax a bit, and Alastair certainly seemed as happy as ever.

Richard loped down the path. His flask was outside the shed where he had sat to eat his lunch in the shade. He picked it up and turned to head back to the lane. As he turned he heard a quiet ripple of laughter. Kate. He crouched, hoping she wouldn't see him. There must be someone with her. Richard peered cautiously through the rows of sweet peas in the direction of the sound. He saw Kate, sprawled on the garden seat. Behind her, bending over her, his lips on hers, was a tall, dark-haired man. Richard stood perfectly still. What a fool he'd been. They must have been meeting alone for weeks.

"No, no, Nick! Not here! Someone might see us," Kate whispered as Nick dropped to his knees in front of her and started to unbuckle his belt.

"Kate!" Nick cried in frustration, as she pulled her skirt down and sat up.

"Nick, Richard only left a few minutes ago. And Alastair could be back at any time – he took the car today."

"Look, Kate, I can't go on like this. I want you so much." Nick sat down on the seat beside her. He looked at her. "You're not changing your mind?"

"No, Nick, of course not."

Her eyes shone with desire.

"Can you doubt it?" she gasped.

"Let's meet tonight. Come to the barn!"

"Nick, I don't know if I can get away. But," Kate hesitated. "Alastair will be out late tomorrow. One of his friends is getting married soon and they are having an early stag night for him. He said he'd be on the last train."

"Perfect! Jo is going to Toulouse tomorrow evening. She's negotiating to open one of her fitness centres in France. Meet me by the barn on the other side of the wood. I'll come there straight from dropping her at the airport. Meet me at ten – it'll be dark by then. In the barn."

"Yes," Kate breathed. "I'll be there. Now we'd better go and pick the peaches you came over for."

Richard watched as they got up from the seat and strolled towards the kitchen garden. He stood perfectly still until they were out of sight. He had heard every word.

****

Kate lay in the geranium-scented water for a long time. She could feel a gentle breeze coming from the open window. The day was starting to cool down now as the sun finally slipped out of sight. She sat up in the bath and pulled the casement window shut. Gazing down into the garden, she tried to relax and control her mounting excitement. What had happened to her since she'd met Nick? She loved Alastair. He was the only man she had ever been with. As a teenager, she had never even had a boyfriend. Men had frightened her. She wasn't sure why, but she recoiled from contact with them. Then she had met Alastair. He was different. Gentle, seeming to understand her fears. They had married young and she had never looked at anyone else. She didn't have any other friends. Just Alastair. He had been all she needed. But when she met Nick, even the first time, she knew here was another special person for her. It was nearly five months since they'd met and that time had been magical for Kate. She had seen Nick most days, getting to know him, laughing with him, enjoying his interest in his house and his new garden. He had filled her days with something special, something extra, a missing ingredient that until now she hadn't known was missing. And gradually, inevitably, she had fallen in love with him. Not only that, but, to her surprise and consternation, she'd felt an overwhelmingly physical attraction. She longed to touch him, feel his skin brush hers, feel the warmth of his body near her. Then one day, they were standing close to each other, surveying the layout for his herb garden. It was early, a slightly chilly June morning. She was wearing a pair of old gardening trousers that were miles too big, and a thin lilac sweater. Her hair was pinned up neatly on top of her head, as usual when she was working in the garden. As he pointed out where the next wall would be built, Nick's arm rested gently on her shoulder. She shuddered involuntarily and turned quickly towards him, her lips parted slightly. What happened next Kate could not remember clearly. Only suddenly his lips were on hers, her hands were in his hair, pulling him towards her. She pressed her body along his, shamelessly, wanting him. His hands were at her waist, then up under her light sweater, caressing her back, moving upwards and around her body. Then the sound of a truck climbing laboriously up the lane had made them both freeze.

"Oh God," Nick had gasped, swiftly dropping his hands. "The builders! I'd forgotten they were coming back today."

Kate had pulled away hastily, smoothing her sweater and backing away from him. As Mrs Fletcher, the Carslows' housekeeper, came into the garden to announce the builders' arrival, Kate bent quickly over one of the borders, pulling at weeds. But not quickly enough before Mrs Fletcher's eyes had passed over her entire body, taking in her dishevelled hair and flushed face, catching her guilty expression.

Since that morning they had grasped every moment they could to be alone together. It was not easy, with all the work that was being done at the manor, and Richard working most days at the cottage. They were careful, too, when Mrs Fletcher was around. Over the next couple of months they spent most of each week in each other's company, happy working together on the garden, but frustrated by the need to be on guard, unable to fulfil their desire for each other. She could feel Nick's frustration building and sensed that if things went on like this much longer, they would take too much of a risk.

Already they had come close to being caught together. Last week they had gone down to the hay meadow to dig out some wildflower bulbs for Nick's garden. He had pulled her to the ground, under a thick hawthorn bush, heavy with blossom. They were only a few metres from the orchard where Richard was working. Taken by surprise, Kate gave an involuntary cry as Nick tumbled down on top of her. Her cry carried on the still air. Richard heard her and called back.

"Kate, is that you? Are you OK?"

"Yes, fine!" she managed to call. "I just grabbed a nettle by mistake."

Nick had laid back on the ground, cursing.

"Kate," he whispered. "This cannot go on. I can't take it. I want you now."

They had agreed to meet after dark, as soon as they could arrange it. The next day, Nick had come up to her in the garden just after Richard had left. They'd agreed. And tonight was the night.

****

Kate climbed out of the bath and slowly dried herself in front of the mirror. She didn't want to think about Alastair. It was all so odd. She did love him, but she did not feel guilty about Nick. She had sex with Alastair and it was good. Alastair was a considerate lover. But nothing came close to the excitement she felt for Nick. She sighed. Alastair would be devastated if he found out. She didn't ever want him to know. She just wanted both of them. She didn't want to have to choose.

She brushed her hair and let it hang loosely down across her shoulders. She thought for a moment then put on a close-fitting dress of thin black jersey and looked at her reflection in the big, ornate mirror on the bedroom wall. She was of medium height, with a well-proportioned figure. The dress pulled tight across her full breasts and buttocks, outlining her body. She ran her hands down her sides. Yes, Nick would like this. She hoped it would be light enough for him to see her. She hadn't worn the dress for a long time, feeling it was too tight and too short, and the scooped neckline was too low. It wasn't really her at all. Far too sexy. But perfect for tonight! She checked the time. Nearly a quarter to ten. It was still just light enough outside to see the lane. It would take her about five minutes to get to the barn. She decided to set off. She wanted to be there when Nick arrived. Alastair would be back by eleven thirty and she had to be home, showered and in bed before then. But she wanted to spend every minute possible with Nick. So she went downstairs, slipped the latch on the cottage door and set off quietly down the lane. She walked past the end of the drive to the manor, glancing towards it, seeing its dark bulk at the end of the drive, the white plaster infills between the old oak beams glowing slightly in the twilight. A few hundred metres further on she turned off the lane along a narrow path through the dense beech wood. It was darker along the path, but she knew the way and the moon would be rising soon. Ahead she could just make out the shape of the barn, on the edge of the wood. She went up the two uneven stone steps to the barn door, lifted the heavy wooden latch and slipped inside.

Inside the barn it was dark and it took Kate a few minutes to adjust her eyes. She could make out the hay loft up above, and underneath it bales of hay were stacked on one side. New straw had been laid on the floor in front of the bales. Kate smiled to herself. Nick had already been here. She sat down on the straw to wait. It was hot and stuffy in the barn. Glancing around, suddenly she felt a strange foreboding. Her palms began to sweat and she felt sick at the thought of betraying Alastair. She needed air, she must get out of here. She should go home now, before Nick arrived. Just as she started to stumble towards the door, she heard the sound of a car. She recognised the throaty purr of Nick's TVR, then the sound of a car door slamming. It would only take a few minutes for him to walk here from the manor. Kate sat down again, her heart pounding now in anticipation, her desire for Nick overwhelming her anxiety and feelings of guilt.

She thought she heard footsteps, and then a scrabbling noise that could have been mice or rats, then a slight thud. Kate could feel the perspiration on her face trickling down her neck into the folds of her dress as she lay back against the hay bales, waiting. What was going on? She sat up, listening. She was sure that someone was out there, but if it was Nick, why hadn't he come into the barn? Had he changed his mind? And if it wasn't Nick, who was it? Suddenly another noise outside startled her. She scrambled to her feet and listened again. It was quiet now. She crept to the door and opened it slightly.

"Nick," she whispered. "Are you there?"

There was no answer.

Kate hesitated in the doorway, peering out into the gloom. It was now quite dark, the moon low and just visible through the trees.

"Nick," she whispered again.

A low groan made her start. Looking round in panic she saw a figure, lying on the ground near the barn door.

"Nick! Oh, Nick, what's happened?"

Kate dropped to her knees beside him, her heart hammering against her ribs. Nick was struggling to sit up.

"My head," he gasped. "Whatever happened?"

Kate tried to help him to his feet, but Nick swayed and collapsed again onto the ground.

"I must have slipped – hit my head on the step, I suppose."

"Do you think you can get up?" Kate asked.

She glanced down at her watch, but it was too dark to see the time. She must be home before Alastair got back, but she couldn't leave Nick. After a few minutes, Nick managed to stand and Kate helped him back down the path. They made their way slowly along the lane towards the manor, not speaking. Kate struggled to support his weight as he seemed to sag just as they turned the corner of the drive.

"Come on, Nick. We're nearly there. You can make it. You've got to!"

Kate's voice cracked with anxiety as she strained to catch any sound of an approaching car or the flicker of headlights. At length they reached the house and stumbled up the steps. Kate pushed the door open and dragged Nick inside. He staggered into the kitchen and slumped into a chair. Kate gasped as she saw him clearly in the bright lights of the kitchen. His face was ashen and there was a long open gash at the back of his head.

"My God!"

Kate felt faint seeing the depth of the gaping wound and the blood on the collar of Nick's shirt. Panic seized her again.

"You need a doctor! I must clean this up. Where's the first aid kit? Have you had a tetanus injection – there looks to be soil in the cut!"

Kate looked round the kitchen wildly. Nick caught her hand.

"Kate. I'll be fine. You have to go now."

"I can't leave you like this," she protested.

"Kate," he cut her off. "Go. This is only a cut. I must have fallen really heavily and caught my head right on the edge of the step. It'll be a thousand times worse if you're not back before Alastair gets home – or if he sees you coming out of here…"

He paused and smiled weakly.

"…in that dress!"

****

"Ouch!" Nick winced as the nurse dabbed disinfectant onto the back of his head.

"Yes, it's a nasty cut. You'll need a couple of stitches. How long were you out?" Dr Grey turned to the nurse. "Get things ready for me, would you, please? I'll stitch it up now."

"I don't really know," said Nick thoughtfully. "Is it important?"

"Probably not. Any double vision? I'll have some X-rays done just to be sure. You certainly gave it a rare old bang. Were you running when you slipped?"

Well, he had certainly been in a hurry. Nick remembered walking quickly up the path to the barn where he knew Kate would be waiting. But he couldn't remember anything else until coming round with her bending anxiously over him.

****

By the time he got home, his head felt much better. The telephone was ringing as he came into the hall. It was Joanne.

"Nick! Why weren't you answering your mobile? I want you to come over here. Today. I've found just the place!"

"What on earth are you on about?"

"You never listen to me, do you? The last thing I said when you dropped me off at the airport yesterday was that I was going to look at the château today. And I have and it's beautiful. I'm having the preliminary contract drawn up tomorrow, but I need you here to sign it."

Of course. Nick remembered now. She was in France. They'd taken their last few holidays there, scouring estate agents' files for Joanne's perfect château. Since childhood she had dreamed of owning her own castle and now, a rich woman, a château in France was easily within her reach. This trip had been planned to include looking at a particular property whilst clinching her deal to open a new branch of her business in France. Usually with Joanne, business came first and Nick hadn't expected to hear from her until the weekend.

"That's great, Jo. But why do you want me over there?"

"God, Nick! What's the matter with you? We've been through all this. You know it's the tax thing. On paper you have to buy the château."

"Oh yes, I forgot. Actually, I really have had a bump on the head. I slipped on the barn steps yesterday."

"Well, never mind that. If you phone now you should be able to get on the early Air France flight in the morning. I'll meet you at Toulouse."

"OK. I'll see you then."

Nick put the phone down. Damn. He had to see Kate. She would be worrying about him, and anyway, last night hadn't turned out exactly as he'd planned. Alastair should be at work by now, he reckoned. It was a hot day so perhaps Richard would have stopped work until the evening and gone home. So Kate ought to be alone at the cottage.

He stopped briefly to take his painkillers, then, perching a straw hat gingerly on his head, he strolled off down the lane. As he walked, he thought about Joanne and Kate. How long could it go on? He hoped a long time. He loved women and was no stranger to the odd affair. But he loved his wife the most. And Joanne needed him, for all her self-confidence and success. He knew how much she loved him and how much of a stabilising force he was in her life. And she was such fun. And so rich. He smiled involuntarily. Never a dull moment with Joanne. He couldn't help feeling excited about the château. If Jo said it was beautiful, then it would be.

As he neared the cottage, he saw Alastair's car standing outside. Perhaps he'd gone to the station on his bicycle. Nick thought of Kate and her quietly smouldering sensuousness and instantly felt his passion rising. God, he hoped she'd be alone.

"Hello, Nick."

A deep voice made him jump. He was now level with the car outside the cottage and had been so immersed in his fantasies that he had failed to notice Alastair coming out of the front door and walking towards the car carrying a holdall.

"Oh, hello. Lovely day, isn't it? I was just coming to see if Richard was around," Nick lied. "I wanted his advice on my fig trees."

"He's gone home. It's too hot to do much this afternoon. But Kate's in. She might be able to help. I'm afraid I've got to dash. We're having a bit of a problem with a survey one of the partners did in Cornwall and I've got to go down there to try and sort things out. Can you believe it, in the middle of August! I expect there will be traffic jams all the way. Come in anyway. I'll call Kate. She's just packing a few things."

"Oh, is she going too? Be a nice break for her," Nick smiled.

Damn again, he thought. It just wasn't his week. He took his hat off and wiped his forehead. He wasn't feeling all that brilliant after all.

"No," Alastair grinned. "It's just that I'm hopeless at packing. And I'm only going for tonight – back tomorrow. It's not worth Kate sitting in a traffic jam as well. God, Nick! What on earth have you done to your head?"

"Oh, it's nothing. I somehow managed to slip and cracked my head on the barn steps." Nick winced a little as he touched the dressing. "Hurts like hell. Dr Grey said I was lucky not to have concussion. Not sure how long I was out for."

"Surely it couldn't have been long!" Kate had appeared in the doorway. "I mean, surely you would have had concussion if it had been," she added quickly. "Here Alastair, your bag. Time for some tea before you go? Nick?"

"No, thanks, darling." Alastair kissed her lightly on the top of her head. "I'd better be off. I'll call you when I get there. Should be back by tea time tomorrow. Bye, Nick. Don't go falling over again!"

"Better not," Nick replied. "I've been summoned to France. Jo's found her dream château and I've got to go over to sign the papers. So you'll be back before me."

"Wow, that's great. Does she need a survey? I could recommend an excellent chap!" Alastair laughed.

"Yes, I'm sure she does, but if this château is the one she's really got to have, she'll buy it even if it's falling down and got every sort of rot you can imagine!"

"Well, have a good trip anyway."

"Thanks, and you. 'Bye, Alastair."

"'Bye." Kate kissed him quickly. "See you tomorrow."

They waved as Alastair drove off down the lane.

"Come round into the garden," Kate said. "I'll bring some tea."

Nick went down the path and sat on the wooden seat under the arbour of roses, now almost over but still retaining a slight memory of their heady perfume. Kate emerged from the kitchen door a few minutes later, carrying a tea tray. Nick noticed that she had untied her hair and was wearing a pink cotton dress with a low neck and a row of small white buttons down the front.

"You look lovely," he said.

She smiled.

"How are you? I was worried."

"So was I! But don't be. I'm fine. I'm sorry about last night. But," Nick leant forward and cupped her face in his hands. "I'll make it up to you. Tonight."

"What?" Kate's eyes were wide. "I thought you were going to France."

"That's right. But not until tomorrow morning."

He took the tea tray from her and put in on the ground. Then he lifted her in his arms and carried her back into the house.

****

As light started to appear through a crack in the curtains, Kate lay back on the pillows, dreamily reliving the last few hours. Nick had carried her straight upstairs and slowly undressed her, kissing every fraction of her skin as he undid the long row of buttons down the front of her dress.

Later she'd prepared a simple meal. Both of them were hungry and, as they drank chilled champagne, sitting close together on the wooden settle outside the kitchen door, looking at the sky as the stars started to appear, Kate felt a euphoric happiness she had never felt before.

They had gone upstairs soon after and made love again before drifting off to sleep. Just before dawn Nick had woken her again, nuzzling and stroking her tenderly. Now the sun was rising quickly. Nick sat up.

"I'm going to have to go," he said. "The plane leaves in three hours."

"I know," Kate sighed. "Nick, you were wonderful. I love you so much."

"I hope this makes up for yesterday," Nick grinned ruefully.

"Oh yes," breathed Kate.

****

Richard sat on the edge of the bed, his head in his hands. He wasn't sure what day it was. He hadn't been to work since the day when he'd heard Kate and Nick planning their tryst at the barn. All he'd meant to do was warn Nick off. He couldn't remember exactly what had happened. But he knew he'd been so enraged at Kate's betrayal of his best friend that all he could think of was stopping her and Nick. He'd gone to the barn to stop them. He knew he'd hit Nick. Hard. Perhaps he'd killed him. He hadn't dared to watch the news and he hadn't dared to go outside in case the police were looking for him.

3

Toulouse, France. August, the next day.

The first passengers were starting to come into the baggage reclaim area. Joanne stood near to the clear glass screen, scanning the faces for Nick. Groups of babbling French school children darted around as the carousel started to move and a jumble of suitcases, holdalls and packages appeared, amongst which Joanne spotted Nick's dark green leather bag. A few minutes later, she recognised the tall, dark, tanned man sauntering into the hall from Immigration, chatting to a very English-looking middle-aged couple. He was wearing a turquoise blue, short-sleeved cotton shirt, sunglasses hooked over the breast pocket, and stone coloured trousers. A cream Armani jacket was slung over his shoulder. Joanne smiled involuntarily. He suited the summer. He returned her wave and the English couple both smiled and looked in her direction. She could imagine he'd have told them her life story by now. She watched him grab his bag and, with much hand-shaking and smiling, detach himself from his new friends and head for the exit. He passed straight through Customs, calling a greeting to the surly officials. Joanne smiled again and shook her head as they returned his greeting. That never happened to her, although she spoke good French and Nick's was awful, if fluent. It was just that his charm seemed to work on everyone.

"Hello there! You look great."

Nick put his arm round her shoulders and kissed her on both cheeks.

"Oh, come on, Nick. Hurry up. It's going to take us nearly two hours to get there and I want you to see it before we go to the notaire's to sign the contract."

Nick followed in her wake as Joanne headed out of the terminal and into the car park. Several heads turned and Nick unconsciously quickened his pace and placed a proprietorial hand on Joanne's back. He knew, although he didn't always like to admit it to himself, that he enjoyed being seen with Joanne. He knew they made a very glamourous and handsome couple.

Once outside in the baking heat of the car park, Joanne swiftly located a silver rented car and within minutes they were out of Toulouse and heading north. Joanne drove fast and soon they were leaving the autoroute and crossing a wide, arched bridge over the river Tarn. The road climbed, then dropped down into the next valley, following a small river through quiet hamlets of white stone houses. Orchards gave way to fields of sunflowers as the road wound along the valley, passing ancient hill-top villages until finally they approached a hill topped by an almost intact keep, the village nestling around its feet. Here Joanne turned abruptly off the main road, heading into the village. They skirted a boules pitch shaded by huge, gnarled chestnut trees, then the road widened into the village square. It was mid-afternoon by now and the square was almost deserted. A couple of tables in the two cafés that faced each other across the square were occupied by tourists enjoying a lengthy lunch. Joanne slowed the car slightly.

"This is Fromac. The notaire's office is up that little street. And the estate agent's is over there. We have to be back here at five. We'd better get a move on."

They were off again, raising the dust as she drove fast down the narrow street on the opposite side of the square, past a church, straight over a crossroads and up, climbing again until they reached the plateau. Here there was rough grass and bright blue chicory growing in the chalky soil. The plateau was criss-crossed by tracks, some leading to isolated farmhouses, some just disappearing into the distance.

"What a view!" Nick exclaimed, taken by surprise.

"Yes, you can see where the river is, down there. And that's Cahors, that town you can just see. We haven't far to go now."

They dropped down the side of another valley, passing a few vineyards, the vines already heavy with dark bunches of grapes. Another hill, another plateau, then another valley and the road finished at a T-junction. Nick could see a village to the left, but Joanne swung the car right. Just ahead was a small sign: *Château de St Geniès-Lafontaine.* Joanne turned sharply to the left off the metalled road, following the sign onto a track. They passed a couple of newish bungalows, small, square, ugly blocks, each with its white plastic table and chairs and striped parasol. The unmade road had forced Joanne to slow the car and Nick glanced at her as she drove. Her eyes were sparkling now and he could sense her rising excitement. The track had got narrower and as Nick looked back, he could no longer see the road they had turned off, nor the houses they had passed. On either side were scrubby meadows, scattered with small juniper bushes, sloes and a few tiny Mediterranean oaks. Then dry stone walls and thicker woods. Ahead were more trees. The track started to descend through the woodland. Nick looked from side to side. The track had been cut into the hillside. To the left the forest was thick, and quite dark, dropping away steeply. He could see patches of dappled sunlight here and there, but the trees seemed to go on for ever. On the other side, they were close to the rocky bank, down which a few small streams trickled. Ferns were sprouting out from crevices in the rock and at the edge of the track in a clear pool, Nick spotted watercress growing vigorously.

A few minutes later they rounded a bend, and there was the château, lying below them, glimpses of gleaming white stone visible through the trees. They carried on, approaching a stone archway over the track, with a large square building to the left. Joanne drove up to the arch and stopped the car. They got out in silence. Nick looked around, puzzled. The building was made of lovely large stone blocks, but looked more like a barn than a château. This didn't look up to much, he thought, surprising himself by how disappointed he felt.

"Come this way," Joanne said, taking his hand and pulling him under the archway and further down the track.

Nick stopped, speechless. The square building they had seen first was obviously a coach house or something. In front of him now was a magnificent view across a beautiful valley. Immediately on his left, the château rose up above him. Dazzling white stone topped with shimmering turrets. Long, shuttered windows facing across the valley, and huge, wooden double doors at the top of a short flight of semi-circular stone steps.

"And that's not all," Joanne said. "What is really amazing about this place is it's got two fronts – sort of."

She led him along the gravel in front of the château, but instead of going up the stone steps to the door and inside, they went through a wrought iron gate in a wall at the corner of the building. Now Nick was speechless again. The side of the château was built into the rock of the hillside and the land fell away steeply from the terrace, sloping down to the valley bottom where there was a small lake, surrounded on one side by willows and open to the valley on the other. In front of them, the balustraded terrace ran the length of the building, flanked at either end by twin towers, their round turrets clad in silvery grey tiles.

"I think it was this terrace that sold it to me." Joanne gazed down towards the lake.

"The view from it is superb, and it faces south so it gets the sun most of the day. But this isn't all. You're going to love the barns and the coach house, and the pig sties! Come on, we haven't much time."

They walked back around the château, back to the archway where Joanne had parked the car. A cobbled passage led into a courtyard flanked by a row of low stone buildings on one side and the wall of the château on the other. Joanne produced a large iron key which she turned in the lock of a tall wooden door whose blood-red paint was peeling and blistered. They went inside in silence, crossing the worn stone doorstep, in from the heat of the August afternoon to the coolness of the centuries-old building. It took a few seconds for Nick to adjust to the dim light after the sunlight outside. They were standing in the kitchen of the château. The room ran the full width of the building. At one end, the entire wall was a gigantic fireplace with a carved stone mantel and a huge iron grate. The floor was old terra cotta tiles, worn and polished with the passage of feet through the ages. The ceiling was vaulted, unplastered stone. On one side of the room, double doors opened onto an inner courtyard, partly bathed in sunlight, with a beautiful vine growing out of the stone floor and running along three sides of the courtyard. At the opposite end of the room, another door led into a huge salon with tall windows along its length, facing the terrace.

Joanne led the way though the French windows out onto the terrace. Nick followed and leaned against the low balustrade. Looking down he could see the château had been built directly onto and into the rock. Dropping away from the balustrade, the rock face was sheer but, towards the bottom, clumps of pink valerian sprouted from narrow fissures in the rock. A thin carpet of sun-scorched grass stretched away from the base of the rock on which the château sat to another low stone balustrade, beyond which lay meadows dotted with a few orange poppies lingering on from the early summer. A broad grassy walk lined with poplars led to the lake, shimmering like a mirage. The silence of the sultry afternoon was broken briefly by the distant sound of a car chugging uphill, somewhere out of sight. Small lizards basked in the sun, clinging to the wall effortlessly, undisturbed by their visitors. Nick breathed a deep sigh. Paradise!

He heard Joanne's light step behind him.

"So what do you think?" she asked breathlessly.

He could tell she was captivated by the beauty of the château and the serenity and peace of the place. Her usual business-like manner had disappeared as she stood close to him and put her arm quietly round his waist, leaning her head against his shoulder.

"Jo, I think it's wonderful."

He turned and kissed the top of her head. She looked up into his eyes and smiled, sliding her arms round his neck.

"I'm really glad you like it."

He smiled back and kissed her gently on the lips.

Back in the car as they drove towards Fromac, Joanne was chattering non-stop.

"Of course there's loads of work to be done. The walls all need repointing and some of the tiles have gone. The whole place needs rewiring and we'll have to do something about heating – it can get quite cold here in winter. And the coach house and the big barn are both in a really bad state, probably need rebuilding. And the wine cellars are a bit dangerous. Then there's everything to do inside. There's hardly any plumbing and nothing's been done to the bedrooms. The floors are all OK though. And then there's …"

Nick let her carry on, half-listening, sharing her elation. He loved the heat and sun and was delighted by the beauty of the setting of the château as well as the magnificent old building. He lay back in his seat, eyes half-closed, dreaming of the sun-filled days and balmy nights he could spend here. It would be wonderful here with Jo. But she was so busy. He'd need to have a bit of additional company. Already he was planning extra pleasures. He'd find a way to bring Kate out here. A weekend or two when Jo was away working would be fun! His head didn't seem to ache at all anymore.

4

Kent, England. October.

Kate sat by the kitchen window staring out at the russet colours of autumn now tingeing the whole garden and turning the orchard ablaze. She could see the clusters of apples and pears still unpicked on the trees. This was usually her favourite time of year, when all the months of hard work were rewarded by the harvest. She would be out picking damsons from the trees in the lane, making jam and wine, freezing blackberries for winter pies, making soups and chutneys from the vegetable garden. But this year was different. At first she hadn't been worried. She had thought the waves of nausea she had felt on a few mornings must be a stomach upset and her periods had always been very irregular. But there was no doubt about the bright blue band in the little white plastic container. She was pregnant. And worse still, she was sure that the father wasn't Alastair. Kate felt cold all over. At her age, how could she have been so careless! In the early part of their marriage, both Kate and Alastair had wanted children. But as the years went by, pregnancy eluded Kate and she began to feel almost frightened at the prospect of being responsible for another life. So she and Alastair agreed perhaps parenthood was not for them, although she was sure that secretly Alastair was disappointed. So Alastair had always been very careful, whereas with Nick........Kate knew in her heart that the child she was carrying must be Nick's. She tried to clear her mind. She must look at all the options and then decide what to do. Easy to say, but what a hard decision. One thing was for certain. Kate would have the baby. Whatever choices she had to make, getting rid of the child was not an option for her. Here was a life, created by her and therefore her responsibility.

Kate got up and pulled on her jacket, going out through the front door into the lane. She set off down the bridle path. She didn't want to go down the lane and risk meeting Nick yet. She hadn't seen much of him recently. He had been in France again to sign the *acte de vente* for the château and to organise the restoration work. She smiled as she remembered how excited he'd been when he got back from seeing it for the first time. Immediately she thought of Alastair. Suddenly she felt overwhelmed with guilt. The deep pang of remorse was almost like a physical blow, the blade of a long knife tearing into her. How could she have been so stupid, thinking she could have both of them and never have to choose? Now she was going to have to hurt one of them or both of them, not to mention Joanne. Kate shuddered. She hardly knew Joanne. They had little in common and, Kate realised to her shame, she had given no thought to Joanne when she had started her affair with Joanne's husband. Worse still, she now remembered something Alastair had said about Joanne and Nick. Nick had once told him how much Joanne wanted to have children.

For the first time in her life, Kate wished there was someone she could confide in. Alastair, she remembered ruefully, had always been her friend and confidant as well as her husband. Perhaps she could talk to him, perhaps he would understand. But how could she expect him to? She had betrayed him. She had to face it now, after all these months when she had persuaded herself that it wasn't betrayal because she loved them both. Kate walked on, hardly noticing the brambles heavy with fruit and the bright red hips on the dog rose bushes that normally would have delighted her. There was no doubt in her mind that she did love both Nick and Alastair. She knew she would lose one or other, probably both. Did Nick really love her? Would he leave Joanne? She was sure that he still loved Joanne.

Arriving at a bend in the path, Kate leaned heavily against the fence, looking down over the fields. The air was very clear and she could just see the bright line on the horizon that was the sea. She thought over the options. She could lie to Alastair – tell him that she was pregnant and that the baby was his. She could tell Nick the same. Tell him it wasn't his. He'd believe her, she thought. She'd just fallen into his arms and she was sure she wasn't the first. She'd lose him, of course. But she would always be living a lie with Alastair and the child. Would she ever tell the child the truth? Kate sighed deeply. There was only one thing that she could do. She would have to tell the truth now – tell Nick it was his baby. She wondered what his reaction would be and realised with a start how little she actually knew him. Would he choose her? Would he leave his comfortable, idle life with Joanne for her and a baby, when he seemed indifferent to children? Where would they go? If he wouldn't leave Joanne for her, what would she do? She'd have to leave Alastair and her beloved cottage. It would be too much to expect him to let her stay. Another thought came to her. Quite suddenly the answer was obvious. Nick said he loved her. She and Nick had to leave together. She'd have to make him come with her. Otherwise it would be too awful for Alastair, not only losing his wife but having to live next door to the man who had ruined his life, or having to move away from the cottage he loved so much. And she was fairly sure anyway that Joanne would send Nick packing the moment she found out.

Her mind made up, Kate turned to head back towards the cottage, giving one last glance towards the distant sea. Beyond the thin grey-blue line lay France. And the château. Of course!

The sound of a car coming up the lane caught her attention. That must be Nick now, just back from the airport. She would tell him straight away, before she lost her nerve. Kate took a deep breath and hurried back up the path and into the lane. By the time she reached the manor she was slightly out of breath, cheeks glowing and panting slightly. Nick was unloading his bags from the car. As she approached, he heard her step on the gravel and looked up, a broad smile crinkling his eyes.

"Hey, you couldn't wait! You look great!"

He stepped towards her kissing her on both cheeks. "Missed me?"

"Oh, Nick, of course."

Tears welled up in her eyes.

"Come on, come on. I'm here now," Nick said, glancing around warily. "Mrs Fletcher's probably got her eye on us. Come in and have some coffee and I'll tell you all about it."

Kate followed him into the house.

"Go into the sitting room. I'll get coffee organised. Mrs Fletcher!" he called up the stairs.

Kate crossed the hall and opened the heavy oak door into the sitting room. She walked carefully across the dark, polished wooden floor and stood in front of the inglenook fireplace, gazing sightlessly at the log fire, laid ready for lighting. She took a deep breath and turned at the sound of a step outside the open door. Mrs Fletcher bustled in carrying a tray set with china coffee cups and a silver coffee pot with a wooden handle. She put the tray down on a low oak table. She glanced at Kate.

"My, you're looking a bit peaky," she said.

Predictably, Kate thought. Mrs Fletcher didn't miss much.

"I'm alright," replied Kate. "Just a caught a bit of a cold I think."

"Probably the change in the weather." Mrs Fletcher eyed Kate again. "Shall I light the fire for you? If you're staying, that is," she added with a disapproving look.

Oh God, thought Kate. She hasn't forgotten that day in the garden, and who knows if she's seen us together since then? It's not going to be long before she notices that I'm pregnant. Before she could reply, Nick came into the room whistling, clutching a packet of photographs.

"No, stay," he said to Mrs Fletcher as she started towards the door with the empty tray. "Come and look at the photographs of my château."

"Yours, huh!" Mrs Fletcher snorted. "She's too good to you, that wife of yours."

"Yes, isn't she?" Nick smiled cheekily at her. "Don't deserve it, do I? Come and look. That's the front, that's the view from the front door, that's the terrace. The terrace is brilliant! You can see the lake from there and right across the valley."

On he went, excitedly flicking through the pictures. Kate was too preoccupied with what she had to tell him to take much in, but it looked so beautiful, like something out of a fairy story. Perhaps they would have a happy ending after all.

"Very nice, I'm sure," said Mrs Fletcher. "But I don't know why you have to go all Frenchie," she sniffed. "There're perfectly good castles in England, you know. Anyway, I've got work to do."

"You'll be the first one out there," Nick laughed. "I'll have you up there polishing the tiles on the turrets."

As the door closed behind her, Nick turned to Kate, still laughing.

"So what do you think? It's fantastic, isn't it? You should see the coach house as well. The structure is magnificent. I've never seen carving like it. The estate agent thinks it must have been built by a journeyman carpenter. You know, as a showpiece to demonstrate to the locals what he could do. You know, like his portfolio."

"Nick."

Kate was still standing in front of the fireplace.

He looked up at her from the photos.

"What's the matter? Come over here and look at these pictures of the pig sties! You'll love these, they're really cute!"

"Nick, there's something I have to tell you. I'm pregnant. And I know it's yours," Kate blurted.

It was so quiet in the room that Kate could hear the ticking of the grandfather clock from the hall. Nick was sitting completely still, frozen. Looking not at her, but at the photographs in his hand. Several minutes passed. Kate realised she was trembling. Nick eventually looked up at her in disbelief.

"Are you sure?" he said. "Well, don't worry. We can sort it out. You can say you fancied a couple of days away – at a health farm or something. Don't worry, I'll give you the money."

Kate looked at him in disbelief.

"No, no," she cried, losing her composure. "I can't do that. I have to keep it, it's a human being. I can't murder it to suit you!"

She turned away from him, her face in her hands. Nick was at her side in an instant.

"Kate, Kate, calm down. I don't want Mrs Fletcher coming in to see what's up."

Kate wiped the back of her hand across her eyes. She turned and looked into his eyes. She must stay calm and make him see what they had to do. She couldn't even let herself think perhaps he'd reject her now.

"There's only one solution to this, Nick," she said evenly. "I've thought about it really hard. I love you and you love me."

She looked up at him, challenging him to deny it. To her relief, he said nothing, but looked down again at the photographs.

"The only solution," she went on, "is for us to go away. We have to go away together and start a new life. Just the two of us – then the three of us."

She smiled down at him. He gave an uneasy smile back.

"But what about Alastair – and Joanne?"

"Look, Nick," Kate answered, surprised by her own coolness. "We have to do this. It's all our fault and we are going to hurt people, whatever we do. People that we love. But this way at least we'll be together and not living a lie."

"Yes, but…," Nick broke off, shaking his head.

To her surprise she saw tears suddenly appearing in his eyes.

"I'm sorry, Kate. But I do love Joanne and she," he swallowed hard. "She needs me. And she'll be devastated when she finds out you're having a baby. It's what she's always wanted and she always said it was my fault we didn't have children. You are sure? Oh God, Kate. What a mess."

He stood up, then sat down heavily in the big leather chair.

"Why won't you just get rid of it?" he cried. "That would solve everything and we could just go on as before."

"Nick, no!" Kate's face was white with anger. "Nothing can ever be the same. You can't bury your head in the sand. I'm having this baby. I could never live with myself if I had an abortion."

Kate knelt on the Persian rug on the floor in front of him. She felt calm again now.

"Nick. I am having this baby," she repeated quietly. "I want you to be with me, with us. I want you to share our lives. I shall have to leave Alastair anyway. I can't let him suffer more than he has to. If you don't want to leave Joanne, I'll understand."

They sat there for some time. Then Nick touched her hair.

"Of course I want to be with you," he whispered. "Jo would throw me out anyway," he grinned weakly.

Then he sat up and grabbed both her hands, smiling deep into her eyes.

"And I know exactly where I'll take you to have the baby," he said, looking towards the pile of photographs.

****

The next few months passed by in a daze for Kate. She said nothing to Alastair as she and Nick made their plans. By November she was beginning to thicken around her waist and, when she stood naked in front of the bathroom mirror, she was thrilled by the sight of the changes in her body. She had never expected to feel like this, but the prospect of having her own baby filled Kate with delight. Winter meant she could conceal her swelling belly with the long, thick woollen jerseys that she normally wore. Alastair was working very hard and fell asleep as soon as he climbed into bed. Recently there had been more problems in Cornwall and he had had to go back there frequently and so was away from home often. Guiltily, Kate felt relieved by his absences. Soon he was bound to notice, and she dreaded the day when she would have to tell him and destroy his world. On the rare occasions when he made love to her now, she was surprised at her own enjoyment of him and pushed thoughts of leaving him to the back of her mind.

With Nick it was different. They were caught up in the excitement of planning their escape to the château in the south of France. They saw each other as often as they could, like children excitedly plotting a great adventure. She was impatient to be with him without having to hide her feelings, and she often sat day-dreaming of long, lazy days in the warm sun, her child playing at her feet. She had never been to France, but Nick had described the vibrant markets and the small cafés where everyone spent hours eating marvellous simple lunches washed down with local wine, sitting at tables shaded by parasols and ancient chestnut trees. She could imagine the beautiful old villages, with the smell of freshly baked bread around every corner. She couldn't wait.

They were going in January, after New Year. It had all happened so strangely. After weeks of indecision and heart-searching about how they would tell Joanne and Alastair, suddenly it had all fallen into place. They had finally decided what to do, and the idea had come from Joanne, of all people. The four of them had been talking at a cocktail party given by a neighbour and the château, as usual, came into the conversation. Nick was describing the work that had been done, and how by Christmas it would be ready for them to move in, apart from some decorating and furnishing. The host had come over to them at that moment, and, catching the end of the conversation had asked Joanne if she was going to get in an interior designer. Joanne had laughed and said she supposed so. Then she had looked at Kate.

"But what I really need is someone to do the garden – at least plan it. It's a complete wilderness. Interested?"

So that's what was agreed. Nick could barely conceal his delight as Joanne suggested that he and Kate should go to the château together so that she could plan the garden and he could engage workmen to do it. The next day Nick had come over to the cottage bursting with excitement.

"It's perfect, Kate!" he exclaimed. "We'll go out in January. If we can make sure that no one knows you're pregnant by then, we'll just go. We'll go to do the garden, just like we've agreed with Jo. It really needs doing and you are just the person to do it! Then after a few weeks we can write to Alastair and Joanne and tell them about the baby. We can tell them we're not coming back, tell them we're going to live together in the château and bring up our baby there. That way no one will be able to stop us!"

"Nick, we can't do that!" Kate stared at him, horrified. "That's so cowardly, so deceitful!"

"Kate, the whole thing is deceitful. However we tell them it's going to hurt them both. At least if we've already gone, it's done. It'll be better this way! It'll be much more civilised! And anyway, you might change your mind about me when you've lived with me for a while," he added with a grin.

So Kate had eventually agreed. She hated the idea of leaving Alastair without even trying to explain, but perhaps she could put it better in a letter. She sensed that Nick was terrified of telling Joanne and obviously he didn't want to make a scene. Behaving in a civilised way was Nick all over, she thought ruefully. At least a civilised appearance. It occurred to her too that perhaps Nick was frightened of what Joanne might do. Joanne, she thought, would want vengeance. It might be better if they were already well away from England when she found out.

5

Kent, England. December.

Christmas came and went, with the usual visit from Alastair's mother, who remarked on Kate's having put on a bit of weight. No one took much notice as Kate was not a favourite with Alastair's dour Scottish mother. She had hoped that Alastair, her only son, would marry a Scot, or at least someone who did a decent day's work instead of mooning around in the garden all day long. Mrs Black would have liked a grandchild too, but knew better than to make any mention of the subject. Kate felt on edge more than ever this year, under her mother-in-law's scrutiny. She was beginning to feel quite tired and heavy. She had not seen a doctor since she knew of her pregnancy, fearful of the news somehow leaking out. It was a relief when they took Mrs Black to the railway station and put her on the train for Aberdeen.

A couple of days later, Alastair received a call from his office. He was needed again in Cornwall.

"It looks like I'm going to be away for New Year's Eve," said Alastair. "Why don't you come with me? One of the partners is lending me his cottage. You'll love it, it's right on the beach. We could stay down for the Bank Holiday and then come back on Saturday morning. It would still give you plenty time to get ready for going to France. And it would be nice to have some time together before you go."

Kate hesitated. She had made plans to see Nick for lunch on New Year's Eve. He had promised to take her out to an old pub hidden away somewhere in the Kent countryside where no one knew them. Alastair, she had assumed, would be at his office.

With three out of four partners being Scots they usually started to celebrate Hogmanay early in the day. And Joanne was away opening her latest fitness centre. Nick would be disappointed, she knew, being left on his own. But then, in less than two weeks they would be on their way to France and a new life together. A weekend alone with Alastair would be a good way for her to say goodbye.

"Yes," Kate smiled at him. "I'd love that."

****

It was a long drive to Cornwall, through the bright, frost-covered fields of Kent in the early morning, then west along busy motorways until they finally turned off towards St Austell and Truro. They followed the coast road for a while, then wound down a steep hill towards the small village of St Veryan. The road ran straight through the cluster of houses, ending abruptly at the beach. A small general store faced a café across the street just before the beach, and on the corner was The Mermaid, a white-washed, stone-cobbled pub with its old-fashioned inn sign creaking above the door. Alastair pulled into the small car park alongside the pub and switched off the engine. Kate opened her eyes and blinked.

"Are we here already?" she asked.

Alastair laughed.

"What do you mean, already? It's taken us over seven hours! But you've been asleep since we hit the M20! Come on, the cottage is just over there."

Kate looked around, following Alastair's pointing finger to a narrow lane leading uphill parallel to the beach. There was a row of rather unprepossessing terraced cottages on each side.

"Ours is the second one on the right," said Alastair. "It's right on the beach."

They climbed out of the car and, gathering their bags from the boot, headed for the cottage. Alastair turned the key in the front door and they went into the small hallway. In front of them was a wrought iron spiral staircase, painted salmon pink. To their left was a cloakroom, the stripped pine door to which had a frosted glass panel with 'Saloon' etched in a flamboyant art nouveau design. On their right was a cosy kitchen with a wood burning stove and a small pine dining table.

"Leave the bags here, Kate. Come upstairs – this is the best bit," Alastair enthused.

Kate climbed the spiral stairs carefully. She stepped off the top rung onto white-painted floorboards. Any disappointment she'd felt when she first saw the outside of the cottage had started to disappear the moment they'd opened the door and she'd seen the 'Saloon'. But now she let out a delighted yelp as she took in the details of the room. The ceiling was open to the rafters, with thick beams across the room, all painted primrose yellow. At one end of the room was a bright green enamel French wood burning stove. In front of it were two easy chairs, upholstered in turquoise blue. In the centre of the room stood a huge brass bed, covered in a blue and white patchwork quilt. A giant brass diving helmet stood near the fire, and an old anchor was propped in one corner. At the other end of the room, a door led into a large bathroom, in the middle of which stood a cast iron bath, painted maroon, with brass taps and large brass claw feet. The bathroom was filled with potted plants, and a mirror in an ornate gilt frame covered almost the entire wall opposite the bath.

"It's terrific!" Kate gasped. "It's so unusual. I love it!"

"You haven't even noticed the best bit yet. Turn round," Alastair said.

When Kate turned, she caught her breath again. She was looking out of three large sash windows in the back wall of the house. The beach was about three metres directly below her, a line of seaweed almost up to the wall of the house indicating where the high tide came to. The sea was now about fifty metres down the beach, well inside the harbour wall that curved round the base of the cliffs on both sides. It was a spectacular setting. A couple of small boats were tied up within the shelter of the harbour and outside the mouth Kate could just see the white crests of waves in the December twilight.

"Glad you came?" Alastair stood behind Kate with his arms round her waist.

"Oh yes," breathed Kate. "I'd no idea it would be like this."

"Well, it's pretty awful in the summer," said Alastair, looking over her shoulder at the deserted beach. "There are a few caravan sites nearby and it's very popular with day trippers."

"Yes, I suppose so," said Kate. "But what a fantastic location. And the cottage is great. It has a lovely atmosphere."

Kate sat down on the window seat looking out across the sea as Alastair fetched their bags and busied himself in the kitchen making cups of tea.

"I'm going to make supper," he announced. "You have a bath and just enjoy it here."

****

The next three days flew past for Kate. Alastair left early in the morning for St Austell to work on the surveys of a row of houses that had been built on the site of former china clay mines and were now showing signs of subsidence. Each day Kate walked along the beach, round the harbour wall to the end where she could see right out around the rugged coastline. The weather was perfect, cold and bright and clear. Later she returned to the cottage and sat drinking coffee at the window overlooking the beach. In the evenings they ate simple meals by candlelight in front of the wood burning stove, before falling asleep in the beautiful brass bed. To her relief, Alastair didn't seem to notice her gently protruding belly, other than remarking on how well she was looking, putting it down to the sea air. On New Year's Eve, Alastair came home at lunch time and they had lobster at the pub across the road from their cottage. In the afternoon they climbed the path leading out of the village and walked for miles along the cliff top until the light started to fade. That evening, as Kate lay in a scented bath, she could hear Alastair downstairs, whistling as he prepared their supper. A few minutes later he came into the bathroom balancing a small tray on which were two glasses and small bowls of olives and nuts, and a frosted bottle of champagne.

"Here, darling," he said, handing her a glass of champagne. "Happy New Year."

"Happy New Year."

Kate's voice caught in her throat and her eyes misted over. Oh God, she thought. Can I go through with this? Have I made the right choice? She looked at Alastair through a veil of tears. Dear Alastair. She did love him so much and she was going to hurt him so much.

"Kate," Alastair was looking at her closely. "Is something the matter?"

Kate swallowed. Should she tell him now? Make a clean breast of it and hope he'd forgive her? What about Nick if she did? Did she really care? And the baby? But now she didn't think she could bear to lose Alastair. She'd made the wrong choice. She couldn't go through with this charade.

"Alastair," she started. Her voice broke. "Alastair, I ……"

The knock at the door in the street below them had Alastair darting to the window.

"Back in a minute," he called, clattering down the stairs.

Kate sank back into the warm water. She heard the door open and a muffled exchange between Alastair and another male voice. The door closed and Alastair was calling to her from downstairs.

"Ready yet, Kate? Come on down when you're ready."

She climbed out of the bath and, wrapping herself in a big blue bath towel, softly padded to the window and stood looking out into the blackness. The moment had passed and she hadn't been able to do it. She hated her weakness, but she knew things had gone too far now. She couldn't turn back. Kate took a deep breath and started to dress quickly.

At the bottom of the spiral stair, she caught a glimpse of herself in the long mirror in its heavy gilt frame. Her shape really had not changed so much yet, although the low-cut bodice of the deep blue velvet dress that she wore tonight fitted more snugly than usual, exposing the creamy swell of her breasts. The dress hung loosely down, almost to the floor. Her face glowed from the days spent outdoors in the gentle winter sunshine, and her hair seemed to have taken on a new shine. Despite her worries, Kate was pleased with her appearance. She owed Alastair this much, she thought. If she didn't have the courage to tell him about Nick, at least she could make sure that their last days together were happy.

Entering the kitchen, Kate gasped with pleasure. The knock on the door was now explained. The whole room was filled with the perfume of spring flowers, bringing a wonderful promise of better things to come.

PART II

This year

1

France. January.

As the Volvo sped through the deserted roads of northern France, Kate glanced sideways at Nick, blinking to reassure herself that it wasn't just a dream. They had left at four in the morning to make sure they arrived in a day. Nick was keen to reach the château and now Kate just wanted to put as much distance between herself and her old life as possible. Leaving so early had meant a hurried farewell to Alastair, which was, she knew, the best way. They had arrived at Folkestone in less than half an hour and were on the train and through the Tunnel before Kate had time to think. Now dawn was starting to break over the flat landscape. Soon they were skirting Paris, just as the early morning rush hour was starting. Then out of the congestion and heading south down the autoroute, towards Orléans. Nick pulled off at a service station and they ate the most delicious pain au chocolat that Kate had ever tasted, washed down with strong black coffee. Then back into the car and on southwards, leaving the autoroute. There was a bit more traffic around now, and Kate looked out with interest as they drove through villages starting to come alive for the day. Old women on bicycles heading for the baker's, men in berets and blue overalls talking on the street corners, a baguette in one hand, gesticulating with the other. Kate smiled to herself with pleasure. It all seemed too much of a cliché – she almost expected someone to appear in front of her in a striped jersey with a string of onions.

They drove through the centre of Blois, Kate gazing in awe at the château that dominated the town, and crossed the Loire. It was nearly three in the afternoon by the time they reached Valençay, driving down the tree-lined avenue towards the château. Here Nick turned left and came to a stop outside a small café.

"Let's have lunch here," he said. "They do good soup and baguettes all day and you don't have to have a full four course meal like in most places! Not that most places would still be serving lunch at this time!"

"Great. I'm hungry now," said Kate. "Have you been here often?"

"Once or twice," Nick smiled sideways at her. "Always on my own, of course," he added.

They got out of the car and went into the café. Inside Kate was slightly disappointed to see that there were two pinball machines and a bar billiards table at the end of the small, rather dark, room. In front of her and to the right was a bar, behind which was a coffee machine and rows of bottles, some of strange, bright-coloured liquids amongst the more recognisable bottles of whisky and gin. There were a few small plastic-topped tables with orange plastic chairs around them, and two bar stools. There was no one at all in the café. As Nick walked up to the bar, a short, dark-haired woman appeared.

"Bonjour, Monsieur," she nodded at Nick.

Nick ordered at the counter and they sat together at a table near the small, grimy window. The woman brought their coffees over, then reappeared with a baguette, filled with Brie and cut in half.

"Voilà! Vos sandwiches!"

She plonked the plates down in front of them with a flourish. Kate bit into hers immediately, realising how hungry she was.

"Mmm. It's delicious," she exclaimed.

Nick grinned at her.

"Don't I bring you to all the best places?" he enquired.

"Well, this is the first place you've ever brought me to and I was beginning to wonder! It's not exactly my idea of a romantic French bistro."

"Don't worry," Nick patted her knee. "There'll be plenty of time for those later."

After they had finished and Nick had paid the bill, they walked back towards the château. It was closed to the public until May, but the gates to the grounds were open and they walked around to the front of the château where they could see right across to the hunting lodge on the opposite side of the valley. The day was cold and overcast and they walked quickly, glad to be able to stretch their legs after so many hours driving.

"It shouldn't take us much more than five hours now," said Nick. "We've made good time so far."

"It'll be dark when we arrive. That's a pity. I am so looking forward to seeing it."

"Well, I'm afraid it's not quite as grand as this." Nick looked up at the façade of the château. "But I know you'll love it."

"Come on then," Kate grabbed his hand. "Let's not waste any more time."

Back in the car, Nick drove quickly on, by-passing Limoges and Brive. It was quite dark by the time they wound down a long, wooded hill into Souillac and across the Dordogne river. Half an hour later they were crossing the Lot, both rivers full and swiftly flowing.

"Not long now." Nick looked out of the window. "That's Cahors down there. It's our nearest big town. I think you'll like it. There's a good market there twice a week."

Kate peered out into the gloom. She could see the lights of the town spread out below them. She felt a mounting excitement.

"So we're nearly there?"

"Yes, about another half hour should do it."

As they left Cahors behind, Kate was surprised by the intensity of the darkness. Although they were still driving along a main road with plenty of other traffic, when she glanced out into the countryside she saw nothing. No street lights, no glow of neon indicating a town. Nick slowed the car and turned right off the main road, down a much smaller road. Here there was very little traffic and complete darkness around them. They drove along in silence, passing a few houses here and there, but none showed even the merest chink of light. Rounding a bend in the road, ahead of them Kate could see a few lights of a hill-top village outlined against the dark sky. The road climbed quite steeply upwards. At the top, on one side was the large dome of a church, on the other, the high wall of an imposing house. Then they were driving through a large open square with chestnut trees and covered arcades in white stone, glowing in the half dozen street lights. The road ran along one side of the square, then narrowed again, the street lined with tall stone buildings that Kate assumed were shops. They were out of the village within minutes, passing a large cemetery, the massive granite tombs looming eerily out of the darkness above the high stone wall surrounding them. A short way further on, Nick swung sharply to the left, off the road and down a narrow track. Kate glimpsed the small signpost: *Château de St Geniès-Lafontaine.*

As they bumped along down the track, the car headlights caught a white shadow, silently flitting through the branches.

"An owl!" Kate whispered in delight.

A final bend in the track and Nick stopped the car. To her left, Kate could just make out the outlines of buildings, towering above them. Nick had stopped just before a high stone arch that spanned the track.

"I'll get the torch," Nick said.

Kate got out of the car and stood looking about her. The air was cold, and absolutely still. Looking up into the blackness, she could see a few stars, but the night was cloudy and silent. Nick came round her side of the car carrying a large torch.

"We'll go in through the kitchen," he said. "Follow me."

The torch picked out a narrow path across wet grass, through an arch into a cobbled passage. Kate followed him into a courtyard and held the torch while he fumbled with a large iron key. In moments he was pushing open a heavy wooden door and light suddenly flooded the courtyard.

"Welcome to St Geniès-Lafontaine."

Nick bowed in front of her.

"After you, Madame."

Kate giggled and stepped over the threshold. She stood looking around in amazement. The kitchen was huge, cold and gloomy. Kate's footsteps echoed as she crossed the tiled floor to the enormous stone fireplace. It wasn't the cosy, welcoming room she'd expected at all.

"Fantastic, isn't it?" Nick pointed at the empty grate. "You'll see, when we've got a roaring fire going, it's wonderful. Takes almost half a tree. And the ceiling – have you seen it? The floor tiles are all original too. The agent said it was just what a French country château kitchen should look like! And he was right!"

Kate stood there shivering as Nick enthused about this feature and that. To her it all seemed so cold and forbidding, so big and inhospitable and drab. She shook herself. She was just tired. Tomorrow it would seem wonderful to her too.

"Nick, I'm exhausted," she said. "Let's just go to bed."

"Good idea. It's quite late now. I'll show you the bedroom and bring a few things in. We can unpack in the morning. Come on."

Nick led the way through shadowy rooms to a stone-floored hall from where rose an imposing, sweeping stone staircase. They climbed to the first floor, then along a wide corridor of broad, uneven floorboards. Near the end, Nick stopped and flung open a tall, panelled wooden door.

"Here we are, darling. Make yourself at home! I'll be up in a few minutes."

Kate listened to the sound of Nick's footsteps on the bare wooden floors, receding into the distance. She could hear him whistling as he descended the stairs, then gradually the sound faded and everything was totally silent again. It was even colder, if anything, in the bedroom than in the rest of the house. The room was actually quite small, but with a very high ceiling, crossed with big oak beams. In the centre of the room was a four-poster bed in dark wood, heavily carved and curtained at the sides with deep maroon, figured brocade. There was a dressing table and chest of drawers in the same heavily carved and polished wood. The floor was of cold stone slabs like the hall downstairs, but a couple of exquisite Persian carpets in blue and red lay alongside the bed, one on each side. There were three tall windows along the wall opposite the bed, tightly shuttered. A door led off the room to a modern bathroom, fitted with an ivory suite with gold taps. Kate brightened up a bit. A hot bath would do her good. She turned on the taps but, to her dismay, a trickle of brownish water was all that she got. Too tired to bother anymore, she went back into the bedroom and, taking off her coat and shoes, climbed between the icy satin sheets of the four-poster bed, fully dressed. Despite the chill, she was asleep as soon as her head touched the pillow. She stirred once when, sometime later, Nick climbed into bed beside her and kissed her neck.

"Good night, darling. You're going to love it here. I know you are!"

****

When Kate opened her eyes, the room was completely dark. She lay still for a moment, disoriented by the blackness and silence of the strange room. Tentatively she stretched out a hand towards Nick before realising she was alone in the big, high bed. Moments later she heard the familiar whistling, very faint at first then getting louder until the door burst open and Nick appeared in the doorway.

"Aha! The princess awakes!"

He crossed the room and threw back the shutters. Light flooded into the room. Kate could see bright blue sky and small misty clouds.

"It's a beautiful day," Nick enthused. "You just don't get days like this in the winter in England! Come on, sit up. I've brought your breakfast."

Nick placed a tray with coffee and fresh croissants in front of her.

"What time is it?" Kate blinked in the bright light. "You must have been up for ages."

"Oh well, if you're not down at the baker's before nine, Madame Chomez has sold out of just about everything. So here we are. Tuck in."

Nick sat on the bed and picked up a croissant. Kate lay back against the pillows contentedly and sipped her coffee, gazing round the room, transformed by the sunlight. Nick was right. She was going to like it here.

****

The next few weeks passed quickly. Days spent planning the renovations to the château and its garden, evenings spent in front of the huge log fire in the kitchen, drinking the coarse red wine of the area, Kate listening drowsily as Nick enthused about everything. The weather was cold and wet most of the time and, inside, the big, old château remained draughty and chilly despite the newly-installed central heating and the big fires that Nick fed constantly with logs from the surrounding woods. Whilst Nick supervised the workmen, Kate was happy to spend her days in the kitchen, working on her garden designs at the long oak table in front of the fire. She was beginning to feel very tired and heavy as her pregnancy progressed, but otherwise she felt happy and content, marvelling to herself at how she seemed to have adapted to her new state and how she was looking forward to the birth of her child. She tried not to think about Alastair. When she did, she was filled with a tremendous sorrow. If only they could have all lived together, her and Nick and Alastair. She knew most people would be horrified at her thoughts. But that wasn't how it was. It wasn't immoral. Kate knew she genuinely loved both of them. Still, the world as it was had made her choose and, as she sat gazing into the flames one afternoon in early February, she knew that soon she and Nick were going to have to tell Alastair and Joanne that they weren't coming home. It was something neither of them had mentioned, not wanting to spoil the magic.

At that moment, Nick came into the kitchen from the courtyard where he had been chopping logs for the evening. He came over and sat beside her, his arm round her shoulders.

"Kate. We're expected back in the next week or so. We're going to have to tell people something soon."

He didn't look at her directly and for a moment Kate was seized with panic. Had he changed his mind?

"Yes," she answered steadily. "And we need to make arrangements for the baby. I'll have to contact a doctor or a hospital here soon."

"I was wondering," Nick looked into the fire. "You are sure it's what you want, aren't you?"

"Yes, of course." Kate tried to keep her voice calm. "Aren't you?"

There was a slight, almost imperceptible pause before Nick replied.

"Well, yes." Nick hesitated again. "It's just, well, you know Jo has been paying for the renovations. And she's not likely to go on doing so when we've told her about us. I just thought, maybe we should keep quiet for a bit until most of it's done."

"Oh."

Kate relaxed. So that was what was worrying him. Money. She had a bit of her own, and she knew Nick had transferred large amounts to his account in France.

"Well, I think that's a bit much really," she laughed. "I know Joanne is absolutely loaded but that'd be rather like rubbing salt into the wound, don't you think? I'd be happier, Nick, if we told them now. There's plenty of money in your account. Let's write today."

"Yes. OK. You are right. Let's do it. Then let's go out and celebrate! We haven't been out at all since we got here and there are some amazing restaurants around!"

Nick went into the salon and sat down at the Louis XIV desk. He raised his pen, then threw it down again. This was going to be harder than he'd expected. He glanced around the room and out of the long windows onto the terrace and beyond. It was a clear day and in the winter sun he could see the lake below the château now that there were no leaves left on the trees. He remembered the first time Joanne had brought him to see the château. How excited she had been. He knew she had fallen in love with the place. It would be difficult enough to tell her he had left her, but to tell her that he was going to live in the château with Kate was harder still. But the worst for Jo would be to know that he would soon be a father. He knew she had always blamed him for their failure to have children. He'd been surprised to say the least when Kate had announced that the baby was his. But she was adamant, and why should she lie?

Suddenly he knew he couldn't write the letter. In fact, he didn't want to. He wasn't at all sure he wanted to leave Jo. Having an affair was one thing, leaving Jo for good wasn't something he'd ever really considered. As he sat there gazing out of the window, Nick realised that he hadn't thought any of this through. Yes, he found Kate attractive, but was there much more to it than that? It had all happened so fast and he'd been caught up in the excitement and romance of running off to the south of France. But he knew he'd always pushed the reality to the back of his mind. Somehow, he'd expected something to happen, for it all to sort itself out without him having to do anything much, definitely not leave Jo for good! He found himself smiling as he thought about Jo. She meant so much to him. Then he thought about Kate. He sat up with a start as the truth hit him. He really didn't love her after all. And not only that. He admitted to himself that it was her calmness and slightly vague air that had attracted him to her in the first place, being so different from his vivacious wife. But already it was starting to grate. She never wanted to do anything or go anywhere. He knew he was starting to find her a bit, well, boring. If he felt like this now, after a few short weeks, what would it be like if he was on his own with her at the château forever? And with a snivelling baby? Another thought came to him again. Was the baby really his? The last tests Jo'd insisted he take had been inconclusive, although Dr Grey had been encouraging and told them to keep trying.

He walked over to the window, thinking hard. It was his fault as much as hers that they were in this mess. If only she'd not insisted on having the baby! But she had and now he'd just have to think of a way out. He didn't want to hurt her. But he certainly didn't want to hurt Joanne. And he definitely didn't want to leave Jo. It was now the middle of February. They had been in France for exactly four weeks and were due back by the end of the next week. Joanne's plan had been that Kate would design the garden and he'd engage workmen to start in spring, when they'd return to France to check on progress. As Nick gazed out at the winter landscape, he noticed that, despite the cold, buds and shoots were appearing on some of the trees. An idea came to him as he stood there. What if he told Joanne that they had decided to stay on so that Kate could supervise the start of the landscaping? After all, they were six hundred miles or more south of Kent, so spring should arrive earlier. And Kate had heard from Alastair that he'd be in Cornwall most of the time for the next couple of months, so why not just tell Jo they were staying on to oversee the garden and the rest of the renovation? That would give him a bit of a breathing space. He could pop back to see Jo for a few weekends. Kate could have the baby and maybe get it adopted, or something. They wouldn't have to tell anyone. Perhaps she'd want to stay in France anyway. Buy herself a little place. She seemed to like it here. Then he could just visit her now and again when he was over on his own, when Jo was working. Yes, that'd be much more fun. He could see the baby and so on. Although he wasn't too bothered about that. Of course he'd help with money....

"I'll take the letters down to the post office," Nick said, walking back into the kitchen, whistling jauntily. "Have you finished yours?"

Kate looked up, surprised at his cheerfulness.

"Yes."

She smiled sadly.

"Don't worry," Nick stroked her cheek. "It'll be alright."

"I suppose so. Can we stay in tonight after all? I don't really feel much like celebrating."

"Of course, darling. I'll collect a few things on the way back from the village and make us a special supper. Now things are sorted out."

That evening they sat in front of the fire, drinking champagne by candlelight, eating a wonderful simple meal that Nick had prepared for them. Kate gazed fondly at him, his handsome profile lit by the firelight, and wondered why she had ever doubted that he loved her and wanted to stay with her.

2

Kent, England. April.

"Y ou know, I'm getting a bit worried." Alastair looked across the kitchen table at Richard. "I haven't had a letter from Kate now for well over a month. And I know there's no phone or internet yet at the chateau, but I thought she might have called from the village or something."

"But Mrs Carslow hears regularly from her husband, doesn't she? I think he calls her almost every day," said Richard. "They must be alright. She told me he'd emailed some photos. Kate doesn't use the internet or texts, does she? Perhaps the letters have just got lost in the post, or she's sent them to Cornwall. She's probably really busy if the gardeners have started already. Probably doesn't get a chance to go to the village and your phone didn't work down in Cornwall, did it? She's probably tried to call."

"Yes, I expect you're right. Anyway, I finish in Cornwall in a couple of weeks. How do you fancy a trip to France? We could drive down and surprise Kate!"

Richard looked at Alastair quickly, with a feeling of apprehension. He had been horrified when Alastair had told him Kate was going to France with Nick and had done all he could to get Alastair to stop her. But Alastair had just laughed and said she'd have a great time, Nick was good company and it would be a real challenge for her to design such a prestigious garden. He also felt it would do Kate good to have her own project and get some recognition for her talents. But Richard knew that Kate and Nick were having an affair. After all, he had seen them with his own eyes, that day back in the summer. He'd cursed himself for not being able to stop them. He felt sick whenever he thought about that night. He could only thank God that he hadn't killed Nick. He had not told Alastair about Kate and Nick, hoping it would all blow over. Even when Nick and Kate were going to France together, Richard couldn't bring himself to tell Alastair what he knew. Now he sat looking at the table, his mind in turmoil. He didn't want to tell Alastair, but would that be better than arriving unannounced to find – what? He felt his anger towards Kate rising again. His hands started to tremble and his face flushed deeply. Alastair glanced at him with concern. He knew Richard never travelled far from home, but he was surprised to see the look of alarm on his friend's face. He hadn't expected that the prospect of a trip across the Channel would upset Richard so much.

"Richard? You don't have to come if you don't want to. I just thought it might be fun. I can easily go on my own and bring Kate home."

Richard struggled to take deep, calming breaths. He had to go. He couldn't let Alastair go alone. And yes. He had the answer. They would go and get Kate and bring her home, but he would make sure that Nick stayed in France. He'd have to work out a plan. Perhaps he really should have hit Nick harder when he had the chance.

3

France. April.

Kate shivered slightly and moved a bit closer to the fire. It was early April, but the nights were as cold and damp as ever. She glanced at her watch. It was after eleven and still no sign of Nick. He was out a lot of the time, more so recently. At first, he invited Kate too, but she preferred to stay in. Now he just went on his own.

She was beginning to wonder where he went, but she really didn't want to go with him. She hadn't expected to feel so tired all the time. And anyway, she hadn't enjoyed the few times she had been out since they had arrived here. Nick had enthused about the picturesque villages and the local restaurants so much and she had been keen to try them and get to know the French way of life.

For the first few weeks, Nick always went to the village on his own to buy bread and croissants. Once she had gone with him to the local supermarket but was surprised and disappointed by the lack of choice and high prices and so, the next time, they had gone to Cahors to one of the big hypermarkets. It had been a mild, sunny day and the winter landscape was starting to show signs of spring. There was blossom on the almond trees and Kate noticed small blue grape hyacinths dotting the meadows as they drove through the countryside towards the town. She had been delighted to step outside into the courtyard that morning and see a carpet of violets under the trees outside. The signs of spring had lured her further away from the château than she had been before, walking down to the lake and scrambling back through the woods where a few early orchids were in bloom. She had felt quite tired when she got back to the château, but they were both in high spirits and set off immediately for Cahors. They drove into the large car park and headed for the entrance to the supermarket. As they approached and the automatic doors swung open, Kate stopped abruptly.

"Whatever is that smell?"

She wrinkled her nose at Nick.

"What smell?" Nick was already heading for the fish counter. "Oh, that sort of stale, slightly rotting smell? All French supermarkets smell like that. So do Spanish ones. It's because of all the fresh fish and meat and veg they have in them. You know, it's not all in little sealed packets like in England."

Kate clutched the trolley. A wave of nausea came over her.

"You OK?" Nick glanced at her.

"I think I'd better get some fresh air." Kate staggered, almost losing her balance.

"Yes, come on. You look awful. Let's get you outside and I'll go back and do the shopping. It's not the baby, is it?"

"God, I hope not." Kate managed a smile. "I don't really want to have 'Carrefour Hypermarket' on the birth certificate."

Outside in the car park, Kate started to feel better. The baby wasn't due for well over a month and the doctor who had come to the château to see her last week and been very reassuring. Speaking to her in perfect English, he had explained what she should expect to happen and when. He had told her just to take things easy now until after the birth. She should have listened. On the way home, Nick had suggested they go out for a meal instead of cooking. That was the last thing Kate wanted, but she knew he wanted to show her what France had to offer.

"Let's go tomorrow. I feel really tired now, but I'm sure I'll be fine in the morning."

"All right," Nick sighed. "But I'm going to keep you to that! We haven't been out since we got here."

So the next day they had set off for Fromac, for what Nick promised would be a truly French experience.

"You'll love it," he'd enthused. "We're going to the village café for lunch. It's a four course menu and you get a choice for each course. It's real, authentic French country cooking. Nothing pretentious at all. Then we can walk it off around the village and go and look at the remains of the old castle before we come home."

It was another mild sunny day. After the weeks of cold and rain, Kate was glad to see the sun and felt happy and content that her baby would be born when the spring was well under way and the days were warm and dry. She imagined sitting out on the terrace of the château, looking down onto the lake, rocking the baby gently in its cradle in the clean, warm air. She would have to think what to do about the balustrade before the baby started toddling. It was quite low and there was a sheer drop down onto grass and rock below.

Nick was in high spirits again. He loved to be out and about and was glad that at last Kate was prepared to come with him. He knew she must be tired, lugging around all that extra weight, but he felt disappointed and irritated at her reluctance to leave the château. Most mornings, after visiting the baker's, he called in at the Café de France in St Geniès, the village from which the château took its name. He and Joanne had stopped there on their first visit and ever since, whenever Nick had been at the château on his own in the early stages of its renovation, he'd eaten there. He spoke bad French very fluently and his easy manner and charm had established him in no time as a favourite, not only with Madame Chomez, the baker's wife, but with the café owner, the bar-tender and waitress and the regulars at the café. Sometimes he had lunch with the architect who was advising him on the renovation of the château or with the doctor who was now looking after Kate. There were a few English residents appearing in the cafés now the weather had improved a little, resolutely sitting outdoors despite the still chilly days. Nick was soon known to them all and was turning down dinner invitations daily. He wished Kate would agree to at least one or two of the invitations. Nick couldn't help admitting to himself that he was getting more and more bored staying in night after night at the château, particularly now that Kate was dropping off to sleep as soon as supper was over. What was the point of being there with her when she was such a wet blanket? So today he felt happy. Perhaps it had just been the bad weather that had made Kate reluctant to go out. Anyway, it wasn't long until the baby would be born and then he'd be able to extricate himself from the situation. Yes, he admitted to himself, he'd definitely made a big error of judgement with this affair.

They drove down the long hill towards Fromac. In front of them they could see the village, its white stone houses clinging to the slopes of the small hill on top of which sat a square tower, all that remained of the fortified castle that had once dominated the valley. As Nick paused at the crossroads at the entrance to the village, a well-dressed woman standing outside the bank waved to him. Nick smiled and waved back. Now there was a woman he'd like to know better! Kate glanced at him.

"Who is that?"

"Oh, she's the notaire's wife. We had dinner with them a couple of times when we were buying the château."

Kate said nothing and, for some reason she couldn't explain, felt a quick flash of jealousy. There was so much she didn't know about Nick, or about his life with Joanne. It occurred to her again that they were still strangers in many ways.

Nick parked the car under a large chestnut tree and they walked down the hill into the small square. The lady from outside the bank met them at the edge of the café terrace.

"Nick! It is so lovely to see you! I had no idea you were back! Why haven't you been to see us?" she exclaimed in heavily-accented English, shaking his hand and kissing him on both cheeks, to which Nick responded readily. She turned her elegantly-coiffured head towards Kate, her glance sweeping over Kate's untidy hair and make-up-less face and looked quizzically at Nick.

"Oh, I'm so sorry. Where are my manners! Marie-Claire, er, Madame Lacombe, this is Kate. Kate, Madame Lacombe."

"*Enchantée.*"

Madame Lacombe held her hand out towards Kate with a polite smile.

"Kate is our neighbour from England. She's a garden designer and is helping us to sort out St Geniès-Lafontaine. Madame Lacombe is the wife of the notaire, Kate."

Madame Lacombe smiled again, this time at Nick and this time warmly, with a playful chuckle.

"Oh Nick! You make me sound like I am just the wife! I am too a person," she protested. Turning to Kate, she said, "I have my own little shop in Cahors. If you would like to buy some of our beautiful French couture, I can help you. But now I must be running. I am due at my husband's office ten minutes ago. It is so nice to see you again, Nick. I hope you will come over to see us soon. Any time. And you will give my regards to Joanne. I hope we shall see her again very soon. It will be so nice for her to have a garden already done for her!" she added, her gaze resting briefly on Kate.

She kissed Nick again on both cheeks, and nodded to Kate.

"So nice to meet you. I hope your work here goes well."

And with that she turned up the narrow street alongside the café, her high heels clattering on the cobbles. Nick waved as she turned into the doorway of an ancient half-timbered building, glancing back at them.

"She's such a nice woman. So elegant – a typical French woman. You should have a look in her shop, you know. Well, once you're back to normal size, I suppose!"

Glancing at her expression, he stopped laughing.

"Kate! What on earth's the matter now?"

"What do you think?" she gasped, her face flushed with anger. "Our neighbour from England!"

"I could hardly say, oh, by the way, this is my current girlfriend, to someone I really respect and who's a friend of Joanne anyway. Now could I? Oh come on, Kate, don't be silly."

"I am not being silly!" Kate was close to tears. "You don't want to tell people."

"Oh, for goodness sake! Be sensible. You know how people gossip."

"Yes, I do know. I thought that's why we had come here, where no one knows us. But you seem to know everyone anyway. And everyone knows you – and your wife!" Kate spat the words at him.

Nick glanced around.

"For crying out loud! Don't make a scene. Calm down and let's enjoy our day. After all, this is France. It's no big deal. Men are expected to have mistresses!"

Kate glared at him. He wasn't joking. He really meant that – how could he! She could not believe it. Alastair would never have thought, let alone said, a thing like that. Nick put his arm round her.

"Please, Kate," his eyes twinkled as he smiled down at her. "You're going to have to learn when I'm joking! Just don't take everything so seriously. Relax and enjoy life a bit, for God's sake!"

"Oh, all right."

Kate laughed in spite of herself. She felt slightly foolish, over-reacting as usual.

"I expect it's just my hormones!"

"Well, I'm glad you said that, not me! Come on, let's go and eat. It's a pity it's too cold to sit on the terrace."

Nick pushed open the half-glazed door of the café and they stepped inside.

The small room seemed dark after the bright sunshine outside. There was a bar covering the wall opposite the door and a number of small, dark brown, varnished tables and chairs, most of which were occupied. The air was thick with strong cigarette smoke and there was a pause in the buzz of conversation as Kate and Nick walked in. Nick beamed around.

"*Monsieurs, 'dames,*" he said to the room at large.

Heads nodded imperceptibly in his direction then turned back to their conversations. A large florid man stood up and approached them.

"Bonjour, Monsieur Carslow! Ça va?"

Nick reached over and shook the man's outstretched hand.

"Ça va bien, Monsieur Lefèvre. Et vous? Les affaires vont bien aussi?"

"Pas mal, pas mal."

Monsieur Lefèvre smiled and shrugged, regaining his seat.

Nick steered Kate towards an empty table under the window, close to the bar. A few men in blue overalls stood at the bar, glasses of beer in front of them. Kate was surprised to see the majority of customers were drinking beer, although one or two solitary male diners had small brown jugs of red wine on their tables. A couple of middle-aged women at a table in the front window, sharing a now almost empty pitcher of white wine, looked up with interest as Nick and Kate settled themselves. Kate noticed one whisper something to the other and as the waitress came to replace the empty pitcher with a full one, realised from their accent that they were English. She felt slightly uncomfortable under their gaze.

"So who is Monsieur Lefèvre?" she asked Nick.

"He's the estate agent."

"And those two?"

Nick glanced towards the window table.

"No idea."

"Well, they seem to know you, or at least they seem to find us very interesting!"

"You know what people are like," Nick shrugged. "Particularly in a place like this – the expats are always on the lookout for gossip. Nothing else to do."

He turned towards the approaching waitress, who, Kate noted, also seemed to know him. The waitress addressed Nick in fast-flowing French, pen poised above her pad.

"Right, Kate. What'll it be? First course is *rillettes* or *charcuterie*, then it's *magret de canard*, or *brandade*, that's salt cod.........."

Kate shuddered.

"Is there anything that's not offal?" she grimaced.

"'Fraid not," Nick grinned wickedly. "This is France! But you do exaggerate – of course it's not all offal. Cod's not offal and there's no tripe on the menu, is there? I'm having the *charcuterie*. You get a great selection. Why not try that, you're bound to like some of it!"

"Yes, all right. Then I'd like the *brandade*. That sounds nice."

"Good, and we'll have red wine."

Nick turned back to the waitress and ordered.

A jug of wine and a basket of fresh bread arrived within seconds. Kate broke a piece of baguette and, looking up, noticed that the two English women were paying their bill. As they left the café, they both glanced again at Kate and Nick. Once outside she saw them talking animatedly, their heads together, one of them looking in again through the café window as they walked off in the direction of the bank. Thank goodness they'd gone. Kate sat back and relaxed. No one else was taking any notice of them. Most of the clientele were men, a mixture of workmen and a few businessmen in suits, eating alone. She looked round the room, noticing for the first time that it was decorated almost entirely in brown, with varnished wooden panels up the walls and brown curtains at the windows. The floor was well-worn dark wooden boards and the walls above the panelling had once been cream but now were stained dark brown from years of nicotine. The whole effect was quaint and appeared not to have changed for years. She sat back and smiled.

"It's just like what I was hoping for," she said. "Now those awful women have gone, it's like the real France, no tourists or anything."

"Yes, it is. I'm glad you like it. Here," Nick filled her glass. "Let's drink to that. What we came to France for!"

Kate raised her glass and took a sip of wine. Her mouth puckered involuntarily and she nearly spat it out again. Nick took a good mouthful of his, and swallowed.

"Mmm. Lovely. You can't beat the local plonk, can you!"

Kate took another sip, trying not to grimace. The thin, raw acidity of the wine was overlaid by a slightly mouldy flavour that made her wonder if it was corked. She swallowed and felt her eyes water slightly.

"Is it meant to taste like this?" she asked.

Nick laughed.

"You'll get used to it. The stuff you get in the cafés is bulk wine that they buy for a couple of euros a litre from the vineyards after they've done the bottling of the good stuff that we've been drinking at the château. But it's still characteristic of this region. Cahors was once famed for its dark wine and there's been a lot of interest in it recently. I want to lay some down. We've got a brilliant wine cellar, after all, although it needs a bit of work. And there are so many châteaux around here. We could have a trip around and buy a few cases. The countryside along the river is breathtakingly beautiful. That's where most of the big châteaux are.

"That sounds fun," said Kate. "I didn't know we had a wine cellar."

"You are impossible," Nick laughed. "But I do need to improve the access. The door's blocked up at the moment but you can get in through those big circular holes in its ceiling. You know, in the floor of the outbuildings off the left side of the kitchen courtyard? But the roof's a bit dodgy, so the builders say."

Kate looked at him blankly.

"I've never noticed those!"

"You really are hopeless! I thought you'd have explored the whole château by now, but all you've done is curl up in front of that fire."

"Well, you try being pregnant then!" Kate retorted. "And anyway, it's been so wet and cold, I haven't fancied going out much. But now that spring is really here I can't wait to get out. I was beginning to feel a bit claustrophobic," she admitted.

At that moment the waitress reappeared bearing two large plates that she set down in front of them.

"Bon appetit," she said, smiling at Nick.

Kate looked at her plate with interest, then growing horror. Thin, bright pink, slices of something were laid out, alternating with dark brown slices of some sort of salami, large, greasy white blobs of fat glistening between the thin brown veins, with a third set of slices of something pale pink with green and red blobs in it. She tentatively cut a small piece from the bright pink something and tasted it gingerly. School Spam was the nearest she could get to it, complete with gristle. She laid down her fork and took a gulp of wine. The wine tasted better now somehow, and she took another large gulp. Nick was paying no attention to her, tucking into his plateful, tearing pieces of baguette and enthusiastically planning their forthcoming wine buying trip.

By the time they had got home late that afternoon, Kate was feeling thoroughly ill. The *brandade* had been tasty at the time of eating, but with an overwhelming amount of garlic. During the night, she awoke with the strong taste of it still in her mouth. She felt disgusted knowing that she must smell dreadfully, and not only that, but her mouth was parched from the rough wine and her head ached dully. She slipped out of bed, taking care not to wake Nick, who was sleeping heavily alongside her, and sat on the edge of the bath with her head against the icy wall of the bathroom, feeling utterly dejected. It wasn't just the food and wine that she had hated, but she remembered the catty looks the two Englishwomen had given her. And how Nick had passed off her presence as a temporary hired help to his friend, the elegant Marie-Claire. And the way that Marie-Claire had looked at Nick. Almost as if they were a lot more than just friends. And had he really said he couldn't introduce her as his current girlfriend? Current? All her dreams of starting a new life where no one knew their past and no one would judge them had been tarnished by that visit to the restaurant.

So, after that, Kate made more and more excuses whenever Nick suggested an outing to a café or a restaurant, or an invitation from one of his many friends and acquaintances. So now he'd stopped even asking if she'd like to go out and just went on his own. Kate was glad he did, knowing he enjoyed company, and sure that he put her behaviour down to her advanced state of pregnancy. She felt more and more depressed as the weeks went on. Depressed by the dreadful, gloomy weather, with its unremitting drizzly rain, the cold château and her own lack of energy. Tonight she gave the fire another poke and decided not to wait up any longer for Nick.

4

France. May.

The sound of a car approaching down the lane aroused Kate. She was lying under a large umbrella on the château terrace, watching the small white clouds flitting across the deep blue sky. The end of April had brought better weather and the first few days of May had been wonderfully warm. A number of small, striped lizards were making the most of the sun, lying along the top of the low stone balustrade at the edge of the terrace. The big wooden table was covered in a blue and white check plastic cloth. The remains of their lunch were still on the table, the almost empty bottle of wine attracting a few small flies. Nick was sprawled in a low wooden chair, his feet resting on the balustrade. His tan was getting quite deep after only a few days of sunshine. He looked relaxed and peaceful, his hat down over his eyes. Kate stretched like a cat and got to her feet slowly. Her baby was due in the next couple of weeks or so now, and she rather hoped that the car she had heard might be the doctor coming to check up on her. She walked over to the edge of the terrace and peered round the corner of the château where she could see the break in the trees, high up on the track. The car was just coming into view. Kate stared in disbelief. In a few seconds the car was out of sight again behind the dense canopy of leaves. But she was sure of it. It was Alastair's car! It was a distinctive bright metallic blue Saab. She had never seen one like it in rural France, where almost everyone drove a grey or white Renault. And the car was being driven slowly, as if by someone unused to the track. She turned to Nick in panic.

"Nick, wake up! I'm sure I've just seen Alastair. Didn't you hear that car? It's him!!"

"Calm down," Nick drawled without opening his eyes. Why did she have to be so jumpy? Of course it wasn't Alastair.

"Nick, it is him. I know it is!"

Nick sat up, pushing his hat back.

"Kate, for goodness sake! It's too far away to tell who it is. Anyway, why on earth would it be Alastair? You haven't heard from him, have you?" Nick looked at her quickly.

"No."

Kate had to admit that there had been complete silence since she had written telling him about the baby and about her and Nick. Nick settled back in his chair and pulled his hat back down over his eyes. Kate grabbed his arm.

"What are we going to do?" she cried. "What's he come here for now? Do you think he wants me to go back to him?"

Kate was close to tears. Nick shook her off and stood up, swaying slightly from the effects of wine and hot sun.

"Get a grip, Kate," Nick spoke harshly. "It won't be him, but I'll go and see anyway. Sit down at the table, then if it is him, at least he won't be able to see you're pregnant!"

He strode through the open French windows into the salon and Kate could hear his footsteps echoing on the stone floors, then the sound of the heavy front door being unlocked. A few minutes later, she heard the sound of tyres on the gravel drive, and a murmur of voices, Nick's raised in greeting. Then, to her horror, the sound of Alastair's deep voice. She gripped the edge of the table. What did Nick mean, Alastair wouldn't know she was pregnant? She had told him in her letter explaining why she had left him. And Nick had told Joanne.

A few minutes later, Nick appeared at the French window, all smiles.

"Look who I've found, Kate!"

"Alastair."

The colour drained from Kate's face and she sat rooted to the spot, still clutching the edge of the table.

"Hello, darling! You look great! France must agree with you!"

Alastair strode over and kissed her cheek.

"Richard and I thought you would be just about finished here by now so we'd come over and surprise you! You can drive home with us, since I know how much you hate flying."

Kate gaped at him in amazement. What on earth was he talking about? Hadn't he got her letter explaining about her and Nick? Even if he hadn't, Joanne would have been sure to tell him. What was going on? She thought back to the day that they had decided it was time to let Alastair and Joanne know about them. She remembered Nick's hesitation, she remembered doubting his resolve. Then she remembered how his attitude had changed, how cheerful he'd been as he set off to the post office. Suddenly it all fell into place. No wonder she hadn't had any letters from Alastair since then. She looked at Nick in horror. He couldn't have posted the letters. And he must have been intercepting Alastair's letters since then, so she wouldn't realise what had happened. And Alastair wouldn't have known that the phone and internet were now connected at the château. Kate felt as if she was going to faint. She clutched the edge of the table, her knuckles white.

Nick was pulling up chairs and getting more glasses, ever the perfect host.

"You must be hungry, both of you. We've just finished but I can rustle up some bread and cheese and of course I do have the odd bottle of wine!"

Kate was staring at him, fighting the realisation that he had betrayed her. She couldn't believe his deceit. He didn't love her after all. He hadn't told Joanne about them and he had made sure Alastair didn't get her letter. He didn't mean to stay with her. She remembered how he'd introduced her to the notaire's wife as his neighbour from England, and how she hadn't met any of his other friends. True, she hadn't wanted to, but, she reflected, Nick had never pressed her to go with him. It was only the doctor who appeared to assume that Nick was the father of the baby. And now he was trying to bluff it out, act as if nothing had happened between them.

She felt a surge of anger and hate. How could Nick have deceived her like this? How could she have chosen this, this creep, over strong, dependable Alastair? But it was too late now. She couldn't hide her pregnancy from Alastair forever and why should she shield Nick? He'd have to admit his guilt. Alastair had to know. She couldn't keep him in the dark any longer. She felt an unbearable pang of love and pain when she thought of how he must have trusted her, how he must have believed the lies about her designing the château garden, how he'd let her go her own way and do what she wanted, without a thought for himself or any concern that she might betray him. At that moment Kate hated herself more than she would ever have believed. She didn't deserve anything, let alone to be loved by such a good man. Here she was, almost on the point of giving birth to another man's child and there was her innocent husband laughing with the man who had cheated him. And she was just sitting there, letting the deception continue because she was too weak to let him know the truth. Kate made up her mind. She'd think about the future later. If she had a future it wouldn't be with Nick, and maybe not with anyone else after this. But for now the important thing was to sweep aside the charade and at least stop pretending to Alastair that everything was normal. She got to her feet and walked unsteadily towards the edge of the terrace where Nick was standing, pointing out the lake to Alastair and Richard. She stopped just before she reached the little group.

"Nick, shut up!" she screamed, losing control as she heard him chatting and laughing with them. There was silence as Nick broke off in mid-sentence and all three turned to face her.

"Yes, look at me. All of you. I'm having a baby. And it's Nick's. And we've been having an affair for nearly a year and, Alastair, I was too scared and too weak and too selfish to tell you face to face. So I ran away with him. Not because I didn't love you, but because I thought I loved him as well and I was having his baby and I knew I'd have to choose between you and I didn't want to have to but I wanted to start again where no one knew me so that I wouldn't hurt you anymore." Kate broke off and gulped for air, tears now streaming down her face. "Don't you say anything," she screamed again at Nick. "It's all your fault that it has happened like this. I wrote to you ages ago, Alastair, to explain. I know it was cowardly and I should have come home to tell you. But I didn't and I thought it would be alright in the end and he was supposed to tell Joanne, except he didn't and he mustn't have posted my letter and I haven't heard from you since so I thought you were really angry and hated me, but now I know he must have kept your letters. And I didn't want you to find out like this, and he is still trying to pretend it hasn't happened."

Kate broke off again, her voice giving out as a stab of pain shot through her. She clutched her belly and staggered, falling awkwardly onto a deck chair.

"Oh no. It's the baby," she gasped, waves of pain racking her body.

Alastair stood stock still as if hit by a thunderbolt. Nick took a step away from him, backing towards the stone balustrade at the edge of the terrace.

Afterwards, Kate could not be sure what had happened next. No one had been paying any attention to Richard, standing slightly behind Alastair. As Kate collapsed, he had thrust Alastair aside and lunged at Nick, his fist smashing into the side of Nick's head. As he staggered under the blow, Richard drove his fist again at Nick, this time catching him on his collar bone. Kate heard the snap of the bone and saw, out of the corner of her eye, Nick's knees buckle under the blow. Losing his balance, he fell heavily against the balustrade. There was a sharp crack and the crumbling stonework gave way under him. The next moment they heard a dull thud as Nick's body hit the rocky ground way below the terrace. Then silence again.

Kate was first to come to her senses, struggling to her feet.

"We must get an ambulance, quick. Alastair, go back through the kitchen, out of the courtyard – that leads down to the lawn where he is. Take the towels from the kitchen in case he's bleeding a lot. I'll phone for the ambulance."

Alastair did as she said, calling up to her from the lawn.

"He's out cold, but he's still breathing, thank God."

"The ambulance is on its way. Come back up here, we need to look after Richard."

When Alastair reached the terrace, Richard was crouched on his haunches shaking his head in disbelief at what he'd done. Kate was bending over him.

"What's he saying?" asked Alastair.

Kate looked up. "I'll tell you later. Now, listen, both of you. Richard, listen to me."

Kate was very calm now as she turned Richard's face towards her. She spoke very slowly.

"The gendarmes will come with the ambulance – they always do round here if you call the emergency number. It was an accident. Richard, you did not touch Nick. There was no fight, no argument. Alastair, we're Nick's neighbours from England, you and Richard came to take me home now I've finished my work here. Nick had been drinking at lunchtime and he tripped and fell against the balustrade while he was pointing out the view to you two. Like much of the rest of the château, it needed repair. It was an accident. Richard?" Kate lifted his chin so that their eyes were level. "You understand me, Richard?"

Richard nodded.

"I'm sorry," he mumbled. "I couldn't help it, I just wanted to stop him …I never meant to …"

5

Nick was walking towards her down the narrow, cobbled street in Fromac. She smiled at him and held the baby up in her arms so he could see it. He didn't seem to see her, but carried on walking, smiling and waving, right past her, so close that she could feel the warmth of his body. She stretched out a hand to touch his arm, in case he hadn't noticed her. But her hand touched only the air. She saw him glance up and smile again. She followed his gaze and there, in the window above the notaire's office, was the wife of the notaire. Marie-Claire. She was naked. Nick turned towards the heavy oak door of the office and disappeared. Kate rushed to the door and rattled the handle, but it was firmly locked.

She opened her eyes and stared at the white ceiling with its slow moving fan. She knew that Nick had died. They hadn't told her yet, but she knew. It was two days now since the accident, two long days and two even longer nights that she had lain in the hospital bed. She had gone in the ambulance with him, going into labour as they sped towards Cahors through the narrow country lanes. She couldn't remember much at all except the wail of the siren and the slow progress through the crowded early evening traffic of the town until the ambulance turned very sharply to the left and down a steep ramp and the doors were flung open and Nick was wheeled away by a team of nurses and doctors and she was left in the ambulance. She thought they'd forgotten her, then the doors slammed shut again and they roared off around a car park to a different building. Where Nick had been taken was bright and modern. The maternity wing was an old stone building with tightly shuttered windows. But Kate didn't care by this time. The next few hours passed in a

83

blur and it was just midnight when the midwife held up a small bundle to her and said something in rapid French to the nurse. They took the baby away and put it in an incubator, allowing Kate to look at it through a screen. She sat looking at it for a long time. It was a boy.

Kate kept asking the staff about Nick, but no one seemed to understand her. She was frantic with worry. The next day, her own doctor arrived with the midwife. He explained in English that Kate had lost a lot of blood and was to stay in hospital for a few days. The doctor spoke reassuringly. Monsieur Carslow was still unconscious and very ill, but they were hopeful. In the meantime they must look to the future. First they must register the birth of her child. This had to be done within three days of birth in France. He said that the nursing staff had called him in because he was Kate's doctor and he spoke English.

"You see, Madame. The midwife needs to complete the birth registration certificate, but she is unsure," he coughed politely, "of the name of the father. The gendarme who made the report on the accident told her that your husband had just arrived from England with his friend to take you home and she assumed, *naturellement*, that he is the father of your child. I have intervened, Madame, since when I attended you for the antenatal, I myself of course have only seen Monsieur Carslow, who, forgive me, Madame," he coughed again. "I assumed was the prospective father. You will understand that it is important to be correct on the registration for many reasons. In France, we have a strong respect for succession, if not so much for marriage itself!" He laughed quietly. "It is not a scandal here to have a child when you are not married to the father, Madame. And anyway, there is no need for people to know. But I think Monsieur Carslow was a wealthy man. His son – if it is his son – has a right to inherit that wealth."

"But he's not dead!" Kate sat up in alarm. "You said he wasn't! Please don't say he's died!"

"Calm yourself, Madame. No, Monsieur is still alive. But let me explain how our laws work. I do not know what arrangement you may have with your husband," he shrugged. "A *ménage à trois* is not unusual in France. Often a wife will be friends with her husband's mistress and his children by her, or vice versa. Take our recently deceased president, Monsieur Mitterand, for a good example. His wife and mistress and all the children standing beside his grave, united in grief! And all the children benefitting from his wealth!" The doctor smiled. "So civilised, no?"

"I'm sorry," Kate shrugged wearily. "I'm not sure I understand what you are saying."

"Madame, in France it is not possible for a parent to disinherit his children. A proportion of the estate is reserved for all natural children, born in or out of marriage. So if, and please forgive me, but I have your son's interests at heart, if your son is the son of your husband, then it makes no matter. But if he is the son of Monsieur Carslow, then we have a different situation. Monsieur Carslow owns the Château de St Geniès-Lafontaine, no?"

Kate nodded.

"When Monsieur Carslow dies, the château will succeed to his heirs according to French law, as does all property in France. These heirs are his blood relatives. Not, you must be aware, his wife, or his mistress. So even if he has made a will leaving all his assets to the dog's home as you English like to do, it does not matter. The law in France overrides this – he cannot disinherit his child. So Madame, you see it is important for your child. If, as I have assumed, Monsieur Carslow is the father, then you should tell me so that I can register it on the birth certificate. If your child is the only offspring of Monsieur Carslow, then he will, by law, inherit half of Monsieur's estate in France. It is not a time to think of convention and what people will say. People in England will not know unless you tell them. If you intend to return with your husband and the baby then that is up to you and Monsieur Carslow. But I urge you to think about the future for your son's sake."

The doctor paused, then opened his briefcase and took out a form.

"Now, Madame. Father's name?"

Kate took a deep breath.

"Nicholas James Carslow."

****

That had been yesterday. Kate had realised then that the doctor thought Nick was dying. She felt numb, confused, unable to sort out her thoughts. Nick had let her down so badly, but she loved him and his easy charm, for all his faults. And yet he hadn't been able to tell Joanne about them. And he'd lied and schemed so no one would know about them. She didn't know what it really meant. Did he still only love Joanne and would he have left her and gone back to Jo? Or was it Joanne's money he loved? She knew she would never know for sure, but in her heart she knew he'd only ever truly loved Jo. And what of Alastair? They hadn't had a chance to talk. She couldn't expect anything other than his anger and hate. Even if he did forgive her, she couldn't forgive herself for betraying him. He wouldn't want her back now. And then there was the baby. Born into this turmoil and drama, a weak, helpless little creature, but Kate's responsibility. She vowed to herself that the baby would never have to suffer.

There was a soft knock at the door and the doctor came into the room.

"Madame. I am sorry. Monsieur Carslow died at four o'clock this morning. There was nothing we could do. He never regained consciousness."

Kate nodded and closed her eyes.

"I am sorry to disturb you. But your husband is here and he would like to see you, if you feel well enough."

"Yes," Kate said. "Let him come in."

The doctor left the room and Alastair appeared in the doorway. His face was pale and he needed a shave. It looked as if he had slept in his clothes.

"Hello, Kate."

He stood at the end of the bed.

"I suppose they told you?"

"Yes."

Kate looked past him, out of the window across the car park at the faceless building where Nick lay.

"I came as soon as I could," Alastair said. "After the ambulance had left, the gendarmes took me and Richard down to the police station in St Geniès. We had to wait for hours until another gendarme from Fromac turned up. He seemed to be the only one who spoke English. I think they believed our story," he added wryly. "Then we all had to go back out to the château for them to examine the balustrade. It's badly cracked further along, you know. It's a wonder it hasn't given way before. They seemed satisfied with our explanation of what happened, but then we had to go back yet again to the Gendarmerie in order for them to fill in all the forms. So finally they let us go at about eleven o'clock and we stayed the night in the little hotel in the square at Fromac. Anyway, yesterday morning, we were just getting ready to leave to come over here and see what was happening when the gendarmes arrived and arrested us both. We were marched out of the hotel in handcuffs! It certainly caused a stir in Fromac!" he laughed drily.

"But why?" Kate asked anxiously.

"Well, by that time you had had the baby and the midwife lives in St Geniès and she had been talking to the gendarme and he got the idea there was more to this than we'd told him. You know, it had to be the *crime passionnelle*. And she also told him Nick was dying, which meant it might be murder."

"Oh no!" Kate cried in horror. "But what happened? Richard didn't say anything did he? And they've let you go?"

"Yes. They don't have any evidence and Richard kept quiet. We stuck to our story. They let us go this morning, rather reluctantly. It's ironic really, but you know it was the truth, apart, of course, from what Richard did."

Alastair was staring out of the window, not looking at her.

"Until that moment just before Richard hit him, I certainly didn't know there was anything wrong."

He sighed.

"Funny though," Alastair frowned and went on, almost to himself. "Richard seemed to know something was up. He was really edgy all the way here. And," Alastair broke off for a moment, then went on in a rush. "I wasn't going to tell you, but after you'd gone off in the ambulance and the gendarmes had brought us back to the château, I was fixing some tape along the balustrade to stop anyone going too near the edge, and I saw something glinting in the grass, down near where Nick had fallen. So I went down, and look what I found."

Out of his pocket, Alastair pulled a small bundle wrapped in a handkerchief.

"What on earth is it?" Kate peered at the bundle.

"Look." Alastair pulled the handkerchief away. "It's a knuckleduster. And I think it's Richard's. On the way down here, we stopped in Cahors to get some lunch. While we were looking for a café, we passed a shop in the main boulevard that sells guns and knives and stuff. Richard was looking in the window and, after we left the café, I went to the bank and he went back to the car on his own. But when I got there he hadn't turned up, and I saw him coming out of the shop. He had a small packet which I saw him put in his pocket. When I asked him what he'd bought, he said nothing! I didn't pursue it, because you know what he's like. I just thought it was probably some air gun pellets or something that he uses to frighten the birds off the garden. But now it seems it's almost as if he knew about Nick and you, and he'd come prepared to teach Nick a lesson."

Kate sat silent for a minute.

"Did anyone see you pick it up?

Alastair shook his head.

"No. The gendarmes were all up on the terrace."

"Good," she spoke quietly and urgently. "You and Richard must get away from here, now. Straight away, before the gendarmes at St Geniès bring in the Police Nationale from Cahors and they start asking more questions. Get rid of that thing," she pointed at the knuckleduster. "Chuck it in the lake."

"Yes. I suppose you are right. But, Kate," Alastair was looking at the floor now, avoiding her eyes. "There is the baby. Your baby. No one knows," he paused and swallowed.

Kate could see the tears behind his eyes.

"No one knows," he said again. "That it's not mine. You can put my name on the birth certificate if you want to. I'll go along with it. I've had time to think, in that cell overnight. Kate, I love you," Alastair turned to her, grasping both her hands. "I know it must be all my fault, going away so much and leaving you on your own. Joanne doesn't know, and we'll have to tell her Nick's death was an accident, so let's just say the baby is ours. Please, Kate," he implored. "I don't want to lose you."

This was too much for Kate. She clung on to his hands, sobbing. How could she have made such a mistake, so many mistakes? She deserved all that had happened and more. She longed to say yes to Alastair, but it was impossible now. He had forgiven her so much, but there must be a limit. And now, unwittingly, she'd put Alastair in danger, by naming Nick the father of her child. The police would suspect him, not Richard. He'd be the one with a reason to want Nick dead. Exhausted, she raised her head.

"It's too late," she whispered. "I've already told the doctor that Nick was the father of the baby. So everyone will know, including Joanne. And when the police get to know, they're going to want to ask more questions. They'll think you did it, not Richard. You must not tell Joanne or anyone what Richard did. Never," she added vehemently. "You must go. Go while you still can. Please," she begged. "Now, before it's too late."

6

Kent, England. November.

Joanne reached forward and put another log on the fire. She finished her brandy quickly and looked at Alastair. She remembered it as if it were yesterday. That day last May when he had sat in the same chair, with the same expression on his face. The day that he'd come to tell her that Nick, her husband, had been having an affair with Kate, his wife, for months. That there had been an accident. That Nick was dead. That Kate had a baby and Nick was the father.

"Yes," she said quietly. "I remember. It was only afterwards that I realised how awful it must have been for you. How brave you were to come and tell me yourself, particularly when none of it was your fault. Did you know they held an inquest? The local gendarme was convinced that you and Nick must have been fighting, or that you'd pushed him over the balustrade deliberately. But the verdict was accidental death. His skull was fractured in two places from falling on the rocks, but there was hardly a mark on his face. You know, nothing to suggest any fight. I knew it was an accident. I knew you wouldn't have hurt Nick. When you told me what had happened, I didn't want to believe any of it. I didn't blame you ever, but I was so confused and hurt and angry with Nick, and more so with Kate. Then later, after they'd sent Nick's body home and we'd buried him, I felt so sorry for you. I felt pretty sorry for myself, but more so for you. After all, although the only man I've ever loved was dead, at least I knew he'd still loved me. Even though he cheated on me. I expect you know Kate wasn't the first by any means, although there weren't any other children. And he always came back to me. Even with Kate and a baby, he still couldn't tell me it was over between us. He would have come back. Although, I suppose if he'd lived, the baby might have made a difference and he might have stayed with Kate. Still, we'll never know, will we?" Joanne smiled sadly.

"But you, Alastair. Kate had betrayed you and left you and even so you gave her another chance after all that happened and she'd had Nick's baby and everything. And even after she turned you down when the baby was born, you went back in August and gave her another chance! I thought you were so generous, so kind and forgiving to still want her, and another man's child. How you must love her. I still remember you coming here to tell me what you were going to do. I really appreciated that – most men wouldn't have had the guts to do it, but you did. And planning to sell the cottage and move to Scotland with her if she'd come back to you – to make it easier for me so I didn't have to see her and the baby. You were so sensitive and considerate to me." Joanne smiled at Alastair. "And then when you came back on your own and said she wouldn't come with you. Well, I was outraged! I was really, really angry with her then. In a way I could understand her falling for Nick, after all, I did, and so did quite a few others! And he'd let her down too, I know. But for her to reject you again when you were still willing to forgive her! I decided then that somehow she must be after my money and the château. Scheming little bitch!"

Joanne slammed her glass down on the table.

"And it seems I was right. So," her eyes were bright and hard now. "What is she up to now?"

She picked up the magazine again.

"Just look at this! She cannot sell my château! You know as well as I do that even if half of it legally belongs to Nick's child, none of it belongs to her! Nick left me everything in his will, and I'm his legal wife. No court, not even in France, is going to award the other half to her. And anyway, until the child is eighteen, it'd be extraordinarily difficult, if not impossible, to sell property it owns in France. I'll have to get my lawyers on to it first thing in the morning. She can't do it!"

Alastair had been gazing into the fire all the time she'd been talking. Now he turned slowly to face her.

"Joanne. She can do it – maybe."

Joanne looked at him in surprise.

"What do you mean? Of course she can't!"

Alastair didn't reply. Joanne scanned his face.

"What else do you know, Alastair? You'd better tell me everything this time."

Alastair took a deep breath. A look of such anguish crossed his face that Joanne hesitated, unsure she really wanted to know.

"When I went back in August to ask Kate if she'd come back to me, I saw the baby. It was very weak and sickly – it was born prematurely, and it had," he paused, searching for the right words. "Various – problems. The only explanation is – it must have died."

"Oh, no." Joanne couldn't help herself from giving an involuntary gasp of sympathy. "But surely," she frowned. "Surely that means the whole château reverts to me. I was Nick's wife and his will leaves it to me. The notaire, Maître Lacombe, told me the other half was mine, that a French court would validate the English will. That's why we decided to wait until the child was old enough to be legally responsible then we would sell it. So if it has died, that means the whole château is mine again.

"Well, no."

Alastair was staring into the fire again. With an effort he turned back to look at her.

"Legally, Kate inherits the child's share because she is its only living relative."

"What! You mean to say that me and Kate now own half each of MY château!" Joanne was beside herself with rage. " I have to share my own château with my husband's mistress!"

"Yes," Alastair replied. "You would have to. Except for one thing."

He stopped. Joanne looked at him expectantly.

"Well?"

"The baby wasn't Nick's."

"What!"

Joanne gasped, her eyes wide. Then she shook her head.

"Of course he was. He must have been. Maître Lacombe checked the papers. He told me Nick's name was on the birth registration as the father. And I saw it for myself, to make sure! He sent me a copy. Remember, I wanted to know what would happen if Kate went back to you."

"I know," Alastair nodded. "That's what Kate told them at the hospital. The doctor there had assumed that Nick was the father because they were both living at the château and he'd been there with her for all the antenatal checks. When the birth was registered, the doctor specifically asked her who the father was, because of all the trouble and the accident. The midwife, touchingly," he smiled wryly, "seemed to think it was mine. The doctor was a friend of Nick's anyway and he wanted to make sure that if it was Nick's child, it got its rightful inheritance. So he deliberately asked her to confirm the father's name. And she said Nick was the father. But he wasn't the father. I know he wasn't."

"But how do you know for sure?"

Joanne suddenly realised the awful implication of this for Alastair.

"You've told me you didn't think it could be yours. You can't mean Kate had a string of lovers at the same time?" Joanne could hardly bring herself to say it. "And anyway, why did she lie about Nick being the father if she knew he wasn't?"

Alastair looked into the fire again as if trying to draw strength from its warm, comforting brightness.

"Oh, Joanne. I've been trying to explain. She lied to make sure her child got half of your château and half of any money Nick had in France. She stole it from you."

Joanne sat silent for a few minutes. Then,

"The cow!"

She spat the words out.

"Jesus, if it wasn't bad enough stealing my husband!"

She flopped back into the leather chair and gazed sightlessly at the beamed ceiling. Alastair remained motionless, staring into the fire. After a while, Joanne sat forward in her chair, a puzzled frown wrinkling her brow.

"But I still don't understand how she thinks she can sell it now. Even if the baby has died, which would make its share hers – if Nick had been the father. And she must still think I don't know Nick wasn't the father. But surely the other half is still mine?"

"I don't think she would be able to sell it without getting the other half formally handed over to her. My guess is that, soon after the child was born, she probably applied through another notaire to get the other half of the estate for her child. As Nick left no French will, and the French are very strong on succession within the family, a court may well award the other half to the child as Nick's only blood relative, rather than you, particularly if you have not instigated proceedings to validate the English will. They might not even consult you since you are not resident in France and we are talking only about French property. Now, if the child has died, and the courts are in process with her application for the whole of the estate to go to Nick's child, or if the application has already succeeded, then Kate will inherit the whole thing as the child's only relative. Then she can sell it."

Joanne's jaw dropped and she started to protest but Alastair went on.

"She might have already got it through, although it seems unlikely given the length of time things take in France, and, although they may present you with a *fait accompli*, you should have been contacted by the French authorities to let you know you have no further claim on the French estate of your husband. Although, as you haven't already made a claim, they might not bother. My guess is that it hasn't happened yet and she's taking a gamble that the courts will find in favour of the child – then by the time she finds a buyer, she'll be the legal owner. Since there was no French will, she's probably hoping that you won't find out about it until it's too late, and, or, since you've let her live there so long without doing anything, and you still think the baby is Nick's, she may think that you actually want Nick's baby to have it, and therefore won't contest it."

"Won't contest it! She's got another think coming! It's my château. I loved that place. But I never want to go there again, because of her. She'll pay for this. I'll bankrupt her, I'll have her in jail for deception!"

Joanne jumped up and started to pace the room.

"I'll get my lawyers on to it now! But," Joanne turned to him, her face softening. "She's right, of course. If the baby was Nick's, I don't suppose I would have done anything. But, Alastair," she hesitated and her eyes sought his, her voice dropping into a gentle whisper, so full of sympathy and compassion for him that Alastair almost broke down.

"Can you really be sure that the baby wasn't Nick's? I'd have to prove it in a court of law."

"I'm sure."

Alastair couldn't meet her gaze.

"For one thing, Nick once told me when you and he were trying to have children that he was pretty sure it was his fault. He'd finally had the tests you wanted him to have, and although they weren't conclusive, they did point that way. Dr Grey can probably provide evidence for you on that. But anyway," he paused, rubbing his hand across his eyes as if still trying to erase the sight from his memory.

"I knew who the father was when I saw the baby myself."

He seemed to be talking to himself now.

"It was the night of the storm, in August," he murmured.

Alastair paused again, then turned to Joanne, a look of pain in his eyes so intense that Joanne now looked away. He took a deep breath.

"As soon as I saw him I knew. He's mine. I'm his father."

"Good God!" Joanne sat back in her chair, staring at him in horror.

"Yes, I know. Can't trust anyone these days, can you?"

Alastair's voice broke as he attempted a wry laugh.

There was a small silence.

"But why did she tell you at all?" Joanne asked, puzzled. "No one would have known. I'd never have known and she'd have had half the château anyway even if I had got my half back – even though that seems a bit unlikely from what you say. But why say anything?"

"She didn't have to tell me. I knew as soon as I saw the baby in August," Alastair sighed. "When I went back to try and get her to come home with me. I thought we could start again. I still loved her, Joanne, and I wanted her back. I was prepared to treat the baby as our own. But when I found out it was mine all along…" Alastair's voice tailed off.

Alastair sighed.

"I'm afraid there's more to it than that," he said. "I know you must be furious with me for not telling you before that Nick was not the father. I'm sorry Joanne, but I suppose I've just been protecting Kate – and myself. But after all that's happened, I owe you the truth. Just listen to me, then you can do what you want. I want it all to be over."

"Alastair, for goodness sake!" Joanne looked at him in alarm. "I can't believe there's more."

"Oh, but there is. I'll tell you everything that happened last August. On the night of the storm."

PART III

This year

1

August.

It was only seven o'clock in the morning but already the motorway to the Channel ports was busy. As he turned off down the slip road to the Channel Tunnel, Alastair was wondering if he'd made the right decision. Ever since he and Richard had left France in May, driving through the night, not using the autoroutes for fear of being stopped by the gendarmes, he had been haunted by what had happened at the château. For a long time, he had nightmares in which it was he who was hitting Nick, then pushing him over the balustrade. It was always the same and he always woke up just after Nick's body hit the ground. The sound of that dull, final thump would stay with him forever. He knew it had been an accident, but he also knew that hitting Nick very, very hard had been what he himself had felt like doing, and probably would have done, if Richard had not got there first. He and Richard had not talked about what had happened at all. And it made it worse that Alastair knew that Richard had attacked Nick out of loyalty to him. So they hadn't talked much at all.

****

Alastair sighed as he joined the long queue at the Eurotunnel check in. How he hated all the lies. The worst thing, of course, had been telling Joanne. She knew Nick was dead before she saw Alastair. The police were at her house as Richard and Alastair arrived home. He had half expected to be arrested himself when they came off the ferry, but the French police had recorded Nick's fall as an accident after all. When he saw Joanne, he realised how much she loved her handsome, lazy, unfaithful husband. She still didn't know about Nick and Kate. As far as the police were concerned, it was a straightforward accident. It was left to Alastair to explain the cruel, unforgivable facts about his own wife. Joanne had surprised him, in a way. She was grieving deeply for her husband, but she listened to Alastair's story of Kate and Nick's deception, the baby, and Nick's reluctance to tell Joanne and Alastair about his affair, with a kind of detached compassion, for Alastair certainly, but also for Kate. She took strength and comfort from knowing that Nick could not bring himself to leave her. She forgave him everything because, at the end of the day, he could not give her up. And she loved him for all his faults. But it was her attitude to Kate and the baby that Alastair found the most surprising. Joanne seemed able to forgive Kate sufficiently to let her stay on in Joanne's own château to bring up her baby with enough money and a roof over its head, even if it was Joanne's money! Alastair supposed it was because the baby was Nick's that Joanne was being so kind when she could have forced a sale of the château and left Kate and the baby homeless and penniless. Joanne herself refused to admit that she had any good intentions and claimed her decision was purely economic. As Nick's child owned half the château she would have had to go through the courts to force a sale before the child was eighteen and this could have cost her a fortune if she had lost her case. So Joanne maintained that her decision to let Kate and the child stay on was purely practical and that when the child was eighteen she would act.

Since fleeing France in May, Alastair had done a lot of thinking. He had trusted Kate completely, so her betrayal had come as a total shock. She had said she loved them both, him and Nick, and the baby had forced her decision to choose Nick and leave him. When he saw her last, in the hospital in Cahors, she had not said anything more, but he knew she still cared about him, urging him to leave in case the police changed their minds about the accident.

Alastair knew he had to see Kate again. He still loved her, despite what had happened. Now that things had calmed down, he wanted to see her. At first he wasn't quite sure why, but something told him he wouldn't rest until he was sure she was coping with her baby and was happy in France. She must feel so isolated. On the long summer evenings that he spent sitting on the bench outside the kitchen window, staring out over the familiar countryside, he eventually realised that what he wanted more than anything was to have Kate back with him. He missed her more than he would ever have imagined. He didn't know if she would come back. He knew they would have to move, but it could work out if they went back to Scotland. So Alastair made up his mind. He would go to France again and ask Kate if she'd come back to him. He'd tell Joanne what he was planning and he'd ask Richard to go with him. No more lies.

That had been two weeks ago. Now Alastair and Richard were on their way. The queue moved slowly. The cars and caravans surrounding them were packed with picnic boxes, lilos, coats and boots, surf boards, bicycles, excited children, bored teenagers glued to their phones, food, maps, tents. It was early August and the holiday season was well underway. Alastair nosed the Saab forward. There were one or two businessmen amidst the throng, a few foreign cars returning home, but mainly the great British rush to the sun was underway. As usual, the temperature in Kent was rising to its highest all year to add to the shortening of tempers and occasional boiling radiators. Alastair watched idly as a beaten-up old Land Rover limped into a side lane. Improbably, not only did it have a roof rack stacked with battered canoes, but it was pulling a caravan to which were attached three equally battered bicycles. Clouds of steam were puffing from under the bonnet as the Land Rover came to a halt. A tall man with longish, unkempt dark hair got out and opened the bonnet, followed by a boy of about twelve or thirteen and a girl a few years older. Alastair watched as they clustered round the front of the vehicle. He heard the man say something to the boy and girl and they all laughed. The sound of the man's deep musical laugh reached Alastair above the noise of car engines and children arguing and parents screaming in other cars. Alastair smiled involuntarily. The girl glanced towards him. She was about fifteen years old, pretty, slim and quite tall, with curly dark blonde hair, tied back from her face. Her brother also looked in his direction. He was a smaller, thinner version of her, with an open, bright, cheerful, freckled face. Alastair realised they were not looking at him at all, but past him to a car behind him in the queue. It was a smart, silver-coloured cabriolet, with a lone woman driver in dark sunglasses. The boy said something to his father, who also looked at the car. They both laughed again, the father in a rueful manner as he turned back to his boiling radiator and clapped-out Land Rover. Alastair glanced in his mirror at the car that had attracted their attention. He gave a slight start as he took in the heart-shaped face and blonde hair of the driver. Joanne!

It was Alastair's turn at the check-in booth and he lost sight of the silver car as he followed the stream of vehicles into the car park. They were early and had almost an hour to wait before their train. Richard went off to buy a newspaper and Alastair got out of the car. Standing leaning against it, he looked around for the silver car. Joanne hadn't mentioned that she planned to be in France when he had told her of his decision. She might be going there on business, but usually she flew. And she wasn't driving her usual Porsche. It seemed almost as though she didn't want to be recognised. Alastair frowned slightly. He hoped she wouldn't show up at the château, even if it was hers. Perhaps she was going to make trouble after all. Alastair remembered how excited she'd been when she first found it. Even Joanne, who had everything, seemed to have lost her heart to the place. And he had to admit it was hard on her that, just because of an archaic legal system, she had lost half of her beloved château to her husband's bastard son! Joanne could afford a legal battle to get Nick's English will recognised in France if she wanted to. But it seemed unlikely that she would go to France herself for that. She could get her lawyers to do it all. Then another thought occurred to him. He wiped the perspiration from his face and tried to think rationally. Why hadn't he thought of it before? Maybe she didn't believe the story of Nick's accident after all! She wanted to get the case reopened. She knew he and Richard would be there, he had told her himself. She would want justice for Nick. Joanne might also see it as a way of getting back at Kate. She would be jealous – who wouldn't – if your husband's mistress gets taken back by her own husband and they live together happily ever after with your husband's baby, while you are left alone, robbed not only of your husband but of your château! Alastair shook his head to clear away his racing thoughts. He was getting paranoid. There was probably a perfectly innocent explanation for Joanne's presence. It was just that he couldn't think of one.

Richard came loping back through the crowds. He liked busy places where no one knew him almost as much as he liked total solitude. So long as he could lose himself and not attract attention, he was happy. As he waited to cross the road into the car park, a silver car passed him slowly. He glanced in at the blonde woman driver. She looked vaguely familiar. When he got back, Alastair was pacing around the vehicle distractedly. He too had seen the car pass Richard and had watched it draw into a parking space about a hundred metres away. The woman had got out and stretched. Then, taking a large, orange leather handbag from the front seat, she headed off towards the shops.

"I'll just be a minute, Richard," Alastair said, already on his way after her. "I need the loo after all."

"OK. There's plenty time," replied Richard, leaning in to get a straw hat out of the car to shade his pale skin from the bright sun. Settling himself against the front wing, he opened his newspaper.

Alastair set off across the car park in pursuit of Joanne. Groups of holidaymakers, sauntering along, got in his way and he almost lost sight of the blonde head as he dodged between baby buggies and supermarket trolleys loaded with duty-free beer. Suddenly she was standing just in front of him, picking up a copy of a free newspaper.

"Hello there, what are you …?" Alastair started to say, his hand lightly touching her shoulder, then stopped abruptly as she glanced up.

"Oh, I'm so sorry. I thought you were someone else!"

The woman turned, and smiled at him radiantly.

"I'm sorry I'm not!"

She straightened up, still smiling at him. At close quarters Alastair could see that the woman, although similar in appearance to Joanne, had none of her bright attractiveness, but instead had a more languid, classical beauty. She glanced at Alastair and smiled.

"Come and have a coffee with me anyway," she said. "I hate being in these places on my own. Do you have time?"

"Er, yes. Of course," Alastair replied, flustered. "Look, I'm really sorry. You just look so much like a friend of mine. My neighbour, actually."

"Well, my name is Chloe."

She held out her hand.

"Alastair."

They made their way to the coffee bar. Alastair brought the cups over to the table that Chloe had commandeered near to the exit.

"So where are you heading, Alastair?" she asked as he sat down.

"Down to the Lot, just west of Cahors."

"Really? So am I! I've got a little place near Fromac. Between Fromac and St Geniès actually. Do you know the area?"

"That's a coincidence," said Alastair. "I'm going to St Geniès."

"Really?" she said again, laughing. "How funny us meeting like this! It's a lovely area, isn't it? I've had my place for about five years now, but I'm selling this year. I suppose I've got a bit bored with it, and the weather isn't too great. Awful most of the winter. Unless you are really lucky, if you go down for a weekend you nearly always spend most of it glaring out at the rain! And even in the summer it's unreliable. And the whole area is becoming overrun with old, retired policemen from Todmorden!"

Alastair laughed. She grinned back at him.

"Yes, I am a bit of a snob, I suppose. The trouble is, they invite you to all these awful dinner parties and lunches where they sit around getting drunk and congratulating themselves on having got out of England! As if anyone was stopping them! Smug – you wouldn't believe it! And none of them speak proper French, and they all watch Sky TV and listen to the BBC and have nothing whatever to talk about except where you can buy the cheapest plonk! But," she went on, suddenly serious. "Did you hear about the terrible business at the château there? At St Geniès-Lafontaine? You must have heard. You might even have known Nick."

Alastair looked up sharply.

"Nick? Well, yes.. I did.. a bit…"

But Chloe seemed not to have heard him. Her eyes filled briefly with tears. She took a sip of coffee, then put her cup down.

"It's part of the reason I'm selling. I knew Nick quite well – very well I suppose." She smiled again, this time to herself.

"We were good together."

Alastair stared at her.

"You mean – you and Nick….?"

"Yes. Well no, not really."

She smiled again, her eyes on her coffee cup. She shrugged.

"It just sort of happened. It was nearly a year ago, I suppose. There he was, tall, dark and handsome – and not from Todmorden! I was sitting in the Café de France in the square at St Geniès, drinking a coffee and wondering why on earth cafés in the villages in France never sell croissants or pain aux raisins and trying to decide if I could be bothered going across to the boulangerie and buying one. And this man sits down at the table next to me and says, 'Would you care to share my croissants?'"

She laughed, her eyes sparkling at the memory. Turning to Alastair she said,

"How could I refuse? We had a marvellous time. Of course nothing happened then. He was over with Joanne to buy the château. But he was terrific company. Well, you must know that. You said you knew him?"

"Yes," said Alastair.

He felt stunned. Surely he had misunderstood? Was Nick having an affair with this beautiful woman at the same time he was living with Kate at the château – even before that?

"When did you – er – meet him again?" Alastair asked as casually as he could.

"Oh, it must have been early March this year, I suppose," Chloe answered. "It was just warm enough to be outside. I was sitting in the café again and there he was, again! We had such fun! I didn't see him that often, just now and again, it was nothing heavy, but I really liked him and we got on so well!"

She laughed again, then blushed a deep red. She looked down self-consciously and took a sip of coffee.

"Look, forget I said anything. I shouldn't be telling you this – I'm not sure why I am. You're probably a great friend of Joanne, and I really don't want to hurt her. She's had enough to put up with. But," she looked up at him, fixing her large, blue eyes on his. "I still don't really believe it's happened – I mean Nick being dead. And I just thought, you know, I needed to talk about him to someone who knew him…"

"I understand," Alastair nodded. "In fact I know exactly what you mean."

She smiled up at him. They sat in silence for a couple of minutes. Then Chloe put her cup down and turned to him again, her eyes alight again.

"But did you know about the woman he'd brought out with him from England? He told us all she was his garden designer. His neighbour from England. That's how he introduced her to

Marie-Claire – that's the Fromac notaire's wife – you probably know her too. No one ever saw her – the gardener woman, that is, apart from Marie-Claire that one time, and Phillippe – he's the doctor. Nick was always out on his own. Or with me! So I hadn't a clue about her and Nick! Phillippe knew, but he never said anything. I really thought she was just the gardener! But anyway, she was pregnant when she came out to the château and it turned out it was his baby! I only found that out afterwards – you know, after the accident. I mean, you probably think it was awful of me and Nick – after all he was married and I knew he was married. I'd met Joanne last year and really liked her. She's a lovely woman. But we were only having a bit of a fling, we both knew that. I knew he only loved Joanne and I'd no intention of trying to take him away from her. It was just great fun! But, like I said, I'd no idea about this other woman being anything other than the gardener! And according to Phillippe she was, well – so, so…." she searched for words. "So serious and intense, I suppose! Not really Nick's style at all! I can't imagine he had much fun with her! But apparently she expected him to leave Joanne for her. Of course he never would have. But can you believe it! Men! And women, of course!"

Chloe laughed, then her eyes filled with tears again.

"But it was a terrible accident. Poor Nick. There was a rumour that her husband – the pregnant gardener woman's – or his friend or someone did it – you know, actually pushed him over the balustrade. But the police said it was an accident and Joanne told me it couldn't have been the husband. She was devastated of course, but she says he – the husband – has been marvellous. It must have been awful for him too. It seems he didn't know anything about the affair either – just thought she was designing the garden. Awful." Chloe shook her head thoughtfully.

"Anyway," Chloe looked up at Alastair. "If I needed anything to make me take a decision on selling, it was that. I've got bad memories now. I can't drive past the road to the château without thinking about it. So, that's the purpose of my trip. Well," she blushed slightly. "Part of the purpose anyway. To sell my house. What a coincidence that you're going there as well and that you knew Nick!"

"Yes," said Alastair, forcing a smile. "Well, I really must get going."

He got up hurriedly.

"It's been a pleasure meeting you," he said.

Looking into her deep blue eyes he meant it. He could see a man like Nick wouldn't have hesitated with Chloe, wife and pregnant mistress notwithstanding.

"And you," she smiled. "Thank you for listening. Perhaps we'll meet on the road. Or in St Geniès. Come over for a drink. My place is the first turning left off the road out towards Fromac. By the way, you don't want to buy a beautifully restored cottage with two hectares and swimming pool, do you?"

Alastair managed a laugh and made his way out of the café, back into the throng of people in the main concourse. Poor, poor Kate, he thought. He wondered if she had known. He wondered if Chloe was the only one. He rather suspected not.

Back in the Saab, they were soon following the long lines of vehicles towards the trains. Alastair looked out for the silver car, but didn't see it again. The old Land Rover with the man and his two children was at the end of the queue adjacent to him. He glanced over and saw the man telling the children something that had them in fits of laughter. Then the silver cabriolet passed them in the next queue. Alastair watched as Chloe waved to the children and slowed to exchange a few words with their father. They all laughed and waved. Alastair caught a glimpse of his own reflection in the rear view mirror. Oh God, he thought. What a glum, miserable old bugger I look. I'm surprised she even spoke to me.

2

"Y ou know, I think I might like to live in France."

Alastair looked at Richard in surprise. They had just negotiated Rouen and had stopped for lunch in a picnic area just off the main road. They were lucky to find an empty table. The car park was full of vehicles from every northern European country: Dutch caravans, bicycles strapped to the back, French and Belgian people-carriers, English family cars, many with trailers or towing caravans, German saloons, one or two smart new sports cars (usually German) and a few old sports cars with drivers in goggles (always English). It was busy and noisy and hot. The opposite of what he would have expected Richard to like. But then, you never knew with Richard.

"Yes, I think I'd like it."

Richard tore off a large piece of baguette.

"I've just been talking to that guy over there."

Richard jerked his head to their left, in the direction of what Alastair now recognised as the old Land Rover from the Channel Tunnel.

"He bought an old barn and thirteen hectares of land a few years ago for £25,000! He's a school teacher. Comes out every holiday with his kids. When they've finished school, they are all going to move out here and run it as a campsite. Sounds really good. Thirteen hectares all of your own! With wild boar and lots of woodland, mushrooms and stuff. And he says the birds are fantastic – kites, woodpeckers, even hoopoes. All that land! You could be really self-sufficient!"

"Yes, and you'd have to speak French all the time too!" Alastair laughed.

"Oh, no." Richard cut a piece of cheese.

109

"He says you don't need to know much to get by. And if you can't speak it, then you don't have to talk to anyone. So that way," Richard looked at Alastair earnestly. "People wouldn't even try to talk to me. I'd like that. They'd accept me more easily. They wouldn't expect me to be able to chat if I was foreign. People wouldn't know anything about me. I could make a new start."

Richard continued chewing for a while.

"Funny thing as well. It's a real coincidence, but his place is at St Geniès! His land joins on to the château's, just at the end of the lake. He's got the river from the lake running along the border of his meadow. He said he'd meet us in the café in St Geniès for a coffee tomorrow and tell me more about what it's like and how you find places to buy like his."

"It's a big step though," Alastair said, surprised at Richard's enthusiasm. He had obviously hit it off with the Land Rover family. "Very different culture and outlook from ours."

"Yes, I'd have to think about it carefully. And then there's the money. Like the guy over there – John – said, £25,000 isn't much for what you get, but it's a lot if you haven't got any cash!" Richard paused. "Yes, I'll have to think hard about ways of raising it."

He was silent for a few minutes. Then, looking past Alastair into the distance, he spoke again.

"Anyway, Kate must like it here."

"Yes," said Alastair thoughtfully. "Yes, you're right. Enough to stay on."

They sat in silence for a few minutes, watching the Land Rover family clearing away the debris of their lunch.

"What do you think, Richard? Do you think I'm doing the right thing, asking her to come back to me? Back to the UK?"

There was another short silence between them. Richard chewed his bread and cheese slowly, still looking past Alastair towards his new friends.

"You know, Alastair, we've never really talked about the last time we were here. But I knew Kate and Nick were having an affair before they went to France."

Alastair looked at Richard in surprise.

"But I didn't say anything because I thought I could stop them. I know I tried," Richard rubbed his hand over his eyes. "And then you, and Mrs Carslow – Joanne – seemed so certain that there was nothing odd about them going off together I didn't want to say anything in case it was over," Richard paused. Then he went on, "Kate must have very bad memories of France. Awful things happened. And yet she has stayed on. In the château. I think you need to know why."

"Well, I don't think there's much mystery about that," said Alastair. "Kate can be pretty practical...."

"Yes, it's possible that's the reason," Richard agreed. "But perhaps it's more that she feels, well – at peace. It's where she feels she will be left alone. Because of what's happened, she thinks that no one will want to have much to do with her. Maybe that's what she wants as well. If she moves somewhere else, she'll have to explain, people will pry. I can relate to her feeling like that."

Alastair looked at Richard's earnest face, his usual pallor now tinged quite pink from the sun.

"So you do think I'm doing the wrong thing, asking her to come back to me? Even to Scotland? Just as a normal family as far as anyone else is concerned?"

Richard looked at him seriously.

"I don't know. But I can see why she might want to stay here, even if she does still love you. No more questions, no more explanations......... You need to know why she has stayed. But the real question for you, Alastair, is not really do you still love her, it's more have you really, really forgiven her? The worst possible thing for you both would be if you took her back and realised you had made a mistake. You might find it harder to forgive her completely than you think. And," Richard paused again, looking at Alastair for a long time. "I'm not sure you know all there is to know yet. I just think, I have this feeling, there might be something else...." he paused again. "Something you couldn't forgive. Something she might not be able to forgive herself for."

Alastair slept badly that night. They had stopped outside Blois in one of the many hotels that line the main routes into the bigger towns of France. What Richard had said had had a peculiarly disturbing effect on Alastair. It also gave him a new respect for Richard. So many people wrote him off as being a bit weird, but in fact in many ways he was the sanest of all of them. Alastair went over it all again and again. Having an affair was hardly unusual, and although Nick's death had been tragic, it was not Kate's fault. If he was prepared to give their marriage another chance, surely what Kate had done wasn't so bad that she would feel too guilty even to try? But Richard had said that he thought there might be other things that he, Alastair, would find worse than her having an affair with Nick. What on earth could be worse? Alastair tossed and turned. He knew he still loved Kate. He knew how much he missed her being around. He thought he wanted her back. But perhaps, after all, she didn't love him anymore. Or perhaps Richard was right. She might have found some sort of peace locked away in the French countryside. Perhaps he wouldn't be helping any of them if he disturbed that fragile peace. Alastair turned over and lay on his back, staring up at the illuminated red switch of the television, suspended from the opposite wall. A red light. Stop. It seemed everything was telling him to stop, go home, leave Kate alone. Eventually he fell asleep. He dreamed of beautiful blondes in fast cars driving past him, not even slowing as he frantically waved his arms and shouted at them to stop. He woke up with a start once more during the night, overcome by a feeling that, after all, this trip was a mistake: a premonition that something awful was going to happen again. He lay awake a while longer, turning it all over in his mind. Then he gave up and closed his eyes. He'd decide what to do in the morning. He'd see what Richard had to say.

Next morning at breakfast, he told Richard he thought they should go home and let Kate be. Richard looked at him thoughtfully.

"No," he said slowly. "No, Alastair. I think we should go and see Kate. I've been thinking too, and it's the only way for you. Otherwise we'll never know. We have to go and see her."

And so they did.

3

The previous week had been unbearably hot. Kate looked up at the sky. It was hazy today, and in the distance, beyond the lake, she could see large thunder clouds were building up on the horizon. It looked like a storm was on the way. She hoped so. It would clear the air. Turning back towards the château, she went into the salon through the open French windows. She crossed the large room to the glass doors on the opposite side that led out to the interior courtyard. Her bare feet made little sound on the stone floor, pleasantly cool now in the heat of summer. The baby's pram was parked in the shady courtyard, close to the vine-covered wall. It was a large, old-fashioned pram with a hood. A heavy net was fixed across the front of the hood to protect the sleeping baby from flies and wasps. Kate preferred to keep the pram here in summer. The sun only ever reached half of the courtyard, even at midday. Most of the year it was cold and dismal, but, for a few weeks at the height of the summer, it was a cool refuge from the blistering heat. She always kept the baby well out of the sun. Now she looked down at him with a tender smile. He was nearly four months old, but still very small. Born prematurely on that fateful night, he had been a weak, quiet baby from the start, but now Kate was becoming concerned. He fed little, slept most of the time and did not seem to be growing as he should. There seemed to be no energy in the tiny, listless frame and his eyes were dull and only very occasionally did he seem to smile, or recognise her. Kate feared for him now as the weeks went by and he didn't seem to change. She watched as he moved slightly in his sleep. Then, turning away with a sigh, she padded into the kitchen. Collecting a glass of cold white wine from the fridge, she went back out onto the terrace and sat down again under the large parasol, looking out over the woods and lawn down to the lake.

Since the baby had been born, much to her surprise, she had eventually settled down into a pleasant routine at the château. The first few weeks had been a nightmare. Not only the shock of Nick's death, the fear of what would happen if the police decided it was not accidental, and the dreadful feeling of guilt, but, she realised now, like so many women before her, how totally unprepared she had been for the demands of a new baby. In fact, as she looked back on it now, the aftermath of Nick's death had hardly touched her. The local gendarmes had reluctantly let Alastair and Richard go on the orders of the national police from Cahors, and the coroner had confirmed it as an accident. Everything had been dealt with by the police, and, she supposed, Joanne. No one had told her anything, but she had eventually asked her doctor. He had told her that Madame Carslow had had her husband's body flown home for burial. This was usual and anyway there was not much room in the only protestant cemetery in the area. It was filling up rapidly, on account of the increasing numbers of elderly English retiring to the region. If she was thinking of staying, the doctor advised her in all seriousness, she should apply now and reserve her plot.

At first Kate was dismayed that Nick's body had been returned to England. With no grave to visit, she would have no focus for her grief. Joanne had won him even in death. But then, she had in life. Slowly Kate had come to terms with the fact that Nick had not been able to give Joanne up. Even the baby had not been enough for him to choose her. This realisation only served to make Kate hate herself even more. He, at least, had stayed true to Joanne, in his own way. Whereas as she, Kate, had renounced Alastair, as well as betraying him. She'd thrown away all they'd had together.

After Kate and the baby left hospital, her doctor had helped her to find a lawyer who explained the alien system of French succession law to her. Kate knew she must provide for her child now and had started proceedings to ensure that the baby inherited all Nick's property and possessions in France. She was warned this would take a while, but, thankfully, in the meantime it meant that payment of death duties was deferred until the ownership of the half of Nick's estate in France not reserved for his child was established. In the absence of a French will and with the presence of Nick's tiny successor, the old advocate had assured Kate that a French court would find in favour of the child over a spouse. The fact of the existence of the English will, with Joanne as beneficiary, appeared to make him even more certain that a French court would find for the child. The rationale seemed to be that an English will had no legality in France and was therefore less than worthless, being English. And the child at least was born on French soil and was, therefore, more fitting to own French property. Kate had smiled to herself despite everything, and almost said out loud that it was fortunate for her case that Joanne had no French blood in her. The advocate, however, was deadly serious and clearly considered the invasion of foreign property owners to be barely tolerable, let alone desirable.

Kate had returned to the château on a warm day in late May. Her doctor had given her and the baby a lift. As they pulled up outside the arch leading to the kitchen courtyard, Kate noticed the grassy verge was covered in purple orchids. Wild honeysuckle was festooned over the small bushes alongside the track and the sweet, fresh smell made her smile. The doctor looked at her as he helped her out of the car with the baby in her arms.

"It is good to see that you can still smile, Madame."

He spoke gravely.

"Yes," Kate replied. "I feel much better now. You have been very kind."

"Madame, I did not know Monsieur Carslow for very long, but he was a good friend to me. I too was a stranger here. This was my first post in France since leaving Paris. It can be a mistake to move to the provinces where you know no one. And it is strange. Monsieur Carslow, a foreigner, was accepted by all, whereas I," he shrugged. "I was labelled, as you say. A *Parisien*. You know," he smiled slightly. "In these rural parts that is a term of contempt!"

"Surely not as bad as being English!" Kate smiled back.

"Oh, maybe not. Although no one seemed to consider Monsieur Nick as English – he was an honorary Frenchman!"

The doctor shrugged again.

"But Nick was a good friend and he helped me to become accepted. I have been here nearly two years now. One day in January this year, I overheard Madame Chomez, you know, the baker's wife, tell an old lady, one of my patients: 'Oh, the new doctor is OK. I have the word of Monsieur Nick, *l'Anglais*. He has told me how good the doctor was to him when…' and so she went on!"

He chuckled.

"Oh yes, Nick was a very good friend to me. In many ways," he smiled and shook his head at a private memory.

"Anyway."

He held his hand out to Kate.

"I must be on my way. I have had my housekeeper come over and clean up a bit here. She has done some shopping for you also, particularly things you will need for the baby. Now," he held up his hand as Kate started to thank him again. "Remember, this child is still weak. You must take care of him and yourself. You are now responsible," he added severely.

Getting into the driver's seat, he turned the small car neatly in the drive and leaned out of the window.

"Telephone me at once if you are worried."

And with that he had driven back up the track, leaving Kate standing with her baby in her arms outside the château, in the sunshine. She had looked up at the dazzling white stone walls and whispered to the baby.

"Welcome home. This is our home now. We are going to start afresh, on our own."

****

Kate put on her sunglasses against the glare of the afternoon and leaned back in the wooden chair, sipping her wine. She felt almost content. Despite speaking very little French, she managed the routine of life with surprisingly few problems. It was interesting, she mused, how much could be done these days without having to communicate verbally with your fellow human beings. If, that is, you didn't want to. Her main concern was always for the baby. Since returning to the château after the birth, she had devoted herself to his wellbeing. She had been surprised how time-consuming and completely demanding such a small creature could be. But that was not the problem. Kate was happy to spend every hour of every day taking care of her baby, but whatever she did seemed to have no effect on his progress. Although he was not exactly ill, with no colic or fever or any definable symptoms, he seemed sickly all the time. At first the doctor had been reassuring, telling Kate the baby was premature and small and weak at birth, so she mustn't expect too much too soon. As the weeks went by and he gained a little weight, Kate was relieved to see a tiny smile every so often and began to think he was progressing and that she was just not sufficiently patient. A few weeks ago she'd taken him into Fromac to the doctor's surgery for a check-up. To Kate's alarm, this time the doctor had looked worried. Again there were no real symptoms suggesting that anything was amiss, but clearly the baby's progress seemed to have stopped again. Since then, the doctor had called by every week to check on the child. His visit was due that afternoon. Kate thought the baby was looking a bit stronger this week, and he had been eating better, but now he seemed as if he had a cold, snuffling and coughing slightly.

She found herself looking forward to the doctor's visits. He usually made the visit his last, on his way home to St Geniès from the surgery. He sometimes stopped for a drink after he had examined the child and they sat out on the terrace, talking. Kate had begun to think he might be interested in her and found herself making sure she had washed her hair and changed her clothes ready for his visits. She had to admit to herself how much his visits had started to mean to her. She lay back now, conjuring him up in her imagination. She actually knew little about him except he came from Paris originally and his name was Phillippe de la Bernière, which Kate thought had an aristocratic ring to it. He had the dark, aquiline good looks to go with the name. His manner was very polite and formal, but he also had a kindness and gentleness about his manner that made him a perfect doctor. His English was good, and she knew he had lived in England for a while, but that was about all she did know.

The sound of a car interrupted her thoughts. She could just see the doctor's white Renault coming down the track, almost obscured by the summer foliage. She got up quickly and, smoothing down her hair, checked her appearance in the large, gilt-framed mirror that hung on the wall of the salon. Greeting him at the kitchen door, they shook hands and Kate wheeled the pram into the kitchen for the doctor to examine the child. He did not speak until he had finished and the baby was restored to his pram and his position in the courtyard.

"Well, doctor? What do you think?" Kate asked anxiously.

The doctor paused before he spoke.

"I cannot pretend, Madame, that I am not concerned. The little one is just not progressing. His breathing is very shallow and to make matters worse, he has caught a cold. I think we must see what happens this week, by which time you will have finished the course of vitamin supplements. Then if there is no progress and the cold persists, we may have to take him into the hospital for observation."

"Oh, no!"

Kate was crestfallen. The last thing she wanted was to go back to that hospital.

"Do not upset yourself," the doctor said. "If we have no change by next week it will be necessary to make sure that the cold does not lead to complications. This is a danger with a weak child. However, we do not know yet what will happen. Keep on with the course of supplements and keep him warm and dry, in the fresh air whenever the weather is good, but keep him out of draughts and keep him indoors if it is chilly or, particularly, if it is damp. I will call again next week."

"Thank you," Kate smiled at him, reassured by his calm manner. "Are you be able to stay for a drink?"

"Certainly," he bowed slightly. "Thank you. But I do not have much time this evening."

"Come and sit down," Kate indicated the terrace. "I will bring the drinks through."

She took the cold bottle of rosé from the fridge, opened it and put it on the tray that she had already set with glasses and a small bowl of olives. She followed him out onto the terrace, where he stood leaning on the balustrade looking out at the lake. The balustrade had been completely replaced since that awful day earlier in the year. Despite everything, the terrace was Kate's favourite spot in the whole château. Even she was surprised that it was where she spent most time. Actually at the scene of the crime, she had once thought wryly.

The doctor turned round as she approached and set the tray down on the round wooden table. He had taken off his jacket and was wearing an open-necked white linen shirt then set off his tanned olive skin. She noticed his hair was streaked with a few reddish lights from the sun and as she picked up the glass of wine to pass it to him, her hand was shaking slightly. She felt a familiar tug of desire that she had not felt since Nick. His fingers touched hers briefly as he took the glass and he glanced up, his eyes resting briefly on her half-exposed breasts. He quickly, and very obviously to Kate, averted his gaze. He indicated a chair.

"May I?"

"Of course, do sit down."

Kate, flustered and embarrassed, sat down herself and took a large gulp of wine, trying at the same time to adjust the neckline of her T-shirt. Oh God, she thought, I've got it all wrong. He's not in the least interested in me. I feel such an idiot.

"Madame, there is something that I would like to say to you," the doctor began, looking down into his glass of wine. "It is a little difficult, as you are my patient."

Kate's heart was hammering against her ribs. Perhaps she was right! He was interested in her! She felt her face flushing and her knees and thighs seemed to melt. He looked up at her, his deep brown eyes liquid as he scanned her face.

"You see," he spoke quickly now, his usually faultless English more heavily accented than normal. "I am in love. I need to speak to you about this now, because of Nick. He was a good friend to me in many ways and I do not want you to think that I take advantage of his situation for my own ends."

"Oh no, I would never think that," Kate breathed.

She reached out across the table and covered his hand with her own, stroking the smooth olive flesh with her finger tips as she gazed at him, her lips parted and moist. The doctor withdrew his hand quickly and sat back in his chair, smiling at her earnestly.

"Thank you, you are very kind," he said. "But let me explain. You see, I was deeply in love, even while Nick was still alive. In fact, he knew – he told me I was!"

The doctor grinned. Kate looked at him in puzzlement. The doctor continued.

"It was very surprising for me too. And to tell a rival that your own *amour* is in love with the rival! And for an Englishman to even notice he had a rival! Or to notice that his *amour* loved the rival! Oh là là là là!"

The doctor chuckled away to himself as Kate sat and looked at him, mystified. What on earth was he talking about? How could Nick have thought she was in love with the doctor? It was only recently that she had even got to know him. She had liked him, and there was no denying that he was very good looking in a Gallic way, but Kate had never ever thought of him in that way while Nick was alive. But to think that the doctor had seen himself then as a rival for her affections. Kate couldn't help feeling flattered.

"But let me explain," he said again, turning his eyes once again on Kate. "I have to tell you this now because it is important to me that you still trust me. Your little one is not well and I would not want you to lose confidence in me as a doctor. You see, the woman I love was Nick's *amour*. Today I will ask if she feels the same, and if she will marry me."

Kate gasped. Marry him! She was still married to Alastair! Surely the doctor knew that? Maybe he thought they would be divorced by now.

"I don't know what to say..." she began.

"I am sorry, Madame, if this is difficult for you. But Nick always told me he was only having, as you say, a fling."

Kate started. Her and Nick a fling! How could Nick have said such things behind her back? Not telling Joanne was one thing, but telling other people she was just a fling! Then she remembered the notaire's wife and the whispering English women in the café in Fromac. So everyone had thought she was just a bit on the side, including the doctor! And obviously including Nick as well. She remembered his comment about her being his current girlfriend! And she'd thought that he was joking! All the feelings of betrayal and hurt towards Nick welled up in her again and, despite her excitement at the doctor's declaration, her eyes filled with tears.

"Please, Madame. Do not upset yourself," the doctor smiled at her. "Men do these things. In France, it is so common. I do not say it is right, but you should not distress yourself. He did not love her."

"Her?" Kate looked at him. "Who do you mean?"

"Chloe, of course," the doctor smiled.

Kate stared at him in bewilderment, then embarrassment and horror as she realised he was talking about someone else. How could she have been such a fool as to think Phillippe meant he loved her? Inwardly she cringed and flushed deeply with shame.

He did not seem to notice her discomfort and went on rapidly.

"Nick told me he did not love her and she did not love him. They were having a fling. Fun. And she really still loved me! I was so surprised and so elated! But then, next day, the terrible news of the accident. She went back to England then. But afterwards I wrote to her and tonight I will see her!"

Kate looked at him in confusion. What was he talking about now? She didn't know anyone called Chloe. But obviously Chloe had known Nick.

"I'm sorry," she stammered. "But I don't quite follow."

"Of course not, Madame. I am not explaining well," he laughed. "Let me start at the beginning. After I had completed my training here in France, I took a secondment to the famous John Radcliffe hospital in Oxford. I wanted to improve my English and to specialise as a paediatrician. I was there for nearly three years. And there I met Chloe. She is the daughter of a professor at the university and we met at a party. She took me punting on the river at midnight and I fell in love with her. We had a wonderful time in Oxford and, when the time came for me to return to France, I asked her to marry me and come back with me. But she said no," the doctor paused here, and shook his head sadly. "I was devastated. I had to return for my work. And she loved me – I know she did. But," he paused again and shrugged. "She did not want to live in France. Her father was not well, her mother was dead and there was no other family. She said she couldn't leave him. And she knew I would have to work first in the provinces for some time. It's the only way for a new general practitioner in France. And she said she could not face that all year round. Too boring, too depressing. Too muddy! So we parted. But she had a small house near St Geniès, so when I saw a job advertised in Fromac, I applied. That way, I thought, at least I might see her in the summer. For the first year I was here, I was so busy and although I would often drive past her house, I only saw her car once, last July. I was too frightened of a rebuff to call in. Then, earlier this year, I think it was about March, I saw her and Nick together in St Geniès. It was so funny! Nick introduced us! Then several weeks afterwards I told him all about it. And Chloe had told Nick all about it as well! So Nick told us both that we both still loved each other! But then, the terrible accident.....she went back home and I thought I might never see her again. But today she has come back. I am meeting her at eight! So I must be going. But, Madame," he turned to Kate again. "I know you must have been aware of Nick's 'fling' with Chloe, and there may have been jealousy between you and Chloe. I needed to explain my situation in case you may see us together, me and Chloe, and think, what is he doing? My doctor who tends my child, with the lover of my child's father!"

"Yes, I see," Kate said faintly. "Thank you for explaining."

"And now, I must go."

The doctor got up and put on his jacket. Kate tried to get up but somehow her knees seemed to buckle.

"No, no, Madame, do not move. I will see myself out. Take care of the little one. Remember, keep him warm. It is important for him not to be exposed to big changes in temperature. I shall call again next week. But do not forget, you must keep a close eye on him, and telephone me if you are concerned. And thank you for your understanding."

He held his hand out to Kate. They briefly shook hands and he left, his footsteps echoing on the tiled kitchen floor. She heard his car chugging away up the steep track. Kate leaned back in her chair and closed her eyes. Hot tears rolled down her face. She'd made a fool of herself alright. Not only thinking the doctor could have any interest in her, but being too blindly in love with Nick to see the truth. She was just one of many. He'd been seeing this Chloe since March! Less than two months after she and Nick had run away together. She remembered how she had refused to go out with him, how he'd gone out on his own, how he'd known everyone, how Marie-Claire had looked at him, and the memory of the whispering English women in the café came back to her again.

Kate wiped her eyes and looked out into the distance. The sky had become quite dark, tinged with pink and purple in the direction of the lake. She could hear the occasional rumble of thunder. She shook her head sadly as thoughts of the time she'd spent with Alastair in Cornwall, and then thoughts of her happy, quiet life in Kent came unbidden into her aching head. The time before she had met Nick. She wished to God she never had. The baby's cry interrupted her thoughts. She sighed and got up. She loved the baby, but she was worried about him. If it hadn't been for Nick, none of this would have happened. Kate paused at the balustrade and looked down at the grass below. She could see Nick's body lying there. Quickly she turned away as the baby's cries got louder. She shouldn't blame Nick. It was her own fault as much as anyone's.

Half an hour later, Kate wheeled the pram out onto the terrace. The baby seemed to be sleeping peacefully again. The wind was starting to stir the tops of the poplar trees that lined the walk down to the lake. It looked like the rain would start soon, but at the moment the breeze was a welcome relief to the sultriness of the day. Kate glanced at her watch. A few more minutes and she would go in and start running the baby's bath.

Suddenly the sound of a car coming down the track startled her. She had so few visitors she thought perhaps the doctor had left something behind. She hoped it wasn't him coming back. She went over to the edge of the terrace from where she could just see the bend in the track. After a few seconds, she saw a flash of blue as a large car passed the gap in the trees. Kate frowned. She didn't know who this could be. A couple of estate agents had been round shortly after Nick's death to see if she was going to sell the château, but apart from the doctor and the postman and the occasional lost tourist, no one ventured all the way down the track as far as the château. She wheeled the pram through the salon and into the courtyard. As she walked back through the kitchen, she heard the car stop outside. Slipping her feet into a pair of old espadrilles that she kept by the door, Kate went outside and through the old stone arch by the coach house. There she stopped short. The car was parked about thirty metres away from her and two men were getting out. Now that she could see it clearly, there was something uncomfortably familiar about the bright metallic blue car, and about the men. Both were wearing sunglasses. The taller of the two, the driver, got out of the car and passed a hand through his fair, sandy hair before turning towards the archway where Kate was standing, hidden in the shadows. The other man was very pale with a shock of bright, white hair.

"Oh God," Kate gasped. "What are they doing here?"

4

Richard and Alastair were glad to be out of the car after the day's long drive south. Neither had spoken much since breakfast. But now they were here. And in a few minutes, Alastair thought, he would be confronting Kate and seeing her with her child. He felt a strong pang of jealousy and hatred for Nick. He hesitated as he turned towards the courtyard. Was he doing the right thing? He wasn't even sure now that he really wanted to see Kate again. He should have left well alone. At his elbow, Richard spoke quietly.

"Let's go in, Alastair. You need to see Kate and the baby."

****

For a long time afterwards, Richard's words would come back to haunt Alastair. But at that moment he caught sight of Kate, coming towards them through the archway and it was too late to turn back. She was looking quite normal, Alastair thought, although he could not have said what he was expecting. Her skin was lightly tanned and her auburn hair was loose, and looked longer and more ginger than he remembered. Perhaps that was the sun. She was wearing clothes he recognised and, he noticed with a slight shock, she still wore his wedding ring. She looked so familiar. He could almost have believed that it had all been a bad dream. Kate smiled uncertainly.

"Hello," she said, stopping in front of them.

"Hello, Kate," Alastair answered awkwardly. "We thought we would come and see how you were."

"I'm fine."

They stood looking at each other for a few moments. Then Kate said,

"Please come in. I was," she paused and looked at the floor. Then she raised her head defiantly. "I was just about to bathe my baby and put him to bed. Perhaps you would like a drink while I do that."

And she turned and led the way into the château, through the kitchen and the salon and out onto the terrace. Alastair glanced sideways at Richard as they followed Kate.

"Sit down, please."

Kate pulled another chair up to the table. Alastair sat down, noticing the two half-drunk glasses of wine on the table.

"I'm sorry," he said formally to Kate, his heart sinking. We shouldn't have come, he thought. She's made a new life for herself. It looks like she doesn't need me. "I didn't know you had company. We can come back tomorrow. Come on, Richard."

"Oh, no," Kate answered quickly. "It's just the doctor who was here a while ago. To see the baby."

Alastair saw her expression change. The concern on her face and anguish in her voice touched him.

"Is there something the matter with him?"

"Yes, well, no. Oh, I don't know. No one seems to," Kate almost whispered. "It's just that he's so weak and isn't making progress. He's almost as tiny and frail as when he was born. The doctor is worried now too. He thinks possibly there could be some inherited problem..."

She broke off, flushing crimson. Alastair shifted uncomfortably. This wasn't going to be easy. Everything reminded him of Nick. He looked at the new balustrade and shivered. Kate, meanwhile, had hurried off to fetch clean glasses from the kitchen and was pouring wine into them. He watched her movements and looking up at her face, he felt tears coming to his eyes. She was still his Kate, still as lovely as ever. He hoped he could forget the last year. He hoped they both could. He knew he did love her, after all that had happened. But did she still love him and would she come back to him?

"If you'll excuse me," Kate straightened up from the table. "I'll just go and see to the baby."

A loud crack of thunder overhead made him glance up at the sky. He hadn't noticed how dark it had become. Thick, black clouds were massed across the valley and a strong wind had got up, bending the tall poplar trees and raising small waves on the usually flat surface of the lake. A jagged fork of lightning lit the sky at the moment Alastair turned back towards the château. Silhouetted against the white stone façade, framed by the open French window, stood Kate, and in her arms was the baby. Alastair rose slowly to his feet as the rumble of thunder resonated round the valley. He took a step towards them, as if in a trance. He must be mistaken. But with the second flash of lightning there was no doubt. Kate was holding the baby up and the two of them seemed frozen in a tableau, looking at Alastair. The baby's bright blue eyes were open. There was no mistake. The small face was a replica of his own.

For a few seconds there was utter stillness on the terrace as the storm raged around them. Then the spell was broken and Alastair was back in the real world, the all too real world. He hissed:

"It's my baby! Why on earth didn't you tell me, Kate? No wonder Richard thought there was something I wouldn't be able to forgive! What were you thinking!"

Alastair stood rooted to the spot, unable to believe what he was seeing. Richard stood beside him, staring at Kate and the baby. Then Richard's face darkened with fury. He lunged towards her, the blow catching her on the jaw. She staggered backwards, and fell to the floor, still clutching the baby, her head hitting the stones of the terrace with a crack. As Richard lurched forward again, fist raised, Alastair came to his senses. He grabbed Richard's arm, pulling him away from Kate and hit him in the face. Blood spurted from Richard's nose. For an instant he stood still, gazing in horror at Kate, lying motionless on the floor, the baby beside her. Then, pushing Alastair away, he make a dash for the door. Alastair stumbled and fell, catching the side of his forehead on the corner of the table. A cut opened above his eye, blood running down his face. He scrambled to his feet and flung himself at Richard, raining blows down on his head.

"Stop it, Alastair! I'm OK. You'll kill him!"

Alastair turned to see that Kate was struggling to sit up, still clutching the baby who was now whimpering quietly.

"It's my fault, Alastair. Leave him alone. He did it for you!"

They heard Richard cry out, "Yes, I'm sorry, Kate. I'm sorry. I just couldn't help it. I did it for Alastair. And I did want to kill Nick! I just can't help myself sometimes. I don't deserve to live!"

Richard slumped over on the floor. It had started to rain and, as Alastair took a step back, breathing heavily, a trickle of blood ran from under Richard's head across the old stone blocks of the terrace, the rain washing it away.

"No! You've killed him! He's dead!" Kate sobbed, clutching the baby to her.

There was an eerie silence on the terrace. All around them the storm raged, forks of lightning illuminating the scene. Alastair, gasping for breath, turned a murderous gaze on Kate.

"So why didn't you tell me?" he rasped, his voice breaking with anguish. "Did you know all along that it was mine? Did you pretend to Nick just to keep him? Or was it just greed, to get the château? Or do you hate me so much? Did you want to get your own back for Richard killing Nick because of his loyalty to me?"

"Alastair, I know what it must look like," Kate sobbed. "But you have to understand. I didn't know until he was born. Then I knew you wouldn't take me back. I couldn't tell you! I had to say that he was Nick's son! It was the only way that I could provide for my baby!"

At that moment there was a purple flash and a shower of sparks lit up the trees behind the coach house. A bolt of lightning had hit the electricity cable to the château. The lights that had been on in the kitchen went out. Alastair spoke again, quietly this time.

"Don't bother, Kate. I don't want to hear it. I came here to see if you'd come back to me. I still loved you and I missed you so much I thought I could cope with bringing up Nick's child. I wanted to believe what you said the day Nick died – that you loved us both and had only chosen Nick for the child's sake. I even felt sorry for you when I found out Nick thought of you as just one of his 'flings'. But how could you lie about the baby? My baby! Well, it's over now, Kate. I should never have come back. And I should never have dragged Richard along. Look what we've done to him. Phone a doctor for him. Quickly. And get the baby inside out of this rain. He'll catch his death."

Alastair turned on his heel and moved towards the kitchen.

"Alastair, please! Please wait," Kate cried. "There's no power so the phone will be out as well. Have you got a mobile?"

"Yes, in the car." Alastair looked down at Richard, who had now pulled himself into a sitting position, propped against the château wall. "I'll get it."

Kate watched him hurry through the salon and out across the courtyard. She followed him into the kitchen and sat down in the big armchair by the fireplace. She cradled the baby in her arms, her tears falling unheeded onto his little head. Her own head was throbbing and her jaw ached from Richard's blow. Suddenly she realised that the child was shivering violently. His blanket and clothes were soaking wet from the rain. She hurriedly grabbed a torch and made her way upstairs to get dry towels from the airing cupboard. A few minutes later, Alastair came in and held the phone out to her.

"Here, you call the good doctor," he said with a sneer. "I'm sure he'll be out here *tout de suite* for you."

Kate dialled the familiar number with a shaking hand, conscious that Alastair noticed that she didn't need to look it up. She heard the ringing tone. No answer, then the doctor's voice in a gabble of French. She panicked for a moment. What on earth was he saying? Then it dawned on her. Of course, it was the answerphone! She had forgotten he was out, proposing marriage to one of Nick's 'flings'. In despair, she turned to Alastair, the phone still in her hand.

"There's no reply. He's out. What shall I do? If I call an ambulance they'll send the gendarmes as well! They always do!"

"Oh God," sighed Alastair. His anger had evaporated and a cold, empty void now filled his heart. "We've been here before, haven't we? But your gendarmes won't let me get away a second time!"

"Here! I don't know how to switch this thing off." Kate thrust the phone at him. "Let me see how Richard is. Perhaps I can drive him to the hospital – say I found him lying on the pavement in St Geniès, been mugged or something. Let's see if he can walk."

Alastair just had time to think fleetingly how good a liar Kate had become, when her cry had him running out onto the terrace.

"Alastair! He's gone!"

A trail of fresh blood led across the terrace to the wrought iron gate in the wall. In the failing light it was impossible to see which way Richard had turned. The grassy steps cut into the hillside led down below the terrace towards the lake in one direction and back along the gravel at the front of the château in the other.

"We've got to find him," cried Kate. "He's losing blood and he needs a doctor. In this weather, he could die from exposure!"

"You go round the front and see if you can see any blood on the gravel. Take the torch – he might be trying to get to the car. I'll see if he's gone this way."

"No, no, go back onto the terrace first. If he's gone down towards the lake you'll probably be able to see him from up there. Even in this light, you might be able to see which way he goes."

"OK," Alastair agreed. "Shout if you see him round the front."

Kate grabbed the torch and made her way along the gravel terrace, frantically scanning the small white stones for blood. A few minutes later she heard a shout from Alastair.

"Kate, I think I can see him! Come back onto the terrace."

"I'm coming! No sign of him this way," she shouted, turning and running back through the gate to the edge of the terrace, where Alastair stood peering into the gloom.

"Look, down there, just by the first poplar."

"It looks like him. Richard! Richard! Come back!" Kate's frantic voice was carried away on the wind.

"Come on! Bring the torch! And hurry, before we lose him!"

Alastair was already across the terrace and running down the slippery grass steps. Once he stumbled and slipped on the wooden edge of a rough-hewn step, almost losing his balance. Kate was close behind, calling out to Richard above the whining of the wind in the trees and the crashing thunder.

"There he is!"

As Alastair and Kate reached the bottom of the steps, they could just make out a stumbling, hunched figure, about a hundred metres ahead of them.

"Oh no, he's heading for the lake!" Kate screamed to make herself heard above the wind and rain. "He might fall in. The bank's not stable and the lake's deep and full of weeds. And there's the weir! In this weather, he could be swept away if he falls in! Richard! Richard! Stop! Come back!"

They ran, slithering and sliding over the wet grass towards the lake, trying to keep Richard in view. He was moving quickly, despite his injuries. Suddenly a flash of lightning illuminated the lake and they could see him, clearly silhouetted against the dark sky, poised on the edge of the bank. Then he disappeared as the thunder cracked overhead.

"He's jumped!"

Alastair's heart was in his mouth. Richard had said he wanted to die. But none of this was Richard's fault. It was all his – and Kate's. He had to save Richard.

"No, look. He's got into the boat."

Kate pointed to where, tossing around in the rough waters of the usually mirror-like lake, was the small, black shape of a rowing boat. The next bolt of lightning lit up Richard's white hair, slumped in the bow of the boat. The wind was blowing the boat rapidly away from the bank, out into the centre of the lake.

"What are we going to do? There's no other boat! It'll capsize in this wind and he'll drown. There's no way he'll make it to the shore in his state."

"I'll go in after him and see if I can drag the boat to the bank."

Alastair was already taking off his shoes.

"No, no, you mustn't. That'd be madness! The wind's too strong and it's too dark. He's being blown towards the weir. We'll have to go round and see if we can get there before the boat hits it. He won't have a chance if he gets swept over the weir."

"Alright."

Alastair could see she was making sense.

"Which way?"

He peered into the darkness.

"Oh God, I don't know," Kate gasped. "Through the trees is shortest, but in the dark, I don't know. But the other way is too far, even in the daylight we wouldn't get there in time. The wind's too strong. The boat's moving too fast. We'll have to go that way."

She pointed at a mass of dark shapes, bending in the wind like waves on the lake. "Through the willows."

The narrow path along the edge of the lake twisted and turned around the trunks of the old willow trees that grew out over the water. The slender fronds that usually draped languidly onto the surface were now whipped into a mass of wiry tentacles, grabbing at their clothes and faces and arms as Alastair and Kate fought their way along the path. The chalky path, baked hard by the summer sun, had turned into treacherous slime. Tree roots protruded across the path and fallen branches obstructed their way. The storm was moving away now, and with it the lightning that had lit their path. The small torch threw a feeble beam ahead of them. Alastair was in front, desperately fighting his way through the luxurious summer growth of the willows, with Kate hard on his heels. Suddenly he heard her cry out. Turning, Alastair saw Kate sprawled in the mud, her foot wedged in a lattice of tree roots. He ran back to her, shining the torch on her white face, twisted in pain.

"I can't move it," Kate groaned. "My foot seems to be stuck and my ankle.. .,"she broke off wincing. "You must go on, there's no time to lose. Come back for me when you've found Richard."

"I can't leave you like this. It might be broken."

"Alastair!" Kate's voice was desperate. "Go and get Richard! He might be unconscious again by now. I've told you the weir will be dangerous. If you can get to the end of the lake before the boat, it's our only chance! Go in off the bank just before the weir. It'll be rough, but it's not deep there, only a metre or so, all the way up to the weir on this side. If you can grab the boat there, you might be able to drag it ashore."

Alastair didn't hesitate any longer. He had to save Richard. Everything Richard had done had been for him. If Richard died, it would be his fault. He turned and set off again along the treacherous path. Soon he was out of the trees and right on the edge of the lake. Ahead of him, where the lake tapered slightly, he could just make out the dark shape of the weir. Above the noise of the wind, he could now hear a more sinister sound – the roar of the water in the weir. Peering into the darkness, the wind and rain beating into his face, he thought he saw the boat, still out in the middle of the lake, just about on a level with him, but moving quickly towards the end of the lake and the weir. It looked as if he would be able to get to there before the boat. He allowed himself a small sigh of relief. Thank goodness! He stood a real chance of saving Richard.

He reached the end of the lake a few minutes later and paused on the edge, out of breath. He could make out the boat, about twenty metres away from the weir, out in the middle of the lake. Water was surging over the weir, waves slapping up at the sides. Even on the bank, the waves were splashing water over Alastair's already sodden feet and legs. The current was very strong towards the weir. Alastair didn't think he'd have the strength to haul the boat to the shore. But if he could wade out into the middle of the lake, close to the weir, he could grab Richard out of the boat as it went past, before it hit the weir. He looked dubiously at the churning water. He hoped Kate was right and that it wasn't very deep. Quickly taking off his shoes, Alastair plunged into the icy water. His feet found the bottom through a tangle of weeds. The water was up to his thighs, the waves washing up his chest. He struggled through the dark water, keeping parallel to the bank at the edge of the lake. When he was opposite the end of the weir, he stopped. It took all his strength to keep his position and not get swept towards it. He knew he would have to try to stay to the side of the weir and grab Richard as the boat went past. From the strength of the current, he couldn't risk getting between the boat and the weir or he'd go over with it. He had been keeping an eye on the boat as it was tossed towards him. Now he looked again, to locate it clearly. For a few seconds, he could not make it out at all and panic seized him. Surely it couldn't have gone over the weir while he'd been wading into the lake. He peered through the driving rain, heavier now, although the storm had moved on. Then there it was, very close to him, on his left, directly in line with the weir. As he moved towards it, a huge wave hit him in the chest and he lost his footing and went under. In seconds he surfaced, choking and wiping water from his eyes. Oh God, where was the boat? There it was, a bit further away now, but there was still time. Alastair lunged towards it through the waves and grabbed at the stern. It was only then that he realised with horror that the boat was upside down. The last wave that had floored him must have capsized the boat. He looked around wildly, shouting out to Richard. But there was no sign of him. Alastair took a deep breath and dived under the boat. Although the water was only a metre or so deep, it was thick with weeds, and pitch dark. He could see nothing.

Surfacing again he scanned the lake, trying to catch a flash of lighter colour that might indicate Richard's hair. He could see nothing but darkness. Again and again he dived, but nothing. Alastair could hear his own voice as if it belonged to someone else, screaming out to Richard. He thrashed through the water searching vainly. Then he stumbled to the shore, grabbed his torch and swept it over the water, time and again. But there was no sign of Richard. A faint hope seized Alastair. Perhaps Richard had been swept over the weir straight after the boat capsized. If he'd been in the water before he went over, he might have survived. Kate had said the river was quite shallow, and there were small shingle beaches along its banks. So, with luck, he'd be thrown clear and washed ashore. But he'd certainly have been injured going over the weir. A loud crash followed by a sharp, splintering sound made Alastair focus on the weir. The boat had just been swept over. The force of the water hurled it into the air. It landed broadside-on, crashing into the vertical stone side of the weir, smashing the bow. Alastair let out his breath slowly as he watched the jagged black shapes tossing around in the foaming water.

He played the torch along the edge of the lake. The path finished in a small, rickety, wooden landing stage by the weir. A low, dry-stone wall stretched back along the margin of the woods, marking the boundary of the château's land. Alastair climbed the wall and made his way through the wet grass to the river bank. From this side he could see for the first time the true deadliness of the weir in flood. Even in the dark, the churning water showed up like a bubbling cauldron of foam and he could hear the noise of the torrent above the howling wind. There was no sign of the battered boat. His heart froze with fear for Richard. Could he really have survived being tossed like a helpless matchstick in this? Alastair knew there was no time to lose. If he had come over the weir, Richard must be badly hurt, as well as nearly drowned. Ahead of him, further down the river, he could just see where the banks flattened as the river turned south. On the bend he could see a pale glow that looked like a shingle beach. He thanked God that the river bed was limestone and the beaches showed up clearly, even in the dark. This was where he should look. If Richard had been washed over the weir, he would eventually end up on one of the beaches. Alastair just had to find which one. The rain had eased to a steady downpour and the wind was dying down a bit now. Alastair called out at the top of his voice, again and again.

"Richard! Can you hear me? Where are you? Answer me! Where are you?"

5

The neighbour's story

"Susie! Come on, will you!" John Nicholson called to his daughter across the car park. "Dan, go and get her, for goodness sake, or we'll be here all afternoon."

John glanced up at the heavy sky. He wanted to get to the barn before the storm broke. The track down from the road was pretty difficult at the best of times and he knew only too well how a summer storm would turn the parched limestone soil into a skating rink. He kicked one of the tyres of the old Land Rover. Pity he hadn't had the money to replace them. The tread was barely legal. Not a lot of grip likely, even in four wheel drive. Oh well. He sighed and hefted the last of the plastic shopping bags into the back and slammed the door. Where were those kids? Towing the caravan down the track would be a nightmare if they didn't get there before the storm.

Susie had been distracted by a large white Pyrenean mountain dog tied to the railings by the trolley park. She had stopped to talk to it and was now laughing with a stout middle-aged man with a curly beard, who appeared to be the dog's owner. Dan had joined the conversation and seemed to have forgotten his mission to retrieve his sister. John strolled over, in time to hear the man finishing what was obviously a very funny story from the way his children reacted.

"Now off you go, you two," the man said, grinning at John. "I can't be held responsible for you getting stuck in the mud!"

John smiled back.

"Sorry to drag them away, and I'm afraid it'll probably happen anyway! Just look at those clouds."

"Yes. Still, it'll be a bit of a relief. It's been so hot recently. Oppressive. Jim Munro, by the way," he said, holding out his hand to John. He gestured towards the dog. "And this is Ferdie. Fernando. He's Spanish."

"Nice to meet you both. John Nicholson," John replied. "Been living here long?"

"A few years now," Jim nodded. "Nice place, plenty of bits of work around with all the English and their second homes. And the Dutch, of course. They don't like to pay for anything though! Worse than the Scots," he grinned, exaggerating his soft accent. "So you've got the barn up on the hill near the château – St Geniès-Lafontaine?"

"That's right. Bought it a few years ago now. Do you know it?"

"Yes. I do a bit of work with the Fromac estate agent, Dominic Lefèvre – you know, with the English clients who don't speak French. Actually, I've been over to the château recently. We thought she might want to sell up after what happened."

"Oh? What did happen?" John asked. "We never hear anything. We're only here during the school holidays and then we seem to spend all our time trying to make the barn habitable and keeping the grass under control."

"Or canoeing on the river, or horse-riding, or swimming at the *plan d'eau* or…"

Dan broke off giggling as John cuffed him gently on the ear.

"That's why we've had this place for ages, but I still have to sleep in the caravan!" added Susie, grinning at her father.

John shrugged and smiled ruefully at Jim.

"What can I say! And if we don't get there soon, your caravan will be stuck in the mud, miles from the barn and you'll have to use the bushes instead of our nice, new, clean, warm bathroom!" John turned to Jim. "We'd better be off. Maybe see you around."

"Sure. I'm often in the café in St Geniès. The first one on the right, on the square as you come in from Fromac. The Café de France. Do you go there? I like it. Food's good. I eat there a lot.

Ever since the wife left. Oh, don't worry," Jim lifted his hand as John opened his mouth to commiserate. "We're still married. She just couldn't stand the weather here. All the rain got her down. So she went back to Scotland! Can you believe it? West coast too! She comes out in June and July. I go back for the winter. Well, see you!"

They shook hands. Susie patted the dog one more time and the three of them made their way across to the Land Rover. The children piled into the front seat and they were on their way, soon turning off the main road, following the twisting side road to St Geniès. The village came into view, perched on top of its rounded hill. Instead of following the road up into the village, they skirted the hill along an even narrower road that followed the meandering path of a small river. Crossing an old stone bridge, the Land Rover slowed to a crawl as the road climbed steeply. On one side, open fields swept down the valley to where the river snaked its way into the distance, sometimes hidden by the clumps of trees along its banks. As they neared the top of the hill, John shifted down a gear and swung the heavy vehicle in a wide arc to the right.

"You're not going to make it in one, Dad," Dan chortled.

"Yes, I am!"

John eased the protesting Land Rover round, watching the caravan behind move jerkily over the ruts at the side of the road. Straightening up the wheel, he just managed to edge into the narrow track leading off the road.

"See!" he grinned at his son as the caravan slid round into place behind the Land Rover.

"Well done, Dad!" Susie cried, just before they all heard a loud scraping noise as the side of the caravan grazed the old gatepost, hidden now under the summer's growth of honeysuckle.

"Damn!" John swore softly as his children convulsed with laughter. "Oh well, nearly!"

He joined in the mirth as Dan said,

"That's five euros you owe me, Suse! I said he wouldn't do it without hitting something!"

They bumped down the track and soon were negotiating the final bend. John noted with relief that everything looked normal. As usual he'd half-expected the place to have burned down in his absence. He stopped the car and they all piled out. John stood in front of the small, stone barn and felt the usual glow of pride and pleasure, mixed with sadness that Gerry was not here to share it with him. His wife Gerry had died of cancer when Dan was two. He still missed her and saw her clearly in both his lovely children. Susie brought him back out of his reverie.

"Dad! Come on! It's starting to rain. Can we get my van parked properly, please?"

John walked over to the edge of the flat, grassy area in front of the barn and looked out across the meadows. Big black clouds were hanging low over the valley, obliterating the tops of the trees on the opposite side. A rumble of thunder made him hurry over to his daughter and he and Dan manoeuvred the caravan into position as heavy, slow drops of rain started to patter more rapidly on its roof. It didn't take long before they had the bicycles and canoes off the roof rack and stacked in the shelter behind the barn. Susie took all the food inside and was methodically unpacking and putting things away in the kitchen corner of the large upstairs room in the barn. The barn had been just a shell when they'd bought it. No water, no electricity, no nothing. John and the children had come out at every school holiday and worked on it, so that now it was nearly finished. It had been Dan's idea to have the living room upstairs. French windows opened onto the covered wooden veranda they had built out at the front, looking across the valley. The river was in the bottom, marking their boundary. Two large meadows dropped away from the flat area in front of the barn, at first quite steeply, then gently levelling out into a lovely flat water meadow by the river. To the left of the meadows was their wood, in which the children played endlessly. Even now, with Susie coming up to sixteen next month, they still loved the freedom of the empty countryside. On the right, some scrubby land sloped up to the road, scattered with small juniper and oak trees. The barn was perfectly situated, unseen from the road and far enough away down the track so that they rarely even heard the few passing vehicles. On the opposite bank, meadows stretched along to the right, following the river, and up the valley sides to more trees on the skyline. To the left, the trees came right down to the river, by the weir. Where these trees started marked the boundary of the grounds of the Château de St Geniès-Lafontaine. In the winter, they could just see its beautiful, silvery turrets. Now the summer foliage hid the château completely from view.

Thunder was rumbling round the valley, surrounding them. They all loved storms here. The drama and excitement of natural forces so beyond anyone's control impressed and thrilled them. Susie had already laid the table on the veranda and had put out the storm lanterns and candles in big glass bottles to protect the flames from the wind. Dan and John were finishing preparing supper when the first bolt of lightning flashed across the sky.

"Brill!" yelled Dan, rushing out onto the veranda.

"Come on, Dan," called John. "Help me get the rest of the food out and then we can eat out here and all watch the storm."

They sat together, dry and warm in the shelter of the veranda, watching the theatrical storm rage all around them. They were hungry after the day's long drive south and the salad and quiches disappeared in seconds. Dan was stuffing large wedges of baguette and cheese into his mouth between cries of delight. A particularly brilliant flash of lightning was followed instantaneously by a crash of thunder right above their heads.

"Wow!" Dan's eyes were shining with excitement. "The storm's right over the valley now."

"I hope it doesn't hit us." Susie was a bit apprehensive.

"Scaredy-cat!" Dan taunted.

"We'll be alright," John reassured her. "If it hits anything, it'll be the château."

At that moment, just as he spoke, lightning blazed across the sky again. To their left the trees by the château were suddenly lit up with an incandescent purple light as the thunder roared and echoed away down the valley.

"It's their power line!" Dan shouted above the storm. "You were right, Dad!"

"Our's is OK," Susie said. "I can still see the fridge light."

They sat and watched the sheets of rain sweeping down. It was almost dark, but they didn't switch on the lights. Sitting in the candlelight on the veranda, finishing his glass of wine, John felt very contented. The storm moved slowly away, chased by the strong wind. Gradually, it became a bit calmer. John was almost dozing, the sound of the rain on the veranda roof beginning to lull him to sleep. Dan was leaning over the wooden rail peering into the darkness below, where he could just make out the whiteness of the water where it came over the weir. The rivers would be really exciting tomorrow. Perhaps he could get his father to take them canoeing. It was nearly too dark to see anything now. Dan was just about to turn away and help his sister clear their supper things when a small flash of light caught his eye. At first he thought it was a glow worm. They got quite a few of them in the meadow in summer. But then he realised that it was something bigger, much further away, down at the bottom of the meadow, on the other bank of the river. There it was again.

"Dad, look."

Dan shook his father's shoulder.

"What's the matter?"

John sat up, rubbing his eyes. He must have been more tired than he had realised.

"See over there," Dan pointed. "There's someone down there! I can see a light. It looks like a torch. Look, there!"

"Oh yes!" John could just make out the small, feeble light. "It looks as if someone's going along the river bank. I wonder what they're doing, out in this weather?"

"Perhaps they're checking up on their animals." This was Susie.

"Oh, trust you!" Dan scoffed. "Always think everyone's as bad as you, only thinking about animals."

"So!" Susie retorted. "The world would be a better place if they were!" she sniffed.

"Come on, you two! Stop bickering." John was peering through the gloom. "Perhaps I'd better go and see if there's a problem."

"Can I come too, Dad?" Dan asked eagerly.

"No, you stay here and help your sister clear up and get the beds made up. We haven't even done that yet, and I'll be ready for mine soon. And put the immersion heater on too. I'll need a hot bath after I've been out in this weather."

"OK," Dan sighed. "The big torch is by the door. Flash it three times if you want me to come and help!"

John went downstairs and took his waterproof jacket from the hook by the door. Collecting the torch, he stepped outside. It was still windy, but the rain had nearly stopped. He made his way down the rough steps below the barn into the meadow, setting off towards the light. It seemed to be moving slowly down river, away from the weir. John headed for the bank, a little way downstream from where he could see the occasional flash of the light. He judged that, by the speed the person with the small torch seemed to be moving, they'd be just about opposite each other when John reached the bank. It looked as if the person on the other side was searching for something. He seemed to be flashing the torch around, over the river as well as the banks. Perhaps Susie was right. It could be the farmer checking his livestock. There were often cows in this meadow. He was on the point of calling out to ask if help was needed when he heard a shout from the opposite bank. The man's voice was carried away on the wind, but then it came a second time. John was sure he heard him call out in English:

"Richard! Richard! Can you hear me? Where are you? Answer me! Where are you?"

****

"So what happened next?" Jim Munro stirred his coffee thoughtfully.

The morning sun was already warm on his back. He sat facing John across the small table outside the Café de France. The big white dog was sprawled under the table, lying on Jim and John's feet. Across the square, the clock on top of the *mairie* had just struck eleven. He could see John's children on the other side of the street, heading off towards the boulangerie, chattering excitedly to each other.

"Well," John paused and smiled up at the pretty waitress as she plonked his cup of café au lait down on the table. "I wasn't sure at first what he was saying, but when I got a bit nearer, I could hear him quite clearly. He was definitely English. Well," John grinned at Jim. "Scottish, anyway. And he was calling out 'Richard, where are you?' I'm sure that's what he said. When I was nearly at the river, I shouted out to him to see if I could help. You know, it sounded like he was looking for someone, this Richard, and in that weather I was a bit worried. I could hear the river was running really high and it was pitch dark. He didn't seem to hear me, or notice my torch. So I called out again and when I got to the bank I could just make out his shape, so I shone the torch on him. And, you know, it was really weird. I recognised him."

"Yeah?" Jim looked surprised.

"Yes, I was really taken aback. We don't know anyone out here. I'd hardly recognise the café people if I saw them out of context and we come in here a lot. But the funny thing is, it was a guy we'd met on the way down. On the road, I mean. He was travelling with his friend and they were going to the château, seems they know the owner. And, you'll never guess, but his friend was called Richard. I remember that because it was him that we were talking to – this Richard – and he was really interested in hearing about our barn. You know, buying a place out here for himself. Said he'd like to move here. Well,

I said I'd meet him here, in the café, today, at ten and tell him all about it."

"And he hasn't shown up?" Jim asked, a look of comprehension and then concern crossing his face. "So the guy was out looking for him last night? He'd got caught in the storm and got lost or something?"

"That's what I thought. I was sure he called out Richard, and I was getting worried that he thought this Richard had got lost out there somewhere. But when I called out to him, asked what was up, he said he was looking for their cat! He said it was terrified of storms and had run off and he was frightened that it had fallen into the river. He told me the cat was called Ricard. I said I'd help him look, but he was adamant he didn't need help, said he was giving up because it was probably hiding somewhere and would turn up when the rain stopped. So that was that, at the time. He seemed to be fairly desperate to get away from me, kept backing away out of range of my torch. Just before I left, I shone the torch on him again. I'd noticed at first that he was soaking wet, but so what? It had been pouring down. But I was nearer to him by then, and when I shone the torch on him, I could see that there was blood on his face and shirt. He might have fallen or something, but in fact he looked as if he'd been in a fight. Then he turned back towards the lake and I went back up the hill to the barn. When I got home the kids had both gone to bed and I felt like a bit of a nightcap so I went out onto the terrace again. I was sitting there for a while, then I noticed the flashlight down by the river again. At the time I thought, that guy must really love his cat. Then I got to thinking it was pretty odd really. It couldn't be his cat, although he kept saying 'my cat', because he'd only come over to France the day before, on holiday, according to his friend. Then I thought if it belonged to whoever owns the château and the guy had let the cat out into the storm by mistake, then perhaps he would be pretty desperate to find it. Perhaps he didn't really mean it was his own cat. And I thought although he looked as if he'd been in a fight it was probably when he was thrashing around in the undergrowth round the lake, or slipped over, that he'd cut himself. Anyway, I didn't think too much more about it last night. I was really tired after the drive and a couple of brandies later I was in bed fast asleep myself." John took another sip of coffee then went on. "This morning I told the kids what had happened and Susie said it couldn't have been his cat. No one who owned a cat would go out looking for it in the middle of a storm. Cats, according to my daughter, have superior intelligence to us humans and would always hide somewhere dry until the storm was over. According to my daughter, everyone knows that! Anyway, I got to thinking about it all again. I was absolutely sure that the guy was calling 'Richard'. I mean when he said 'Ricard', it was a completely different sound. I know it looks nearly the same on paper but, with a Scottish accent as well, it sounded completely different. And another thing. He was soaking wet, and he wasn't wearing a coat or anything. You'd have thought that if he'd really gone out to look for a lost cat, he'd have put a raincoat on at least. Then when Richard didn't turn up this morning, I just got to thinking about it again. Thing is, I don't really know what to do. It seems a bit far-fetched, but I got to wondering if something had happened. You know, because the guy looked so beaten up, maybe…Well, I got to wondering if this guy and Richard had maybe been involved in a fight about something. Perhaps they were outside before the storm really started, got into some sort of argument, Richard headed off on his own, missed his way in the storm or something. But I'm sure I'm just being a bit melodramatic. And I don't want to make a fuss in case I'm wrong and the guy really was looking for a cat."

"Sounds a bit odd alright," Jim agreed. "But I expect there's a perfectly normal explanation. I suppose the best thing would be just to pop round to the château and ask if Richard's OK."

"Yes, that's what I thought," John nodded. "I expect you are right. He's probably just overslept. It is a long drive. I think I'll go over there now. This is worrying me. Are you staying here long?"

"I need another coffee before I can really start the day," Jim grinned. "And Salome there," he jerked his head in the direction of the waitress, "will be so upset if I go before she gets the chance to ask me again if I can get her a job in the UK."

"I'd rather go without the kids, just in case something is up. Will you tell them where I've gone and to wait here for me? Here," John fished in his pocket. "Pay for what we've had and give the kids the change – and tell them not to spend it all."

"Sure," Jim nodded. "Thanks, John. I'll wait for you to get back. There's been some funny things happen recently at that château. I just hope there hasn't been another one."

John walked over to the Land Rover and set off, taking the road to the right of the café, out of the square towards the cemetery. He passed the end of the small road that led up to the Gendarmerie, then followed the curve of the main road as it headed out of the village into the open countryside. He soon came to the small signpost: *Château de St Geniès-Lafontaine*. Turning off down the narrow lane, John reflected on what he was going to say. Hell, he thought, I've no idea of the Scottish guy's name. And although we've been neighbours for a few years, I've no idea who lives at the château. I'm assuming they'll be English. If they're not, God only knows how I'm going to explain what I want. Should have brought the kids. They speak much better French than me.

The Land Rover bounced round the final bend in the track and John caught his first glimpse of the château. He'd seen its turrets from the barn, but now that he could see the whole thing from above, through the trees, he was impressed. As he drove down the final length of the track he was relieved to see the UK plates of a blue Saab parked on the gravel where the track finished. He recognised it as the car that Richard and the Scotsman had been travelling in. Pulling up alongside it, he climbed out and looked up at the château towering above him, blinding white in the sunlight. John followed the sweep of the gravel round the front of the building and eyed the massive oak door set at the top of a short flight of semi-circular stone steps.

Oh well, here goes, he muttered to himself, climbing the steps and, grasping the brass, hand-shaped door knocker, rapped loudly on the door.

As the sound died away, there was total silence. John waited, looking around. No birds sang. There was no breeze today, just this deafening silence. He knocked again, harder this time. Still nothing. John sighed. Perhaps there was a back door, tradesman's entrance or something. Bound to be. It was such a big place they probably couldn't hear the door if they were at the other end of the building. Funny there was no bell. He stepped back and looked up at the blank windows, all tightly shuttered on this side of the building. He walked back to his car. On his right there was what he took to be a coach house and by the stone arch over the track there was a cobbled passage that seemed to lead into a small courtyard. This looked more like it. He went into the courtyard and glanced around. The shutters were open on two ground floor windows and, glancing in through the nearest window, he could see a big stone chimney breast. This must be the kitchen. He hammered on the blood-red painted wooden door set between the two windows.

Again, nothing. He listened intently, but could hear no sound from the house. Knocking again as hard as he could brought no response. John moved closer and, getting a toe-hold in the rough stone wall, peered in through the window. It was quite dark inside, but he could clearly see a long table. On it were a breadboard and half a baguette, the bread knife lying alongside and crumbs on the board. A half-full jug of milk stood nearby. On the far side of the room, John could just see a coffee percolator on the hob. In the shaft of sunlight that fell on it, he could see a curl of steam rising. Good God, he thought. It's like the Mary Celeste! Then he heard it. For a second he froze, his blood running cold. It seemed to come from far away, in the bowels of the château. Then he realised the scream was the shrill, agonised cry of a baby in distress. John jumped involuntarily and lost his footing, dropping back down onto the cobbles. He hammered again on the door. Now he knew someone was at home. Still no answer. Someone had to be there. They couldn't have left a baby on its own, surely. Something odd was going on here. He was beginning to wish he hadn't come. He should have left well alone. But he was here now. He might as well try and find out what had happened to Richard. John stepped back from the door and started to haul himself up to see in through the second window, hoping for a sign of life.

"Can I help you?"

The voice behind him made John start violently and, losing his grip for the second time, he slithered back to the ground, landing in a heap at the feet of the Scotsman.

"Oh, yes. Hello. It's me, do you remember ? We met last night in the storm. Before that we saw you at the Tunnel yesterday, then in the picnic stop. I was talking to your friend," John spluttered and gabbled in his embarrassment at being discovered peering in through the window.

Getting to his feet, he added, "I've been knocking on the door for ages."

"Yes. It's a big place. I'm afraid it's difficult to hear when people knock if we're not expecting them," the man said. "Can I help you?" he repeated.

"Well, yes. I hope so," John said. "I've come to see if Richard's OK."

"What? Richard?" The man looked startled. "Why shouldn't he be?"

"It's just that we'd arranged to meet this morning in St Geniès at ten. I waited for over an hour, but no sign of him. So I thought I might as well pop over and see if he'd just forgotten. Is he in?"

"No. He's – he's not here. He left early this morning. Had to go back to England suddenly. Business, you know. Sorry I can't help," the man spoke in a hurry and was already turning away from John, about to close the door.

"Hey, just a minute!" John called after him, surprised and a little annoyed by the man's abrupt manner. "Are you sure about this?"

"Yes, of course I am. Look, I have to go. We've got a sick baby."

"I heard it," said John slowly. "I'm sorry to have troubled you. Thanks."

He turned to leave, then said,

"Oh, by the way, did you find your cat?"

"Cat?" A pause. "Oh no, I'm afraid not."

"Pity. I expect he'll turn up. Animals are usually good at self-preservation. So my daughter tells me!" John grinned. "Thanks again."

As he reached the archway, John turned to wave goodbye, but the man had vanished. Bloody odd, he thought. Richard had seemed really keen to hear about moving to France. And going back the minute you've arrived on holiday? And on business? When Richard had told him he only worked as a part-time gardener for the Scotsman? It looks more like they've had a falling out, John mused. And it seems as if there might be a woman in it somewhere, he thought. Usually is. Anyway, it must be someone's baby.

He strolled back to the Land Rover and got in. For a few minutes he sat looking at the silent château. He didn't like it. There was something funny going on here. But it was none of his business. He shrugged and turned the key in the ignition. He reversed the heavy vehicle and drove slowly back over the gravel towards the track. As he passed the parked car, something caught his eye and he paused alongside it. On the back seat was a black holdall and a dark green jacket. John could have sworn it was the jacket that Richard had been wearing when they saw him at the Tunnel. Glancing around to make sure the Scotsman was out of sight, he jumped out of the Land Rover and tried the back door of the car. It opened. John reached in and pulled the holdall towards him. He read the name on the small leather tag attached to the bag: Richard Talbot. The front pocket of the bag was open. John stuck his hand in and pulled out a passport. Flicking open the cover, Richard's face peered out at him. Then he heard the sound of another car being driven fast down the track.

He just had time to push the passport back into the holdall, close the car door and leap back into the Land Rover before the small white Renault appeared round the corner. John waited for the car to pass him, pretending he had stopped out of courtesy on the narrow track. The driver, a handsome Frenchman, acknowledged him with a cheerful wave.

Fifteen minutes later, John was back in the Café de France, holding a large glass of brandy. Jim, Dan and Susie sat looking at him in silence. The children's eyes wide, Susie's with concern and a hint of fear, Dan's with excitement.

"Was there any blood, Dad? I mean on the jacket, in the car?"

"Honestly, Dan!" Susie exclaimed. "You're such a .. a .."

"But Dad!" Dan persisted. "You said the guy looked as if he'd been in a fight last night. You said he was covered in blood!"

"Not exactly," John replied. "But well, yes, he did look as if he might have been fighting. And this morning, even more so I suppose, when I could see him close up. He'd got cuts on his face. Those could have come from the trees and stuff in the storm but one of them over his eye was quite nasty and I noticed his right hand was all bandaged round the knuckles, as if he might have hit someone really hard. Yeah, the few cuts and grazes on his face mostly really did look like what you'd have got just from tree branches and stuff. They didn't look as if they'd have bled much. They weren't deep. But last night his clothes did have a lot of blood on them. I mean I noticed in the dark, just by the torch light. Far more blood than I'd have expected now that I've seen the cuts on his face clearly. And it all seems so odd. That guy Richard seemed so keen to talk to us about moving here, seemed, you know, really pleased that we said we'd meet him today. I can't believe the story that he's gone back home. I mean, how can he have, leaving his coat and bag and passport?"

Jim Munro stirred his coffee thoughtfully and nodded.

"Yes, I agree it seems as if there's something very strange going on. There's something about that château. It seems to be jinxed."

"What do you mean?" asked Dan, his eyes alight again. "Murders?"

"Well, no. Not exactly anyway. You must have heard about it?"

"No," John shook his head. "Like I said, we don't know anyone down here, so don't ever talk to anyone much."

"It's a sad story really," Jim said. "An English couple bought the château not long ago. Just over a year now, maybe. I didn't know them well, but I'd met them a few times in the estate agent's office in Fromac where I work sometimes. Good-looking couple. Stunning in fact, especially seen together. He was dark, tall, a real charmer. She's blonde, really sparky, fabulous figure. Loads of money, of course. But nice people. Anyway, they got stuck into the renovations on the château. She didn't come out much. It seems she was the brains, a real business woman. She made the money and he spent it. He was out here a lot. Made a lot of friends. He had that knack of getting on with people – with anybody. He spoke fairly bad French really, but it was the way he said it. Had all the women weak at the knees! But the men liked him too. He used local craftsmen for all the work and was a good carpenter himself. He earned a lot of respect round here. Then, early this year, he came out again, just after Christmas. This time he brought another woman with him. She was a garden designer, apparently, who lived next door to him in England. She was supposed to be getting the grounds sorted out for them. She was a funny woman, bit of a drip really. Quite pretty, but in a droopy sort of way. You know, seemed to be sort of in a bit of a dream all the time. And she always seemed a bit hostile. Well, perhaps not that, more aloof, like she didn't want to have anything to do with anyone. I mean," Jim shrugged, "no reason why she should if she was just here to do a job. I only saw her once in Fromac with Nick – that's the guy who owned the château. Anyway, to cut a long story short, she stayed a few months, then her husband arrived to take her home. Now the next bit's the good bit, Dan. And what actually happened depends on who you talk to, but the official version is that the police get an emergency call to the château. Nick seems to have fallen through the stone balustrade of the terrace. I don't know if you saw it, but there's a drop of about ten metres, straight down onto rock. So he's more or less a goner. Died a day or two later in hospital. But the woman, it seems, was pregnant, she goes into labour and gets rushed to Cahors where she has this kid, and announces it's Nick's! The gendarmes start investigating Nick's death. You know, was it really an accident after all? Did he fall or was he pushed? Meanwhile, her husband scarpers back to England sharpish! That's not all – news spreads here like a disease – nothing else to do but gossip!" Jim snorted and took a sip of his own brandy.

"Go on!" Dan urged him. "What happened next?"

"Well, like I said, news travels fast. Next thing is, Chloe's in our office in Fromac saying she wants to sell her house. She's in floods of tears – can't stay here now after what happened to Nick."

"Who on earth is Chloe?" John asked.

"She's a lovely Englishwoman who has a holiday home here. I look after it for her while she's away. She's another stunner. Rumour has it she had an affair with the local doctor when he was in England and he only came to St Geniès because she's got a house here – but that's another story," Jim laughed. "Anyway, it seems that Chloe was also having a bit of an affair with Nick! Straight after he died, she put her house on the market and went back home. So now the doctor's walking round looking like the end of the world is nigh! But Chloe got back today. Her first visit since Nick died. So that should put a spring back into the doc's step! But I digress," Jim stopped grinning. "A couple of days after Nick died, the notaire's wife disappeared. Yes, you've guessed it. She left a note saying she couldn't go on living now she knew Nick was dead. She also swore to her husband that Nick was not to blame and he knew nothing about her infatuation. It was a very Gallic gesture – very theatrical. But she was like that, Marie-Claire was – very passionate and impulsive. Her car was found abandoned near the château. But no one has seen her since."

A small silence descended on the table.

"Blimey!" Dan was the first to speak. "That's really creepy. It's like there's a curse on the château. But what happened then? Who lives at the château now? Who's that Scottish guy that Dad saw – the one who was with Richard?"

"After she'd had the baby, the woman garden designer went back to live at the château with the child, and she's still there. It would have been her kid you heard today, John. Apparently it's quite poorly. The doctor's there all the time. It seems likely it won't live long."

"Oh dear," Susie sighed. "How awful. What happened to her husband?"

"Well," Jim paused. "It sounds to me as if the guy you met might be her husband. I never saw him, but he'd been to the hospital after the baby was born, just before he disappeared back to the UK. I know one of the nurses and she told me the husband talked English like me! So I assume she meant he was Scottish! And when he came down last time, when Nick died, he had a friend with him. Could have been this Richard."

"So," John said slowly. "Are you saying there might be some connection between Nick falling over the balustrade and Richard disappearing? And the link is the Scottish husband of this woman who's the mother of Nick's baby?"

"Dad!" Susie exclaimed. "You've got a weird mind! That's really far-fetched! And you shouldn't jump to conclusions about people you've never met. That's the trouble with gossip!" she sniffed, glancing at Jim.

"Hey, young lady!" John tapped her knuckles with his coffee spoon. "Watch what you're saying and mind your manners. You shouldn't be impolite even if you don't agree with people."

"Sorry," Susie mumbled, blushing.

"No, no." Jim patted her on the shoulder. "You're quite right. Nick's death was declared an accident. There's no reason to suspect the husband was involved."

"Except if he'd just found out his wife was on the point of having another man's baby…" John mused.

"Yes, maybe. But that doesn't seem to have anything to do with Richard," Susie put in.

"Unless, unless," Dan said excitedly. "Richard was there, right, when Nick died? Then if he saw the Scottish guy, like push him or something, then the Scottish guy might want to get rid of him too. You know, 'cos he was a witness!"

"So why wait till now? And if he did take Richard out, he wouldn't have gone looking for him in the storm shouting, would he, Stupid?" Susie retorted scornfully.

"Perhaps he'd pushed Richard over the balustrade too, in the storm, then couldn't find the body or something! Thought he'd got away, but wanted to finish him off! Serial killers often come back to the scene of the crime to do it again, you know," Dan added authoritatively.

"Don't be silly," Susie said. "If he'd been going to kill Richard, he'd have made sure Richard didn't talk to anyone on the way here. He wouldn't have let him make a rendez-vous with us for today, would he? That'd be really stupid. He couldn't have planned it!"

"Yes, he could! He might not have known Richard was planning to see us today. I mean, how often do you meet people in lay-bys and arrange to see them next day? It was a real coincidence that we live next door. He couldn't have foreseen that, and he'd have had to act normal or Richard would have been suspicious. If he'd tried to stop him chatting to people, it'd have looked really weird!"

"Come on, you two. That's enough," John put a hand on the shoulder of each of his children. "Let's calm down a bit. All we know is that Richard was supposed to meet us today and hasn't turn up. According to the Scottish guy, he's gone home. But without his jacket, bag or passport. And last night I think

I saw him looking for Richard in the storm. So it could all be very straightforward. Richard most probably got lost out there in the dark, sheltered under a tree or something and just hadn't got back to the château by the time I arrived today. It's none of our business."

"Dad!" Susie and Dan cried in unison.

"You can't just ignore it," Susie added. "Richard's missing."

"Presumed dead!" Dan shrieked gleefully.

"Be serious." Susie glared at him, kicking him under the table. "Dad, I think you should report him to the police as a missing person. This Scotsman must have known he hadn't gone home, without his passport. He lied. Perhaps because he doesn't know where Richard has got to either but didn't want to tell you, in case you jumped to conclusions! Just like Dan is doing!"

Dan opened his mouth to protest, but his father silenced him.

"Susie could be right. Although we don't know that he hasn't reported Richard as missing, do we?" John looked at Jim. "What do you think, Jim? Am I making too much of this? It's all 'ifs' and 'maybes'."

Jim stroked his beard thoughtfully. Slowly he shook his head.

"I've got a bad feeling about this. I think you should report it. Tell the gendarmes everything you told me. There're too many loose ends about this whole business, and too many coincidences. And if that woman's involved, I reckon there's trouble."

"OK," John nodded. "I think you're probably right. I might look foolish when it turns out there's a perfectly logical explanation and the police might already know if he is missing. But I know this will prey on my mind if I don't do something. Which way to the Gendarmerie? Do they speak English?"

"I'll come with you," Jim said.

6

The doctor's story

Chloe was glad that she'd called Jim Munro on her way south that morning. Not only had he been over and opened up the house and pool for her, but he'd done her shopping too! The fridge was full of cheese and fruit and salad and bottles of white wine. There was fresh bread on the table, and one little, individual tarte aux fraises. Her favourite! The windows were open and on the table was a vase of zinnias that Chloe knew would have come from Jim's own garden. He'd even made up her bed and left a small, pink rosebud on the pillow, with a scrawled note attached: 'Just what the doctor ordered!!!' Chloe smiled. Good old Jim. He was a dreadful gossip but he'd been a good friend to her, as well as an excellent house-minder. She dropped her bags on the floor of the bedroom and walked back through the living room and out onto the terrace. The sky was heavy and the air sultry. It looked like a storm was brewing. Chloe sighed slightly. She'd been looking forward to a swim but the wind was getting up and she knew before long it would be raining. Oh well, she thought, it is August. I should have come earlier. She went down to the car and drove it into the garage. She walked back up the stone steps onto the terrace and into her living room. She plugged in the kettle in the kitchen and wandered into the bathroom. Turning on the taps she started to run a bath. She had a bit of time before Phillippe was due. In the bedroom, she unpacked her clothes and hesitated about what she should wear tonight. Phillippe was still very much a Parisian at heart, despite his months in the country. He would appreciate a bit of sophistication, she knew.

Suddenly remembering, she grabbed the plastic carriers from the Duty Free Shop and went back into the kitchen. Opening the fridge again, she moved the bottles Jim had put there, making room for the Dom Pérignon from the carrier bags. She glanced at Jim's choice of wine and smiled. She didn't think Phillippe would be too keen on the five euro Muscadet! But she didn't mind. She and Jim could drink it together.

Taking her cup of tea into the bedroom, Chloe stripped off her clothes and slipped on a silk dressing gown. A crash of thunder reminded her to get candles out in case the power went off. It nearly always did when there was a storm. It used to infuriate her that the EDF, the French electricity company, would turn off the power in the out-of-town areas in a storm. They said it was to prevent damage to the overhead cables. Chloe thought that seemed unlikely but had always lost the argument. It was just something they always did. So now she was always ready with the candles. On reflection, she decided a candle-lit bath was probably just what she needed to help her unwind after the long drive. Perhaps the EDF had a point.

Once soaking in the deep tub, she lay back and thought again of the last time she'd been here. Even now she found it hard to believe what had happened. Poor Nick. And poor old Joanne. Chloe felt guilty when she thought of Jo. Jo didn't know about her and Nick of course, although Jo had no illusions about her wayward husband. Chloe knew that Nick, for all his philandering, had really only ever loved Joanne. Chloe frowned slightly as she thought of the woman at the château with the baby. The baby the woman claimed was Nick's. Chloe remembered the first time she and Nick had made love, up in one of the towers of the château, on the bare wooden floor. She'd been a bit worried because, although she was on the pill, and never forgot to take it, a dish of moules a couple of nights previously in that awful cellar-like restaurant near Cahors had given her food poisoning. But Nick had reassured her that they didn't have to worry about rushing back to Fromac to buy condoms because he knew the chances of his fathering any children were very, very small. Something hereditary. She'd laughed, and said how convenient. But she also remembered, rather guiltily, the intensity of their passion and how they couldn't have stopped themselves anyway.

But it wasn't like Nick to lie, certainly not about something like that. Chloe half-suspected that this woman must have been pregnant with someone else's child and had just seized the opportunity to pretend it was Nick's so she could get her hands on the château. Marie-Claire Lacombe had explained all the complications of family succession law to Chloe when she had been buying her own house and Marie-Claire's husband had acted for her. Chloe sighed sadly as she thought about Marie-Claire. She hadn't known how much Marie-Claire cared for Nick. No one had, least of all Nick. Marie-Claire had never said anything to anyone. And she was such a flamboyant character, the last thing you would expect would be for her to commit suicide over an unrequited love. Jim had told her that, after Marie-Claire went missing, her husband had refused to believe that she had killed herself, despite her note. He told everyone it was typical of her to be so theatrical and she would turn up. But she hadn't done yet, and it was about four months since she had disappeared.

Chloe sank lower into her warm bath and glanced up at the clock. Nearly half past seven already! Phillippe would be here soon. In fact he'd probably be leaving home about now. Outside the storm was raging. She hoped none of the roads would be flooded. She smiled to herself as she wrapped a large blue bath towel around her body and padded into the bedroom. Nick had been right. She did still love the doctor.

****

Phillippe kissed her gently on the lips. His deep brown eyes were moist with tears.

"You have made me so happy," he murmured. "I thought you would never change your mind."

"Phillippe! Lots of things have changed. And I don't think I ever stopped loving you. It took Nick to make me realise that."

"I know. And I owe him much also. I have wanted to get away from here myself. I do not have good feelings anymore about St Geniès."

"No," Chloe shivered involuntarily. "I wish you'd told me about your new job before! I was worrying all the way here about how much I wanted to be with you, but how much I really didn't want to live round here."

"I wanted to surprise you," he smiled. "I wanted to show you just how much I, a Frenchman, was prepared to do for you. Even return to your cold and wet country!"

"Ha!" Chloe snorted. "Cold and wet! Just look out of the window! It's August for God's sake, and look at it!"

Phillippe laughed and stood up. Peering out into the darkness he said,

"Well, at least it's nearly stopped raining. I think I'd better set off for home now. I'm supposed to be on call tonight from midnight. And it's likely that there may be problems because of the storm."

"What a pity you can't stay," murmured Chloe, putting her arms around his waist and resting her head on his shoulder.

"I know, chérie."

He turned and took her in his arms again, kissing her deeply and passionately. Then he picked up his jacket and car keys.

"I will see you tomorrow," he said. "My surgery finishes at midday. I'll meet you in the café."

"Good," Chloe nodded. "I need to see Jim about selling the house so I'll go to the café a bit earlier, then I can see him first and then wait for you."

She opened the door and they walked out onto the terrace together. The rain had almost stopped and the wind had died down. There were several branches scattered over the lawn from the row of trees that separated the house from the lane outside. One of the cast iron garden chairs on the pool terrace was on its side. The storm had obviously been quite wild.

"Take care driving home," Chloe said. "It looks as if there will be a lot of debris and trees down. I expect the road'll be flooded at the bottom of the hill."

"I'll be careful. *A demain, ma chérie.*"

Chloe stood and watched as the doctor reversed his car out into the lane and drove off into the blackness. She turned and went back indoors, hugging herself with pleasure. She was so happy. Nick would have been over the moon, she thought sadly. He'd have taken all the credit for getting her and Phillippe back together. Why did he have to die?

The road back to St Geniès was more or less clear and Phillippe was soon parking his car in the square and hurrying towards his apartment. He rented two floors in one of the old buildings that formed the left hand side of the square, opposite the *hôtel de ville* and at right angles to the Café de France and the Café des Sports that sat side by side on the third side of the square. The fourth side was shorter than the rest and this was where the road leading up from the valley reached the village on the crest of the hill. The square itself was deserted. The lights were on in the two cafés and Phillippe could see one or two drinkers still sitting at the bar. He crossed the road and, in the shelter of the colonnaded pavement, rummaged in his briefcase for his house keys. Once inside, he bounded up the steep flight of wooden stairs and into his living room, dropping his briefcase on the sofa and, walking over to the long windows, closed the shutters for the night. He glanced down into the square as he did so. Leaves and a few branches now decorated the petanque pitch below his window, but the old chestnut trees that lined the square seemed to have survived the storm well. Stepping back into the room, he walked across to the desk in the corner and sighed when he noticed the red light of the answerphone winking at him. Glancing at the machine, he could see there was only one message. That wasn't too bad, he thought, and went through into the kitchen to take a can of beer from the fridge. Then he returned to the living room, sat down on the dark brown leather sofa and pressed the flashing red button.

At first he couldn't make out anything, just echoing and crackling that made him think a mobile phone was being used. Then he clearly heard a woman's voice, speaking in English.

"They'll send the gendarmes as well! They always do!"

Faintly in the background he could just hear a man's voice. The man was also speaking English, but Phillippe could not catch the words. He replayed the tape, listening intently to the man. He thought he could make out the last few words the man said:

"…won't let me get away a second time!"

Then the woman's voice again, faintly. Then more noises and the phone was switched off. Phillippe frowned. How strange. He thought he recognised the woman's voice, but he couldn't place it immediately. He had many English patients. The region had a large expatriate community, mainly English, so once word had got round that Phillippe had spent two years in England, his patient list had doubled overnight. He didn't see much of most of them, which was why he was surprised that the voice sounded familiar. He thought carefully of the hypochondriacs amongst them. The voice sounded relatively young, which ruled out a lot of his patients, most of whom were retired. Perhaps it was one of the air crew, he thought. There were a few of them around, taking advantage of their concessionary fares to have homes in France and the UK. One of them was in his surgery frequently with minor problems. But it didn't sound like her. He thought hard. Then he had it. Of course! Why hadn't he thought of her straight away! It was Madame Black from the château. Something else must be wrong with that poor child of hers. Phillippe shook his head. He'd be surprised if the child survived much longer.

He reached for his briefcase and took out his phone. As he flicked through his contacts for the telephone number of St Geniès-Lafontaine, he idly wondered who the voice in the background belonged to. He smiled to himself. She'd certainly been dolled up when he'd called there earlier. It had looked as if she was expecting a lover! He was just about to dial when something else occurred to him. He put down the mobile and played the house answerphone back again. What a very strange conversation! They must have phoned him because they needed a doctor, presumably for the child. But why hadn't they left a proper message? And what had all the talk about gendarmes and getting away with it got to do with anything? Phillippe felt uneasy all of a sudden. What Jim Munro frequently said was right. There was something about that château that gave him a bad feeling.

The phone made him jump.

"Allo, oui?"

"Hello, doctor? It's Kate Black here."

"Ah, yes, Madame." Phillippe sat up, alert. "What can I do for you?"

"It's the baby." Kate's voice was anxious. "He's very hot and feverish. And he's coughing a lot more."

"I see," Phillippe said.

That explains the earlier call he thought, feeling slightly guilty that he had been out. He should have left his mobile on when he was at Chloe's, but he hadn't wanted anything to interrupt them and he wasn't officially on call until midnight.

"How long has he been like this?"

"I'm not quite sure," Kate hesitated. "I've only just checked on him."

"Oh?" Phillippe said in surprise. "But you called earlier? I recognised your voice on the answerphone, although you did not leave a message."

There was a pause. Then Kate said hurriedly,

"Yes, well, actually that was about something different."

"Dear me! The baby has more problems?"

"No, no. Actually," Kate said again. "That was me. I've hurt my ankle, twisted it."

"I see. Can you walk on it?"

"Not easily. It's quite swollen and painful. But it's the baby I'm worried about now," Kate said. "Could you come out and look at him, please? I'm sorry it's so late but I'm so worried. He's very flushed and seems to be in such discomfort. He seems to be having difficulty breathing."

"Yes, of course. I'll be over in a few minutes."

Phillippe put the receiver down with a sigh. This was all he needed. The child was so weak, any infection was going to be more serious than in a healthy baby. Possibly fatal.

Ten minutes later, he was parking the Renault outside the château. As he got out and grabbed his bag from the back seat, he noticed another car parked on the opposite side of the gravel forecourt. That was good. It must be the man on the phone. If he was still here, he could help look after the child if Kate couldn't walk properly.

Phillippe knocked on the kitchen door. The château was in darkness, but Kate opened the door immediately. The kitchen was lit by candles and a couple of oil lamps. She was leaning on what looked like a tree branch, with all her weight on one foot, the other raised slightly. Phillippe could see even in the dim light that the ankle was very swollen.

"Thank you for coming," Kate said quickly. "He's over there, in front of the fire. We've no power. The lines were struck during the storm."

The kitchen was smoky and cold. A small, miserable pile of logs was smouldering in the big fireplace. As Phillippe looked at the child, lying in a carrycot in front of the fire, his small body heaved and shook with a dry, rasping cough. His face was red and he was breathing quickly, in shallow gasps. Phillippe lifted the baby out onto the table and examined him rapidly. Then he turned to Kate, who had limped over to the table and was looking at him anxiously.

"I'll make him as comfortable as I can. It looks as if his cold has developed into bronchitis," Phillippe frowned. "But I am surprised at how suddenly this has happened. When did you notice the change?"

Kate coloured.

"Just now, when I phoned," she stammered. "I, er, I hadn't checked him for a while because," she seemed to search for words. "Because of my ankle!" she finished suddenly.

Phillippe looked at her curiously. It seemed as if she'd been trying to think of an excuse for why she hadn't checked her child earlier.

"Madame," he said, frowning again.

He broke off, thinking hard. He could hardly believe that the child's condition had deteriorated so rapidly. When he had examined him that afternoon he had had a cold, but that was all. Phillippe thought for a moment, going over all the symptoms in his mind to see if he had missed something.

"Madame," he said again, looking at Kate. "Has anything happened to trigger this? Did he get very cold during the storm, for example, when your power went off?"

Kate shifted uneasily, adjusting her makeshift crutch.

"Yes," she said quietly. "I'm afraid so. In fact," she took a deep breath. "In fact, he got rather wet. I……, I left the pram out in the rain when the storm started."

The doctor stared at her. He just did not believe how careless people could be. The last thing he'd told this woman to do was to make sure she kept her sick child warm and comfortable.

"I see," he said coldly, unable to disguise his contempt. "When the storm started? And you have only just checked on him? So he was outside all through the storm and has been, I suppose, soaking wet until now?"

"Oh no! No!" Kate cried. "He got wet when the storm started, but I brought him in and dried him then. But then…" Kate broke off, almost in tears.

"I see, I see," said Phillippe quickly, remembering the answerphone. The time on the message had been not long after the storm started.

"This was when you called earlier? He was ill then?"

"Yes, er, no! No! I fell," she said, looking at the floor. "I was in a hurry, you know, trying to get him dry. I was very upset because of leaving him outside. The power was off and I tripped in the dark…I could hardly walk."

Phillippe's momentary anger disappeared. He felt sorry for her now. He could imagine the panic, realising she'd left the pram outside, finding the baby soaking wet, no power, groping around in the dark, falling, fumbling around in pain, trying to get the child warm with no heating. He turned back to her and said quietly,

"Now, Madame. I have done all I can for now with your child. He needs to rest and be kept warm, in a well-ventilated room."

He glanced round the smoke-filled room.

"This is not ideal," he said. "I will carry him up to the nursery for you. Do you have any heat there?"

"No," said Kate. "But in summer it's not as cold as down here."

"Very well. While I go to the nursery, you sit down and place your ankle on the chair so that I can examine it."

He was back in a few minutes. Kate's ankle was badly swollen and she winced as the doctor checked it.

"You are lucky," he said. "No bones broken. But there is not much bruising. This generally means the ligaments are not torn badly, although from the pain I would have expected much more bruising. When did you do this?"

"Oh, er, several hours ago," Kate answered, not meeting his eye. "When I phoned earlier. The storm had just started. I told you, I fell in the dark when the power went off."

"That's unusual," muttered the doctor, starting to bandage Kate's ankle. "So little bruising! But I can find nothing out of the ordinary. It seems like an uncomplicated sprain. I will strap it up for you, which should make it more comfortable. It should not take long to heal. There you are, Madame."

He finished the bandage with a flourish and stepped back.

"Try to keep the foot raised when you are sitting and don't put too much weight on it for a day or so."

He looked at her curiously.

"You fell on your face?" he enquired.

"Not really," Kate answered. Then quickly added, " Well, yes I suppose I did hit the side of my face as I fell. It feels a bit sore."

Phillippe took a closer look. She must have fallen very hard, he thought.

"Put an ice-pack on it to reduce the swelling. Now, I would like you to check on the baby frequently if possible, and telephone me if there is any change."

"Yes, I will." Kate nodded. "I feel so bad about leaving him outside. But I'll be fine."

She lifted her foot gingerly off the chair. "That feels better already."

"Don't try to walk on it yet," Phillippe warned. "Now how are you going to be able to manage to look after him? He'll need lots of drinks to keep him hydrated so you'll have to go up and down to the nursery a lot. You must be very careful in the dark too. If I know the EDF, you won't get any electricity until tomorrow at the earliest and even then you may have to wait all day. It was a bad storm. Oh, but it is fortunate," he exclaimed, remembering the car outside. "You have visitors. You must make sure they help you. You need to rest the foot for a while at least."

"Visitors?" Kate started. "No.. oh, I mean, yes! Yes, but they went out. They aren't back yet. They might not come back… I'm not sure," she stammered.

Phillippe looked at her curiously. She seemed very flustered. He smiled inwardly to himself as he packed his instruments back into his bag. He knew there had been a man here, he'd heard his voice on the answerphone. Why did the English have to be so coy!

"I shall call again tomorrow morning to see the child, on my way to the surgery. If you have any problem with him, please telephone. I am on duty for the practice tonight, so if there is a problem, call the emergency number, not my personal number. No, do not disturb yourself," he said as Kate tried to get up.

"I will see myself out. And don't forget, call me if there is any change. Goodbye."

Phillippe closed the kitchen door behind him and crossed the courtyard. It was fine now and there was even a bit of moonlight appearing through the scudding clouds. He glanced at the parked car as he threw his bag into the back of his Renault. English plates. It must belong to the mystery man on the answerphone. Good, he thought. It was time Madame had some company. It had been hard on her: Nick's death, living alone in a strange country with no friends and a sickly baby. Phillippe put the car into gear and set off up the track. He was worried about that child. He'd been worried before, but tonight he was seriously concerned. It had definitely got bronchitis now and the chances were, unless they were very lucky, that it might develop into broncho-pneumonia. And in such a weak child that could well be fatal, even in this day and age. He shook his head as he approached the paved road and turned right towards St Geniès. How could she have left the child outside in the storm! What could she have been thinking about! And how could she have fallen so heavily onto her face? Phillippe wondered idly if she had a drink problem. He'd never noticed any signs before, but living alone like she did, he wouldn't be surprised. It happened to a lot of the English who came to live in France. His thoughts drifted back to Chloe and he was back in the square parking the car before he knew it.

Once inside the apartment, he turned on the electric fire and drew the big leather armchair up to it. He was on duty now so he might as well write up his notes on Kate and the baby before he tried to get a few hours' sleep. He glanced at the answerphone first to make sure there were no more messages, then on impulse played back Kate's first phone call. He listened carefully again. The time on the answerphone showed 7.35 pm. Minutes after he had left for Chloe's. He replayed the message and shrugged. So she'd sprained her ankle and didn't want to make a fuss by calling 15 as a medical emergency. That must be what the conversation was all about. And she was right: all emergency calls got routed to the St Geniès Gendarmerie. Mystery solved. He listened to the male voice in the background:

"…won't let me get away a second time.."

He shrugged again. Could mean anything. He took up the file on the child and carefully completed his notes. It was a sorry little soul, he thought. And so pale and fair – it didn't look anything like Nick. He wondered if there was anything in Kate's family history to account for it being so weak. Then he turned to Kate's file and began writing. He was still puzzled by her injury. According to the time of her message, she must have fallen well over four hours before he saw her. It was most unusual that the ankle was obviously so painful still, but showed so little bruising. He hoped there was no more serious injury to the ligaments. Perhaps he'd better get it X-rayed after all, he pondered. But there was no evidence of a break. He leaned back in the big chair and rubbed his eyes. What a day! He hoped there'd be more no emergencies tonight. Taking his mobile phone into the bedroom, he put it down on the bedside table next to the photograph of Chloe he'd taken in Oxford, three years ago. She was smiling out of the picture at him, with the sun behind her highlighting her golden hair. He'd never have believed it possible that now he was going to marry her and go back to Oxford with her. The letter from the Radcliffe lay next to her photo. They were looking forward to welcoming him back – this time as Consultant Paediatrician! But Phillippe's joy was tinged with regret that Nick was not here to be his best man.

****

The alarm clock was ringing loudly in his ear. Phillippe rolled over and lay on his back for a few minutes. Surgery was at ten, but before that he had to call in at the château. Then at midday he was meeting Chloe. He'd still got to hand in his notice but he'd do that on Monday. He climbed out of bed and stood for a moment in front of the long mirror in the bathroom,

171

checking his body for any signs of flab. He'd have to do a bit more swimming to make sure he kept his muscles toned. And did he need a haircut? He shaved carefully, showered, patted on his usual St Laurent cologne and, glancing out of the window at the blue sky, selected a deep turquoise polo shirt and a pair of light khaki chinos.

Outside in the square, the cafés were opening for business. It was fresher today after the storm and Phillippe decided to take his breakfast inside the Café de France. Greeting the patron, he sat down at one of the small tables near the door. The waitress came over almost instantly, carrying a small white cup of strong black coffee and a croissant, still warm from the baker's oven.

"Thank you, Martine." Phillippe smiled at her.

"It's a pleasure, Doctuer Phillippe," Martine beamed. She was the pretty eighteen-year-old daughter of the patron. "I fetched your croissant myself when I saw you coming out of your door. I am very happy today. I got my letter confirming my place at the Sorbonne!"

"Congratulations!"

Phillippe almost told her his own news. But first he had to tell the partners at the surgery. He knew just how fast news travelled in the country and it wouldn't do for the other partners to hear from village gossip. Martine moved off to wipe the tables outside the café and remove remnants of tree branches and leaves blown onto the chairs during last night's storm.

"What a night!" said Thierry, the owner of the Café de France as Phillippe paid at the counter. "These summer storms get worse!"

"They certainly do," Phillippe replied. "Thanks. See you later. I'll be in after surgery."

He walked quickly back to his car and headed out of the square towards the château. As he passed the road leading up to the Gendarmerie, he was reminded of the answerphone and the strange message. Something about it really bugged him. Not just the odd message that obviously wasn't supposed to be a message at all, but there was something about the man's voice that seemed familiar. The man was speaking English, but he didn't sound English. Phillippe was still pondering what it was about this voice that he recognised when he turned down the track towards the château. He was relieved and pleased to see the blue English car from last night was still there. So at least Madame had someone to help her.

Knocking at the kitchen door, Phillippe was surprised when it was opened almost immediately. He had expected to wait while Kate hobbled in from somewhere. He was even more surprised to recognise the tall, fair-haired man who opened the door.

"Good morning." Phillippe tried to keep his astonishment out of his voice. "I am the doctor. We have met before I think. At the unfortunate accident of Monsieur Carslow. Monsieur Black, isn't it?" Phillippe held out his hand.

"Yes. Good morning, doctor," Alastair shook his hand formally. "Please come in."

"I have come to check up on the baby and on Madame's ankle."

"Yes. Kate is in the nursery with the child. I expect you know the way."

Phillippe caught a slight inflexion in the other man's voice, but wasn't sure how to interpret it. Alastair stood aside as the doctor went through into the nursery. After a few words with Kate, he examined the child.

"Good, good," he murmured. The baby seemed a little brighter today. "So he has spent a peaceful night? Not too much coughing?"

"No, not too bad," Kate answered.

Phillippe noticed her eyes were red and her face drawn and quite swollen.

"And you? How is your ankle? You look as if you have not had very much sleep."

"Oh, I'm fine. Do you really think he's looking better?"

"Yes, I do. But there is no doubt that he has bronchitis. Maybe not too badly, and let us hope he will get better soon.

But you must be vigilant and watch him very, very carefully. It is not uncommon for complications to develop in children."

Phillippe stood up. "Keep an eye on him and let me know straight away if there is any change."

"Thank you, doctor. Thank you so much for coming out." Kate tried to stand. Phillippe put his arm out towards her.

"Here, take my arm. No electricity yet, I suppose?"

Kate laughed and shrugged. They made slow progress back towards the kitchen. Phillippe noticed that Alastair was watching them, a strange expression on his face.

"Doctor, you've met my....," Kate hesitated. "My husband, Alastair."

"Yes, indeed, Madame. And we have met before of course. Very briefly." Phillippe himself hesitated, not wanting to refer again to Nick. "Well, I must be on my way. Surgery starts at ten today. I shall call in again on my way home with some medicine to help with the baby's cough."

He moved to the door, which still stood open. He turned to Alastair and held out his hand. The bright sunlight shone on Alastair's face. Phillippe looked at him curiously.

"You seem to have been in the wars too, Monsieur," he said. "That cut above your eye looks quite deep. Would you like me to see if a stitch is needed?"

"No, thank you, doctor," Alastair replied curtly, drawing away from the doorway into the gloom of the kitchen. "It's nothing."

"Well, if you're sure." Phillippe had seen the scratches and cuts on Alastair's arms. "What happened to you? These cuts look recent."

"Yes," said Alastair shortly. "I got them last night during the storm. I had to go searching for a lost cat."

He shot Kate a meaningful glance, not lost on Phillippe.

"Yes," Kate agreed hurriedly. "Somehow the cat had got out and I was worried about it."

"Oh dear. Did you find it?" asked Phillippe.

"No," replied Alastair, his hand on the door, ready to close it behind the doctor.

"What colour is it and what's its name? I'll ask around in the village," Phillippe said.

"It's white," said Alastair, his face blank. "Its name is Ricard."

"Right, I'll keep my eyes open. Goodbye, and don't forget. Contact me if the child's condition changes."

The door closed behind him immediately. Phillippe got into his car and sat there for a moment, thinking. It was definitely Alastair Black's voice on his answerphone. That's why it had sounded familiar. It was the Scottish accent that he'd remembered. After Nick's accident, the St Geniès gendarmes had been convinced that Alastair and the friend who had arrived with him had somehow been responsible for Nick's death, so perhaps that explained all the talk about gendarmes. But why did Alastair say he wouldn't get away a second time? What had he done this time? And why had Kate behaved so oddly yesterday? Leaving her precious baby out in the storm? Phillippe was puzzled by the whole affair. He was convinced that in fact she hadn't sprained her ankle until much later on that evening. Certainly it didn't look as if she'd done it several hours before, as she had said, when she'd made the first phone call. And her swollen face – most people automatically throw out their arms to save themselves when they trip. And the husband looked as if he'd been in a fight. Phillippe had noticed that his knuckles on one hand were bandaged, and that cut over his eye could have been made by a branch, but it seemed unlikely. It seemed more likely that the husband had hit her and she'd fought back. Perhaps not so surprising, given the circumstances. But why had the husband come back at all? And the story about looking for a cat! Kate had never mentioned it the night before, but they were British, so Phillippe would have believed them mad enough to have spent the night out in the storm looking for their cat. Except he knew that Kate didn't have a cat. And there was something else about the husband that Phillippe couldn't quite put his finger on. He hadn't taken too much notice of him the last time they'd met, when Nick had died. But something about his looks seemed very familiar.

****

On his way back to St Geniès after morning surgery, Phillippe remembered just in time to turn off the road to deliver the baby's medicine. As he approached the château, an old Land Rover coming up the track pulled over to let him pass. Phillippe noticed the English plates. Good, he thought, at least Madame Black has some friends. As he entered the small passage leading to the kitchen door, he nearly collided with Alastair. He seemed to be in a great hurry. Phillippe caught a glimpse of the expression on the man's face and a car key in his hand, and for a moment he thought that the child must have had a relapse and that Mr Black was on his way to fetch him.

"Monsieur!" Phillippe cried. "Is everything all right?"

"Yes, yes. No problem!" Alastair stopped suddenly in his tracks.

"You are in a hurry," said Phillippe. "I will move my car, I fear I am blocking the road."

"Oh no, no, it's OK," Alastair said. "I'm not going anywhere. Just need something from the car."

He hesitated, then in a rush went on,

"Thought I might move it, er, under the arch. In case....in case it rains again!"

"Let me give you this medicine for the baby," Phillippe said. "The instructions are on the label. I will not hold you up. Goodbye."

Getting back into his car, Phillippe shook his head in bewilderment. What on earth was going on here? The man had obviously been in a tearing hurry to do something that involved his car, but definitely didn't want Phillippe to know what he was up to. Once out of sight of the château, Phillippe stopped his car. When he thought about it later, he wasn't sure what had made him do it. He wasn't a snoop by nature, but his curiosity was aroused. Getting out of the car, he walked quickly back down the track, until he could look down through the trees to the château. He could see the back door of the blue car was open, but no sign of Alastair. Phillippe shrugged and turned to go back to his own car. What in earth was he doing, spying on these people? Then he remembered the message on the answerphone, all that talk about gendarmes.

Stopping again, he took one last look back through the trees. As he watched, Alastair suddenly appeared from the dense undergrowth at the top of the bank, above where the blue car was parked. He climbed down the muddy bank, closed the car door and got into the driver's seat. Phillippe, realising with horror that he could be discovered if Alastair drove up the track, fled back to his own car and sped off as fast as he could up the muddy lane. Not daring to glance in his rear view mirror until he was nearly at the junction with the main road, Phillippe was relieved to see that there was no sign of the blue car. He let out a deep sigh and turned the Renault toward St Geniès.

****

The clock on the *hôtel de ville* struck one. There was silence round the two tables outside the Café de France. All eyes were on Phillippe. Jim Munro was the first to speak.

"Before you got here, Phillippe, John and I were just about to go to the Gendarmerie. I think you'd better come with us. From what you've just told us, your story and John's together certainly make it look like there's something badly wrong up at the château. Again."

?

The wife's story

Kate lay still on the wet, chalky gravel for a few long minutes. She had fallen headlong, the full weight of her body crashing down, wrenching her ankle round as her foot stayed put, held as if in a vice by the tree roots. A searing pain shot up her ankle as she tried to extricate her foot. In an instant she realised not only was she stuck, but her ankle might even be broken. She urged Alastair to go on without her. If he went on alone he might have a chance of reaching Richard before he was swept over the weir.

As she lay there helplessly, the pain in her ankle started to ease off a bit. During a short lull in the roaring wind, she could hear Alastair crashing along through the trees. He should be reaching the end of the lake soon. If he got there in time, he may be able to grab the boat and save Richard. Kate struggled into a sitting position and looked at her foot. She had rushed out of the house still wearing her old espadrilles. The rope sole of the shoe had bent round her foot as she tripped and was now wedging her foot in the roots of the tree. Perhaps if she wiggled the shoe round she'd be able to tear the old canvas top and pull it free, then there might be room for her to pull her foot out. Gingerly she started to work the sole of the shoe round, wincing every time it pulled on her foot. She could see the edge of the canvas was frayed where it met the sole. Grabbing the canvas with both hands, she took a deep breath and pulled as hard as she could. It ripped more easily than she'd expected and she fell back onto the path as the canvas gave way. After several minutes of wriggling and pulling at the rope sole, that too was almost out of the space between her foot and the tree root. Once last heave and she cried out in pain as the shoe came out of the hole, jerking her foot violently. In a few seconds the jolt of pain subsided and Kate was able to lift her foot free. Her ankle was already swelling rapidly and she knew it wouldn't take her weight. She turned over and managed to get up onto all fours, then slowly, painfully, she inched her way back along the path in the dark, her hands slipping on the mud.

At first it wasn't too difficult as the path sloped slightly, but was fairly flat. After a while, she reached a point where the path ran alongside the water's edge. She was exhausted. She sank down on the grass bank and closed her eyes. Her ankle throbbed and she was soaked to the skin. Her arms and legs were coated in the sticky white mud from the path. Her jaw and all down the side of her face ached from Richard's blow. Her hair was plastered to her head with a mixture of rain and mud running down into her eyes, making it even more difficult to see. Kate manoeuvred herself into a standing position, grasping a branch to keep her balance on one foot so she could see down the lake. Alastair should have reached the weir by now. At first she could hardly see anything, but gradually she made out the line of the bank and the weir at the end of the lake. She scanned the water for a sign of the boat. Then, very close to the weir, she caught sight of it. She could see another shape, nearer the bank. Then the shape seemed to merge with the boat. Her heart leapt. Alastair had got there in time!

A searing pain shot up her ankle and everything went black. When Kate came too again, she was lying on her side on the bank, her foot bent under her body. In her anxiety to see if Alastair had reached Richard, she had forgotten about her injured ankle. Desperately, she pulled herself up again. She had to see if Richard was safe. If Alastair had managed to grab the boat, he would have tied it up at the landing stage by the weir. Kate strained her eyes but the rain and dark and the waves on the lake made it impossible to see. The storm had all but passed now, but one final flash of lightning suddenly lit the scene. There was no boat tied up. And no sign of anyone. Kate's heart thudded against her chest. She clung to the tree, gasping for breath. Where were they? She was sure she'd seen Alastair reach the boat. Oh God, she thought, sinking to the ground. What's happened to them? Surely they haven't both gone over the weir?

Kate started to crawl back along the shore searching for them when suddenly she remembered the baby. She uttered a small, anguished cry. She'd left him lying on the rug in front of the fireplace, where she'd put him before she'd returned to the terrace to discover that Richard had gone! That was hours ago. Anything could have happened to him!

What seemed like a lifetime later, Kate crawled in through the kitchen door. The room was in darkness, but she could hear the baby whimpering, somewhere in the direction of the fireplace. Crying with relief, she groped her way round the furniture until she eventually found the cupboard where the spare candles were kept. Thank God that for once she had remembered to keep the matches with them. Still on her knees, she lifted the lighted candle above her head and scanned the room as best she could in the direction of the baby's cries. There was no sign of him on the rug where she had left him, although his blanket lay there. Then she saw him. Somehow, he'd rolled off the blanket and rug and lay huddled on the tiles close to the fire grate. She scrambled over to where he lay and, setting the candle down in the fireplace, gathered him into her arms. As she clutched him, sobbing, to her breast, she realised he was icy cold, as cold as she herself was. She was also soaking wet and the baby now started to howl as cold water dripped off her hair onto him. The candle guttering in the fireplace showed her that he'd been lying in the draught from the big chimney. Kate found the blanket and wrapped him in it again. He was breathing rapidly and coughing. His body was frozen but his face was flushed red and hot to her touch. Wild with panic, she lit candles and tried to get the few bits of firewood in the grate to catch light. Hobbling to the phone, she called the doctor's number. It was not long after midnight.

8

The dark blue squad car bumped its way along the track towards the château. In the back seat sat John Nicholson, Phillippe de la Bernière and Jim Munro, wedged together behind the two gendarmes. It hadn't taken long for them to persuade Jules Espinet that there was something to be investigated at the Château de St Geniès-Lafontaine. Jules remembered all too well what had happened earlier in the year. He had thought the whole incident very, very fishy. But they had questioned the two foreigners thoroughly and their story was plausible. The woman corroborated their story. That was significant. If there had been any foul play in the death of Monsieur Nick Carslow, would the woman who had left her husband for him have lied to protect the husband? Anyway, there had been no evidence that it was anything but an accident. Jules shook his head as he concentrated on manoeuvring the squad car down the rutted track, through the puddles and mud slides from the previous night's storm. He'd always thought there was something very odd about the case. Something to do with the coincidence of the 'accident' happening just when the wronged husband appeared. Something to do with the woman, the husband and his friend telling such identical stories. Something to do with the woman staying on in the château and filing a case for her son to inherit the whole of Monsieur Carslow's French estate, despite his wife in England having paid for the château. Oh yes, Jules was well-informed. A village gendarme always had his sources and his ear to the ground. And he happened to be quite close to the midwife who had attended the birth of the child. But the Police Judiciaire in Cahors had taken over the case. They always did if it was something worth investigating, Jules thought bitterly.

And they'd decided it was an accident. No evidence to suggest otherwise. Jules was furious, but there was nothing he could do about it. And now, this strange turn of events. He ran over in his mind what he had heard today. It was just as well the doctor was involved, he reflected. At least it meant he could understand everything, without having to involve that jumped-up little anglophile Jean Joubert from Fromac. Jules snorted. Wet-behind-the-ears little runt! Only got the job because he could speak English. Hardly out of training, the new *sous-officier* at Fromac had been sent over to St Geniès to interrogate *his* suspects! He who had been *adjutant* at St Geniès for three years now! No wonder it never came to anything. But he'd got the doctor to translate the foreigners' statements for him because he didn't trust young Jean and Phillippe had confirmed Jean's report. That made Jules even more annoyed. And Capitaine Lolmède from the Police Judiciaire in Cahors had made such a fuss of Jean. What an asset to the region, what with all these foreigners coming to live here! What an arsehole more like!

Jules snorted again. His partner, Bernie Rousseau, glanced at him curiously. Bernie was the opposite of Jules, in every way. Short, fat and balding, he'd never risen above the rank of *sous-officier* and was now coasting towards retirement. Jules wished he had a thousand euros for every time Bernie had told him about the little apartment near the coast, just east of Montpellier, where Bernie and his lady wife would be heading come October. Bernie glanced at his partner now, taking in the sharp, dark profile and olive skin of the younger man. He was ambitious, Bernie knew this. He liked Jules, but he had had enough of this game. Time to put his feet up now. But no chance with Jules around. And Bernie knew how Jules felt about the death of Monsieur Carslow. Bernie sympathised. He too felt the case had had an unsatisfactory outcome, typical of what happened once the Police Judiciaire were involved. But for Bernie, it was more personal. A life-long supporter of Le Pen, he had a characteristically Gallic attitude to foreigners: they were all inferior to a native Frenchman. A few, however, earned

Bernie's approval. Jim Munro, for example. He was alright. And this other bloke with the long dark hair. He seemed alright as well. Bernie had seen him around with his two children for the last few summers and had approved of the way the father treated them as adults, and the way they behaved themselves. Not like most of the foreign kids. And Bernie had really liked Monsieur Carslow, who had always bought him a drink when he saw him in the village. Bernie also liked Madame Carslow, though he had only met her once. She had spoken to him in beautifully correct French, with such a charming way about her. He could have fallen in love! He was not, however, enamoured of the other woman, the one up at the château. She was pretty enough, he conceded, but aloof and silent, although not, he also conceded, as smug and arrogant as many of the resident foreigners. He agreed with Jules that the arrival of the husband just at the time the balustrade decided to give way was too much of a coincidence. Bernie didn't like the husband, who had described Bernie as "that fat French bastard" when the husband and his friend were in the cells earlier in the year, waiting for young Jean to come over and translate. They didn't think Bernie could understand, but Bernie had watched enough American films to have picked up a few useful phrases of English. He also thought he had heard the husband telling his friend something about getting rid of a knuckleduster. He knew that word too. Bernie's theory was that the husband and his now missing friend had come to the château ready to beat up, if not to kill, Monsieur Carslow. A *crime passionnelle*. But Jean poo-pooed this, saying he'd asked them if either of them owned a knuckleduster, and they'd said no. Well, they would do, wouldn't they. Bernie shook his head. What a naïve little prat! Bernie didn't like Jean much. Jumped up little English-lover. The police in Cahors were just as dismissive of Bernie's theory, but that's what you'd expect from them. To Bernie it had been a missed opportunity. If only he and Jules had been able to pin murder on the two foreigners, it would have been a feather in their caps, and there would have been a big bonus in it for them. Jules wanted promotion, to make a name for himself, get transferred to the city. Bernie wanted the money.

The château came into view.

"Here we are again, old son." Bernie turned to Jules. "Let's see if we can nail them this time, the bloody rosbifs," he muttered, anxious that Phillippe did not hear.

He knew the doctor was keen on the other blonde Englishwoman, Chloe. Jules nodded grimly.

In the back of the car, John Nicholson shifted his position slightly and craned forward to see if the blue Saab was still there. He felt a bit uncomfortable now at the thought of having to face the Scotsman again and more or less accuse him of..... what? John hoped against hope that Richard would be at the château and it would all have been a misunderstanding. He hadn't expected the gendarmes to make him and Phillippe accompany them. It was all going to be a bit embarrassing. He supposed that was just the way the French system worked. They rounded the last bend in the track and, to his relief, John could see the blue car was still there. But he was sure it had been moved. It was now parked underneath the stone arch that spanned the track, near to the cobbled passage that led to the kitchen door. The squad car slowed as they passed it and parked on the gravel beyond, on the windowless side of the château. Jules turned round in his seat and spoke to Phillippe in French.

"Monsieur Phillippe, I would like you to translate everything they say. I would be most grateful if you could explain to Jim and Monsieur here that they should stay in the car. I want them to take a look at the English car with Bernie, but I do not want the Blacks to know they are here. For now they must not think we suspect anything, or even know that the Englishman seems to have disappeared. Also, I do not want anyone to discuss things without my understanding fully what is said. I shall explain your presence as my interpreter. I shall not mention that you have come to me because of your concerns. We are officially investigating a suspected drug smuggling outfit. Don't look so surprised, *Docteur*! It is true. It is an important case for us at present. We know they use English couriers who drive down to Spain and collect North African kif. We know that sometimes the couriers pose as tourists and we suspect that somewhere in our area there is at least one house where the dope is either stored or where cars are exchanged. Actually, we have good evidence that the house is over near the aerodrome at Lalbenque, and that sometimes they fly it in and out. But it will not hurt to be checking out these two English men and their English car!"

"Thank you, Jules. I know you realise it is important for a doctor to maintain his patient's trust. If it had not been for the story that Monsieur John told, I doubt I should have come to you at all."

"I am grateful that you did. Your information is intriguing. After we leave here, I should like to recover the tape from your answerphone. I may need it as evidence."

Phillippe nodded. He felt apprehensive. Evidence of what?

Jules and Bernie were out of the car now, adjusting their caps. Jules strode into the courtyard and rapped on the kitchen door with his baton. Bernie stood behind him, looking up at the shuttered windows above. There was no sign of life. Jules rapped again, louder. From inside, they all heard the cry of a child. A few minutes later, the door opened. Kate looked nervously at the two gendarmes.

"Yes?" she asked. "Can I help you?"

"We certainly hope so, Madame Black," Jules replied. "I would like to speak to your husband and also to his friend, Mr Richard...,"Jules consulted his notebook. "Mr Richard Talbot."

Phillippe moved forward.

"You have understood, Madame? I am here to interpret for the officers."

"Yes, yes. Come in."

Kate opened the door wide and stepped aside. The three of them filed into the large kitchen.

"This way, please."

Kate led the way through the house and out onto the terrace. Jules and Bernie glanced at each other as they stood gazing at the new stone balustrade.

"My husband," Kate said quietly as Alastair stood up to meet them.

"Yes. Good afternoon. We have already had the pleasure of meeting."

The irony in Jules' voice was not lost on Alastair.

"Officers, doctor," Alastair nodded to Phillippe. "How can we help you?" he asked, moving forward to stand alongside Kate.

"We should like also to speak to your friend Monsieur Talbot. We understand that he arrived with you yesterday evening."

"Yes, that's right," Alastair answered. "But I am afraid he had to leave, early this morning. He had to return to England urgently. But can I help you? What is this about?"

"It is merely routine, Monsieur," Jules smiled reassuringly. "We have had a report from the *Douaniers* that two men travelling together in a blue English-registered car are involved in a smuggling operation. A car answering this description was seen yesterday afternoon turning down the road to the château. We wish, of course, to eliminate you from our enquiries. Perhaps I could see your passport, Monsieur, then I shall need to ask a few questions. The blue car outside, it is yours? At what time did you arrive? And have you been out in the car since? Have you kept it locked? Could anyone have opened the car or moved it without your knowledge?"

Phillippe translated, his eyes on Alastair and Kate.

Alastair nodded.

"Yes, it's my car. We got here about, oh, maybe five o'clock yesterday. Maybe a bit later. Just before the storm. I locked the car after we'd taken our stuff out when we arrived and haven't been out to it since. Well," Alastair suddenly hesitated, glancing at Phillippe. "That is, I did move the car down under the arch after the doctor had called. You know, in case it rained again. I thought it would be better protected."

"But you did not go out in the car?"

Alastair shook his head.

"Good. I would be most grateful if you would hand your keys to my colleague who will search your car. To eliminate you from our enquiries of course," Jules smiled again.

"Here are the keys. And my passport."

Bernie took the keys and went back into the kitchen. He paused to glance out of the windows. The blue car could not be seen from here. Bernie hurried back to the squad car.

"Come along, Monsieurs! I need your help. Here are the keys to the blue car. I am to search it. I need you, Monsieur," he nodded to John, "to identify the jacket and holdall. If," he paused melodramatically, "they are still there!"

John and Jim followed him under the stone arch.

"Does anything look different, Monsieur?" Bernie asked John.

"Yes, the car has been moved. Jim, can you translate for me, please? My French isn't up to explaining."

Jim nodded.

"The car was further down the track this morning. And it wasn't locked," John went on, peering in through the back window. "That's funny! There's nothing there! The bag and jacket were there, in the back, I swear it! I saw them first through the window and then I tried the door to see if it was open. Richard's passport was in the bag. I shoved it back in when I heard a car coming down the track. It was the doctor arriving."

"Let's make sure."

Bernie unlocked the car and searched carefully. He stood back a few minutes later and shook his head.

"Nothing. Nothing at all. Very strange!"

John shook his head.

"Look, it was definitely there this morning. Only a few hours ago."

"I believe you, Monsieur," Bernie laid a fat hand on his arm. "Now, Monsieur. Tell me what is strange about this car?"

Jim translated but still John looked puzzled and shrugged. Jim suddenly spoke.

"I know just what you mean," he said. "It's clean. There's nothing in it. What normal person manages to arrive after an eight hundred km drive with a totally clean and empty car? It should be full of rubbish and crumbs and God knows what. Someone has cleaned this car out. Like they were trying to make sure there was no evidence of who or what had been in it."

"But that's daft," John said. "We know Richard was in this car. We all saw him. So why bother to clear it out to make it look like he was never here at all?"

"Search me," Jim said.

Bernie rocked on his heels.

"We must not jump to conclusions. However, we can establish that someone has removed the bag and the jacket of Richard, sometime between your visit this morning and now?"

"Yes," John agreed.

"So." Bernie thought for a moment. "Why could it not have been Richard himself? He might have still been here when you came to look for him."

"No," John shook his head. "According to Alastair, Richard had already left when I called."

"Perhaps he did come back," Jim put in. "You know, realised he'd forgotten his stuff?"

"Jim, *mon ami*! Who leaves for a long journey without their bag, their jacket, their passport, then remembers they just might need these items? Poof! No. Someone has removed these things so it appears that Monsieur Talbot has gone home!"

"But why move the car?"

"Because after your visit, when you came looking for Richard," Bernie paused. "Someone realises that if it is to look like Monsieur Talbot has gone home, the bag and jacket must not be seen here. So someone goes outside to move the evidence, and at that moment, *quelle horreur*! The doctor arrives! So someone has to improvise! Pretends that he is going to move his car.....but, the doctor sees the car door is open, he sees Monsieur Black coming back to the car out of the bushes, he sees him get into the car and move the car under the arch because that is what he has told the doctor he will do, and he knows the doctor will come back, so it must look right ...”

Bernie shrugged, raising his hands.

“So what now?” Jim asked.

“You two get back into the squad car and you stay there. We do not want our friend to see you. At present he thinks we are investigating a smuggling operation!” Bernie smirked with self-satisfaction. “That was my idea! So that he is not on his guard!”

Jim and John glanced at each other but walked quickly back to the squad car and got in. Bernie went back into the château through the kitchen door. As he emerged onto the terrace, Jules was writing in his notebook.

“So, to go over this again, for my colleague’s benefit. You arrived last night, you went out into the storm to look for a lost cat, you fell and cut yourself and got scratched by branches etc etc in your search, the lightning struck the power lines, in the dark your wife had fallen and sprained her ankle, when you got back the doctor had been and gone, and the child had caught pneumonia. The cat is still missing and your friend decided to leave early this morning and return home. Can’t say I blame him.”

Jules snapped his notebook shut.

“Now, Officer Rousseau,” he turned to Bernie. “What news of the blue car?”

“Nothing,” Bernie said. “Absolutely nothing. In fact,” he paused dramatically. He was enjoying this. “It looks to me as if the car has been deliberately cleaned very thoroughly inside.”

“This is interesting. Monsieur, you told me you did not go to your car after you arrived except to move it to a sheltered place?”

“Yes, that’s right,” Alastair replied slowly.

“And your friend. Could he have taken your keys without your knowledge?”

“Well,” Alastair hesitated. “Yes, I suppose so.”

"And now your car is empty, completely empty. And your friend is missing. Tell me, how did he leave? Did he call a taxi, or walk? Is he flying home, taking a train?"

"He called a taxi," Kate put in quickly. "On his mobile phone. He had a mobile phone. I think he was going to take a train. I'm not sure."

"I see. Tell me, Monsieur Black, how well do you know Monsieur Talbot?"

"I've known him for a long time," Alastair replied. "Since university."

"And are you aware of any involvement he might have had with drugs?"

Alastair coloured.

"Well, yes. I know Richard did take drugs. But then a lot of people did....," his voice tailed off.

"Monsieur, Madame." Jules looked at Kate and Alastair sternly. "It seems to me that your friend might well be who we are looking for. And you, Monsieur Black. I must ask you not to leave the area until we have made further enquiries. I shall be keeping your passport for the moment. When we have found your friend we shall, no doubt, be able to establish your own innocence in this matter. Smuggling is a serious crime in France," he added. "Particularly where drugs are involved. Thank you for your cooperation. I hope we shall clear this matter up most quickly!"

Jules bowed slightly and strode off the terrace, Bernie and Phillippe following.

Kate and Alastair stood on the terrace watching the squad car round the final bend in the track before disappearing from view. There was silence. The hot air hung heavily and even the lizards lay still on the stone walls.

"I just don't know what to make of this," Alastair said, breaking the silence at last. "What made them come here?"

"I suppose the doctor must have seen your car and told them. If they were looking for a blue car they'd probably asked him to be on the lookout. They often seem to do that. He acts as the doctor on call for them. They know him well and he sees a lot when he's out on his rounds. This is awful, Alastair! When they find Richard, they'll want to know what happened! And I don't think they believed our story about the cat! The doctor knows that I haven't got one! They'll know we've lied, obstructed their enquiries and Richard might tell them what happened and they might arrest you ….."

"But Kate, think about it!" Alastair broke in. "If they find Richard," he paused, catching hold of Kate's hands. "We've got to face it, he's probably dead. Then if they really think he was involved in some sort of smuggling ring, they'll assume he's been killed because of the drugs. Why would they think we had anything to do with it? And it's just as well we cleaned the car out so thoroughly. Now they think Richard did it to remove any trace of drugs or his whereabouts!"

"But that doesn't mean they won't suspect us of being involved with the drug smuggling!" Kate wailed.

"They would have to find some evidence! We're clean. There's nothing to link us to drugs. If they find Richard and he's alive, it'll be OK. He'll tell them he had an accident, that's all. They won't be able to link him to drugs either. If they don't find him, then they haven't got any case and they'll have to let me go."

A sudden thought struck Alastair. He held onto Kate's hands, tightening his grip, his stomach churning.

"Kate, you do believe me, don't you? About what happened? I tried to save him!" Alastair's voice broke. "I know I was angry, furious that he'd hurt you. I just saw red when he hit you. I was so shocked by seeing the baby… I couldn't believe it. I still don't….I can't believe you lied…! And Richard's my friend. Everything he's done has been out of loyalty to me."

"I know. Alastair, I know how it must look to you, but I had to do it. How else could I provide for my baby?"

Alastair sat down and put his head in his hands.

"I don't want to know, Kate," he spoke quietly. "I just can't take any more at the moment. I've got to go out and look for

Richard again myself. It's still my fault he went out into that storm. I should never have come here, never brought him with me. But if there's the smallest chance he went over the weir and has been washed up somewhere down that river, I've got to do what I can."

9

Capitaine Lolmède stood by the grimy window looking down into the narrow street below. It was raining again. A steady, relentless downpour. The gutters were full and dark yellowy puddles stood along the edges of the street, lapping the broken pavement. The municipal dustbin just outside the gate to the police yard was overflowing. One or two bags of rubbish, carelessly tossed into the already full bin, had spilled their contents into the street. A thin, ginger-coated dog was nosing around amidst the blue plastic bottles. The Capitaine sighed and glanced up at the sky. The heavy grey clouds showed no sign of breaking. Well, no point in putting it off any longer. He'd better get over to St Geniès and see how things were going.

The telephone rang as he was putting on his jacket.

"*'Allo, oui?*"

"Capitaine Lolmède. Jules Espinet here. Gendarmerie St Geniès. We have an interesting development. Could you come over to the station instead of meeting at the château?"

"Certainly." Hubert Lolmède glanced at his watch. "I was just leaving. I'll be with you in about half an hour."

He replaced the receiver. Good, he thought. At least no more hanging around in the rain today. He slammed the office door on his way out and clattered down the concrete stairs, out into the yard where his car was parked. He nosed the small car through the narrow, wet side streets, turning right into the main boulevard, practically deserted except for a few groups of disconsolate tourists. Across the bridge, then heading west towards St Geniès. Once he was out of the town and on the main highway, he began to go over the case in his mind. He really didn't like this sort of thing. Too much speculation, not enough fact. Just what always seemed to happen when he got called in on a case in a rural area. Nothing happening out there, so the local gendarmes try to make mountains out of molehills. Had a crime really been committed? He didn't think so. He sighed. As if he hadn't got enough to do, trying to catch these drug smugglers. They were real enough. They had to be stopped. He didn't want to divert resources to some unimportant missing tourist who probably wasn't really missing at all.

Driving through the empty square at St Geniès, he began to feel quite sorry for the tourists. Here a few of them were huddled under the awning of the Café de France. There wasn't much to do in a place like this, especially when it was raining. He drove out of the square, passing the cemetery on his right, then turned immediately into the small road that led to the Gendarmerie. It was an ugly, square building set incongruously in the quiet street of low, modern bungalows. Three storeys high, its flat, dirty-beige concrete walls punctuated by shuttered windows, it had a gloomy and forbidding air. It looked deserted. Hubert drove in through the open metal gate and parked in the empty yard. Climbing the steps to the main door, past the sodden Tricolour hanging limply above the entrance, he was reminded of his own first job after he had joined the force. He shuddered. That had been in Brittany, as far west as you could get. He'd been there for four years and it had felt like forty. Thank goodness he'd transferred into the police and, later when he got his promotion, into CID. That guaranteed him a city posting. The countryside didn't suit him at all.

Inside the Gendarmerie, he walked down the grubby corridor to Jules' office. The door stood open. Bernie Rousseau and Jules looked up as he rapped on the door jamb. They were standing by the window, on either side of a long table. Between them, on the table, lay a number of objects: a holdall, a jacket, a British passport, some clothes. All of them were wet and covered in mud.

Hubert Lolmède pushed his chair back from Jules' desk and stood up.

"OK. Let's go over it all once again. We have a missing person. Richard Talbot. Last seen yesterday. We have recovered his passport and personal effects from the grounds of the Château de St Geniès-Lafontaine. They had been dumped there where no one would have found them, had they not been looking. Had the good doctor not been suspicious. We have the statement of Docteur de la Bernière. We also have the statement of the Englishman, Nicholson. So we know that both Monsieur and Madame Black have lied to us about what they were doing last night in the storm. You have your suspicions that something, you don't know what, happened to our Mr Talbot last night. So, what do we do? There is no evidence to connect him with our drug smugglers and anyway the Drugs Squad made several arrests this morning at Lalbenque, at the house we have been watching. We were nearly too late. Most of the stuff had gone. We think they sent a shipment out yesterday evening. There's an alert out at all the ports. That means if our missing boy is one of them, he'll get picked up when the shipment is intercepted."

He walked over to the table and looked down again at the mud-caked objects.

"However, we also know that, earlier this year, this same Talbot was present when the accident occurred that killed the other Englishman, Carslow. We know that he is the friend of Monsieur Black. We have interrogated him in relation to the death of Nick Carslow. There was, however, no evidence to suggest that this death was not an accident. So, Jules? What now? I do not see that there is a case to investigate here. Unless he really is part of the drugs ring, which I doubt, this Englishman has merely decided to go missing. His friends at the château have helped him, and sure, they have lied to you, but so what? You know as well as I do that, under our laws in France, it is everyone's right to disappear, if they so choose. This Richard Talbot is not a minor, he is capable of making up his own mind. If he wants to disappear, why should it bother us?"

He looked at Jules questioningly.

Jules leaned forward, barely suppressing his anger.

"You have your point of view. But, earlier this year, when they were under suspicion in relation to the death of Nick Carslow, we routinely took blood samples and so forth from both of them for DNA analysis. We still have those samples. When we were at the château earlier this afternoon, I noticed on the terrace some very small spots of what looked like blood. I would like to go back there with a forensic team and see what they can find. If it matches Talbot's blood, I think we have cause for further investigation. Also, we saw some recent footprints in the mud on the bank leading up to where we found this stuff."

He gestured towards the table.

"We know the doctor saw Monsieur Black coming out of the bushes there. To prove his connection with hiding these effects, we need to match his boots to the footprints. I realise that I cannot do this without your authorisation. I must therefore ask your permission, Capitaine," Jules spoke formally, doing his best to hide his irritation at the humiliation of having to ask permission to investigate his own case.

"Hm," Hubert stoked his chin thoughtfully for a few moments, mindful of the antagonism in the other man's voice. Relations were strained at the best of times between his department and the Gendarmeries. Only last week, his new boss had issued an instruction that the Police Judiciare should try to promote cooperation, particularly with the rural areas. They'd come close to letting these drug smugglers slip through the net because of rivalry between them and the Lalbenque Gendarmerie. In the event, the Drugs Squad had gone in too late and had only been able to arrest a couple of the couriers and had missed the main shipment. Only a few kilos of hashish had been found. And those seemed to be part of the payoff for the couriers they'd arrested. Hubert had been in his office when the head of the Drugs Squad had burst into his boss's office next door. The walls weren't particularly thin, but Hubert had heard every word of the furious argument that had ensued.

It went against the grain to waste precious manpower on a missing person when the drugs problem was escalating all over France. They hadn't made a significant seizure since 2011. It was possible that this Talbot was involved with drugs, so perhaps he'd better cover his back. It wouldn't do any harm to let Jules have his way on this one.

"We don't have much to go on," he said. "But I think maybe we should make further investigations. OK, let's do it."

****

The next day the sun was shining and Hubert decided to walk to the office from his apartment on the other side of the river. It was only a ten minute walk and as he strolled across the wide bridge, his mind played over the case of the missing Englishman. Jules Espinet had got the bit between his teeth and no mistake. These country gendarmes were apt to try and make the most of anything remotely unusual, Hubert thought, for the second time in as many days. Jules had always been convinced that Alastair Black and Richard Talbot had played some part in Nick Carslow's death. The disappearance of Talbot was certainly suspicious, particularly when you considered the two independent reports from the doctor and the other Englishman. Hubert thought about the message on the doctor's answerphone. Now that really could be incriminating. Or not. Depended if you were looking for trouble. He paused for a break in the traffic, then crossed the road quickly and headed up the main boulevard in the direction of his favourite café. Breakfast would be a good strong coffee and a cigarette, as usual.

Choosing a table in the sun, he ordered his coffee and unfolded his newspaper. Looking up as he lit his cigarette, Hubert was surprised to see Jules Espinet crossing the street and heading for the café. Not in uniform, Hubert hardly recognised him.

"Morning, Jules," he said, standing up and shaking his hand. "What brings you to Cahors on your day off?"

"Capitaine, good morning. May I?"

"Of course." Hubert signalled to the waiter as Jules sat down. "Coffee, Jules?"

"Thank you. I'm sorry to disturb your breakfast," Jules said. "But I had a call from Forensics this morning and I came straight over."

Hubert looked puzzled. Jules must have got on to Forensics pretty smartly yesterday. He himself wasn't an early riser, by any means, but even so, Forensics must have called Jules very early today for him to have got over here so quickly.

"Go on." He looked at Jules through the cigarette smoke. "What did they say?"

"They went to the château late yesterday afternoon and took samples from the terrace and the car. The car was clean. Scrubbed clean. But on the terrace they found some small patches of blood, the ones I'd noticed. Forensics say they were fairly recent and it looked as if someone had cleaned up most of them, just missed a few tiny specks."

"So?" Hubert shrugged. "Alastair Black had cut himself looking for the non-existent cat. The doctor said he had quite a deep cut on his face. The doctor also thought that it might have been the result of a domestic – Madame Black had a swollen jaw, as if maybe she'd been punched, rather than hit her face as she fell when she sprained her ankle. And that wouldn't be so surprising, given that she's just had another man's child."

"Yes, and what if the friend had come to her rescue and Black had turned on him? And remember what I told you. When we had them at the station at St Geniès last year after Monsieur Carslow's death, we took samples from them because we thought he might have died as a result of some sort of fight. Well, Forensics have matched the blood on the terrace. It's not Black's. It matches Talbot's."

Hubert drained his cup.

"Go on."

"The prints in the mud on the bank leading to where we found the holdall and jacket match the boots that Black was wearing. Forensics confirm that the car had been cleaned thoroughly and recently, with the same cleaner that was used on the terrace. My theory is that, on the night of the storm, Talbot intervened when Black had a go at his wife and Black killed Talbot, probably accidentally, possibly not, moved the body in the car, then the next morning – yesterday – dumped the holdall and jacket, cleaned the car and the terrace to remove any traces of blood or whatever – or so he thought – then tells everyone that the guy's gone home."

"Jules, Jules!" Hubert interrupted. "Let's not get carried away! Why should he kill his friend? And didn't the English Mr Nicholson meet Black on the night of the storm, apparently looking for his friend?"

"OK, OK!" Jules held up his hands. "Perhaps he did not kill him. But, there is Talbot's blood on the terrace. Someone has tried to clean it up. They have both lied about what happened during the storm, Monsieur and Madame Black. They tell Nicholson that Talbot has gone back to England. But Nicholson sees his belongings, including his passport, still in the back of Black's car. The doctor thinks Black is acting suspiciously and when we arrive the car has been emptied and cleaned. The doctor's observation of Monsieur Black leads us to where he has dumped the jacket and holdall. And then there is the message on the doctor's answerphone – 'they won't let me get away a second time'. I tell you, Capitaine, this should be taken seriously. And I'll bet whatever you like it's linked to Monsieur Carslow's death!"

Hubert lit another cigarette.

"Suppose you are right. Why did they come down here earlier in the year? To teach Monsieur Carslow a lesson for stealing Black's wife? They came to take her back? Anyway, perhaps there was a fight and he falls against the weak balustrade, or perhaps they – one or other of them, or both – push him over? Whatever, he is dead. They have their revenge. We could not prove then that they had any involvement at all in Carslow's death and we can't prove it now. Then now, several months later, they come back. What for this time? To fetch the erring wife home? And one of them disappears. You suspect Black is responsible for Talbot's disappearance in some way. But why? Jules, unless it was accidental as you suggest and Talbot did try to break up a fight between husband and wife, you have no motive."

He shook his head and went on. "All we have is a missing person, although I grant you missing under odd, if not exactly suspicious, circumstances. We can do no more. We have no reason to search for Richard Talbot. He has disappeared," Hubert shrugged. "That is his prerogative."

Jules frowned, his frustration nearly getting the better of him.

"Capitaine. Listen. I think we may have a motive for Monsieur Black wanting to be rid of his friend. We have a theory, that is Bernie and me, that the two of them came down here earlier in the year intending to kill Carslow. We are fairly sure, but of course we cannot prove it at the moment, that they came armed."

"Armed?" Hubert raised an eyebrow, trying hard to keep the derision out of his voice.

"Yes. Bernie heard them talking when we had them in the cells. Bernie doesn't speak English, but he understands a few words. You know how much he likes American gangster movies."

Hubert smiled, not sure what was coming next.

"Well," Jules continued, irritated by Hubert's smirk. "Bernie heard them talking about knuckledusters."

"Knuckledusters?" Hubert enquired sceptically.

"Yes. And Docteur de la Bernière, who attended Monsieur Carslow at the scene of the accident, said to me that there were marks on him that could have been made by a direct blow, but with an instrument, not by bare knuckles. His collar bone was broken and there were marks which could have been consistent with a blow from a knuckleduster. Bernie asked the surgeon who did the autopsy specifically if they could have been made by such a blow. But the autopsy verdict was that it most likely happened when he hit the ground, because of the force that would have been needed to cause the break. Our theory was always that it was a *crime passionnelle*. The husband killed the lover." Jules paused. "But now, to the present. The friend, Talbot, sees this happen. He's the witness to a murder. But he keeps quiet because he's Black's friend. Now they come back here. Why, I don't know. But Talbot wants to move here, to France, quite desperately, apparently. He wants a new life, a fresh start. This is what the Englishman Nicholson says. But he has no money. So he decides one way to get money is to blackmail his friend. After all, Talbot saw Black kill his wife's lover. Talbot knows we were suspicious at the time, so he threatens to tell us the truth about Monsieur Carslow's death unless Black pays up. So Black kills him. Perhaps he doesn't mean to. Perhaps he attacks him and Talbot tries to escape. That's why Nicholson sees Black searching for him in the storm. Black can't let Talbot get away and tell us the truth about Carslow's death!"

There was a brief silence. Jules sat back from the table, looking expectantly at Hubert. Around them, the café was starting to fill up. The bright sunshine had brought the locals and tourists out. The street was becoming crowded. It was market day. Hubert caught the waiter's eye and ordered two more coffees, groaning inwardly. He didn't like this case one bit. Maybe the gendarmes were right. But it was all too circumstantial for him. His training told him Jules was extrapolating the facts way too far. But, nevertheless, his instincts wouldn't let him dismiss the gendarme's theory as a complete flight of fancy. He too had a bad feeling about this case.

"OK, Jules. I'll consider authorising a search for this Richard Talbot, on the assumption that you are prepared to stake your reputation on there being sufficient evidence to show that his disappearance is connected to a crime. We would start with the château. In fact, we'd start with the lake. Ideal place to dump a body. But first," Hubert broke off as the waiter put two small, white cups of dark brown coffee on the table. "First we go back to the château and we talk to the husband and the wife. Or rather, this time I talk to them. We give them one more chance to explain what really happened during the storm. Then, if I agree with you that there are grounds for suspicion, I'll authorise a search. Remember, Jules, you're asking to use substantial police resources and I've got to be able to justify it to my superiors. You know how they don't like being told what to do by your lot!"

18

Wearily Alastair climbed the flight of stone steps up to the terrace. He could see the top of the small pink and white parasol attached to the baby's pram. His baby. Kate's slim back was towards him as he pushed open the wrought iron gate.

"It's no use," he said. "I've been all the way down the riverbank, as far as the road bridge. After that the banks are very steep. I don't think he could have survived in that gully even if he'd been swept that far alive. But there's no sign of ..."

Alastair broke off. Kate had turned towards him, her hand to her mouth, her eyes huge.

"Kate, what.....?" Alastair started forward onto the terrace.

"Bonjour, Monsieur Black."

The soft voice stopped Alastair in his tracks. A stocky man in his thirties stood up from the table and advanced towards Alastair.

"I don't think I have had the pleasure," he spoke in clear, slightly-accented English. "Let me introduce myself. Capitaine Hubert Lolmède, Police Judiciare, Cahors. At your service. Your wife and I were having a little chat. I hope you will join us."

He resumed his seat, indicating a chair opposite. Alastair sat down heavily. He could see that Kate was trembling. She sat down next to him..

"You will be aware, no doubt," Hubert Lolmède looked directly at Alastair. "That we are now investigating the disappearance of Mr Richard Talbot. We know that Monsieur, or rather, Mr," he corrected himself. "Mr Talbot arrived here three days ago, travelling with you, in your car, Mr Black. You and your wife have told the officers from the Gendarmerie de St Geniès that Mr Talbot arrived at this château with you, just before the storm. You have also informed the officers that Mr Talbot left early the following morning to return to England. This person has been reported as failing to turn up to a rendez-vous on that day. You will also be aware that, acting on information received, the officers of the Gendarmerie searched an area of woodland here, close to the château. With Madame's permission, of course," he added. He leaned back in his chair and looked from one to the other.

"So, Mr and Mrs Black, I am here to inform you that, in the light of their discoveries, the officers of the Gendarmerie Nationale have thought it appropriate to involve the Police Judiciare in the investigation of this case. You may not be aware that in France, investigations by the Gendarmerie that develop such that they require certain resources, or have serious implications, are generally handed over to the police. In this particular case, our involvement is, for the moment, in a joint operation," he explained. "So, to get back to the search made by Officers Espinet and Rousseau. They made some interesting discoveries. Firstly, in the bushes, over there," he gestured towards the track. "They found Mr Talbot's jacket, holdall and," Lolmède paused. "His passport. Secondly, they found that there were some quite recent traces of blood on this very terrace, where we sit. The blood matches that of Mr Talbot. And finally, Monsieur, they found that your car has been cleaned inside very recently, very thoroughly and with the same cleaner that was used to attempt to clean the blood off the terrace."

Lolmède stood up and walked round behind Kate and Alastair.

"You should also know that both Docteur de la Bernière and Mr John Nicholson have been questioned regarding the events at the château during the night of the storm. We are seriously concerned that some harm has befallen Mr Talbot. As our evidence suggests that you two were the last people to see him, and that it appears possible that he may never in fact have left the château or its grounds, I am seeking your permission to undertake a thorough search. We would like to start outside."

Capitaine Lolmède returned to the table and stood in front of them. In the silence that followed, he leaned forward, his fists on the table, looking from one to the other with a penetrating stare. After a couple of moments, he said quietly,

"We would like to start, in fact, with the lake."

Kate's sharp intake of breath was audible to all three of them. The Capitaine gave no indication of having heard her. He strolled over to the balustrade and looked down onto the lake in the distance. How calm and peaceful it seemed. Turning back towards them, he resumed his seat.

"But before we start, perhaps I could hear from you both your own recollections of that night. In case, perhaps, you may have remembered something," he paused. "Something of interest."

There was a moment of stillness on the terrace. No one spoke. Kate thought afterwards how even the cicadas seemed to be holding their breath.

Then Kate burst out, "Yes, I have remembered something. I'm afraid I didn't mention it to the officers who were here earlier. I was too confused and upset."

She looked down at her hands. She could feel the tension emanating from Alastair. She could feel his fear of what she might say. But Kate knew it was now or never. She had to tell the truth, or at least part of the truth, or the consequences could be far worse. Capitaine Lolmède sat silently, waiting. Kate closed her eyes for a few seconds, praying she was doing the right thing. She straightened her back and began to speak, not looking at Alastair.

"My husband arrived here on the day of the storm, in the late afternoon, early evening, just before the storm broke. Richard was with him. I didn't know they were coming. I hadn't spoken to my husband since the spring, the last time he was here. After they arrived, we were having a drink on the terrace just as the storm was starting. Richard's very close to Alastair and he," Kate spoke with difficulty. "He hates me, because of my, er, relationship with Nick Carslow. Well, he suddenly started yelling at me, calling me a whore and worse. Richard's always had a problem with anger. I thought he was going to hit me or the baby. It was very frightening. I really thought I was in danger. So did Alastair and that's why he hit him."

Alastair and Hubert were looking at her intently. She rushed on.

"Alastair hit him to defend me. Richard fell and hit his head on the stone flags. We thought he was unconscious. It was pouring with rain by then, so I took the baby indoors and Alastair went to phone the doctor. The power was off and he had to go out to get his mobile. By the time we came back out onto the terrace, Richard had disappeared. We saw him heading down towards the lake. We were worried because he was hurt and we didn't know how badly. We didn't know what he'd do next. We ran after him and saw him get into the boat that we keep tied up at this end of the lake. He seemed to be rowing towards the other end. He couldn't have known about the weir and how dangerous it is in flood. We knew that we had to get to the weir before he did so we ran through the willows on this side. About halfway along, I fell. That's when I sprained my ankle. Alastair went on, and I saw him in the lake by the boat, right up by the weir. Then he disappeared. Alastair searched all along the river banks but he couldn't find him. We thought he might have been washed over the weir and ended up on the river bank. But he hasn't come back, so that's why Alastair was out looking for him again now, in case he's lying somewhere, badly injured. But we, well, we think he might have drowned in the lake. It was so rough in the storm, and it's quite deep."

Capitaine Lolmède nodded his head slowly.

"Thank you, Madame. This is very helpful. I shall arrange this afternoon for the lake to be searched. In the meantime, I must ask you both to accompany me to the station so that you can make statements. We can do this at the Gendarmerie in

St Geniès so as not to inconvenience you too much, Madame. Do you have someone you can call on to look after your child?"

"No, I don't know anyone," Kate answered. "And he's too ill to bring with me. Do I need to come to St Geniès? I've told you all I know."

"I'm sorry, Madame. I'm afraid you must make a formal statement, given the serious nature of this case, and the, er… inconsistencies …with your previous comments. I shall call one of our female officers. She will stay here while you accompany me to St Geniès. Excuse me while I make arrangements."

He got up from the table and walked to the edge of the terrace. He made a number of calls, in rapid French, before returning to the table. Alastair remained seated, his mind racing. He hoped that Kate had been right to tell the truth. Well, almost the truth. He wondered if the Capitaine had seen the baby. The doctor certainly had. He might not have remembered Alastair clearly from last year, but as a doctor, he'd be certain to come to the same conclusion that Alastair himself had done. And the gendarmes already thought he'd killed Nick because Nick was his wife's lover. And they'd be sure that Richard had been a witness, so now they'd think he'd killed again. It was all beginning to look like a premeditated plot by him and Kate to dupe Nick and get their hands on the château.

Capitaine Lolmède sat down. He would have liked to have had a closer look at the lake, but he didn't want the husband and wife to be left alone now. No more conferring on what story to tell the police. They sat in silence round the table. It was only ten minutes from the Gendarmerie in St Geniès to the château. They were sending Simone over. She was one of the trainees attached to the station and the only female officer they had there. Lucky she lived on the premises. He looked up at the familiar sound of the squad car approaching.

"Good." He got to his feet. "Monsieur, Madame. Let us go."

****

"Just one final question."

Kate looked across the narrow metal table at Capitaine Lolmède and Jules Espinet. It was three hours since they had left the château. Alastair had been interviewed first whilst she had sat in the outer office, watched over by Bernie Rousseau. They'd kept Alastair in there for over two hours. Now it was her turn. So far it hadn't been as bad as she had feared. She'd gone over her story again, just as she'd told the Capitaine earlier. They'd asked a few questions, but on the whole they seemed to believe her. She was beginning to relax a bit. After all, it was the truth. Richard must have drowned in the lake when the boat capsized. She felt sure of it now. If he had been washed over the weir, Alastair would have found him.

"Yes?" she asked.

"You say you saw Mr Black reach the boat in which Mr Talbot was trying to escape, and you saw the boat capsize?"

"Yes."

"Madame, how far away from the weir were you?"

"I'm not sure." Kate thought for a moment. "Probably about fifty metres."

"So, from fifty metres away, in the middle of a storm, when it was almost dark, you could see a small boat capsize?"

Kate hesitated.

"I thought that was what I saw...."

She broke off as Jules interrupted. Lolmède translated.

"My colleague would like you to tell us exactly what you actually saw, not what you think happened. What you can swear that you saw."

"I saw the boat, near the weir. I saw Alastair in the water. At least I saw a man. Then they both seemed to disappear. Then I passed out. When I came to I couldn't see either the boat or Alastair."

"Did you see the man in the water reach the boat before it disappeared?"

"Yes, I did."

"But you did not see the boat capsize? Why do you think that's what happened? I must press you, Madame. Did you actually see the boat capsize?"

"Well, no. But I'm sure it did! That's what Alastair told me!" she cried.

The Capitaine and Jules glanced at each other.

"Thank you, Madame. We have no more questions for you at present. We will take you home now. The police divers will be arriving at the château early tomorrow morning. In the meantime, we have cordoned off the lake and please, keep away from the area for now, if you would not mind. Tomorrow we shall need both you and your husband to show us exactly where you were when you last saw Mr Talbot."

****

Kate and Alastair watched in silence as the squad car climbed the track away from the château and disappeared from view.

"Do you think they believed us?" Kate turned anxiously to Alastair.

"I really don't know," he sighed. "Oh Kate, how have we got ourselves into such a mess?"

"It's my fault." Kate's eyes filled with tears. "I should never have…"

"Don't say it, Kate." Alastair turned away. "You know, I had no idea about you and Nick. Even when you came out here with him. And do you know why I came back this time?"

Kate shook her head.

"I came to ask you to come back to me. I still loved you," Alastair said simply. "But I don't understand you. I just do not understand why you lied to me about the baby. How could you!" He shook his head, turning away from her. "You know, I felt sorry for you a few days ago. Stuck down here, on your own with a new baby. No friends, no money. I supposed you'd loved Nick. And now I know you used Nick as much as you used me! And what about Joanne? You stole her husband and now you've stolen her château. You lied that this baby – our baby – was Nick's just so he – or you – would inherit this place! How could you?" Alastair spoke in a dull, quiet monotone.

Kate stood crying silently.

"And now," he continued. "Does it really matter if the police believe us or not? They thought I had killed Nick. They think Richard saw me do it. They think I've killed him too to keep him quiet. You didn't see the boat capsize. They know you were too far away to see properly on a night like that. They think I pulled him out of the boat and drowned him. If they find his body in the lake, they'll charge me with murder."

They stood staring at each other.

"I'm going now, Kate," Alastair said flatly. "I'll be at the hotel in the square at Fromac. I've told the police that's where I'm staying. I've had enough of this place."

He turned on his heel and was gone. Kate stood for a moment watching the blue car as it drove away from her. Then she went indoors, still hobbling on her aching ankle. She bathed the baby, gave him his final dose of medicine for the day and put him to bed. Then she lay down on the floor beside the cot and cried herself to sleep.

11

Bright sunshine streaming through a crack in the shutters woke Kate. She stretched out and managed to stand up, feeling stiff and cold from the night spent on the floor of the nursery. For once the baby had slept through the night and was still sleeping, more peacefully than she'd ever seen him. For a moment she stood and smiled down at him. Then as she opened the shutters, she was brought rudely back to reality. Outside were several cars, one of which she recognised as the St Geniès squad car. A navy blue police van was also parked near the courtyard. As she watched, two men in wetsuits set off towards the lake, carrying a small inflatable dingy. Going downstairs and out onto the terrace, she looked down on the activity around the lake and shuddered.

****

John Nicholson was frying bacon when he heard his son shout. Dan came crashing out of the woods, rushing across the meadow towards the barn.

"Hey, Dad!" he shouted. "Guess what! The police are searching the lake! There are frogmen and everything!"

John walked out onto the veranda, frying pan in hand.

"And how do you know? I told you to keep away from there for now."

"It's OK," Dan gasped. "I've been up in the treehouse with your binoculars! I got a really good view!"

Susie emerged from her caravan, hair tousled, rubbing her eyes.

"Do you have to make so much noise?" she grizzled.

212

"You're missing all the fun, lazy bones!" Dan replied.

"Fun! So you think someone being murdered is fun!"

"Ha! So now you agree with me! You think Richard has been murdered!"

"Now come on, you two," John intervened. "I've told you, we do not know what happened to Richard and we should not jump to conclusions."

"Yeah, but Dad, it was you who reported it!" Dan retorted. "You started it all!"

"Come and set the table," John replied, ignoring him. "Breakfast is nearly ready."

John retreated to the kitchen and started on the eggs.

"Dad! What are you doing! They're black!" Susie was standing behind him peering at the eggs.

"Oh God!" John jumped and lifted the pan off the gas. "I was just thinking about Richard. And Dan's right. What have I started by going to the police?"

"But Dad, you had to! He's disappeared. Anything could have happened to him. I hope he's alright."

"So do I," John agreed. But somehow he didn't think Richard was alright.

Later that morning, John was sitting in the sun, half-reading a book, half-dozing. Susie was sunbathing on an airbed alongside him.

"Dad, can we go out for lunch?" she asked.

"Yes, that's a good idea. Go and find Dan, will you, love, and we'll go into St Geniès."

"OK."

Susie got up and pulled on her shorts over her bathing suit.

"Dan," she hollered. "Hurry up! We're going out for lunch!"

"Susie, for God's sake! Stop yelling and go and find him. You're frightening the birds!"

Susie threw her airbed at her father and set off across the meadow. John tipped his hat over his eyes and stretched out. When he woke up and glanced at his watch, he was surprised to see it was nearly one. Whatever had happened to Susie? She and Dan hadn't come back and they'd be a bit late for lunch now. John got up and looked down the meadow. No sign of them. Oh well, he thought, they could go out tomorrow. They were probably in the treehouse. He wandered off towards the woods and was soon at the foot of the big sweet chestnut tree that housed his children's den. Looking up through the branches he could see they were both up there, leaning over the side that faced towards the château, peering intently.

"Give me the bins for a minute," he heard Susie say.

"OK, but hurry up! They're pulling it out of the boat now."

"Dan, Susie! What's going on?" John spoke quietly.

"Dad, it's the divers. They are in the lake up at our end, near the weir. It looks like they've found something in the lake. It looks like a body."

****

Chloe and Phillippe were finishing their lunch. The café was crowded as was usual on a Sunday. In the square, the market was finishing and most of the stalls were more or less packed up. Small knots of elderly men still stood around in the sunshine, talking and smoking. Their wives had struggled home long ago with baskets bulging with vegetables. Most of the people sitting at tables on the café terrace were foreigners, a mixture of residents and tourists, predominantly English, but with a good number of Dutch and a few Germans. A group of Frenchmen stood around the bar. They were deep in conversation and as he walked past on his way back from the cigarette machine, several of them greeted Phillippe. As he paused to return their greetings and brush off with a smile their comments on *"la belle Anglaise"*, he caught a few snatches of conversation that stopped him in his tracks.

When he got back to the table, Chloe looked up at him in alarm.

"Phillippe, what's the matter? You look really worried," she said.

"I just heard something. From them," he gestured over his shoulder towards the bar. "About the Englishman who's disappeared from St Geniès-Lafontaine."

"What?" Chloe asked. "Have they found him?"

"Maybe," Phillippe answered. "It seems that the police decided that there was something suspicious about his disappearance and this morning they've had divers searching the lake at the château."

"Gosh!" Chloe's eyes were wide. "What do they think happened?"

"It seems that Madame Black's husband is suspected of having something to do with the disappearance."

"But that's what you thought anyway! Isn't it? Isn't that why you went to the gendarmes?"

Phillippe shifted in his chair.

"Well, yes, it is. But, now, Chloe, they are talking about the police thinking he has murdered this Richard, and not only that, they think he murdered Nick as well."

"No!" Chloe's face paled. "But surely Nick's death was an accident! Oh, I couldn't bear it if all this was dragged up again."

"I know, darling." Phillippe took her hands. "I feel so awful. If I hadn't gone to the gendarmes, none of this would have happened."

"But you had to. If this Alastair Black is guilty, he's got to be punished. Especially if he really has killed two people! It's only fair on Joanne as well. She has a right to know the truth about Nick's death, if it really wasn't an accident."

"Of course, we may all be jumping to conclusions," Phillippe said. "The police have put up posters to see if anyone has seen this Richard. Look."

He handed her the poster, written in English and French. Chloe looked at the black and white photograph and frowned.

"You know, I think I've seen this man somewhere. Yes, Phillippe, I did see him! He was at the Channel Tunnel when I came over. He was with another man. He spoke to me. The other man, I mean. He knew Nick!"

"That must have been Alastair Black!" Phillippe exclaimed.

"What! But he was so nice! I'm sure he couldn't be involved in anything…" Chloe broke off.

"Look, let's stop this. I feel bad myself for ever going to the police, but …I had to… and I didn't expect Nick's death to be raked over again. I wouldn't do anything to upset you. I'd never have said anything if I'd thought this would happen…," his voice trailed off.

"I know," Chloe said. "It's OK, Phillippe. I never loved Nick, you know that. But he was a good friend, to both of us. And if they do reopen the case, well, so much the better. We need to know the truth. So does Joanne. But, I can't believe that Alastair Black is a killer! I'm sure that Nick's death was an accident. And surely he wouldn't harm his friend! I expect he'll turn up, or if anything has happened, I'm sure it will all have been an accident."

She squeezed Phillippe's hand.

"Let's not get morbid anyway. I'm so happy, and I want to stay this way!"

"Me too."

Phillippe leaned across the table and kissed her.

"Now, now! In a public place too! And in front of children!"

A large, strong hand descended on each of their shoulders. Jim Munro stood smiling down at them.

"Jim!" Phillippe cried in protest. "This is France!"

"Come and sit down," Chloe said, kissing him on both cheeks.

"Beer, Jim?" Phillippe had already caught the eye of the waitress. *"Un pression, s'il vous plaît, Martine!"*

"Thanks," Jim smiled up at Martine as she placed the glass in front of him. "Aah…." He took a long draught. "That's what I came to France for!"

"What!" Chloe laughed. "The beer?"

"Well, it's cheap!" Jim smiled, wiping his mouth.

Then suddenly he looked serious. "Anyway, have you heard the latest?"

Chloe and Phillippe looked at each other and shook their heads.

"Go on," said Chloe. "You're dying to tell us, you old gossip."

"You knew the police had decided to search the lake up at the château for this missing Englishman? Well, they had divers up there at crack of dawn and it seems they've found a body!"

"Oh no," Chloe gasped. "Do they know what happened? Did he drown?" she asked, glancing at Phillippe. "At least they've found him."

****

Kate watched as the ambulance doors closed. There seemed to be people everywhere around the château. The divers were loading their dingy back onto the trailer and she could see a policeman talking to Capitaine Lolmède, holding up a plastic bag. Capitaine Lolmède got into the St Geniès squad car alongside Jules Espinet and Bernie Rousseau and the car set off up the track at speed. She turned away from the window. They'd be going to Fromac, she supposed. To arrest Alastair. She'd seen them haul the body out of the lake. It was when they had got right down to the far end, near the weir, that they found it. Richard! She didn't want to believe he was dead. Ever since he'd disappeared in the storm, she had hoped Alastair would find him, washed up on the river bank somewhere. Or he'd just appear at the kitchen door. But now there was no hope. The police would charge Alastair with murder. She felt sure of it. It was all her fault. Everything that had happened. To Nick, and now to Richard. It was all her fault. She had lied to Alastair and she had cheated on him, then she'd lied to get the château for her son. But in the end she hadn't been able to lie convincingly enough to the police to help Alastair. Why hadn't she just told them she'd seen the boat capsize? Why say Alastair was near it? She knew they thought he'd drowned Richard, instead of trying to save him. Kate was in despair. If only she could turn the clock back. She had destroyed Alastair. If it hadn't been for her, both Nick and Richard would still be alive. And she'd done it all because of Nick! Had she loved him so much? Or just been infatuated? She knew now that he had never loved her. She had been just one of many. She looked down over the balustrade of the terrace to the spot where Nick had fallen. It would be quick. She only had to climb onto the stone wall and jump.

Somewhere far away, she heard the baby cry. Kate stood for a moment, unable to identify the sound. Then suddenly she came back to her senses. How could she even think of ending her own misery when she was responsible for a new life? She had to take care of this sickly baby and make him well and happy. Make sure he never suffered as she was doing. Teach him not to be weak and foolish. She'd try to make amends by making sure her baby never suffered, or made others suffer.

12

Jules stood on the pavement outside the glass doors of the hospital and took several deep breaths. The smell of the morgue was still in his nostrils. He crossed the small garden to the car park, walked over to his car and, leaning against it, put his gendarme's cap down on the bonnet and lit a cigarette. He knew he wasn't supposed to smoke in public when he was in uniform, but he needed it. He reflected, not for the first time, on how on earth the doctors and forensic people could stomach their job. When the assistant had pulled the green cover off the body, Jules had retched, almost vomited. He wiped the cold sweat off his face again at the memory. A few drags on the Gauloise and he was feeling more himself. The sun was setting behind the hills to the west of the city. It had been quite a day. Jules pulled on the cigarette. That damned Scotsman was going to get away with it again. He felt it in his bones. He wasn't going to get any more cooperation from CID after this. He looked up as a car drove quickly down the ambulance ramp and stopped close to him. Capitaine Lolmède climbed out hurriedly.

"Sorry I couldn't get here earlier," he said. "Well? What news?"

Jules dropped his cigarette stub onto the tarmac and ground his heel into it.

"You're not going to like this anymore than I do, Capitaine."

"What? Go on, man," Hubert urged impatiently.

"They found the body on the lake bottom, up near the weir at about eleven this morning. Bernie and I had been called away to deal with those burglaries over the other side of Fromac. Forensics called to say that the body was being brought over here to the hospital morgue and they'd do the autopsy straight away. Said it would take several hours to do all the tests and if I could get here by six they'd have the results."

"And?" Hubert asked.

"Like I said, you are not going to like this. The cause of death was drowning. But," Jules paused. "It's not Richard Talbot. The body has been in the lake for about four months. And it's a woman."

"Merde!" Hubert swore softly.

"Yes. The doctor's just completed the tests and the comparisons with women on our missing persons' register. He's almost sure it's Marie-Claire Lacombe, the notaire's wife from Fromac, though it's impossible to recognise her after so long in the lake. Quite turned my stomach. Of course, it's ironic really. She was mixed up in all this in a way. You might not know this, but she left a suicide note a few months ago, when she disappeared, just after the death of Nick Carslow. She said she was in love with him – Carslow, that is – and couldn't go on living after he'd died. We – and her husband – didn't take it too seriously. We thought she'd turn up eventually. According to her husband, it wasn't the first time she'd had an infatuation with some other man and apparently she was given to theatrical gestures. Her husband thought she'd have gone off somewhere on her own to get over it, then she'd be back, as has happened before. He didn't ask us to search for her. In fact he asked us not to. Her sister took over running the boutique in Cahors and we all thought she'd turn up when she was ready. Anyway it wasn't our problem. Maître Lacombe was sure she'd never take her own life. I suppose we might have guessed if she really was going to do it, she'd try and commit suicide at the château. That's where her car was found too."

"Merde!" Hubert said again. "Poor old Lacombe. So he never believed she'd really kill herself. And you're going to have to tell him."

They fell silent for a few minutes. Then Hubert Lolmède spoke again.

"So we still have no evidence that Talbot is dead or alive. He's just missing. We can't hold Black indefinitely. *Merde!* I agree with you now, Jules. I admit I didn't at first, but instinct tells me he's the one responsible for Carslow's death, therefore indirectly for Marie-Claire's suicide, and for Talbot's disappearance. But you know as well as I do that without any more concrete evidence we are going to have to give him back his passport soon. Did they find anything else in the lake?"

"Yes. In fact I really thought we'd got him for both deaths until I saw poor old Marie-Claire. They found this on the bottom of the lake." Jules brought out a plastic bag from his pocket and held it up.

"It's a knuckleduster. Remember what Bernie overheard when we had Black and Talbot in custody in May? And it's been in the lake for several months. Fortunately there's a serial number and a maker's mark that are still partly visible. And it's a bit unusual. Look at these spikes. If it was bought around here we should be able to trace where it came from, and there's a good chance whoever sold it might remember if it was bought by a foreigner. It's not that long ago."

"OK, Jules. I'll get on to it. I'll order the divers back tomorrow to have another look at the lake and the river on the other side of the weir. But we'll have to move fast. We just don't have enough to make an arrest. If we don't find this Richard Talbot in the next couple of days, we'll have to return Black's passport."

****

Next day, Capitaine Lolmède was drinking his breakfast coffee in his usual café. In front of him on the small round table was the list of shops in Cahors likely to sell knuckledusters. Fortunately there were only three. He was going to have to visit them himself. His sergeant was still busy on the drugs case and no one else was available. He was already getting flak from his colleagues for working with the gendarmes. The rivalry between the two services was legendary and, despite the new police chief's directive for better cooperation, old prejudices were hard to break. Lolmède sighed. He didn't want to get a reputation either for cosying up to the rural plods, or for sucking up to the new chief. But now he was sure that Richard Talbot's disappearance was linked to Nick Carslow's death and that it had no connection with the drugs gang, despite Bernie Rousseau's best attempts to persuade him otherwise. It was time Bernie retired. His addiction to American gangster movies was clouding his judgement. Still, he reflected, it was Bernie who had put them on to the knuckleduster. Hubert got up, dropping a few coins onto the table and waving to the patron as he left the café. He'd start with the nearest shop.

The sun was out again today and already it was hot and humid. Most of the shops were just opening up. A few hundred metres' stroll down the main boulevard brought Hubert to the first likely shop. He reasoned that if their theory was right and that last spring Alastair Black had bought a knuckleduster in order to attack his wife's lover, he would have gone into the first shop he saw. So it would be the one in the main boulevard. It was nothing unusual here in rural south west France to have several shops in a town this size selling guns and ammunition for the hunt. Hubert hated these places. Most also sold hunting knives and various other paraphernalia. It was surprising, though fortunate of course, he thought, that there were relatively few murders, given the ease with which anyone could obtain arms and weapons. Above the shop was a sign: '*Frédéric – Tout pour la chasse*'. Hubert looked in the shop window at the array of knives. A small sign read: 'We also supply specialist items: samurais, fighting stars, butterfly knives, flick knives, American knuckledusters.'

Hubert pushed open the door. A bell clanged loudly. Inside, the shop was dark after the bright sunshine of the street. It was small and crammed with racks of combat clothing. Behind the counter, a large glass-fronted gun cabinet was packed with rifles and hand guns. Hubert turned as a small, fat man with greasy grey hair bustled in through a door behind the counter.

"Yes, Monsieur. How can I help?" he beamed at Hubert.

"Police Judiciare," Hubert said tersely, holding out his identity card.

The man started slightly.

"But Officer, I have all the licences. Everything is in order. Only last month I...."

"I'm not here about licences," Hubert interrupted. "I would like your help in one of our investigations."

The man relaxed visibly.

"Yes, of course, anything. Please, take a seat."

He smiled ingratiatingly at Hubert.

"I am interested in your sales of American knuckledusters. Are they a popular item?" Hubert tried to keep the irony out of his voice.

"Oh yes," the man enthused. "I carry the widest range available anywhere in the south west! You'd have to go to Marseille to better it! In fact that's where most of my supplies come from."

"You will have a record of sales for the past year?" Hubert enquired.

"But of course, Officer. It is required by law," the man smirked.

"I would like to see it. Now would be convenient."

"Of course."

The little man hurried off through the door at the back of the shop. In a few moments he returned, carrying a black ledger which he opened on the counter.

"Here, Officer. Sales of American knuckledusters, from January last year."

Hubert took the book and looked down the list of entries. There were only five in the whole period. A very popular line, eh? Still, the fat man was more likely to remember the customers. He looked down the list until he got to May. One entry. He was in luck. He took his notebook out of his pocket. Yes, the serial number Jules had noted matched that in the ledger! He pointed to it.

"This one. Do you remember anything about the purchaser?"

The fat man took a pair of spectacles out of his pocket and looked at the entry.

"Ah, yes. That is a very special item. With the small spikes. Very effective. Quite lethal."

He smirked again, but catching Hubert's expression, hurriedly added, "Of course it is really a collector's item. No one would use such a thing these days!"

"Of course not," Hubert agreed, smiling grimly. "But tell me, can you remember anything about the customer?"

"Well, yes, as a matter of fact I can. He was a foreigner. They often are, the collectors."

Hubert produced a photograph from his notebook. It had been taken last year by the St Geniès gendarmes when they had Black and his friend in custody.

"Do you recognise this person?"

The man took the picture and held it to the light. He shook his head. Hubert's heart sank. His case was falling apart.

"No, never seen him before," the man said. "It wasn't him that bought the knuckleduster. The bloke that bought it had almost white hair and really pale eyes. Looked a bit weird. That's why I remember him. I think he was English."

Hubert silently held out a photograph of Richard.

"Him?"

"Yes, that's him! Definitely. What's he done ?"

"He's gone missing," Hubert answered. "Have you seen him since May?"

"No. I just saw him the once, when he came into the shop. I don't remember anything much about him. He seemed to know what he was after, as I recall. Didn't speak French. Just pointed. Paid cash. Never saw him again."

"Thank you. You've been very helpful. Now would you mind displaying this poster in your window? We are anxious to locate him."

"Certainly, Officer. Anything I can do to help."

The fat man held the door open for Hubert, shaking his hand enthusiastically.

Out in the street, Hubert felt the need for another coffee and a cigarette. He'd have liked a brandy, but it was not yet ten o'clock and he was on duty. This case was going nowhere, except round in circles. He wished he'd never got involved. He should have known better than to listen to Jules and Bernie. His colleagues were right: leave the rural plods to their own farmyards and fantasies.

PART IV

This year

1

Kent, England. November.

"So they gave me my passport back and let me go," Alastair concluded, looking up at Joanne. "They had to. They couldn't find Richard and without a body, they couldn't arrest me. In the end, they couldn't spend any more time searching. The police just said as far as they were concerned, Richard had a right to go missing. They seemed to think Kate and me had made up our stories to help him disappear. The local gendarmes thought differently though. They were convinced that I'd killed both Nick and Richard. I was lucky to get away. Lucky!" he bowed his head, tears pricking his eyes.

Then he looked up. "So now you know it all, Joanne. Please believe me, I've told you the truth. I tried to save Richard. But it was my fault he ran off into the storm. Richard did hit Nick, but his death really was an accident. And the baby really is mine, not Nick's."

Joanne sat silent for a long time. Looking across at her, Alastair saw the tears running slowly down her face, unheeded.

"Nick's got a lot to answer for," she whispered.

"Don't blame him," Alastair said, shocked. "We're all guilty – except you."

Joanne got to her feet and stood looking into the fire. Then she turned to Alastair, her head held high.

"I'm going to go out there myself," she said. "If you are right and the baby has died, I'm going to make sure Kate doesn't get her hands on my château. We can prove that the baby is your's, and I can prove that the baby definitely wasn't Nick's. Our doctor has got all sorts of samples from Nick when I made him have the fertility tests. Not that Nick ever told me the truth about those! Though he managed to tell plenty other people," she added bitterly. "I'll get on to my lawyers now. Kate might have applied to overrule Nick's English will, but they can't actually do it without us knowing. So once my lawyers prove Nick had no descendants, his English will leaving the château to me will be ratified in France. I'm sorry, Alastair, but your wife is the one who is really responsible for all of this and she isn't going to get away with stealing my château as well."

Alastair stood up.

"You are right, Joanne. Kate has a lot to answer for. But I'm sure she only wanted the château to give the baby – our baby – a roof over its head."

"Alastair!" Joanne's eyes flashed. "Don't defend her! Stop making excuses for her. You're mad to take her side after all she's done to you! Just look at yourself! She's ruined your life! She's stolen your child! You don't go out, you look years older than you are, you never smile anymore. You are a mess!" she shouted.

They stood glaring at each other. Alastair shrugged helplessly. She was right.

2

France. November.

November can be a dreary month, thought Joanne, as she roared down the autoroute in the Porsche. There weren't many leaves left on the trees now. She glanced at the clock on the dashboard. She was making good time. With a bit of luck she'd reach Fromac in time for dinner. As she drove, she went over the events of the last week in her mind. Her lawyers had confirmed that Kate Black had made an application, on behalf of her son, for the unreserved portion of Nick Carslow's estate in France. The process had not got very far. Thank goodness for the slowness of French bureaucracy, Joanne thought. A couple of phone calls from her lawyers explaining her case and, just before she left today, she had heard that Kate's application had been thrown out. Her lawyers had also confirmed that the hospital in Cahors where the baby had been born had retained samples from the child, and had handed over their analysis to the Cahors police, at her lawyers' request. Capitaine Lolmède had been most cooperative. Joanne knew that what Alastair had told her was true, and now she could prove it in a court of law: the baby was definitely not Nick's. It was definitely Alastair's. She wondered, not for the first time, if Nick had known, or at least suspected.

It was dark and cold when Joanne got out of the car in the square at Fromac. She had decided to stay in the small hotel that faced the café and the estate agent's office. She had stayed here before, when she had found the château. The place looked deserted, but the front door soon opened in response to Joanne pounding the brass door-knocker.

"Good evening, Mrs Carslow. Please come in."

The small, dark-haired Englishwoman stood aside to let Joanne into the stone-flagged hallway.

"Did you have a good journey?"

"Yes, thanks, not too bad."

Joanne dropped her leather holdall onto the floor and stretched her arms above her head.

"But it's a long drive on your own."

"Yes," Patricia Holdsworth said, nodding sympathetically. "I've made a meal for you. Nowhere in Fromac is open in the evening at this time of the year. If you'd like to come up, I'll show you the room first. I've had the heating on all day, so hopefully it will have taken the chill off by now," she added with a touch of irony. "This way, Mrs Carslow."

"Joanne, please."

Patricia smiled back.

"This way, Joanne."

Joanne followed her up the curved wooden staircase, along a short corridor and up a second flight, at the top of which Patricia stepped onto the landing and opened a heavy wooden door. She stood aside to let Joanne enter the large room, pleasantly furnished in English country style, with a floral wallpaper in peach and green.

"The bathroom is through here," Patricia said, switching on a light. "I've just had this installed, so you should be alright," she laughed. "I'm gradually having all the plumbing re-done. Is dinner in about half an hour OK?"

"Fine," Joanne replied, as Patricia bustled out.

She lay down on the bed for few minutes, exhausted after the long drive. A nice hot shower would do her good. Then a meal with Patricia. This was an opportunity to catch up on the gossip. Patricia would know what was going on at the château. And even if she didn't, no doubt Jim Munro would be able to fill in the details tomorrow. Joanne had met Jim a few times, when she was buying the château. And she knew he was a bigger gossip than Patricia. Which was interesting, Joanne smiled to herself, since the relationship between Pat and Jim themselves was a great source of gossip for the local expats.

Half an hour later she was sitting in front of a roaring log fire in the first floor dining room, a glass of wine in her hand. Patricia appeared from the kitchen and sat down on the other side of the fire.

"I hope you've warmed up a bit," she smiled at Joanne. "Will you be staying long?"

"I'm not sure," Joanne replied. "I expect you'll have guessed why I'm here."

"Well," the other woman hesitated. "It's only gossip, really. But we all know that the château is up for sale. Jim told me as soon as Kate Black had been into the office. We were all a bit surprised."

She broke off, looking into the fire.

"Why?" Joanne asked directly.

"Because we all knew that it was you who had bought the château! I mean, paid for it!" Patricia burst out. "No one here thinks Kate Black has a claim to it at all. Dominic Lefèvre has even refused to take it on! Apparently, according to Jim, he was quite rude to her."

"I see," said Joanne thoughtfully. "That's why it's with the Cahors agency."

"Yes. It's with the Agence Sainte Croix, I think. Dominic went to see them, to warn them that she didn't actually own it, but they didn't listen to him. There's so much rivalry between these estate agents, they just thought he was annoyed that she'd given it to a Cahors agent rather than him. But we couldn't work out how she expects to get away with it. When she gets a buyer and the notaires get involved, it'll be obvious it's owned by you and Nick, so she can't claim more than the child's half at most. And there's plenty people here think she can't even claim that," Patricia added ominously.

"Oh? So tell me about the child, Patricia. What's happened to it?"

"Well, no one is quite sure. When she came in to see Dominic to put the château on the market, she told him that the child had died, so the château was her's, being the baby's only living relative. I don't really know any more about it. It was only about a week ago, maybe two, so she must have been in here the day the baby died, if it really did."

"What on earth do you mean?" asked Joanne. "Do you think it's still alive?"

"No. At first Jim thought she might have just made the story up so she could sell up and get her hands on the money. The château is worth quite a bit now, with all the work you and Mr Carslow did on it," she added. "Jim also thought," she paused for a moment. "I don't like to cast aspersions, but Jim thought she might have killed it herself."

"What!" Joanne stared at her, shocked. "Surely not! No one would kill their own baby!"

Patricia put her glass down.

"The trouble is, everything that has happened over there at St Geniès-Lafontaine is weird, ever since she came to live there. That woman is a curse," Patricia said vehemently. "But I suppose you know that," she added quietly.

Standing up, she turned to Joanne.

"Please, come to the table. Let's eat before I let dinner get over-cooked."

Joanne sat at the end of the table, thinking over what Patricia had said. A few moments later, when a plate of steaming soup was placed in front of her, she realised just how hungry she was. Conversation was easy between them as Joanne changed the subject to Patricia's hotel and its prospects. It was only when they were both ensconced in front of the fire again, sipping coffee, that Joanne went back to the subject of Kate and the château.

"So, tell me, Patricia, what did you mean about Jim thinking Kate could have killed her own baby?"

"Well, I'm sure he's wrong. The baby was always ill, right from the start. Docteur de la Bernière was in and out of the château all the time. He was really kind to her, you know. More than she deserved. Anyway, according to Jim, Phillippe – that's the doctor – gets a call from the château one day a couple of weeks ago, saying its urgent and he has to come right away. So he does, and when he gets there the baby is dead. Apparently he had caught bronchitis a few months ago, at the end of the summer, and that had developed into pneumonia. She had refused to take him to the hospital, although the doctor had warned her that it was very serious. Had got quite hysterical, saying she couldn't leave the château, she was needed there. Phillippe thought she seemed to have gone a bit crazy ever since the summer. Never leaves the château except when she goes shopping. Sandra saw her in Carrefour in Cahors once. She said it looked like she was stocking up for a siege, the amount of stuff she'd got in the trolley. But since the summer, hardly anyone has seen her except Phillippe when he goes to see to the baby. He reckons she's really changed. After what happened, it's not really surprising. I suppose you know about all that?" Patricia looked at Joanne a little warily.

"About what?" Joanne asked.

"Her husband came down here with his friend, and the friend disappeared. No one knows why they came, and it was all very strange. The gendarmes at St Geniès were convinced her husband had killed his friend. Quite a few of us thought that as well," she added.

"Really, Patricia!" Joanne put her cup down rather crossly. "Don't you have anything better to do than to make up stories about people!"

"Look, Joanne, it's not entirely without foundation," Patricia retorted huffily.

"Go on then. Why do you think Alastair Black killed his friend?" Joanne asked.

But she knew what the answer was going to be.

"I personally have never seen her baby. Hardly anyone has," Patricia said, leaning forward. "But someone saw her taking it into the surgery once, not long after it had been born. It was

Sandra. She told me it didn't look anything like Nick. Oh, I'm so sorry, Joanne! I shouldn't have mentioned it. Forget I said anything."

"It doesn't matter," Joanne said. "Go on."

"To cut a long story short, the child is the spitting image of Alastair Black. She told Espinet, who's in charge at St Geniès, and they got really excited because they think it's all some sort of scam that the Blacks cooked up to get their hands on your château. Alastair Black kills Nick, maybe with the friend's help, friend threatens to shop him for some reason, so Black kills him too. But there was nothing they could do. They'd already searched the lake up at the château and there was no trace of the friend, so they had to let Alastair Black go. He stayed here you know, until the police let him go. In fact, I thought he was really nice. I didn't think he could have done it."

Joanne sat back in her chair. She could see why the gendarmes thought what they did, but she believed Alastair's story completely. And it seemed he had been right about the baby dying.

"Patricia, carry on with what you were saying about Kate refusing to take the child into hospital."

"It seemed that she was adamant to keep him at the château with her. Phillippe was really worried that something might happen and he'd be blamed for not insisting she bring him in. He's leaving soon, and it would be bad for him if there was any sort of stain on his reputation. He's taking up the post of consultant paediatrician at the Radcliffe in Oxford in the New Year. He's marrying Chloe, did you know? You know Chloe, don't you? Isn't that lovely? But I digress. Eventually he decided the baby wasn't getting any better and he arranged to send a nurse over to sleep at the château until there was an improvement. She nearly did her nut – Kate, that is. She just refused point blank. Said she could manage and she wasn't having strangers around. She went on and on at him until in the end he gave up. Made her promise to contact him immediately if the baby's condition changed. And the notaire had to go over there and stand over her while she signed a statement indemnifying the hospital and the surgery and the doctor in case anything happened to the baby as a result of it not being hospitalized. She wouldn't even come into Fromac to the notaire's office. Said she couldn't leave the baby and wouldn't even let Phillippe stay with it while she came over! I mean, poor old Maître Lacombe having to go over to that place, after what happened to his wife there! Oh, God!" her hand flew to her mouth. "Oh, Joanne, I'm so sorry."

Joanne sighed.

"Don't worry, Patricia. I can't hide from what's happened. But it does seem as though Kate's losing it. And so the doctor just got called round there one day and found the baby dead?"

"That's right. He wasn't exactly surprised, but I think he had thought the baby was over the worst. They had to do a post-mortem and the cause of death was respiratory failure due to advanced broncho-pneumonia. But it could easily have been caused by a pillow over the head. She seemed sufficiently unbalanced to do it, particularly if she needed money and she thought it was the only way she could sell the château. But she did seem devoted to the baby. She might have just wanted to end its suffering. I don't suppose we shall ever know for sure."

3

It was nearly nine o'clock when Joanne woke up next morning. Climbing out of bed, she was pleased to notice that Patricia had left the central heating on. She opened the shutters and gazed down into the square, two floors below her. There was not a lot of activity. It was too cold for anyone to be sitting out on the café terrace opposite, but, as she watched, Dominic Lefèvre came out of the café and walked next door to his estate agency. He paused to inspect his window display before unlocking the glass door and going inside. Joanne turned away from the window. She had intended to plan her next few days last night, but the long drive, the warm fire, the wine and the good food had had its effect and she had fallen asleep almost as soon as she'd climbed into bed. She was surprised how relaxed she felt this morning, despite what lay ahead. What she needed now was a shower and a nice strong cup of coffee. She's plan her next moves over breakfast.

Sitting at the table in the window of Patricia's little dining room, Joanne could observe the square well. The lace curtains hid her from view, and from her vantage point she could see not only the square, but up the hill to the right, where she had parked her car, and along the main street that led out of the village past the boules pitch. Directly opposite her, to the right of the café, was the narrow, cobbled alleyway that led to the oldest part of the village where the notaire's office and the *mairie* were situated. This was her first appointment. The notaire. Joanne sighed. He was expecting her at eleven o'clock. Her lawyers had arranged it all as soon as they had received the report they needed about Kate's baby from the Cahors police. They had a sheaf of original documents testifying that the baby was not Nick's. The notaire should have formally completed the proceedings to reinstate Joanne as rightful owner of the whole of the Château de St Geniès-Lafontaine. She wasn't looking forward to facing Maître Lacombe after what had happened about Marie-Claire. Still, it had to be done. Once she'd got that over, she would go into Cahors and put the Agence Sainte Croix in its place. The château would be off the market by the evening. Then, of course, came the hard bit. She'd have to go and tell Kate that the game was up. She knew she could leave it to her lawyers, but somehow Joanne felt she had to do it herself. She sipped her coffee thoughtfully. What was going to become of Kate? It sounded very much as if she needed help. Probably getting away from the château would be the best thing for her anyway. How could she have stayed on there for so long, with all those awful memories, Joanne wondered. Probably because she had nowhere else to go. Perhaps she did see her chance when the baby got so ill. Kill it and sell off the château before anyone noticed. It occurred to Joanne that Alastair may have been right: Kate might have lied to Nick about him being her son's father because she wanted to have a hold over him, wanted him to leave Joanne for her. But after he'd died, the only reason Kate could have had to lie about the father of her child was to get her hands on Nick's money and the château. If she was calculating enough to lie then, with Nick only a few hours dead, putting the baby out of his suffering might have seemed a good option, leaving the way clear to selling the château and getting out with a great deal of money. The sympathy Joanne had always felt somewhere deep down in her heart for Kate's predicament vanished. It was replaced by cold anger.

****

The English couple sitting in front of Dominic Lefèvre were trying to describe their dream home, in halting French. Dominic sat back, pen poised, reflecting on how often he had heard the same thing. All of them wanted a place out in the country, quiet and peaceful, no neighbours, two or three hectares or so of land, a view, but only a few minutes' walk from a picturesque village with a baker's, a café etc. Outbuildings, barns (for turning into gîtes for their income when they retired and came to live here permanently), stone house to restore, but not too derelict, with mains water and electricity, original features, fireplaces, bread oven, pigeonnier, bôlet, space for the swimming pool, and all for under 200,000 euros. He felt like saying, get real, you dreamers. Instead he smiled pleasantly and handed them a file containing his cheapest properties and the ones that had been on his books the longest. After noting their name and address, he sat back and reached for the phone. This was one Jim Munro could handle. He'd got a bit of a headache already, trying to make out what on earth these people were trying to say to him. He wished they wouldn't bother. If they just came in and said, we don't speak French, that would be fine, but they'd come in, determined that they can make you understand, don't want to lose face by saying they can't speak French, and it was just a waste of everyone's time.

As he was dialling Jim's number, his attention was caught by a movement across the square. The door of the Hôtel Coq d'Or opened, and out stepped a blonde woman wearing a smart black leather jacket and black trousers. Dominic walked to the door to get a better look. Yes, he was right. It was Madame Carslow. This looked interesting. He saw her cross the square towards him and, craning his neck, he could just see that she was heading up the alley towards the notaire's office. He turned back to his clients, but not before she looked in his direction and gave a little wave. Dominic returned her wave, guiltily, moving away from the door. Back at his desk, he dialled Jim's number again. He answered immediately.

"Jim, can you come over right away?" he asked excitedly. "I have news! And, oh, I also have," he glanced at the form on his desk, "Mr and Mrs Moore, who would like to see a few properties."

Joanne went into the café. It was empty. She walked up to the bar as the waitress emerged from the kitchen clutching place mats and cutlery. Looking at her watch, Joanne noticed that it was only 11.45. Her interview with Maître Lacombe had been short and to the point. He had assured her that matters would be officially, as he put it, regularised, within two weeks. If she did not intend to press charges against Kate. This was something Joanne had been thinking about. Her better nature told her to leave it, let it go. Soon she would be able to sell the château herself and have done with the affair. If she pressed charges, things could drag on and on. And she felt Alastair didn't deserve more pain. She knew, and marvelled at the fact, that he still loved Kate. And there was Kate herself. Joanne thought perhaps she had suffered enough as well.

Settling herself at a window table, Joanne ordered a small jug of red wine. She took the menu from the waitress and looked down it at the *plats du jour*. Her anger at Kate had subsided from this morning and she felt sorry for her again now. Really, Joanne thought, gossip could be very damaging. After listening to Patricia last night, she'd almost believed that Kate had killed her own baby. But, nevertheless, apart from stealing her husband and being partly, at least circumstantially, responsible for his death, she had tried to cheat Joanne out of hundreds of thousands of pounds. Even now, when she didn't have a child to think of. That had always been the way Joanne had thought of it before. Kate had been trying to provide for the child in the only way she could. If she'd had any decency, as soon as the child had died she'd have left, knowing she didn't have any claim to the château. Joanne felt her anger rising again. She took a gulp of wine. Well, she thought, Kate's not getting away with it. But I don't need revenge. I won't press charges, even if she does deserve it. I just want to be able to forget about it all. Although she knew she never could.

She was pouring another glass of wine when the café door swung open and Jim Munro, a large white dog and a thin, pale, bespectacled English couple filed in, leaving muddy footprints all over the brown lino. Jim noticed her right away and smiled warmly in her direction. When he had settled his brood at a table in the corner he came over to Joanne's table, his dog following behind, tail wagging as it approached Joanne.

"Mrs Carslow, good to see you."

He held out his hand, beaming.

"Pat said you were coming out."

"Jim." Joanne took his hand. "Still busy, I see."

"Oh yes," Jim smiled ruefully. Lowering his voice, he added, "And punters like these I could do without. They want to see every last house we've got for sale just in case they miss 'the' one. They'll make a big mistake if they move out here. But you can't tell them."

He laughed and Joanne found herself laughing too as the dog sat down at her feet, sensing the good humour. She reached out and patted its head as Jim looked at her seriously.

"I don't mean to speak out of turn," he said. "But you know everyone is on your side in all this, don't you? If we can help you at all, you just have to ask."

"Thanks," Joanne answered. I might as well tell him straight, she thought. "Look, Jim. Sit down for a minute. I know how tongues wag out here. As I'm sure you already know," she smiled, remembering Dominic's face pressed up against his office door, straining to see where she was going this morning. "I went to see Maître Lacombe this morning. You might as well also know that the maître confirmed that Mrs Black has no claim to the Château de St Geniès-Lafontaine. Her application to over-rule Nick's English will in the interests of her child has been thrown out and Maître Lacombe is submitting the documentation for the re-registration of her child's parentage today. The child was not Nick's, as she erroneously stated at the time of its birth," Joanne said drily. "And I am not pressing charges. I shall be selling the château once the re-registration is complete, and I shall be putting it with the Agence Lefèvre. So you can tell Dominic I shall be coming to see him before I leave."

Jim gaped at her.

"Good God! You know, people said it wasn't Nick's baby. She's a bit of a one, isn't she? Who'd have thought it when she came down here at first to do your garden! Butter wouldn't melt in her mouth then!"

"I'm telling you all this, Jim, because I know what gossip's like round here. You have the truth and I know I can trust you to pass it on. I mean the true story, not a garbled version. This afternoon I'm going over to the Agence Sainte Croix to tell them to take my château off their books. And why. Then I'm going to see Kate to tell her she's had a good run for her money, but it's all over now and she'll have to move out. Nick's death was an accident. The real father, ironically, was Kate's husband, Alastair Black. Alastair Black is completely innocent in all of this: he didn't kill Nick, nor did he kill his missing friend Richard, nor is he in cahoots with Kate to steal my château, as some say. So now you know it all. I want to set the record straight."

Jim looked at her in amazement. Joanne sat back and took another sip of wine. She felt better for telling Jim. Somehow it felt more real now. Everything was going to be sorted out. No more surprises and lies. She was going to finish this business and put it to the back of her mind. Suddenly she felt glad she'd come. She should have come out straight after Nick's death and nipped it all in the bud. It was her own fault for feeling sorry for Kate, alone in a foreign country with no money or job and her new baby to support.

"Bloody hell!" Jim said eventually. "Her own husband was the father! I didn't see that coming!"

"Well, there it is. Truth can be stranger than fiction," Joanne said wryly.

"You're telling me! Look, I may see you this evening if you are eating at Pat's. She's invited me round."

"Yes, I'll be there," Joanne answered. "I'll see you then."

"Looking forward to it," Jim replied. "Now, if you'll excuse me, I'd better get back to the punters."

They shook hands. Joanne watched with interest as he settled himself at the table and started to explain the menu to the English couple. He was just right for this job, she thought. Genial. That described him. And genuinely so, Joanne felt. She knew he'd try his best to make sure these people realised what they would be taking on, even if it meant they didn't buy in the end.

The waitress came over to her table and Joanne placed her order. She looked out of the window as she waited for her food to arrive. It was a bleak, grey day again. The stone buildings around the square that looked so white and bright in the summer sunshine looked cold and shuttered against the winter. A few cars drove through the square as she watched, and an old lady, bundled in a thick, brown woollen coat, emerged from the vet's surgery in the next block to the café. She tottered up the hill past Joanne's car, towing a small grey poodle on a lead. Otherwise, the village was deserted. Even the café, which she had never seen so empty, had only attracted one more customer, a salesman of some sort, despite it being well past noon by now. Joanne had expected Dominic, at least, to be in. Glancing across at Jim's table, she knew why he wasn't there: Dominic hadn't very much patience with his English clients. No matter. She could see him tomorrow, once she had dealt with the Agence Sainte Croix and Kate.

The arrival of the waitress with a large bowl of soup and a basket of bread interrupted her thoughts. Joanne dipped her spoon in and took an experimental mouthful. It was delicious. As she ate, she thought back over what Patricia had told her last night. She frowned a little as she thought about Kate. Perhaps she ought to have a word with the doctor before she went over there. If she was a bit deranged, and Joanne couldn't help thinking she might well be, after all that had happened, she didn't want to be responsible for pushing Kate over the edge in any way. Another thought suddenly occurred to her. Somehow, she couldn't dismiss it from her mind. If she went over to the château and confronted Kate, would she actually be putting herself in danger? If Kate was unbalanced, getting rid of Joanne herself might seem like the solution. Kate didn't know yet that her claim to the estate was void. The letter from Maître Lacombe wouldn't arrive until tomorrow. So if Joanne went round this afternoon, Kate might take her chance to kill her, thus removing the obstacle to her claim! Don't be ridiculous, Joanne told herself. It seemed so absurd, as she sat there in the warm café, half-listening to Jim and his chattering clients. But nevertheless, she shivered. First Nick, then Richard and now the baby. Who next?

Joanne started slightly as the waitress approached to remove her empty soup plate. A few minutes later, she returned with Joanne's salad. At that moment, the café door opened and in walked a tall, dark man. He greeted Jim Munro in faultless English. Jim spoke a few words to him, nodding in Joanne's direction. The Frenchman followed Jim over to Joanne's table.

"Joanne, I'm sorry to interrupt your lunch, but I thought you might like to meet the doctor. Joanne, this is Phillippe de la Bernière."

"Madame," Phillippe bowed slightly as he took her hand. "I'm delighted to meet you. I have heard very good things of you from my fiancée, Chloe. But she did not include the description," he said, smiling at her.

Nick must have been mad, he thought, running away with that weird Kate Black when he was married to this woman. Joanne squirmed inwardly. Frenchmen could be such prats. She smiled back, seeing Jim's smirk out of the corner of her eye.

"I am pleased to meet you at last," she replied formally. "I have never thanked you for doing what you could for my husband."

Phillippe inclined his head, slightly embarrassed by her direct reference to her husband's death.

"I wonder if I could speak to you for a few moments, Madame Carslow?" he asked.

"Of course," Joanne indicated a chair. "Would you like a glass of wine?"

"No, thank you. I am on duty this afternoon. But I will come straight to the point," he said. "I feel I owe you an apology."

"Oh?" Joanne looked at him in surprise.

"Yes. You may know that I am Madame Black's doctor. I am afraid to say that I was under the impression that Nick, your husband, was the father of Madame Black's child. I was responsible for the registration of the birth. Of course, I now know, from the hospital and Capitaine Lolmède, that I made a grave error."

"Yes, you did. Although it was hardly your fault," Joanne spoke coldly. "I assume you asked Mrs Black for the father's name?"

"Yes, of course. But she hesitated at the time. I was surprised by the child's colouring and eyes, but of course that could have come from Madame Black's own family. But I am afraid I assumed that Monsieur Carslow was the father. And I'm sorry to say that I may have persuaded Madame Black that it was in her interests to ensure that Nick's name was on the registration document. I even introduced her to Maître Chevalier, who was to prepare the case to overturn Nick's English will."

"I see," Joanne took a sip of wine. "Well, it's all sorted out now," she said crisply. "Mrs Black should hear from Maître Lacombe tomorrow. By the way, I was actually thinking perhaps I should speak to you. I understand that you think she, that is Mrs Black, has been acting a little strangely of late?"

"Yes, I do." Phillippe wondered who had told her, aware that he shouldn't discuss his patients with anyone. "But it's very understandable, considering what she has been through."

Joanne was silent for a few minutes. What about what she herself had been through? She seemed to be expected to cope.

"I am asking you this, doctor," she said eventually. "Because I intend to go and see Mrs Black myself. I need to know when she will be vacating my château. If Mrs Black is likely to be," she groped for the right word. "Irrational, it might be better if I did not go alone."

"Really, Madame! I am sure that you would not be in any danger from Madame Black!" he laughed. "But if you are concerned, why go at all? Your lawyers can deal with it for you."

"I'm glad you find this amusing," Joanne retorted, feeling slightly foolish. "In fact, if you must know, I felt I would like to give her the opportunity to explain her side of things to me."

"I'm sorry," Phillippe said. "That is considerate of you. I apologise. It's just that I am aware of how some of the gossip in this place can get out of hand."

"Yes. I apologise too. Let's start again," Joanne smiled at him. "You did nothing other than your professional duty over the registration of the birth. But thank you for telling me. I know that Kate has been through a lot. I actually wanted to make sure that me turning up wasn't going to push her over the edge. And yes, I couldn't help thinking that so much has happened, that, well, she might do something desperate. I was thinking of coming to see you anyway to ask your advice. It would be much easier just to get my lawyers to tell her she has to go, but the bailiffs can be really unpleasant. And my lawyers want me to sue her. We could win huge damages and ruin her and her husband. But I don't want to do that. And I just thought it might be better for her if at least she told me her side of things and we tried to be civilised. I could wait until she finds somewhere else to go, maybe."

"I'm sorry," Phillippe said again. "You are being very kind to her. Under the circumstances, although I shouldn't discuss my patients, I will tell you what I can of her present mental state. Remember, I am not a professional psychiatrist, but in my view she is displaying some rather disturbing symptoms. Or perhaps behaviour is a better word. The episode in August was a terrible occurrence. After her husband was allowed to return to England, she was alone again in the château with her ailing son. He had contracted bronchitis, probably partly due to her own negligence," he broke off as Joanne interrupted.

"Surely not! Alastair said she was devoted to the child!"

"It seems that in the confusion of whatever happened on the night of the storm last summer, the baby got left outside for some time. Yes," he nodded. "In the storm. He took a serious turn for the worse that night. In the months since then, the bronchitis developed into broncho-pneumonia, which is very serious in children. The baby got sicker and sicker. I was very worried about it. He should have been hospitalized, but she wouldn't hear of it. She refused to let him be moved to Cahors, saying she couldn't leave him. I arranged for her to sleep at the hospital so she could be with him twenty-four hours a day, but still she refused. Just would not leave the château. So then I arranged for a team of nurses to come over so that there was always someone on hand. But no, she wouldn't have that either. She got quite hysterical at the suggestion that there would be someone at the château with her. I could not understand her reaction, but there was nothing I could do. She insisted that I make my daily visit at a particular time. One day I was early. She was really quite peculiar about it. Ranted on about disrupting her schedule and upsetting the baby and how it mustn't happen again. I can assure you it didn't! I've got too much to worry about without that sort of aggravation. No one ever sees her in the village. Still, that's nothing new. She never went out much. But a couple of people have seen her in the big hypermarket in Cahors, looking as if she was stocking up so that she wouldn't have to come out at all for months! That's all really," Phillippe shrugged. "It is strange behaviour and it could have put her baby's life in danger. That's what is so odd about it. You are right. She was devoted to that child. I can't understand why she took any chances with him, especially when he was so ill."

"But do you really think the baby would have lived if he'd been in hospital?"

"I don't know," Phillippe shrugged again. "My guess would be yes, maybe. But neither do I really think she had anything directly to do with his death. It's possible, of course. She might have reached the end of her tether. But no, she wanted him to live. He was all she had."

"So what do you think about me going over there?" Joanne asked. "I mean, she's not suicidal or anything is she? It wouldn't be surprising if she was."

"No, I don't think so," Phillippe said. "After we got the post-mortem results, I went with her to the *hôtel de ville* to register the death. She told me then that she was going to put the château on the market and move on. She said she wanted to get away from here as soon as she could. She seemed quite positive. But there is something else you ought to know," Philippe paused here, looking at Joanne. "There's a lot of nice antique furniture in the château. I suppose it is yours?"

"Yes," Joanne answered. "We bought quite a lot of stuff locally, and some of it was from Spain."

"Well, it looks as if Madame Black might have started to clear it out already. Last week, just the day after the funeral in fact, I was driving back home after a late night call and happened to be coming along the road that passes the end of the track to the château. It was odd really. As I was approaching, still a way off, I caught sight of headlights coming up the track from the château. There's one spot where the track turns towards the main road and in winter when the trees are bare, you can see the track. It's quite far away, but I saw headlights, just briefly before the track turns again. Anyway, I slowed a bit when I got nearer, expecting someone to turn out into the road. But nothing. I glanced down the track, because I was so sure I'd seen something and it was so unusual for there to be any traffic on that track. I could have sworn that there was a biggish van parked in the shadow of the last few trees before the track meets the road. I thought this was a bit odd, and so I slowed a bit and kept looking in my mirror. I was nearly at the corner where the road bends right just before you get to St Geniès when I took a last look in the mirror. There were headlights behind me, just past the turning. I am sure that the van must have pulled out into the road and then turned its lights on. It seemed really odd. So I pulled off the road myself, just by the cemetery. A few minutes later, an English-registered furniture van passed me. I felt rather foolish. It was nothing odd after all. Just that Madame Black had decided to start sending her furniture back to England. At the time, I thought I was working too hard, imagining that anything to do with the château was suspicious, and forgot about it. It was only when I got the call from the hospital the other day about the samples and it was clear that she was trying to embezzle you that I got to thinking about this incident again. No wonder the van didn't want to be seen coming from the château if she was stealing your furniture!"

"The scheming cow!"

Joanne banged her fork down on the table. There was a small silence in the café as the English couple with Jim stopped in mid-sentence and stared at Joanne. Only the French salesman continued reading his newspaper and chewing thoughtfully on his steak. Joanne took a deep breath.

"I'm sorry," she said. "It's just that I've been trying very hard to look at this whole mess from Kate's point of view. And as soon as I decide to give her the benefit of the doubt, I find out something else! And when it comes down to it, it always seems she's just after my money. For whatever reason," she finished.

She looked across the room at the back of Jim's head. She was glad to see that he was talking rapidly to his clients again. They had lost interest in her and were hanging on his every word. Phillippe spoke again.

"Madame Carslow, if I may make a suggestion. Put off your visit to Madame Black until tomorrow, or the next day. By then, she will have received Maître Lacombe's letter. She will have had time to take it in. You could telephone her so that your visit is expected. If you are seeing the Agence Sainte Croix this afternoon, I fear you may again feel as you do now. Perhaps you should give yourself time to cool down a little."

Joanne opened her mouth but stopped herself before she uttered the sharp retort that came immediately to her lips. She finished off her glass of wine.

"Yes. I think you are probably right," she said, her composure regained. "Thank you, doctor," she smiled at him. "You have been very helpful."

"It was a pleasure to meet you," he stood up and held out his hand. "I hope we shall meet again."

"I'm sure we will."

She watched as he left the café and crossed the square to his car. Dominic Lefèvre came out of the bank at the same moment and the two men shook hands and stood together, talking and gesturing, on the pavement. She smiled. Frenchmen were so, well, French. But Phillippe was right. She had a feeling that her meeting this afternoon with the estate agent could be difficult and most probably would make her forget any compassion she still had for Kate. Joanne went up to the bar to pay her bill. As she turned to leave the café, she touched Jim's shoulder.

"See you this evening," she smiled, nodding to the English couple.

Jim's dog stood up and nuzzled her, its tail whacking against her leg. She patted the thick white fur.

"See you too," she said to the dog.

4

Leaving the café, Joanne crossed the square to her car. She'd be in Cahors in half an hour, just in time for her meeting. She'd phoned from England to make an appointment, to be sure someone would be there. She'd said she was interested in the château, but she hadn't told them why. She expected that they would have recognised her name, but apparently not. So she had decided to confront them after she had the necessary papers from the notaire to prove what she was about to tell them.

Putting the car into gear, she drove slowly out of Fromac, past the bank and the church, turning left towards the main road. The sky was still a heavy grey, with no sign of the sun coming through the thick, low clouds. Joanne drove along the quiet road, thinking over what Phillippe had said to her. She frowned as she thought about her furniture. She and Nick had bought some of it together, although most of it had been her own choice. It was all high quality, antique French and some Spanish stuff. And some of it very expensive. She had thought she might bring some of it back. Joanne felt a seething fury towards Kate. She seemed determined to get every last penny she could out of Joanne. And she wasn't wasting any time either. Shipping the furniture out the day after her son's funeral! Joanne thought about that as she drove on. Phillippe had said it was an English-registered van. So Kate would have had to have made arrangements in advance. It usually took weeks to arrange something like that. Of course she might have been lucky and the company might have had a van coming back empty from doing a removal to Spain or the south of France. That was unusual though. Joanne knew most companies never sent an empty van back. A van wouldn't usually be sent out until it could come back fully loaded. She might have been lucky, Joanne mused. But if not, it meant she had planned it all before the baby's death! So what did that mean, Joanne puzzled. She intended to move back to England with the baby? Unlikely, unless she had decided to go back to Alastair, but he hadn't heard from her since August. She just needed money so had sold the furniture to a dealer who had arranged the transport? Maybe. Or what if she had planned to kill the baby after all? That's why she refused to take him to hospital, didn't want anyone around at the château, had planned it all in advance. Have the furniture moved out after dark so no one would know. After all, everyone knew there was some doubt if it actually was her property so she'd have to do it secretly. She could disappear on the proceeds and then wait for the château to be sold and a small fortune fall into her hands! Joanne gripped the steering wheel tighter. It seemed all too plausible.

She was coming into Cahors now, passing the row of supermarkets and car showrooms on the outskirts. In a few minutes she'd be in the town centre. She must pull herself together and calm down for her meeting with the estate agent. Crossing the river, she turned right and followed the road along the bank. The river was very high, a wide, chocolate-brown ribbon, flowing swiftly. Joanne found a parking space just before the road left the town again. Locking the car carefully, she crossed the road and climbed the steep hill, emerging at the top of the main boulevard that bisected the town. The old quarter with the cathedral and the market place lay between the boulevard and the river. Joanne turned left, heading down towards the town centre. The estate agents' offices were clustered together at the top of the boulevard. The Agence Sainte Croix stood a little way back from the main street, forming one wall of a small courtyard. A low wall with white-painted iron railings and an imposing iron gate separated the courtyard from the bustle of the street. In contrast to some of the other agencies whose windows were crammed with fading photographs, each of its three windows displayed a single large photograph of a sumptuous château. No prices were shown. Joanne was relieved to see that none of the photographs were of St Geniès-Lafontaine.

She pushed open the big wooden door and found herself in a wide hallway, with an office leading off to either side. A perfectly-coiffured woman sat at a desk in the smaller, right-hand office, whose door stood open. A small notice on her desk read *Accueil*.

Joanne stepped into the office. The woman looked up, inspected Joanne from head to toe, decided that she was a suitable customer, and smiled slightly.

"Good afternoon, Madame. How can I help you?"

"Good afternoon. My name is Joanne Carslow. I have an appointment. Regarding the Château de St Geniès-Lafontaine."

Joanne spoke in perfect French. The woman consulted a large diary, the only item that lay on the antique walnut desk at which she sat.

"Ah yes. Monsieur Bertrand is expecting you. If you would like to follow me."

The woman led the way across the hall and entered a huge room that ran from front to back of the building. The ceiling was high, with intricate moulding around the edge and around the large chandelier that hung from an elaborate central rose. There were four splendid desks arranged at the four corners of the room, each with a smartly-dressed man sitting at it. All four desks had two walnut and leather chairs in front of them. Joanne was surprised to see that three out of the four desks had clients occupying the chairs. The room was warm and tranquil. The receptionist led her over the thick carpet to the desk in the farthest corner of the room. She pulled out a chair for Joanne and stood aside.

"Madame Carslow," she announced.

Jacques Bertrand was a tall, large man in his forties with a shock of black, curly hair. He held out a fat red hand to Joanne.

"Madame," he purred. "Jacques Bertrand. How nice to meet you."

His eyes flicked over her expensive leather jacket, the black Gucci briefcase, her Cartier watch. He licked his lips, the only thin thing about him, Joanne observed. This was the sort of client he liked!

"Please," he said, gesturing to the chair in front of his desk.

"So," he settled himself back in his own leather chair. "You are interested in one of our newest properties, I believe."

He glanced down at a folder open on his desk.

"The Château de St Geniès-Lafontaine. Let me congratulate you on your taste, Madame." He leered at Joanne. "We are just completing the particulars for this property, but already we have so much interest! Just this morning I was there showing the property to clients!"

"Oh, really," Joanne bristled. I must keep calm, she told herself.

"I understand, Monsieur," she said. "That there is some question over the current ownership of the château."

Jacques Bertrand waved a hand, airily dismissing the suggestion with a shrug.

"Ah, I see you may have spoken to the estate agent in Fromac! Madame, it is pique on his part, not to be offered the chance to sell the château! His is a small concern. He has a small town mentality. He is not used to dealing with such prestigious properties, but he feels he has a right to all the properties in that area!"

"So, there is no problem? You are sure?"

"Absolutely, Madame. It is to be sold by an English lady who, tragically, has just lost her husband and her son!"

Jacques allowed himself a small sniff and an ostentatious pause while he apparently composed himself.

"So sad!"

He began laying out a series of photographs of the château on the desk in front of Joanne.

"Indeed it is." Joanne's tone was hard. "Monsieur," she said. "I am afraid I must press you on this matter. I am aware of the lady," she almost spat the word out, but softened her voice for his benefit. Don't want to give the game away yet, she thought. Not until I've found out what tales Kate has been telling.

"I understand that her son is believed to have inherited half of the château from his father."

Jacques nodded.

"But," Joanne went on. "What of the other half? I am aware that this lady was not married to the owner of the château."

"You are correct, Madame. However, the lady tells me that the unreserved portion was to be left to her son and she is in the process of obtaining probate to that effect. It is only a matter of time. Now with the unfortunate demise of her son, the entire château will be hers to dispose of in due course. So she has asked us to market her property now. By the time a buyer is found and all formalities are concluded, then the question of ownership and execution of the will can be expected to have been completed. There is no complication, I assure you."

"I'm sorry to have to tell you this," Joanne said icily. "But there is. There is a severe complication."

"Madame?"

Jacques looked up at her in surprise, his ingratiating smile slipping slightly. Joanne reached for her briefcase.

"The complication is," Joanne glared at the round, supercilious face. "That the Château de St Geniès-Lafontaine actually belongs to me! In its entirety! And you have no right to market it!"

The shock on Jacques' face was genuine. The only genuine thing about him, Joanne thought, relishing the moment. He recovered quickly.

"Please, Madame! That is impossible! What are you saying? I think I may have to ask you to leave," he said, lowering his voice and glancing around the room. Rising from the leather chair, his face darkening, he said, "Please, I will show you out."

He glanced uncomfortably around the room again. All the other clients seemed engrossed in glossy brochures. His colleague at the nearest desk looked up questioningly.

"Monsieur Bertrand, sit down!" Joanne commanded.

Her clear voice cut through the subdued chatter in the room. All heads turned in her direction. Jacques Bertrand subsided into his chair. She took a sheaf of papers from her briefcase.

"This," she said, placing a document in front of him. "This is a copy of the *Acte de Vente* for St Geniès-Lafontaine. As you see, the owner is Nick Carslow. My husband. My late husband. This," she placed a second document alongside it. "This is a copy of his English will, the only one he left, in which he leaves everything to his wife. Me. I am the only living relative of my husband. He had no children, no surviving parent or sibling. A French court has authenticated my husband's English will to apply to his French assets."

She held a third document in the air and placed it on the desk. She sat back, glaring at Jacques.

"Monsieur, you have been misled. The 'English lady' to whom you refer is a fraud. She has no claim to my château whatsoever. You were warned of this by Dominic Lefèvre and you chose to ignore him for your own commercial gain! I order you to remove the château from your books. Now. Immediately. I shall be selling it, but I do not wish to deal with an organization such as yours that acts so incompetently and, yes, unlawfully, that it knowingly offers stolen property for sale!"

No one in the room moved. All eyes were on Joanne as she stood up.

"You may keep these papers," she said. "They are copies. My lawyers will be contacting you shortly. You can expect a substantial claim to be made against the Agence Sainte Croix. You can also expect your reputation to be severely damaged, if not destroyed beyond redemption! Good day."

Turning on her heel, Joanne marched out of the room leaving a stunned silence behind her. Oblivious of the scene, the receptionist glanced up from her empty desk as Joanne opened the outside door.

"Au revoir, Madame!" she sang out. *"Bon après-midi!"*

Out in the street, Joanne took a couple of deep breaths. She realised she was trembling. The cold, damp air folded itself round her as if it would swallow her up. She recalled the beautiful photographs of her château that Jacques Bertrand had spread out before her and suddenly she thought of Nick. Her triumph seemed hollow. The boulevard danced before her through the veil of tears that welled up in her eyes. For the first time in ages she just wanted to curl up by herself somewhere, give in to self-pity for her loss, and weep. An agitated voice behind her made her turn, quickly wiping her eyes with the back of her gloved hand.

"Madame, please!"

It was Jacques Bertrand, breathing heavily and sweating slightly from the exertion of running after her up the street. Gasping for breath, he babbled:

"Please, Madame! I cannot tell you how sorry we are that this has happened! I assure you that the Agence Sainte Croix is totally, totally innocent! We had no reason to doubt Mrs Black's word. Nothing could have alerted us to her deception!" He paused for breath. "Please return to our office for one moment, Madame. I am sure that we can sort this out amicably, without the need for lawyers. We have been misled by Mrs Black. It is she who is to blame…."

Joanne allowed herself to be led back to the Agence. As they approached, she saw the receptionist standing at the open door, anxiously peering out. Her haughty indifference had now disappeared as she held the door open and almost curtseyed as Joanne entered. This time she was shown through the receptionist's office to an inner sanctum guarded by the woman, who now brought coffee for Joanne. The door closed, leaving Jacques outside with the receptionist. A tall, distinguished-looking man rose from behind an even bigger walnut desk.

"Fabian Sainte Croix, at your service, Madame."

He spoke in faultless English.

"I cannot begin to apologise to you for this unfortunate incident."

Sometime later, Joanne emerged from the Agence again, this time feeling much better. In her handbag was a cheque for fifty thousand euros. She knew she could have got more, a lot more, through her lawyers but, in a way, this was more satisfying. And it meant it was all over quickly. For some reason that puzzled Joanne slightly, Kate had told the agent not to send any clients to view the château until the following week. That meant no one had yet been round to look at it, despite what Jacques had said. The Agence had agreed to remove all their advertising immediately and to tell any clients who showed interest that the château was no longer for sale through them. Joanne was pleased. She hadn't wanted a long drawn-out legal case. It was nice and tidy now. All that remained for her to do was to see Kate. Then she could go home and wait for Dominic Lefèvre to sell the château. If there was any furniture left, she'd get Jim Munro to sell it for her and that would be that. It would all be over.

5

It was starting to get dark by the time she reached her car. She felt exhausted and glad that Phillippe had persuaded her to postpone visiting Kate until tomorrow. Leaving Cahors, she began signalling right, preparing to turn off towards Fromac at the roundabout. On impulse she cancelled the signal and drove straight on, keeping to the main road. A few miles further on, she turned right down a small, narrow road. Soon she was skirting the hill to which the village of St Geniès clung. She drove slowly up the winding road, past the church and into the big square. The street lights were already on. The big clock on the tower of the *hôtel de ville* struck six o'clock. Everywhere was deserted. Even the two cafés appeared to be closed. A few minutes later, she was out of the village again, and the turning to the château was just up ahead. There was barely enough light, she thought, but at least Kate wouldn't see her. She only wanted to take a quick look at the château, on her own. Turning down the unmade road, she passed the two modern bungalows, both in darkness. Just after the track narrowed where it entered her property, Joanne slowed the car. She'd go on foot from here. She didn't want Kate to hear the car or see her lights and come out. Not today. Joanne wasn't ready to face her yet. She pulled off the road on to a small, grassy track that led downwards through the trees. Cutting the engine, she sat for a few minutes, listening to the complete quiet of the countryside. She pulled on her gloves and got out of the car, leaving the keys in the ignition. She'd only be a few minutes.

It was getting colder now, and the sky seemed to be clearing a bit. There was just enough light left for her to be able to follow the white chalk track downhill towards the château. She was glad it was fairly dry underfoot. Her heart was beating fast as she approached the bend in the track from where she knew she'd get her first glimpse of it. It was so long since she'd been here. So much had happened since that day, a lifetime ago, when she'd turned that corner and seen the château for the first time.

Suddenly, there it was, way below her, a ghostly shape amidst the dark trees. She couldn't see any lights on in the château. Beyond it, where she knew the lake lay, was inky blackness. It made her shiver slightly. She stood on the edge of the track, looking down, for a few long moments. An owl hooted nearby. There was no other sound.

Turning to go, a sudden flash of light caught her eye. The kitchen door at the back of the château had been opened and Joanne could see a figure silhouetted in the doorway. Peering into the darkness, she was surprised to see that it was a man. The man came out into the courtyard, followed by a second, then a third. The door closed, but Joanne could see that they carried a powerful torch. The pinpoint of light bobbed around and then disappeared. Joanne realised they must have gone into the old coach house. It had been Nick's own special project and he had lovingly restored the beautiful woodwork himself, with the help of a couple of local artisans. They had intended to use it as a garage when they were at the château.

Joanne peered down into the darkness, curious to see what was going on. A few minutes later, there was a splash of light as the kitchen door opened again. One of the men went back in, leaving the door open. Seconds later, he came out, carrying a large package, or sack, of some sort, and disappeared towards the coach house. Another figure went into the kitchen, emerging almost immediately carrying a similar load. This went on for several minutes, as Joanne watched, baffled. Did these packages contain all her silverware and ornaments? Remembering what the doctor had told her, it seemed as if they could be being loaded into a van or something parked in the coach house. It was certainly big enough to take a furniture van comfortably.

Was Kate planning on selling off all Joanne's stuff as well as the furniture? It certainly looked like it.

She thought about going back up to her car and calling the police. But what if it was only, say, Kate's own stuff that they were moving? In the end, curiosity got the better of her and she made her way silently towards the château. She branched off down a track to the left which ran round the side of the coach house She moved quickly and quietly, keeping to the edge of the track so that she could easily dodge behind the trees if anyone came her way. She remembered that there was a small, horizontal window only a metre or so off the ground at the corner, on the track side of the coach house. The path from the kitchen door led around the other side of the building to the wide entrance on the lower side, away from the main track. So long as Joanne kept to her side of the building, she shouldn't bump into any of the men, or Kate. She would be able to peer in through the low window and see what was going on.

Everything was in darkness now. When she judged that she was nearly opposite the window, she darted across the track and stood silently against the side of the building for a few moments. Then she crouched down and peered in. The coach house was built into the side of the hill below which the château stood. Joanne's window looked down from some five metres or so above the floor level. Inside the building stood a large removal van, its open back doors facing Joanne. Several of her best pieces of furniture stood alongside the van, and inside it she could just see what looked like the end of her four-poster bed. She had been right. Kate was certainly determined to get as much as she could out of her. Joanne shifted her position to get a better look at what was in the van. Kate wasn't taking any chances of getting caught, she thought. There was no electricity as yet in the coach house, Joanne knew. She wondered why Kate had thought it necessary to wait until after dark to load the van. It seemed excessively cautious when Phillippe had said that hardly anyone ever came to the château anyway.

In front of her, the two men who had been loading furniture into the van by the light of powerful torches climbed out and a third man got in. He seemed to be carrying what looked like a crowbar. Joanne craned forward to see what he was doing. He seemed to be doing something to the floor of the van. He said something to the other two. As she watched, the bigger man took something out of his pocket. She saw the glint of a blade as he split open one of the sacks that she had seen them carrying out of the kitchen. He started passing a series of smaller, plastic-wrapped parcels to the other man, who handed them up to the man inside the van. He appeared to be reaching down into some sort of hole in the floor of the van. Joanne suddenly realised that the floor of the van seemed higher than it should be from the outside. They were filling a compartment under the van floor with the packages. She watched, fascinated, as package after package went in. Then the man inside the van replaced the floor and the other two hauled her Louis XIV armoire into the van, positioning it on top of the compartment. Another few items of furniture went in, then the man with the crowbar climbed in again. There was evidently a series of hidden compartments all along the length of the van. Joanne sat back on her heels for a moment, her heart beating faster. What was going on? It seemed obvious that something illegal was going into the van along with her furniture. What could it be? The parcels were too small for alcohol. Cigarettes? Drugs? Yes, she thought. It had to be drugs. She'd seen plastic-wrapped packages like these on the TV news when there'd been a big drugs raid. God, she thought, not quite able to take it all in. What was Kate mixed up in? Turning back to the window, she could see that the van was about three quarters full now. The last few pieces of furniture in the coach house were going in. Time to make her way back to her car. She'd have to be careful. If she was right and these were drugs, she didn't fancy her chances if she was caught snooping. She'd have to get the van's registration number first though. As soon as they shut the van doors she'd be able to see the plate properly. The two men inside the van jumped out and began to close the doors.

Joanne didn't hear the man with the crowbar coming down the track behind her. She had just got the registration number and started to turn away from the window when she felt the blow across the back of her skull. That was all. She felt nothing more.

****

When she came to, Joanne was lying on an icy-cold stone floor. She tried to move her legs and arms but didn't seem able to sit up. Something was holding her down. Eventually, she raised herself up on to one elbow and finally wriggled into a sitting position. She tried to get to her feet, but fell back onto the hard stone. It was dark, but as she felt down her leg to her left ankle, she touched the thick chain that was wound round it, and could just make out that the other end of the chain was fixed to the wall. She couldn't feel any sensation in her leg. Sitting up as best she could, she rubbed it and gradually a bit of feeling came back. Edging slowly and painfully across the floor towards the wall, she managed to get enough slack in the chain to be able to sit with her back supported by the wall. When the back of her head touched the uneven surface of the rough-hewn stones of the wall, she almost lost consciousness again. Closing her eyes, Joanne dropped her head forward. Where on earth was she? What had happened? She remembered leaving the car to take a look at the château. Then she'd seen the men moving around and had gone down to the coach house to see what they were doing. Then someone had hit her hard from behind. And now she must be somewhere in the château, she was sure. But where? There were so many outbuildings. She opened her eyes again gingerly. Any movement of her head was excruciatingly painful. It was very dark around her, but in front of her there seemed to be a doorway, through which she thought she could make out a couple of areas of dim light in what she took to be the ceiling of the adjoining room. Sky lights? Was she in one of the towers? No, the floor was too cold. She must be in a cellar. She closed her eyes again against the pain. For a few minutes she sat there, unable to think. As she sat silently, she became aware of something else. The smell. She knew that smell. Wine. Old, fusty wine. As her eyes adjusted, she saw the row of oak barrels. She was in the wine cellar of the château! Then another sensation came to her, as she continued to sit against the wall, her head dropped forward onto her knees. There was someone else in the cellar with her!

Joanne sat very still. What if it was the person who hit her, waiting for her to come round so they could interrogate her? They might want to know how much she'd seen. Once they found out who she was, they might – what? Kill her, Joanne thought in panic. They'd find her car. Probably already had. She'd left her bag in it and everything! Oh God, what was she going to do?

A quiet voice from somewhere fairly near stopped her train of thought. Joanne's eyes flew open.

"Joanne?" the voice said. "Are you – awake? Are you all right? Can you move at all?"

She knew that voice. It was Kate.

Now that her eyes had got used to the darkness of the cellar, Joanne could just make out Kate's pale face about two metres away from her. Kate too was chained to the cellar wall. The chains round both their ankles seemed new and shiny. They were attached to the big old iron rings on the wall of the cellar. Joanne remembered Nick telling her that he thought they had been used for hauling the wine barrels into position. Joanne's heart leapt when she saw that she was chained to the old rings. They'd been there for ages and would be rusty by now. She was strong. She should be able to pull the ring out of the wall. But of course she couldn't.

She sank back against the wall and looked over in Kate's direction. Christ, the last person she'd choose to be locked up in a cellar with.

"What's happened, Kate? Who were those men? What on earth is going on?"

"Oh, Joanne," Kate's voice was a whisper. "It's all my fault. The whole thing. And if it wasn't bad enough, now you're trapped here as well. We'll never get out. I don't care for myself, I deserve it. But you don't...."

"Kate, for God's sake!" Joanne broke in angrily. "Stop whining!"

That was all she needed. Kate snivelling all night. What had Nick seen in her?

"Of course we'll get out. You're lucky I am here," she added sarcastically. "People will miss me. They'll come and look for me. Several people know I was coming here tomorrow. They'll find us."

"Oh, I hope so. I've got to get out of here. But I didn't even know this cellar existed," Kate said. "I'd never seen it before."

"Well, we'll just have to make sufficient noise when they come looking for us so that they do find us," Joanne replied briskly. "I suppose you realise we're under the outbuildings on the other side of the courtyard outside the kitchen, don't you? But no one's likely to come until the morning. I doubt I'll be missed before then. So you might as well tell me what's going on. Who are those men?"

A thought suddenly struck Joanne.

"Can we be sure they won't come back tonight?"

"Yes. I'm sure," Kate answered. "They've got what they want. They won't be back now. But I can't wait until morning!" Kate was getting hysterical. "I've got to get out before then and see if Richard is alright!"

"Richard!" Joanne exclaimed. "Richard! For God's sake! What's he got to do with it? I thought he'd disappeared. What on earth is going on? Who are those men? What were they doing? I saw all my furniture going into the van, but I also saw them concealing stuff under the floor."

"No wonder they brought you down here," Kate said. "You probably guessed if you saw it. They're smuggling hashish. Tons of it."

"But what is it doing here?"

"It's a long story," Kate sighed. "But I have to get out of here," she whispered, frantically pulling at the iron ring that held her chain. "I have to get out and help Richard. He was badly hurt in the storm. You know, in August. In fact he's nearly paralysed. I don't know what they've done to him. They might have taken him with them, or just left him. But he can't look after himself. He needs his medicines. I have to get to him, I have to! I can't let him die! I owe him!" Kate's voice broke and Joanne could hear her sobbing in the gloom.

"I don't pretend to see how Richard fits into all of this," Joanne said. "Still, everything seemed to have turned out right for you – up till now. Telling everyone that your own husband's baby was Nick's. It was a good plan to get your hands on my château, and it nearly worked. You even started selling off my furniture, then you thought …yes, of course, you did do it! You did kill your own baby!"

"No, Joanne, no!" Kate cried. "How could you think that?"

But Joanne rushed on.

"You got fed up with it being sick all the time, attracting attention from the doctor and everyone – so you did it! You thought it would all be yours then! Nick's money that he had in France and the château! All the furniture! Well, you were wrong! The French authorities hadn't got round to doing anything about your application to overturn Nick's will before I found out what was going on! I saw the advert for my château in a magazine! That was your big mistake, Kate. You should have put it with a smaller estate agency that didn't advertise outside France. Then I'd never have seen it until was too late. But Alastair has told me everything! And tomorrow you'll get a letter from Maître Lacombe telling you the birth of your son has been re-registered with the correct parental details and telling you to get out of my château! You might as well know that the

Agence Sainte Croix has taken it off its books and you're lucky they aren't taking you to court. You're lucky I'm not, as well!"

"Joanne, please. Please listen. You're wrong, you don't realise ….."

"Look, Kate," Joanne said. "I was prepared to think the best of you. Despite what you did, running off with Nick. I knew he wasn't innocent. I was even prepared to let you stay on in the château because I thought it was Nick's baby and I knew you had nowhere to go. Even when I found out that it was really Alastair's baby and that all you seemed to be interested in was getting hold of my château and my money, I still felt sorry for you, on your own and your baby dying. I'd decided this morning that you'd paid a high enough price. But now, it's all fallen into place! You're a pretty good actress, Kate! Alastair, Phillippe de la Bernière, even me, until now, thought you'd suffered enough. I should have listened to Jim Munro and the others! When we get out of here, I am going to make sure you pay for this, Kate! You planned everything, just out of sheer greed! And to cap it all, you're part of a drugs smuggling gang! I certainly would never have guessed that! And of course the château's an ideal place to hide stuff!"

Joanne sat back against the rough wall of the cellar. She stared up at the vaulted ceiling, her eyes filling with tears. How could she have been so wrong about Kate? She'd never liked her much, that was true. But she'd been totally taken in by Kate's dreaminess, never imagining for a single moment, even right up until now, that it masked such a cold and calculating heart.

After a few minutes, Kate spoke again.

"I don't blame you for thinking this, Joanne. You've got every right to hate me, and to blame me for what's happened. But it's not what you think. Please listen to me. I want you to hear the truth. I don't expect you to forgive me, but at least perhaps you can understand."

There was no reply from Joanne. Kate took a deep breath and started to explain…..

"I fell in love with Nick almost as soon as I met him," she said simply. "I don't know why, but I just wanted to be with him all the time. I still loved Alastair, but I was infatuated with Nick. Anyway, Richard obviously noticed." She gave a feeble little laugh. "Alastair didn't, of course, but Richard did. Richard and Alastair met a long time ago and Alastair is the one person in his whole life that he's formed any real relationship with at all. He trusted him implicitly and would have done anything for him. Of course, I had no idea that Richard knew about me and Nick. But he was outraged and couldn't bear to see me betray his friend. Then one night," Kate swallowed hard. "I had arranged to meet Nick in your barn. It was dark. I was waiting for him inside. I heard a noise outside and thought it was him, but no one came in. Eventually I went to investigate and there was Nick, lying on the ground with a deep wound on his head. What I didn't know, until the day Nick fell over the balustrade, was that Richard had overheard me and Nick arranging to meet in the barn. Richard had been waiting outside for Nick and had hit him with a shovel. He wanted to stop me and Nick. Stop me cheating on Alastair. The only way he could think of was to warn Nick off," Kate's voice tailed off.

There was silence in the cellar. Kate wouldn't see Joanne clearly, but she could sense that she was staring at her in amazement.

"Good God! So Richard had tried to kill Nick, even before you went to France! How did you find out?" she asked.

"It was when he and Alastair came out here to bring me back in the spring. Richard did come out here wanting to hurt Nick. After he realized that what happened at the barn hadn't been enough to stop our affair, he came out with Alastair because he wanted to get rid of Nick for Alastair's sake – I really don't think he wanted to kill him, just really hurt him, enough to warn him off. So he bought a knuckleduster in Cahors on the way to the château. And he hit Nick with it. But the rest was an accident. Please believe me, Joanne. Nick just fell against the balustrade and it gave way. Richard was horrified when Nick fell and it was then that he told me about the barn, just before the gendarmes arrived. They took him and Alastair away for questioning. The local gendarmes were determined to pin Nick's death on them. They held them for as long as they could but in the end they had to let them go. Richard and Alastair just fled back to England as fast as they could before the police dreamed up any other charges. Of course, although I'd been sure the baby was Nick's, as soon as I saw him I knew he was Alastair's. And yes, Joanne, you are right. I lied to the doctor when he asked for the father's name. He assumed it was Nick's and told me not to be ashamed if he was not my husband. He explained about French inheritance laws and how important it was for the child. I know I did wrong, but I had nothing, nowhere to go. I knew that Alastair wouldn't want me back, even if I'd told him he was the father of my baby. I don't think he'd even have believed me. All I could think of was putting a roof over my baby's head. I'm sorry, Joanne. I am truly sorry. When you didn't try to get me out of the château, I thought that you must have been told that the French courts had thrown out Nick's will and given all his French estate to my baby. I didn't tell Alastair, although I wanted to. I knew that I was to blame. If it hadn't been for the way I behaved with Nick, Richard would never have done what he did. I thought it would be better for both Alastair and Richard if they never heard from me again. Then when they turned up on the night of the storm, I didn't know what to think. When they saw the baby they both realised that it was Alastair's."

"I know the rest," Joanne said. "Alastair told me. But how did you find Richard again? And where do those men and the drugs come into all this?"

"It's a long story," Kate replied.

"We've got all night. Unfortunately," sighed Joanne wearily.

PART V

This year

1

France, August.

The wave thwacked into the side of the small boat, tossing it up into the air. Richard was hurled out into the dark water, still desperately hanging on to the oar. The current swept him forwards. Through the driving rain, he just had time to make out the white foam where the water hit the weir before he was dragged towards it and engulfed in the crazy, deafening surge of water. Somehow, he managed to hang on to his oar. It snapped in two as one end hit a submerged rock. He felt a sickening wrench as his left leg caught in something and the rest of his body was swept onwards by the torrent. The pain passed through his body with an intensity that made him cry out above the cacophony of the wind and rain and water. The churning water closed over his head, the force of it dragging him forward.

When he surfaced, he could feel the cold numbness in his leg. Somehow, his head was above the water again. He was in the river on the other side of the weir. The water swept him forwards, onwards and onwards. Richard lost consciousness again for a few seconds, but, coming to, was aware that he still had part of the oar in his grip. Powerless to fight the current, he tried to concentrate on keeping his head above the water, holding his breath when a wave engulfed him again. His remaining strength was ebbing fast. He was swept around a wide bend in the river at a frightening speed. Suddenly, a tree, uprooted by the storm, loomed in front of him. There was nothing he could do. The force of the current flung him at the tree. His head smashed into a thick branch, he lost his grip on the oar and everything went black.

A very long way away, far in the distance, Richard heard a voice calling his name. He opened his mouth to call back, but no sound came. He tried to get to his feet to run towards the voice, but he didn't seem to be able to move his legs. He opened his eyes and felt the steady rain falling on his face. His body seemed to be entwined in the branches of a tree. It was still very dark. He managed to raise himself to a sitting position. His head throbbed painfully and every inch of his arms and back ached. He winced with pain as he tried to wriggle out of the embrace of the tree, his legs dragging behind him. Something was stopping him. Glancing behind, Richard could just make out his left leg, caught on a broken branch. But he couldn't feel anything. With his last remaining strength, he heaved himself forward and eventually he was clear of the tree. Laying panting with the effort of freeing himself, he peered around in the dark. He remembered everything that had happened up until he had hit the tree. Now he was lying on a small strip of white pebbles at the edge of the river, swollen from the storm and flowing swiftly. He sat still and listened. Had he really heard a voice calling to him, or had it been his imagination? All he could hear now was the river and the wind. The rain had nearly stopped and the wind was getting quieter. He strained his ears. There was no human sound. Peering back up river, he could see nothing but blackness. He tried to estimate how far away from the château he had been carried by the current. He had no idea where he was.

Then he remembered John Nicholson, the man in the old Land Rover. He'd told Richard that he had a barn somewhere near the château. He'd said his land joined onto the château's, by the river. Richard felt a glimmer of hope. If only he could find his way to John's barn, he felt sure that John would help him. He remembered that the barn was on a hillside, above the river. If he could make his way along the bank, sooner or later he'd see it. Even in the dark, its silhouette would show up against the sky. He didn't know which side of the river he was on. He thought he was probably on the opposite bank from the barn, but if he could spot it in the dark, he could wait there until morning and John or his children would be bound to see him. Richard looked back up the river. He didn't know how far from the château lake he'd been carried, but somehow he felt it couldn't be far. John's barn must lie further downstream. With a huge effort, he hauled himself up the soft, slippery bank and onto thick, wet grass. After resting a few minutes, he started to wriggle his body forward along the bank, dragging his inert legs behind him, away from the château.

At about the same time, John Nicholson stood watching the small blob of light from Alastair's torch retreating along the river bank towards the château. John stayed on the bank for a few minutes, looking away from the château towards the big bend in the river a couple of hundred metres downstream. It looked like there was a big tree down across the river there, but it was too dark to see properly. It might make the river flood his land. But so what, John thought. The barn was well up the hillside out of range. He'd go down in the morning and see if he could shift it. It might be good for logs for the fire next year if he could get at it. He turned and set off back along the bank and up the hill to the barn.

Downstream, round the bend in the river, Richard made slow but steady progress away from the château and the barn. It was relatively easy going on the cushiony grass if he stopped every few minutes for a rest. It couldn't be very long before he'd be able to see John's barn, so he could take his time. He felt tired, but quite optimistic now. He'd be able to sleep on the bank until daylight, once he knew he could be seen from the barn.

Sometime later, Richard stopped and sat up on the bank. The worst of the storm had passed and a few stars were showing between the breaks in the clouds. He'd lost all track of time, but he was beginning to fear that he must have missed the barn. He was expecting to have come across it by now. Should he turn back and retrace his path, or go on a bit further? He was dog-tired now. He had no feeling in his left leg at all, and his right was cold and numb. But the aches in the rest of his body made up for it. By now his forearms and hands were shaking from the effort of hauling himself along. He needed to rest, to sleep. Now that the rain had stopped, the night air was quite mild. He felt a warm, seductive breeze ruffle through his hair. If he just slept for a few hours, he'd feel so much better, then he could go on. Richard shook his head to clear it. He was sweating profusely, but his skin felt quite cold, despite his exertions and the mildness of the summer night. His mind told him that this was a bad sign and he must get himself somewhere he'd be found as soon as it was light. Peering into the darkness once more, hoping for sight of the barn, out of the corner of his eye he caught a tiny flash of light in the darkness. There it was again. It looked like a torch. Perhaps it was John or one of the children. It was quite a long way from him, and seemed to be on the same side of the bank as he was. It had to be the barn. John had said it was isolated with no near neighbours except the château. There it was again. Then he saw a larger glimmer of light, and then the torch light and it disappeared again. Yes, thought Richard. That's it. That's the barn door being opened and closed behind the person with the torch. He gathered all his remaining strength and set off again, heading directly towards where the light had been.

Quite suddenly, the moon appeared briefly. In its light Richard saw, to his relief, the dark outline of a building, not far ahead, nearer than he'd expected and to his right. This must be it. He knew he'd been moving up a slope, but not a steep incline as he'd expected from John's description. It didn't matter. This was it. He'd just about had it. One last effort and he could make it to the barn door.

The grass was short here, the ground almost bare in places and becoming much steeper. Hauling himself up over the stony surface was excruciatingly painful. Sharp little chips of chalk cut into his hands and arms. The shape of the building above and in front of him started to dance. Richard stopped, his breath coming in wrenching gasps. He was barely four metres from the building now, but he couldn't make out the door. It must be on this side, because this was where he'd seen the light. At that moment, a shaft of light appeared directly in front of him. Richard could make out a rough-hewn stone lintel. A figure ducked out through the doorway and straightened up in front of the building. The figure towered above the top of the building. Richard's heart lurched. The figure was a giant, a monster. Richard collapsed in an inert heap, sending a shower of stones rattling down the slope.

The next thing he knew, he was lying face down on hard, flattened earth, in some sort of stone building. He could hear voices that seemed to be echoing in his head. It was light in this building, a sort of golden, mellow light. Richard groaned. The voices stopped. He closed his eyes again. The voices started again. This time he knew they were real and they were in the building with him.

"So what are we going to do about him?" a man's voice asked.

"Leave him," came the reply. "We don't know who he is. We don't know how long he'd been out there, so we don't know what he's seen. By the looks of him, he won't last too long anyway. We'll just leave him here. No one's going to come down here, that's what we're banking on, isn't it? So we might as well just leave him. Better gag him and tie him up, just in case, although it doesn't look like he's going far."

"Yeah, right."

Richard's arms were pulled roughly behind him and a cord tightened round his bruised and battered wrists. Something was thrust into his mouth. As the gag was tightened behind his head a pain seared though his neck and everything went black again.

Sometime later, he regained consciousness and cautiously opened his eyes. It was dark now inside the building. He was lying on his side, his arms twisted behind him. Gradually his eyes became accustomed to the gloom and he could make out a few random chinks of light. It must be after dawn. Looking up above him, the stone ceiling and the walls seemed to slope inwards. Richard shut his eyes, thinking he was going to faint again. When he opened them again, the ceiling was still sloping. Puzzled, he peered upwards. Eventually he realised that the ceiling actually did slope away from its apex, in a cone shape. He was lying in what seemed to be a small, circular cell, shaped like a pointed dome. Like the Buddhist stupas he'd seen in a film on TV about Nepal. This one seemed to be built entirely of small stones, packed together like in a jigsaw puzzle. Like the dry stone walls you get in Yorkshire, he thought. Only smaller stones. He could make out a couple of rough beams going across the space above his head where the walls started narrowing towards the apex of the dome. There were no windows, just a doorway on one side, with a stone lintel and a dark wooden door. He struggled into a sitting position. The ceiling seemed to slope very close to his head. So the doorway was actually little more than a metre high. No wonder he'd thought he's seen a giant coming out last night. Was it last night? How long had he been here? And where on earth was he? Who were those men who had tied him up? And why? He lay back on the floor. He felt terrible. Every inch of his upper body ached. He could hardly bear to move his head and neck. What worried him most was his left leg. He couldn't feel it at all. His right leg was still numb, but he could move his foot slightly. What an idiot he'd been, running off like that.

Richard looked around his cell. He couldn't help admiring the workmanship of the crude shelter. It was just a pile of stones, no mortar or anything. He could not make out where he could be. Certainly not in John Nicholson's barn. But his cell did seem to be some sort of farm building. Perhaps it was near to the barn. When it was properly light he'd crawl outside and see if he could raise John. It was very quiet. His eyes were becoming accustomed to the dim light now. The cell was about three metres in diameter. He was lying up against the wall. Opposite him was a big pile of what looked like sacks, reaching up to the sloping ceiling. Richard shivered on the damp earth.

He'd work his way to the sacks and pull a few of them over him to keep warm. He could probably manage that, even with his hands bound. It took a few minutes to manoeuvre himself into position, but eventually he managed to get a purchase on the corner of the top sack and pulled. It slipped off the pile easily and flopped down over his shoulder. He wriggled round to grab another. No luck this time. His hands contacted a slippery surface. It felt like plastic. Fairly solid. It must be fertiliser, or some farm chemical, Richard thought. Damn. He'd have to make do with the one sack that had been covering the plastic sacks of chemicals. He edged back against the wall on his side of the cell and arranged himself on the sack. That was a bit better. It was getting lighter now. He took a closer look at the plastic sacks. He could just about make out what it said on the side: *Nitrophoska bleu spécial*. Yes, they must be fertiliser. Phophate or nitrate, something like that. Richard felt a wave of relief. He must be in one of John Nicholson's outbuildings. Or even if he'd somehow missed John's barn, he must be on another farm. He'd be able to get help from the farmhouse. Even with his arms bound, he'd be able to crawl out. Whoever had tied him up was long gone. He'd heard them say 'leave him'.

When he opened his eyes, the shape of the door of the cell was outlined by a narrow strip of dazzling light. He must have been asleep for a while. The sun must be fully up. Richard struggled into a sitting position. His head swam and his breath was coming in short gasps. He felt far worse now. He must get help. Somehow he managed to inch his way across the floor towards the door. Eventually he reached it and lay still for a while, his head resting against the rough wood. Gathering his remaining strength, he pushed against it. Nothing happened. He pushed again, as hard as he could manage. Nothing. In a panic, Richard looked all over the door for a latch or other fastening to undo. But there was none. One final shove and he heard, with a desperate sinking feeling, the clank of a chain on the outside of the door. He was locked in.

2

"So what's going on, Salome? What's with all the gendarmes and police?"

The man in sunglasses jerked his head towards the road out of the square, up which two police vans and a squad car were moving as quickly as the Sunday market crowds would allow.

"Poof! I thought you had not noticed me today!" replied Salome, tossing her black hair back out of her eyes. "It's the missing Englishman. They have decided something suspicious has happened to him and they've started a search. It was on the radio this morning. They're even sending divers up to the lake at the château! And they are searching all the countryside and asking all the farmers around St Geniès to check their outbuildings for him. Exciting, yes?"

"Yes," replied the man slowly. "Bring me another beer, would you, darlin'?"

"Of course," Salome put her tray down on the table. "But don't you want to know all about this scandal? I will tell you. Earlier this year, the man who owns the château came out from England with a woman who is pregnant and isn't his wife."

The man half-listened as Salome told her tale, his mind racing. So, the police were searching the area. This was bad news. More than half the hash was stacked up in the *gariotte* near the château. They hadn't been back since they'd moved the stuff over from the house at Lalbenque on the night of the storm. Just as well they'd split the consignment. With police swarming all over the place it was going to be difficult to move it again and it wasn't safe to do a delivery yet. All the roads in the area and the airports were being watched, as well as the Channel ports. Still, the police here were looking for a missing person, not drugs. But they might still have dogs. Suddenly he was aware of what Salome was saying.

"Salome, you say this missing person is English?"

"Of course! You have not been paying me any attention!" she pouted.

"Of course I have!"

He put down his glass and smiled at her, focussing on her breasts, straining against the thin material of her tight, pink T-shirt. He put out a hand and stroked her wrist.

"Now, Salome! Tell me about this guy. I might know him. What does he look like?"

"Here!" She thrust a small poster at him. "You know him?"

He shook his head.

"Never seen him before in my life."

Shit. It had to be him, didn't it? This job was jinxed. The bloke they'd found outside the *gariotte*, half-dead, just had to be the one the police were searching for.

"See you later, Salome! Keep that beer ready for me, and have one yourself!"

He stood up and dropped a few notes on the table. Salome pocketed them and smiled up at him.

"And you haven't forgotten what you said the other night about getting me a job in England, have you? I have to get away from this boring place before I kill myself!" she ended dramatically.

Before he could reply, the patron called to Salome from the bar.

"Please," she implored. "You see how it is. He is always on at me for something or other. He never criticizes his precious Martine!"

She glared across the café terrace to where Martine was serving the doctor and his English girlfriend. The patron called to Salome again and she flounced into the bar, leaving the man to make his way across the square to his car.

He drove fast, passing several police cars before he left St Geniès behind and was well on the way to Fromac. It seemed quiet here, he noticed. The search seemed concentrated around St Geniès and the château. Shit. He'd wanted to move the stuff over to the house at Fromac, but the others had said no. Not where they'd been staying. Not if it might implicate Mother. Frank had known about this isolated *gariotte* and it seemed like a good idea at the time. He turned off the main road just outside Fromac and headed up onto the plateau. Soon he was bumping down the long track to Frank's mother's place. The German Shepherd announced his arrival long before the big, new house came into view. Mother was sitting on the terrace with a gin and tonic in her podgy, bejewelled hand. Frank and Jimmy were there too, bottles of beer in hand. Looked just like they were on holiday.

"Hello, son!" Dora shouted as he got out of the car and walked over to them. "Come and have a drink!"

"Thanks, Dora."

He swaggered over to them, bending to kiss Dora's flabby cheek.

"Frank, Jimmy. We need to talk. I just heard something in the café and I don't like it one little bit."

"I'll go and get you a beer."

Dora swung her fat legs off the sun-lounger and padded around the edge of the swimming pool and up the steps to the kitchen terrace. She disappeared inside.

"So what's up, Vin?" Frank asked.

When Vin had told them, the three sat in silence for a few minutes. Then Frank spoke.

"No choice then. We've got to move it again. And we can't risk the farmer or the plods finding our friend. We don't know what he saw."

"He might be dead by now," Jimmy said hopefully.

"If he is, and they find him, they'll be after us for murder as well as drugs!"

"OK, but where do we move it to?

"Not here, for a start. Can't have Ma mixed up in this."

"No, 'course not."

"Vin. Any ideas?"

"Yes, as a matter of fact. I've been thinking about what Salome said. The police have been searching the château and its grounds and the lake today, right? That's where they started, yeah? They haven't looked anywhere else yet. And they'll not have found him at the château, so they won't be looking there again. I say we move the stuff tonight. To the château."

Frank nodded slowly. "I see where you're coming from."

Jimmy shook his head in disbelief. "What! Are you both bonkers? That mad English woman who lives there's going to go along with that, isn't she?"

"Don't be daft, Jimmy! She won't know, it's a big place. We can hide it in the grounds somewhere," said Frank.

"Yes, she will know, Frank. That's the beauty of it," Vin interrupted.

They both looked at him.

"We move the stuff and we move the guy. We knock on the front door of the château and we say, excuse me, Madame, but here we have your good friend – remember what Salome said about the gendarmes thinking that her husband might have killed this guy and that she was mixed up in it too – and if you don't let us stash our dope in your château until it's safe to make a delivery, we'll kill him and dump the body where the police will find it. Then the police will arrest your husband, or maybe even you, for murder. And if you go to the police, we'll take you out as well. Then the police will arrest your husband on a double murder charge. And she'll say: 'Come on in, gentlemen. Have a cup of tea.'"

Frank took off his sunglasses.

"I like it," he said. "Yes, I like it. The château is isolated, she's a bit of a recluse, no friends after what she's been up to. And it's handy there's a kid involved as well. More opportunities there for persuasion. Should we need them."

****

A sound like someone putting a key into a lock made Richard start. He had been drifting in and out of sleep, in and out of consciousness. He had no idea how long he'd been lying on the floor of his stone cell. At first he'd tried to keep a tally of the days. Now he wasn't sure if it was a couple of days or weeks that he'd been in the cell, without food or fresh water. He wasn't hungry, and he'd soon discovered that water dripped into the cell through small holes between the stones in the dome. He'd just had to wriggle into the right position, then open his mouth and the rain water had dripped conveniently into his mouth. It tasted awful, but he didn't care. His left leg was still without any feeling, and the rest of him ached, but not so bad now. He couldn't feel much at all. He opened his eyes and focussed on the doorway. A rattle of the chain confirmed that someone was outside. It was dark, but he could make out the edge of the door. The person outside had a torch. They were opening the door, very quietly. Richard lay there watching as two figures ducked into the cell. A torch was shone in his face.

"Get up."

A boot nudged his left leg. Richard saw his leg move, but felt nothing. The boot connected again. His leg was kicked into the air. He felt nothing. From somewhere he heard his own voice, thin, rasping.

"I can't."

"Leave him, Jimmy. Get this stuff out of here and into the van."

Richard watched as the larger of the two figures started to heave the blue plastic fertiliser sacks out through the door. No one spoke anymore. The smaller of the two figures left the cell.

It didn't take long before the whole stack of sacks had been moved. The two men came back into the cell.

"OK. Now him."

It was the smaller figure who spoke. The other one bent over Richard and dragged him, feet first, out through the door. His head bumped painfully along the ground. A nail in the door jamb caught his right leg, ripping through his trousers. Richard felt the pain of the nail cutting into his flesh and gasped with relief. At least his right leg had some feeling in it. Outside, the man released his legs and slung Richard over his shoulder. A few minutes later, he stopped. Richard could see the outline of a waiting car, the boot open. The man bent forward, tipped Richard into the boot and slammed the lid closed.

"Right," said Frank from the driver's seat. "Jimmy, you go with Vin in the pick-up. I'll give you five minutes, then I'll take the back road to St Geniès. Wait for me at the bend in the track to the château, just out of sight of the main road. Turn your lights off when you get there."

****

Kate turned the light out in the nursery and limped back downstairs. Her ankle felt sore tonight. She'd lit the fire, even though it was still August. She'd put her feet up and have a glass of wine before she went up to bed. She sat down and leaned back in her chair, eyes closed. She thought about Alastair. She wished he'd stayed with her at the château, but she supposed she couldn't really have expected him to want to spend any more time with her. At least he wasn't under arrest. The hotel in Fromac was quite pleasant and the woman who ran it seemed very nice. Kate sighed and rubbed her eyes. Just then the telephone rang. Kate started, and looked at the clock. It was nearly 11.30. Who could be calling her so late?

"Kate. It's Alastair. The police have just been to see me. They've identified the body from the lake."

Kate held her breath.

"Kate? Are you there? It's not Richard. It's the notaire's wife," Alastair spoke tersely. "If they don't come up with anything before Tuesday, they'll have to give me back my passport."

Kate let out a long sigh. Thank goodness. There was a glimmer of hope that Richard was still alive somewhere. She knew he was. And Alastair would be free.

"Oh, Alastair. I'm so relieved," Kate was almost sobbing.

"Yes."

There was a small pause.

"Well, goodbye, Kate."

The phone went dead. Kate looked at it as if lightning had struck the château again. The police had made sure the EDF had got her reconnected the day before, for their own purposes. She sank back into her chair, a feeling of utter hopelessness overwhelming her.

A sudden hammering on the kitchen door made Kate start out of her chair again. It must be Alastair! He must have changed his mind. He must want to be with her despite everything! She hopped over to the door and flung it open.

3

Kate's scream brought Richard to his senses. He had fallen almost on top of her when she had pulled the door open. He'd been aware of being dragged out of the car boot and across cobbles to a doorway. His captors had propped him upright against the door before one of them knocked loudly, then took a couple of paces back. Kate was on her knees beside him, cradling his head on her lap.

"Richard, Richard! Oh, I knew you were alive! Speak to me!"

"Kate," he muttered. "Kate, shut the door..."

He must warn her about the men. But all was quiet. Perhaps they'd gone. He couldn't think clearly. Maybe they'd thought he was just a trespasser. Kate was scrambling to her knees.

"Richard, can you get up? Here, lean on me."

"It's alright, darlin'. I'll give you a hand!"

Kate screamed again as the three men stepped into the kitchen, over Richard's inert body, kicking his legs out of their way. One of them slammed the door behind them, and stood with his back against it. The one who had spoken grabbed her arm and hauled her to her feet. He hustled her over to the fireplace and pushed her back into her chair. He took up his position behind her. The third man walked over to the table and perched on the edge, surveying the scene.

"Well, well!" Frank said. "Nice little place you've got here! Plenty of room for everyone!"

"What.... what do you want?" Kate stammered.

"From you, darlin', nothing at all," Frank leered at her. "We found your friend here on one of our premises. So we've brought him back to you. He should be more careful, going out in a storm like that!"

"Thank you," Kate said. "But, how do you know…?"

"We know all about you, darlin'," Frank interrupted her. "We know about these little incidents that have happened here. We know what the police think about you too," he shook his head, wagging a finger at her. "You've been a bit of a naughty girl, haven't you, eh?"

"What do you want?" Kate asked in a low voice.

"Well, it's like this," Frank shifted his weight to settle himself more comfortably on the table and went on conversationally. "We have some items that we need to store for a while. Bulky items, you understand. That we need to keep safe for a while. We need a place that's nice and private. We thought this place looked just right. Of course, because these," he paused. "These items, are very valuable, we need to keep an eye on them ourselves. So we need to stay here too. And since it's such a nice big place you've got here, it seems ideal. We won't get in your way at all."

Kate gaped at him, baffled.

"But you can't do that! I don't know who you are…."

"And you don't need to, darlin'. Now I am going to take a little tour of the premises. You are going to stay here with my nice friends and you are going to keep quiet."

He moved nearer to Kate and placed a hand on each of the arms of her chair. He brought his face up close to hers and continued almost in a whisper.

"You will do exactly as you are told. We're going to be here for a while. If you attempt to contact the police, or tell anyone that we are here, we will kill your friend. We'll make sure the police have the body they are looking for, so you can say goodbye to your husband as well. Oh yes, we know it all," he nodded at Kate's gasp. "He seems to have settled in quite well at the Coq d'Or. And then of course, there's the baby, isn't there?"

"No!" Kate cried. "You wouldn't!

Frank smiled at her in reply and moved back over to the table.

"Of course we wouldn't! Because you'll do just as we say. And then you won't have anything to worry about."

He walked over to where Richard lay, unable to move.

"Now then, first of all we need to find a nice comfortable room for your friend here, where we can look after him. He's not well, you know," Frank shook his head. "Should take more care of himself. Vin, you come with me."

Two hours later, thirty-six fertiliser sacks were stacked neatly in the small cellar under the pantry at the end of the kitchen. The pick-up was parked out of sight in the old coach house. Richard was sleeping in the small dressing room of one of the guest suites on the top floor of the château. The one with the narrow spiral staircase that led down into the main hall, just beside the front door. His door was locked and, in the guest bedroom, Jimmy was sprawled on the bed, a bottle of wine in one hand and the TV remote in the other. Kate was in her makeshift bed in the nursery, the door locked from the inside. Vin was installed in a first floor room that overlooked the track. From his window he could see any approaching vehicles and if Kate left her room, she would have to pass his before reaching the stairs.

And Frank was sitting on the pale blue leather sofa opposite his mother, a glass of whisky cradled in his hand. He glanced round the room, taking in the big gilt chandelier, the bright oil paintings, the tasselled brocade curtains, the cocktail cabinet in the shape of a globe. Yes, he'd been a good son. Dora liked the house, but she'd have preferred to be on the Costa, of course. She was made up with the new villa that Frank had just bought there. But Frank was canny. They'd move there when the job was over. This was the last one. They'd be clean. No point in living on the Costa if there was any heat. Too many narks.

"So it's all sorted then, love?" Dora took a swig of her gin.

"Couldn't be better, Ma. She's going to play ball alright. We've got her by the short and curlies."

"That's nice," Dora smiled indulgently at her son. "She's a bit of a one, by all accounts. The latest is, she's trying to get that château made over to her kid," Dora paused for effect and another swig of gin.

Frank looked puzzled.

"What, you mean the château isn't hers anyway? I thought it must belong to her and her husband."

"Oh no, dear," Dora shook her head. "She had another lover – real gent that one! I could have fancied him myself!"

She broke off to cackle with laughter at the thought.

"He's the one got killed falling off his terrace way back in May, or was it April? It was his château, and she told everyone he was the kid's dad so she'd get the château and the money! But of course nobody thinks he was!"

"Well, well," Frank smiled. "Gets better every minute. Might be more potential there, eh, Ma?"

"You bet! I'll make sure I get all the details, love! Then you can see if there are any more, er, business opportunities, as you might say! Cheers!"

They clinked glasses and settled back in front of the big TV set. EastEnders would be on in a minute. It had been a good move getting that satellite dish.

4

November.

Outside the nursery window, the few leaves left on the trees had turned a deep orange. It was a beautiful day. Kate listened anxiously to the shallow, rasping breath of her son. She was at the end of her tether. The doctor said he had to be admitted to hospital and she should come with him, but how could she? They wouldn't let her go out and anyway, she had to be at the château to look after Richard. He seemed to be getting a bit stronger, although he was barely able to move. Why couldn't they just go and leave her alone? She shuddered with remembered fear. They'd held a gun to Richard's head when they'd seen the nurse drive down the track. And when the doctor had come with the notaire to make her sign the indemnity. The doctor thought she was crazy, she could see it in his eyes. None of them suspected she was being forced to behave this way. Everyone thought of her as more than eccentric and her behaviour was just proving them all right. Perhaps she was going mad. She sat down by the cot and looked at her baby. How long could he keep his feeble grasp on life? What was going to happen to them all? When would the nightmare end?

Kate looked up as Jimmy came into the room. He wandered over to the cot and looked down at the baby, shaking his head. He walked over to the window and checked the track. The baby made a faint gurgling sound. Funny thing was, Kate thought as she looked over at Jimmy, she didn't mind them too much. They were evil, she knew that. But at least she knew where she stood with them. She thought bitterly of Nick. Pity he hadn't been as honest. She half-smiled to herself as the irony of her thoughts struck her.

"That's better! Not all bad, is it?" Jimmy said. "Anyway, I've got news for you. Me and Vin, we're going away. It'll only be for a few days. But don't worry, Frank'll be popping in to look after you, so you won't be on your own! He wants to have a bit of a word anyway."

As he was leaving the room, Jimmy heard the baby gurgle again. He recognised that sort of sound. Then it was quiet. He walked quickly over and looked into the cot.

"You'd better come over here," he said to Kate. "Looks like this is it. Poor little bugger," he added. "Come down when you want to call the doctor. He'll have to do a post-mortem or something. Frank'll need to know when he's coming."

He left the room and clattered downstairs, taking his mobile phone from his pocket and dialling. Frank answered straight away.

"Frank. Jimmy. Listen, something's cropped up here. The kid's croaked. That means the doctor'll be over. I reckon straight away, but I don't know how long he'll be here. He might even have to bring the gendarmes. So can you get here first? Me and Vin need to be out of here if we are going to catch that flight. We can't hang around until the doc leaves in case it takes longer than we think."

"OK, Vin," Frank answered. "No problem. I'm on my way. You and Vin be ready to leave when I get there. Ten minutes."

He put the phone down, rubbing his hands.

"Right, Ma. Good news, eh? Should be able to do a little bit of negotiating over the sale of the château now. She won't want to hang on to it now, will she? Everyone'll understand if she sells straight off. And if we, how shall we say – facilitate – the sale, let her see an agent and that, a little commission will be in order, now won't it? Couldn't be better timing, could it? I mean, if she's selling, she'll want to be moving her stuff back to Blighty, won't she? Nothing could be more natural than getting an English removal company to come and pick up her stuff, now would it? So if the van gets seen, no problem! Any rate, I'll be off now. Don't call me unless you have to. I'll be at the château. Vin and Jimmy'll pick up the van and be on the overnight ferry tonight. They'll be in Spain tomorrow, unload your stuff at the villa and be back up here the day after. By then it should be all quiet at the château again. Just me, the grieving Madame and the boyfriend!"

"You watch yourself, duck," his mother said, looking up from her magazine. "Don't you go feeling sorry for her or anything. She's bad news, that one. Keep her locked up as well, but separate from the bloke. Can't be too careful."

"Ma, I'll have to let her out for the funeral! Otherwise it'd look odd."

"True. But keep an eye on her. Tell you what, I'll go to the funeral as well! Nothing like a good burial! You tell her we're keeping an eye on her! Tell her if she steps out of line, I'll be on the mobile to you from the cemetery and she'll be burying the boyfriend next. And the same when she goes anywhere – the estate agents, anywhere you have to let her go. I'm serious, boy. You just let her know someone's watching her. She could be more reckless now the kid's dead."

"You're right, Ma. Good idea. People are used to seeing you around anyway."

"Sal'll be here next week as well. So I'll just be showing her around, won't I? She might even be wanting to buy a place, eh? So we'd have to go into the estate agent's, wouldn't we?"

"I'll be off then. I'll ring you later, Ma."

"Bye, duck."

****

Frank closed the kitchen door as the pick-up carrying Jimmy and Vin disappeared round the bend in the track. His own car was well out of sight in the old coach house. He turned back to Kate.

"When's the doctor due, darlin'?" he asked.

293

Kate sniffed and wiped her hand across her eyes.

"In about half an hour," she answered wearily. "He had to notify the hospital. They have to send an ambulance. He's not allowed to carry a…" her voice broke. "A dead body, in his car."

"Come on now," Frank put his hand on her shoulder.

She was too tired and too numb to pull away.

"Now, as soon as we spot them on the track, I'll be off upstairs. But don't forget I can hear every word. Baby alarms can come in quite useful, even if we don't have a baby anymore! And you behave as nicely as you've done these last couple of months. We don't want any more unpleasant events today, do we?" Frank spoke quietly. "But don't forget," he brought his face close to hers. "One word out of place and you'll be looking at two funerals, and I'll be long gone down that back staircase before you can say *'Sacré blue!'* Understand?"

Kate nodded. She looked up at him.

"Can I go up and tell him? Tell Richard?"

"No," Frank shook his head. "Not until after the doc and these other people have been and gone."

He walked over to the window and looked up the track. Nothing yet. He took the small black gun out of his pocket and checked the clip. Kate watched him unseeingly. She felt so hopeless. Maybe she'd tell the doctor everything. She didn't doubt they'd kill Richard. Perhaps her too. Maybe that'd be for the best. The kitchen was silent. Frank stood at the window. Motionless, expressionless. Minutes passed, then he stepped away from the window and across the room.

"OK, darlin'. Here they come. Now don't forget what I said. As soon as they've gone, you can go up and see him. He needs looking after, you know. And it seems to me you owe him. Big time. Remember that," he added. "In case you get any ideas."

Kate stood up and went over to the kitchen door. As she stood looking out onto the damp courtyard, she thought, he's right. I caused all of this. Standing there in the gloom, Kate made up her mind. She had to go along with Frank, to save Richard. She had no choice.

Phillippe de la Bernière snapped his black bag shut and reached for his overcoat. Outside, the ambulance doors closed and it set off slowly up the track.

"The post-mortem will be done in the morning. If all is in order, the hospital will then issue the certificate. After that, you must register the death at the *mairie*. This must be done within twenty-four hours of the death. If you prefer, Madame, I will accompany you to Fromac to do this. St Geniès does not have the authority. I will bring the certificate from the hospital. Once you have registered the death, the *mairie* will authorize the closure of the coffin. You may delay this for up to six days, if you wish, for the payment of respects. In this case, you will need to arrange for a transfer to a *reposoir*. In any case, you should contact the undertaker in St Geniès. He will take care of everything," Phillippe spoke formally.

He glanced at Kate's stricken face.

"Or, if you wish, I will contact him for you. So, Madame. Expect me at about three o'clock tomorrow afternoon. We will go to Fromac together to register the death."

Kate nodded.

"Thank you. You've been very kind."

Phillippe held out his hand.

"I'll see myself out."

Closing the kitchen door, he was glad to be out of the château and hurried over to his car. A few minutes later, he was speeding towards Chloe's house. Only a few weeks now and they'd be in England and nearly married. He wondered idly about Kate. The baby's death wasn't exactly unexpected, but he thought he might have pulled through eventually. Especially if she'd let him be taken into hospital. Had she given up and just wanted him to die? Had she even given him a helping hand? Phillippe dismissed the thought. Unprofessional speculation. Still, the post-mortem should settle any doubts.

Back in the kitchen, Kate sat silent in front of the fire. Frank appeared in the doorway.

"OK," he said. "Go up and tell him. Then I want a word."

He followed her upstairs and opened the door to Richard's room, standing aside for her to go in. Leaving the door open, he settled himself on the bed in front of the TV.

"Take your time," he said.

A long time later, Kate walked slowly out of the dressing room where Richard lay. Frank looked up from the TV as she spoke.

"Could I ask you something?" her voice was steady and calm. Frank nodded.

"Let's go downstairs," he said. "I could do with a bite."

Kate led the way to the kitchen and silently started to get food out of the fridge. Frank stood in the shadows by the window, eyes fixed on the track. All was quiet in the darkness of the late autumn evening. He came over to the table and took one of the glasses of wine that Kate had poured. So, he made a mental note as he surveyed the meal that Kate had laid on the table, it didn't look as if Jimmy and Vin had had too bad a time of it over the last couple of months. Kate sat down opposite him. She drew a deep breath.

"I know you know everything about how I come to be here," she began. "I know you know about the château. I mean, it's not mine. I've no claim to it. Up until today, I was going to stay here, with my baby. We needed a home, and," she looked at him defiantly. "Nick Carslow owed it to me. He owed me that much!"

Frank kept on looking at her in silence.

"But now, what I need most is money. Richard needs proper care. And I want to get away from this place. So I want to sell. Now, straight away. I want you to let me go into Fromac and see Dominic Lefèvre. I promise I won't say anything. I promise I'll do anything you ask. Please."

Frank nodded slowly. Was he a mind-reader, or what? Ma always said he should've been a psychiatrist.

"You seem to be forgetting something. Me and Vin and Jimmy, we quite like it here. We might not be ready to move out yet. We like things to be private. I wouldn't feel, you know, comfortable, with a lot of strangers traipsing through here," he added.

"But Jimmy said you'd be gone soon," Kate cried. "He said when he and Vin got back this time, you'd all be gone in a couple of weeks! We could tell them not to send any buyers until you'd all gone!"

Oh, Jimmy said that, did he? Frank's face hardened. He'd have to remind Jimmy about keeping that gob of his shut.

"Well, I'll have to think about this," he said. "I will consider your request. Of course, it would make things inconvenient for me. But under the circumstances, your bereavement and that," he smiled bleakly at her. "We might be able to come to some arrangement that would suit us both."

Neither of them spoke again until Kate had made coffee and Frank had settled himself in front of the fire. Kate sat down and closed her eyes. She just wanted to get away now, with Richard. She must sell the château quickly. She was sure the courts would have nullified Nick's will by now, and the château would belong to her son. Almost all of Nick's money was gone. And she had to get Richard proper treatment. If only they'd let her see Dominic Lefèvre, get things moving, she'd be able to hope, she'd be able to get through the next few days.

Frank looked across at her. She wasn't going to be a problem.

"I've been thinking," he said. "And this is what we'll do. Now that you're moving, I'm going to help you. You'll be wanting to move all this furniture," he gestured. "It so happens that I'm in the removals business. And, quite by chance, I have a furniture van coming through France in a couple of days. So, to help you out, you understand, I'm willing to have it stop off here, and load up your stuff. Of course, it'll be handy for me too. I'll be able to move my own belongings. It's been in storage here long enough! Then the van'll come back in a week or two and take the rest of the stuff. No charge to you, of course. Can't say fairer than that, can I?"

"What do you mean?" Kate asked. "What will you do with the furniture? I've nowhere in England…."

Her voice trailed off. It was all Joanne's furniture anyway. All valuable stuff too. Was she as bad as these criminals who were holding her and Richard prisoner? Was she happy to steal all she could? Then it dawned on her. She'd never see the furniture again. Or the money it would fetch. She sat there silently. What could she do? If she sold the château and moved, she'd have to clear it anyway. Did it matter who stole the stuff? She felt ashamed as a momentary anger passed over her at the thought of losing the thousands of pounds she could have got for the furniture.

"What about the château?" she asked. "Will you let me go and see Monsieur Lefèvre?"

Frank didn't reply straight away. He was thinking hard. If anyone saw the van, it might look better if the château was on the market. Then it'd be clear that Kate was moving. If it wasn't on the market, some busybody might just report it. Think the château was being burgled. What had he to lose? A good story for the van was important, just in case. He didn't want those nosey local gendarmes sniffing around. He only needed a couple of weeks more, max. Then he'd be home and dry.

"OK. This is what you do. Tomorrow, you phone the doctor. Get the post-mortem results. Tell him not to come here. You'll meet him in Fromac to register the death. You go to the estate agent first. Tell him no viewings for two weeks. And don't forget, I'm doing you a big favour here. And my commission will be very modest. So behave. Remember, this is all for him," Frank jerked his head. "And just to make sure you're alright, I'll have someone looking after you. They'll be carrying a silver mobile phone in their left hand. You do anything we don't like, and you'll never see him again. Understand?"

Kate slept better that night than she had for months. In her heart she was relieved that the baby had died. His suffering had been so hard to bear. Now she dared to hope that she could at least partly make amends. With the proceeds from the château, she'd be able to afford to take Richard to the best clinics. Switzerland? He'd like that, she thought. No one would know either of them. It could be a fresh start for them both.

5

They were standing just inside the big iron gates, near one of the grey granite tombs topped with a glass structure stuffed with plastic flowers and memorial plaques. As she passed close to them, following the tiny wooden coffin, Kate heard one of them say to her friend,

"Looks like a bloody greenhouse, Dor! Might as well bury them in the allotments!"

"That's foreigners for you!" Dora giggled.

Kate didn't need a second glance to tell her that these were the two women who had been in the estate agent's when she'd gone in yesterday. They'd been talking to Jim Munro when she had rushed out in tears. She'd heard them tut-tutting at the way Dominic had refused to sell her château on the grounds that it wasn't her's. It was then that she'd noticed the thin, bespectacled man and his wife, flicking through a file of properties. In his left hand was a silver mobile phone.

At the *mairie*, just as she and Phillippe were called into the small office where all business was conducted, she'd seen the French woman in the headscarf, a copy of *Les Dépêches du Midi* on her knee. Kate couldn't see her face, but gave a start as she saw the silver mobile phone in her gloved hand. Her left hand.

She looked again at the two English women. She'd seen them a second time yesterday, in the Agence Sainte Croix in Cahors. They looked like sisters. Well into middle age, with lots of gold jewellery, painted nails, dyed blonde hair. Jim Munro had seemed to know one of them. They looked friendly, kind, salt-of-the-earth types. For a moment Kate thought about asking them to help her, telling them everything. She glanced over her shoulder. She couldn't see them anymore. But she could see the French woman in the headscarf from the *mairie*. And the phone was still in her hand. She was following the small cortège down the central path flanked by tall cypresses towards the far end of the cemetery, past the stone crosses of the older graves to the overgrown area at the very end where the cemetery wall met the fields beyond.

Kate's mind registered the phone again. From somewhere she heard Frank's voice: 'They'll be carrying a silver mobile phone in their left hand. You do anything we don't like and you'll never see him again.' They needn't worry. She wasn't going to do anything to jeopardise Richard. She kept walking. The undertaker stopped in front of a small, deep and freshly dug hole in the ground. The pall bearer deposited his burden unceremoniously into the hole and stepped back. Kate, the doctor and a small, thin figure in a dog collar stood around the grave. The French woman stopped short of them, near the end of the row of Catholic gravestones and vaults.

The man in the dog collar cleared his throat and read in English from his prayer book.

"*....and now we commit his body to the ground: earth to earth, ashes to ashes, dust to dust, in sure and certain hope of the resurrection to eternal life through our Lord Jesus Christ....*"

Kate's eyes misted. She heard the wind in the cypress trees. A few spots of rain fell and she shivered. The small man shut his book. Kate turned away. She couldn't see the woman in the headscarf anywhere.

Dora stuffed the scarf and gloves into her handbag and let in the clutch, turning the car in the direction of Fromac.

"That went well! I couldn't believe it yesterday when that man in Lefèvre's took his phone out just before she walked in! What a stroke of luck!"

"And you looked the part, Dor," Sal chuckled. "I could have taken you for a Froggie myself! And, you know, I saw her looking at us at the cemetery and just for a moment I thought she was going to shop our boys and get us to help her!"

****

When she got back to the château, Jimmy and Vin had returned. Frank was still there. Something seemed to be happening. They sent her up to Richard with his dinner. She heard the key turn in the lock. Several hours later, Jimmy appeared in the doorway and threw a bundle of bedclothes into the room.

"You're staying up here from now on," he said to Kate, and closed the door again. She heard him lock the door and switch on the TV.

Downstairs, Frank and Vin were sitting at the kitchen table, a bottle of wine between them.

"That's everything loaded," Vin said. "There's about a quarter of the stuff left in the cellar, so with what's still over at Lalbenque, we've got one more full load after this."

"Perfect."

Frank was pleased. The van looked good. There'd been no problem at the ferry or customs. Sal's husband had done a good job on the paperwork. The villa on the Costa was looking the business, according to Vin. Ma'd be pleased. Not long now and she'd be down there in the sun.

"Right. Tomorrow night you leave. We'll wait until late, just in case."

****

Kate walked through the empty salon and out onto the terrace. The sun had come out for the first time in weeks. She was beginning to let herself think it would soon be over. All the antique furniture from the ground floor rooms seemed to have gone. Frank came out onto the terrace.

"Not long now, darlin'," he said. "You'll soon see the back of us."

Kate stood silently looking at the lake. She hoped he was right. The longer they stayed, the longer before Richard got proper care.

Later that evening, she heard the van rumble out of the coach house. Frank closed the kitchen door and walked over to where she sat.

"Just me and you again," he said to Kate, leering at her and running his finger along the back of her neck.

****

Jimmy put the van into a low gear and slowly eased it onto the track. No lights once you're in sight of the main road, Frank had said. It was bloody dark. He drove carefully and slowly, following the chalky track. Just after the bend, he switched off the lights. Just as well it was chalk, or he'd have been in the bushes by now. Vin sat alongside, whistling tunelessly.

"Bit late with the lights, Jim!" he said. "Didn't you see those headlights on the road over there?"

Smart arse, thought Jimmy. He stopped the van behind the last group of trees before the track met the main road. Vin was right. There were headlights coming towards them up the road. They both sat in silence, watching the lights. It looked like a small car. Drawing level with the end of the track, Vin tensed as the car slowed. But only for a moment, then it sped on and disappeared in the direction of St Geniès. Jimmy started the engine, and drove to the end of the track. Turning onto the main road, he switched on the headlights. They would be in Dover by this time tomorrow.

6

Frank saw the furniture van before he heard it trundling down the track. Good. Jimmy and Vin were earlier than he'd expected. Things had gone well. The cash was in Andorra already. Ma was a rich lady! Vin and Jimmy could have their cut when the final consignment was delivered. They'd load up now and be off tonight. And that would be that. Goodbye to the Lot! He smirked at the pun. First though, he thought, he'd better sort out these two, glancing over at Kate and Richard.

"Come on," he gestured at Kate. "I need you downstairs."

Kate rose obediently. Frank followed Kate downstairs. Jimmy and Vin were in the kitchen, the kettle was boiling and Jimmy was eating a sandwich. The homeliness and incongruity of the scene struck Kate before the blow to her head. She sagged at the knees. Jimmy and Vin looked on as she fell to the floor.

"Jimmy, put that sandwich down and help me," Frank said. "Get her down into the wine cellar and chain her up. Then come back here and we'll start loading."

Most of the remaining furniture was already out in the coach house, waiting to be loaded. It didn't take long to move the rest of the dope. They worked quickly, by the light of powerful torches. The first two compartments under the floor of the van were soon full, the plastic-covered packages stacked neatly and covered with a triple layer of insulation, before the false floor was replaced and Joanne's furniture was piled in on top.

"Right," Frank said, jumping down out of the van. "Get the last of the furniture in. You'll have to take these pieces out when you pick up the rest of the stuff at Lalbenque. Make sure you get the big stuff right on top of the compartments, so that it covers the joins. Then if you do get stopped and they bring the dogs in, you've more of a chance if they can't get their snouts down where the insulation's thin."

Frank shone his torch around the coach house as Vin and Jimmy struggled with the last pieces of furniture. Clean, except for the slit-open fertiliser sacks. Perfect. Nothing unusual about them. Jimmy had done a thorough job on the château too. No finger prints, no DNA.

He turned back towards the van as Jimmy slammed the doors shut. Something caught his eye as he turned. A tiny movement, a shadow? Frank frowned and stood perfectly still, his torch trained on the van doors, but his eyes scanning the coach house. An owl? A bat? Something was there. A thought struck him. Kate! Had she somehow got out of the wine cellar? He looked up at the heavy beams that supported the roof. It must have been a bird or something up there. His eyes travelled around the ceiling. The window! The small, horizontal window high up at the back of the coach house. Keeping his torch on the van doors, Frank stared up at the window and stiffened. There was enough light outside for him just to make out the silhouette outlined in the window frame. He moved forward so that he was close to Vin and Jimmy who were securing the van's doors.

"Keep on with what you're doing," he whispered. "We're being watched. The window, back of the coach house. You two stay here, carry on getting the van ready. I'll be back in a minute."

Frank switched off his torch and went round the front of the van. Picking up his crowbar, he slipped silently out of the building and up the track.

****

"It looks like she was on her own," Vin said. "Her car's up there, off the track. Quite well-hidden. Keys still in the ignition. I've left the briefcase in the car."

"OK," Frank nodded. "Now we know who she is. Looks like she was snooping, but not on us. But people are going to miss her, sooner or later. Which is a pity. Means we need to get a move on and get the van across the Channel before anyone finds them."

"We could just kill them both," Jimmy said, matter of factly. "Kill all three."

"All the time our Kate thinks we've got the boyfriend, she's not going to talk. And this other bird can't identify us. We were too far away and it was too dark. She might have got the van's number, if she can remember it after the whack on the head I gave her, but you're going to change the plates at Lalbenque anyway. So we leave them where they are. I'm not keen on a murder rap. And you take the boyfriend with you. Dump him when you collect the rest of the stuff. Don't kill him, Jim. I said just dump him. He won't last long. OK, Vin?"

Vin nodded.

"Let's go then. Have a good trip, boys! I'll see you in sunny Spain!"

****

The pick-up was where they'd left it, parked outside the old farmhouse, just off the main road. Jimmy edged the furniture van into the shelter of the Dutch barn. Between them they hauled Richard's inert body out of the cab and into the back of the pick-up. Vin got into the driver's seat and carefully reversed out onto the track, and back to the main road. Jimmy set to work clearing the back section of the van and changing the plates. He was glad they were on their way. He didn't really get on with France. The bread gave him indigestion and he wasn't that keen on French beer. Too gassy. And it rained too much. He looked up at the sky. Looked like it was going to be a wet night.

Vin eased the pick-up off the main road and down a narrow lane, passing slowly through a deserted hamlet. There were a few cars parked near a couple of farms, but not a chink of light to be seen. A couple of miles further on, Vin slowed as the ruined house came into view. He pulled over onto the verge and switched off the engine. Silence. He looked around. He could drive down to the *gariotte*, but that would leave fresh tracks. There were only six sacks to collect. He'd leave the car here.

Richard was no weight at all and Vin trotted the hundred metres to the *gariotte*. He dumped Richard on the ground and climbed the uneven stone steps to the open doorway. Shining his torch inside, he counted six blue fertiliser sacks. In less than ten minutes he had five sacks in the back of the pick-up. One last trip and he'd be on his way. He hauled Richard up the steps and dropped him on the hard earth floor, rolling his body out of sight against the back wall of the small, round, stone shelter. He picked up the last sack. At the bottom of the steps he paused. Twenty-five kilos. You could go a long way on twenty-five kg of good quality Moroccan.

Back at the van, he and Jimmy finished loading quickly and efficiently.

"Right," Vin said. "Let's go. Home, James!"

Jimmy grinned, the engine already turning over. He turned on the windscreen wipers as the first spots of rain started to fall. Shit.

They were making good time. The roads were quiet and, despite the rain, they were keeping up a decent speed. Vin looked at the gps. They were just coming up to Souillac. After that they could pick up the autoroute and it'd be plain sailing all the way back to Calais. The wide road swept steeply down towards the valley of the Dordogne in big, broad bends. Jimmy nursed the heavy van around the curves as fast as he dared on the greasy surface. Vin could see the lights of Souillac below them. He didn't see the car coming straight towards them up the hill, on their side of the road. Jimmy saw it and swerved to the right, missing the car by inches. The front wheel of the furniture van caught the soft, wet verge. The van skidded. Its momentum carried it on in a straight line, through the crash barrier, through the trees, down the steep slope towards the Dordogne.

?

"Jim?" Patricia's voice sounded worried. "She still hasn't come back."

Jim frowned.

"Joanne, you mean? I'll ask around and call you back," he said and hung up. He grabbed his jacket and picked up the dog's lead.

"Ferdie! Come on! Let's go find the lady!"

****

At midday he was back in the café in Fromac. Sitting opposite him were Patricia and Dominic.

"So, no one's seen her since yesterday lunchtime? We saw her in here and she said to me she'd see me at Pat's that evening. Yesterday evening. But she didn't come back to the hotel last night, nor this morning. No one's seen her car since she left Fromac after lunch yesterday. She told Phillippe she was going into Cahors to the Agence Sainte Croix, then to the château. He persuaded her to wait and go over to St Geniès-Lafontaine today."

They all nodded. Jim went on.

"We know she went to the Agence Sainte Croix. Dominic spoke to them. He's checked the hospitals. There was a bad crash up near Souillac last night, but it was two men in a van. No one else was involved."

The three of them looked up simultaneously as the café door swung open. The look of expectation on Pat's face faded as a teenage girl came in. She was followed by a younger boy, and a tall, dark-haired man. Jim's dog opened an eye, then scrambled out from under the table and greeted the girl effusively.

"Ferdie! You remembered me!" she cried, kneeling beside the big dog and burying her face in its thick fur.

"John!" Jim jumped to his feet. "Good to see you back! And you too, Dan, Susie!"

John Nicholson and his family seemed to fill the small, sombre café with a new life.

"So what's going on?" John asked, surveying the anxious faces.

"It's to do with the château. As you'd expect," Jim said with heavy irony. "Only this time it's the real owner, Joanne Carslow, who's gone missing!"

"What! Not another one!"

"Great!" Dan shouted. "It's brill how something weird always happens here, just when we arrive!"

"Dan!" Susie turned to her father in indignation. "Dad, tell him! He thinks everything's funny. This is awful. I think someone must have put a curse on the château," she added seriously.

Jim shook his head, smiling.

"There'll be a perfectly innocent explanation, I'm sure," he said.

Dominic and Pat looked at him.

"Go on then," Pat said. "What is the explanation for my guest not returning to the hotel last night, nor this morning, when she's booked in until the weekend and she promised to have dinner with us last night? When we've asked everyone she knows and no one has seen her? Just where is she?"

"She's at the château. She must have gone there yesterday as she'd planned."

All eyes turned towards Dominic. He hadn't spoken for some time, but now he went on.

"It's the only explanation. Why didn't I think of it before? And if anything has happened to her there, it is I who is to blame."

"Why? What have you done?" Dan's eyes were wide. John shushed him. Dominic went on.

"Yesterday she asked Phillippe if he thought she would be in any danger if she went to see Madame Black. You know, we all thought she had been acting very strangely. Joanne had listened to us all and she asked Phillippe's professional advice. I met him just after he'd spoken to her, and he asked me what I thought, as I'd recently had dealings with Madame Black. Did I think Madame Black might want to harm Madame Carslow, even kill her?"

"Why should she want to do that?" Dan again, eyes like saucers.

"Because of the château, Stupid," Susie said. "If Mrs Carslow was dead, there'd be no one to contest the inheritance."

"Wow!"

"Anyway, Phillippe was beginning to wonder if he'd given her the right advice. He was on the point of going back into the café and telling her not to go on her own, he'd go with her, but I said I thought she was being fanciful. It was my honest opinion that, though she may have her faults, and she has been through a lot recently, Madame Black was not so disturbed as to want Joanne dead, or to harm her in any way. But it looks as if I might have made a complete error of judgement," Dominic looked distraught. "I stopped Phillippe from going with Joanne to the château. No one has seen her since yesterday lunchtime. So she must have gone to St Geniès yesterday on her own. We must go over there and look for her. There is no time to lose."

Jim stood up.

"Pat, you stay at the hotel. We can call you there if we need to and if she comes back, you can let us know. Dominic, you have to go back to the Agence. Your clients need you. Me and John'll go and look for her. Come on, Ferdie."

****

Jim stopped his van. He'd seen it as soon as he'd turned down towards the château. But only because he'd been looking for it. The Porsche was almost hidden from view, parked down a narrow, grassy track, in the woods of St Geniès-Lafontaine.

"Come on, boy," Jim said to the dog, his heart in his mouth. "Let's see what we can find."

Behind him, John had parked the Land Rover on the verge and was already on his way down the track. Jim was glad they'd met. He wouldn't have fancied doing this on his own, even with Ferdie. Ferdie was sniffing around the Porsche, his tail wagging slowly. He probably recognised the scent. He'd met Joanne the previous day, Jim recalled. And Ferdie had a good nose. John peered in through the window.

"The keys are in the ignition," he called to Jim. "And there's a briefcase on the passenger seat. But no sign of her."

"There's no sign of footprints either," said Jim. "It rained heavily last night. So she must have left the car here before it started. That means, yesterday afternoon or   evening. Probably on her way back to Fromac from Cahors."

"Come on."

John was already heading for the Land Rover, glad he'd made the kids stay at the barn. He didn't like the sound of any of this. He could hardly believe that yet another disaster might have happened at the château. He hoped to God it hadn't. Jim followed the Land Rover down the track. All looked quiet as they approached the château. They parked next to the stone arch.

"Let's go to the kitchen door," Jim said to John. "She might just have decided to stay the night here. After all, it's her château."

But he knew John didn't believe that likely. Nor did he. They went through the courtyard, Ferdie's claws skidding on the cobbles as he rushed around, sniffing enthusiastically. John knocked hard on the kitchen door. Silence. He knocked again, then tried the handle. Nothing.

"Let's see if we can find a window open, or something, Jim. I'll try here, you and Ferdie take a look around outside and maybe try the terrace."

Jim walked round the corner of the building, past the front door. It didn't look as if anyone had opened it in months. Grass was growing out of cracks in the stone steps, and a huge spider's web hung over the top corner of the door, glistening as the weak autumn sun caught the gossamer fibres. He went through the wrought iron gates and onto the terrace, shivering slightly as he looked down over the balustrade where Nick Carslow had fallen to his death. Way below, Jim could see the calm shimmering of the lake where Marie-Claire Lacombe had drowned herself, and at the far end, the weir where Alastair Black may or may not have killed Richard Talbot. He hoped they weren't too late for Joanne.

He tried the French doors that led from the terrace into the salon, but they were locked. The shutters had not been closed and, pressing his face up to the glass of the French windows, he was surprised to see that the salon was completely empty. Not a stick of furniture remained. He remembered what Phillippe had said about seeing a furniture van a week or two ago. That explained it. Kate Black must have gone.

John appeared at his elbow.

"No luck round there," he said.

"Looks like it'd be easiest to break a pane in this door," Jim said.

They were inside the château in a few seconds. Their footsteps echoed as they moved through the empty rooms.

"Hello!" Jim called as they reached the kitchen. "Nothing. It doesn't look as if anyone's been here recently. Anybody here?" he called again. "It's me, Jim Munro. Mrs Black, Joanne! Are you there?"

His voice came back to him off the stone walls. John bent down over the fireplace.

"The ashes are still warmish," he said. "Could be last night's fire."

"Not much to go on," Jim mused. "No sign of Joanne. We'd better have a proper look around. This place is pretty big – it'll take a while. But it feels deserted. Let's take a floor each and meet back here. I'll send Ferdie off on his own. I've given him another sniff of Joanne's briefcase from the car. He'll bark if he finds anything interesting."

Two hours later, John and Jim were back in the kitchen. Jim shook his head.

"Nothing. It's pretty weird alright. I mean, it looks as if one or two of the rooms have been used recently, especially that one on the top floor with the TV and that bed in the small room next door. I suppose that's her stuff. Kate Black's, I mean. But where are they both? It looks as if Kate's done a runner with the furniture. But what's she done with Joanne first?"

"We haven't looked in all the outbuildings yet," John pointed out. "I've been into the coach house, but that's empty except for a pile of old fertiliser sacks. It looks as if something's been parked in there. I suppose she used it as a garage."

"Yes, maybe," Jim agreed. "OK. Let's do all the outbuildings next."

8

Joanne rubbed her stiff legs and shifted around so that she had a better view through the doorway. She couldn't quite see her watch, but she knew it was still daytime. She could see shafts of light falling onto the earth floor of the adjoining room. She knew exactly where she was now. She and Kate were in the wine cellar, where the barrels of wine had been kept to mature. When the château had grown its own grapes, the mash would have been brought through the room above the one where they were chained, and tipped into the huge fermentation barrels that would have stood on the dirt floor of the room next to theirs, the fermentation cellar. That's why she could see the circles of light. There were circular holes in the stone floor above the barrels so the mash could be tipped straight down the hole, into the barrels. And there were holes now in the roof of the room above. They had never got round to repairing it. It had been Nick's next project, to restore the whole wine-making building.

Joanne thought hard, trying to remember the exact layout. She knew the cellar that she and Kate were in had no door directly to the outside. That was so that the temperature and humidity stayed the same to help the wine mature properly. Their chains were new, but they were attached to old rings in the cellar wall. She wasn't sure what they'd been there for, but, despite the years, they were still firmly fixed. But some of the stonework was crumbling. Maybe she'd be able to work the ring free from the wall, in time. If she could get the ring out of the wall, how was she going to get out? There had been a door to the outside from the fermentation cellar, but it had been blocked up by the previous owner so that no one could go in there in case the roof fell in. That meant she'd have to climb out through the circular mash holes. But how was she going to do that? The barrels used to be nearly three metres high, and stood on planks to keep them off the floor to stop the base rotting. She knew there were no fermentation barrels there anymore, but maybe, just maybe, some of the planks were still lying around.

She started to scrabble away at the wall around the ring holding her chain in place. Kate was lying slumped against the wall. No point expecting help from that quarter. Joanne gritted her teeth and heaved on the ring. Her fingers slipped on the damp wall and it was difficult to get a purchase. She'd have to try and scrape away some of the crumbling bits. She was crawling over to reach a pointed stone near her on the floor when she heard a noise. It sounded like a car, maybe more than one. From what Kate had told her, it didn't seem likely that the drug smugglers would be back, but could she be sure they'd actually gone? Should she call out, in case it was someone come to look for her? She wished she'd left her car in a more obvious place. It'd probably gone anyway. The gang would have been sure to spot it and would have taken it. So no one would think she was here, even if they did come to look. She sat still, straining her ears for other sounds, but the cellar was almost completely underground and too well insulated by its thick walls and ceiling.

Joanne grabbed the pointed stone and wriggled back to her iron ring. No point waiting for someone find her. Face facts, she told herself. The only way out of here is getting the ring out of the wall and somehow climbing up through the fermentation hole.

A few hours later, she judged, she'd succeeded in scraping away enough of the small stones and mortar around the ring so that she could wiggle it around. She sat back against the wall to rest her aching fingers. She was getting pretty tired now, and her headache was getting worse again. No time for self-pity, she told herself, taking up her position at the wall again.

****

The dog's bark echoed loudly through the cellar. Joanne dropped her stone and jerked around. One of the circles of light in the ceiling next door was obliterated. The dog had its big, white, furry head through the hole.

"Ferdie!" Joanne cried in delight.

The dog yelped with pleasure.

****

"Where's that bloody dog got to?" Jim asked. "There's no point staying here any longer. We'll have to get onto the police. She'd not here. We've looked everywhere."

"Yes, I suppose you're right," John replied.

"Ferdie! Ferdie! Come on! Home time!"

The dog's answering bark came from somewhere nearby.

"Come on, Ferdie!" Jim was getting annoyed. "It's not a game!"

They walked back to the cars. Jim looked around, expecting Ferdie to have got there first. But there was no sign of him.

"Bloody animal! I'll have to go and look for him."

"That's him barking again. It sounds as if he's in there," said John. "You looked in there, didn't you?"

"Yes, it was the last place I went in. I didn't go through into the next bit where the roof's missing. I've never been in that bit. Nick said it was dangerous. But I could see there was no one in there."

"Better go and get the dog, in case he's got trapped there or something," John said.

They retraced their steps into the courtyard and through the big open doorway.

"This is where they used to bring the grapes in," Jim said. "The cellar's under here."

"Cellar?" John looked at him. "Why haven't we looked there?"

"The door's blocked up now," Jim answered. "And as far as I know, there's no other way in. Ferdie!"

The dog's answering bark came from deep within the building. John went ahead, his footsteps echoing down the long room. When he got to the doorway into the next room he hesitated, glancing up at the crumbling lintel. On the other side, the main roof beam had cracked almost in two and big sections of the roof had caved in. Piles of broken roof tiles and stones littered the uneven floor.

"Here he is!" John shouted back to Jim. "What are you doing, Ferdie? He seems to have got his head stuck in a pile of stones," he called to Jim.

"It's not a pile of stones, you prat! It's a hole down to the fermentation cellar! And I'm chained up to the wall of the next cellar!"

The exasperated female voice floating up from the bowels of the earth made John jump out of his skin. Jim came crashing through, nearly tripping over on the stone slabs and rubble in his haste.

"Ferdie! You marvel! You've found her!"

"Jim Munro, get down here and cut me free! You'll need bolt cutters, but I know you'll have some in the back of your van."

9

An hour later they were sitting around the roaring fire in the dining room of the Hôtel Coq d'Or. Joanne's Porsche was parked in the square, alongside the Land Rover and Jim's van.

"You must tell the police," Patricia was saying earnestly to Kate, who sat huddled next to the fire, her hands, still shaking, clasped around a cup of tea.

"I can't."

She shook her head.

"I know you are right, but if I do, they'll kill Richard. I know they will. They are ruthless."

"But how can you be sure he's with them?" Jim asked. "I mean, if they'd got you two chained up in the cellar, no one else knew what they were up to, so why should they take him with them? How can you be sure they haven't already killed him and dumped him somewhere?"

"Jim!" Pat glared at him.

"Jim's right," said Joanne. "And in any case, it's getting on for twenty-four hours since they left. If they were going back to England, they'd have crossed the Channel ages ago. Anyway, what are you going to do, Kate? Wait for them to tell you where Richard is? What on earth makes you think they'll bother? It's more likely they've just dumped him somewhere, probably somewhere near here. There would be no reason to take him with them, but also they'd have no reason to kill him, so long as they left him somewhere he wouldn't be found straight away. I think you should go to the police. Let them start a proper search."

Ferdie shifted his position slightly, keeping his head resting on her feet.

318

"I agree with Joanne," John Nicholson spoke for the first time since they'd got back to the hotel. "It's your best bet. If it hadn't been for Ferdie, we wouldn't have found you. They must know that although you'd have been missed, Joanne, it would have taken a very thorough search of the château to find you both. By that time, they'd be long gone. Richard would just have been a hindrance to them, not an insurance policy."

"But I can't risk it," Kate wailed. "What if they have still got him with them, and they hear that the police are looking for them? If I give the police their names and descriptions, and the van and everything? And then there's the other one. Frank. He seemed to be in charge. And he didn't go with them the first time, so he may be still around here somewhere. And that man in the estate agent's and that French woman in the headscarf who was following me everywhere. They might have Richard. Frank warned me if I ever said anything, Richard would be killed. I tell you, they must still have him. They know I can identify them all, so I can never talk."

"But they aren't going to keep Richard indefinitely, are they?" Joanne said, exasperation showing in her voice. "We know he's nowhere in the château. They've probably taken him away, to make you think they'd still got him and then dumped him somewhere."

"Think about it rationally," John said to Kate.

Joanne glanced at him. Was he being sarcastic? Kate, rational? But his face was earnest, and his deep, resonant voice was full of sympathy. Joanne felt ashamed at her own impatience with Kate.

"If they want your silence," John went on, "they'd have to have a hold over you. And that hold is Richard. If he is their hostage, why did they chain you up and leave you somewhere where you wouldn't be found? If Joanne hadn't been caught snooping around, you'd have been down there alone. Who would have missed you? Remember, they put you down there before they caught Joanne. It was part of their plan. So, what does that mean? I'm afraid it means they expected you to die down there, because you wouldn't have been found."

John went on quietly.

"They could have killed you, both you and Joanne, but my guess is that they'd have come back in a few weeks or months or so and taken the chains away, so it looked like you'd accidentally fallen into the cellar. Which would have been easy to do. Then there wouldn't have been any murder charge, even if they were ever caught for the drugs. I think you have to face it. Richard probably isn't with them any longer. To keep you quiet they'd have to hold him prisoner forever. And that would be more of a risk to them that just dumping him somewhere. But I don't think they'll have killed him either. They could have thrown him down into the cellar with you, but that would seem a bit odd when you were all eventually discovered. They know he went missing and was never found. If he's found now, somewhere out in the countryside, maybe where they found him in the first place, for example, who's to say he hasn't been there all the time since August? From what you say, he's pretty ill and incoherent. I think we have to tell the police what's happened so they can find him, and soon. If you leave it much longer, it'll be too late for Richard anyway."

Kate looked into the fire. She knew it made sense. He was right. She'd have to take the risk.

18

Phillippe turned on the TV just as the local news was starting. He needed a shower before he went over to Chloe's. It had been a busy day after a late night at the hospital and his back ached. Perhaps he'd have a bath.

He was coming back into the sitting room when an image on the TV screen caught his eye. There had been a major crash on the N20 just south of Souillac the night before. One person killed and one severely injured. The ambulance had arrived at the hospital in Cahors just as he was leaving late last night. The TV newsreel showed a large furniture van on its side halfway down the hillside, the van's cab a mangled wreck. The newsreader was saying something about a haul of hashish hidden under the floor of the van. The picture changed to Capitaine Lolmède, standing outside the police headquarters in Cahors. This was the gang they had been searching for since the summer. The van driver was dead and police were at the bedside of his companion. They were both English, and the police thought that the one who was still alive was the boss of the operation. They weren't looking for anyone else. The picture changed again. Back to the van. The camera panned in, showing the hidden compartments under the floor and the parcels of hashish stacked inside. Also stacked in the van was furniture. Phillippe looked hard at the TV screen. There was something familiar about the van and about a couple of pieces of furniture that were lying near the open door of the van. The camera angle changed and the TV showed an aerial view of the crash. Phillippe stared. It looked just like the van he'd seen coming out of the track to the Château de St Geniès-Lafontaine that night a couple of weeks ago. And he was sure the Louis XIV desk on its side in the mud was the same one that had once stood in the salon of the château. He reached for the phone.

****

"Oooh, I say! Dreadful business, isn't it? Makes you ashamed to be English," the blonde woman said.

The flight attendant sitting next to her in front of the TV in the small first class lounge at Toulouse International Airport nodded.

"Doesn't it just?" she said, breaking off as a flight announcement drowned out their conversation. "That's us. That's the crew call. Nice talking to you. I'll see you on the flight."

"See you later, then, duck. I'd better go and find that son of mine, and my sister. They went off somewhere a while ago. I expect she's leading him astray," she cackled.

Half an hour later the two fat, middle-aged, bright-blonde women were sitting either side of Frank in the front row of the first class cabin on flight BA369 to Malaga, watching as the swimming pools of the suburbs of Toulouse receded into tiny blue dots.

"Cheers, Ma, Aunt Sal!" said Frank, raising his glass of champagne.

They clinked glasses and settled back into their seats. Shame about Jimmy, Frank thought. But just as well it was Vin who'd survived. Vin wouldn't talk, but he couldn't have been sure about Jimmy. Vin knew Frank'd look after him when he got out. Shame about the consignment as well. Still, it was fortunate that Frank hadn't quite got around to handing Jimmy and Vin their share of the proceeds from the first shipment. It was always nice to have a bit of extra cash. Frank smiled in satisfaction. He was looking forward to the future. He liked the Costa. And he was clean. It'd been Ma's idea to have a 'stage name' as she put it. No more Frank – back to good old Dennis, just like on his passport. And it was nice to be able to stop wearing the brown contact lenses. Aunt Sal was a dab hand with the spray tan, and she'd done his new blond highlights just the way he liked them. He was definitely feeling more like his old self. Ma's house in Fromac was clean as well. They wouldn't sell it straight away, just in case. They could all go back there next summer for a while. A lot of the expats in France did that – the Costa for the winter but it could get a bit too hot in August. And he was getting out just at the right time, with the bottom falling out of the UK market for hash. You had to keep up with the times and know when to stop. Too many entrepreneurs growing high-strength skunk in their attics all over England.

He settled back in his seat. Pity about those two women in the cellar. Especially the blonde. Still, when the bodies were eventually found, if anyone did make the connection between the drugs and the château, it would be obvious that it must have been Jimmy and Vin who had chained them up while they made their getaway. Poor old Vin. Looked as if he might be up on a murder charge one day as well.

****

At about the same time, the police officer stationed by the bedside of the Englishman in Cahors hospital awoke with a start as the man moved slightly and mumbled something. The officer grabbed his pager and called for the interpreter. Vin moved his head again, beads of sweat appearing on his forehead. His eyes flickered open.

"Jimmy…"

The officer leaned forward to catch his words. The door opened and Capitaine Lolmède rushed in, followed by two nurses.

"Has he said anything?"

"No, Sir."

"OK, you go and get a coffee. I'll stay here. The interpreter's gone home, so I hope my English is up to it," he said. "Switch the tape on."

The nurses bustled around the bed. Vin's eyes flickered again. He muttered something, then again, the same.

"What?" Lolmède strained to catch the words. "What did you say?"

Vin's eyes closed. Again came the same few words. But what was he saying? Hubert Lolmède leaned closer.

"What?"

Vin's breathing was shallow. The nurses looked at each other anxiously, one of them checking the signal on the monitor beside the bed.

"Capitaine, I think we must ask you to leave. The patient is getting weaker," one of them said.

Vin's eyes suddenly opened and fixed on Hubert.

"Capitaine?" he croaked.

"Yes?" Hubert bent forward eagerly.

"Capitaine," Vin's voice was barely audible. "Fuck off."

The monitor went blank. The nurses hustled Lolmède out of the room. Hubert stood in the corridor cursing. He looked at the small tape recorder in his hand. Perhaps they'd get something off it. He wanted to get the man behind this smuggling racket. For some reason he didn't think it was the dead man in the room he'd just left. And he was sure it wasn't the driver.

"He said 'floor', 'got to get the rest', 'we'll share it, Jimmy', 'get the rest, it's underneath', 'we'll share, get it', 'floor', 'under', 'got to get the rest', 'go back afterwards and get it, we'll share it', 'get the rest, Jimmy, it's underneath', 'we'll share, get it', 'go back.'"

"You're sure? You're sure that's all he said?"

Jean Joubert nodded.

"Yes, Capitaine. Definitely all. In that order."

"OK. Thanks, Jean. You've been very helpful. You are wasted in the Gendarmerie."

Jean smirked and bowed slightly before edging out of the office. Hubert Lolmède rubbed his face with his hands. 'Got to get the rest'. It was bad enough that they'd more or less closed the case, thinking all the stuff had been taken out of the area before they'd raided the house at Lalbenque back in August. Now it looked as if it'd been hidden somewhere on his patch all the time, right under his nose. And there was more somewhere. But where? 'Under the floor' wasn't a great clue.

The phone on the desk close to his elbow rang suddenly. It was the duty sergeant downstairs.

"I've got Dr de la Bernière on the line. Wants a word about the drugs case."

"Put him on."

A few minutes later, Hubert replaced the receiver thoughtfully. So from what Phillippe had told him, it looked as if there might be a connection between the drug smuggling ring and the Château de St Geniès-Lafontaine after all. He thought back to his interview with the Blacks after the disappearance of Richard Talbot. He'd known they were hiding something. He remembered ruefully that it had been either Jules or Bernie who'd suggested they might have had something to do with the drugs gang, and he'd dismissed it. As he thought about it now, it seemed more plausible. Alastair Black might just be the man behind it all. If Richard Talbot had been his partner, or even just a courier, and there'd been some sort of dispute, his suspicious disappearance would be easy to explain. Yes, it was beginning to fit into place. The police had been all over the château and the grounds when they'd been searching for Talbot. Black knew that, so it was the ideal place to move the drugs to after the search, then just lie low. Hubert himself had handed back Black's passport. But he'd put an order out to passport control and so he'd be informed if Black ever entered France again. He'd been too clever for them. He'd got clean away with one shipment, Hubert guessed, the one Phillippe had seen that night. They'd recovered the second one, but only by default, because of the crash. And according to the information from the dying courier, there was one more to go. Hubert stood up. He knew what had to be done. Take Phillippe's statement tonight. Get a stakeout organised on the track from the château to make sure nothing and no one left tonight. Get an alert out to all ports and airports to be on the lookout for Alastair Black. First thing tomorrow, a raid on the château. He'd get the bastards in the end. He was out of the office in seconds, bounding down the corridor, calling to his staff. He didn't hear the phone ringing.

11

The Café de France was busy for a winter's evening.

"Capitaine Lolmède is over there, Docteur," the waitress said as she passed him, plates of pasta in her hands.

"Thanks, Martine," he smiled and made his way between the tables to the back of the room where Hubert was sitting with a glass of beer in front of him. He stood up as Phillippe approached.

"Phillippe. Good of you to come. Sorry to drag you out this evening, but I want to move on this one straight away. Everything is set up for a dawn raid. So I need to know all that you can tell me."

Phillippe sat down, facing Hubert across the table.

"Of course," he said. "I hope I can help. There's not much to tell."

****

"And the way she behaved, Madame Black, that is," Phillippe concluded some minutes later. "It was so odd. Or so I thought at the time. But of course now, it's clear why she didn't want anyone at the château, and why she didn't want to leave it herself. And from what I know about her trying to get the château for herself, she's definitely got a crooked streak in her."

Hubert nodded.

"It certainly fits," he agreed. "Have you seen her recently?"

"No," Phillippe shook his head. "Not since the funeral."

"So she might have left already?"

"It's certainly possible. But there's someone who would know."

327

He gestured towards a table near the front of the café where a tall, dark-haired man was holding a chair for a blonde woman. Two teenage children had already settled themselves at the table. Hubert looked. He didn't recognise the woman, but the man and the children looked familiar.

"That's John Nicholson, isn't it?" he asked. "He owns the barn just down from the château? The guy who reported Richard Talbot missing? How would he know about Kate Black? I thought he didn't know the Blacks?"

"I don't think he does," Phillippe replied. "But the woman with him certainly knows Kate. That's Joanne Carslow, Nick Carslow's wife. Owner of the Château de St Geniès-Lafontaine. And what's more," he went on. "She was going to the château today to see Madame Black and re-claim her château."

"Well, well," said Hubert. "I think I might have to interrupt their evening for a few minutes. But first things first," he smiled as Martine placed a bowl of steaming bouillabaisse in front of each of them.

12

Joanne put her glass down to stop herself spilling the wine as she shook with laughter.

"Dan!" Susie spluttered. "That's the worst joke I've ever heard!"

"So why are you laughing so much, Susie?" her father asked, wiping tears from his eyes.

Joanne looked across the table at the three of them. She felt a pang of – what? Jealousy? They looked so happy, so complete in their little family group, such good pals. Susie and Dan were the sort of children she'd always dreamed she'd have herself. And John. She glanced at him appraisingly. Scruffy, yes. Good-looking? Average. Lovely eyes, could do with a shave. Tall, fit, yes and yes. Rich, definitely not. But kind, generous, considerate, gentle, funny. Attractive? Her mind went back to that afternoon and she shivered very slightly. She'd thought she must be hallucinating when she had heard that beautiful, deep, soft musical voice somewhere above her. She had felt so safe in the strong, muscular arms that had heaved her out of the cellar.

She was glad he'd asked her to join him and his children this evening. It was good to get away from Kate. Pat and Jim were looking after her at the hotel tonight. Joanne needed space away from them, and John had guessed. She shifted her gaze as Dan tugged on her sleeve.

"Listen, Joanne. This one's even better. And this isn't a joke, right, this one's true! It was when we were driving down this time, we stopped at one of the picnic places on the autoroute, where they have these funny toilet blocks, you know? And this other English car had just stopped, and this huge, really fat, old woman got out. I think she was with her son. He looked really fed up. Anyway, she goes into the ladies' toilet block, and she's in there for ages. He's standing by the car waiting, looking at his watch, then she comes out, killing herself laughing. And it seems it's the first time she'd been to a French loo on a motorway and she's never seen one of these foot-print ones they have. Well, she didn't know which way round to use it and…."

"Dan!" Susie and John yelled in unison.

"What? It's all true!"

"Yes, Dan. But we are all eating our dinner and that's enough for now," John said firmly. "What will Joanne think?"

Joanne thinks you are the nicest man she's met in a long time, thought Joanne. And that voice is just so sexy.

Across the café, Hubert and Phillippe finished their meal.

"OK," said Hubert. "I think it's time to see how Mrs Carslow got on at the château. I'd like you to come with me, Phillippe. I might need your help with the translation."

Phillippe nodded and the two men made their way through the crowded café. John Nicholson turned as they approached.

"Phillippe!" he smiled broadly, rising and holding out his hand. "It's good to see you again. And," he turned to Hubert. "Capitaine Lolmède, isn't it? You remember my children? And this is Joanne Carslow."

Once the introductions were over, Hubert spoke.

"Do you mind if we join you for a few minutes?" he asked. "I'll come straight to the point. It's about the Château de St Geniès-Lafontaine. Your château, Madame."

Joanne looked surprised.

"Oh, good," she said. "I thought Kate said there was no reply from your office. She must have found you after all."

It was Hubert's turn to look surprised.

"Kate?"

His eyebrows lifted.

"Mrs Black?"

"Yes," John put in. "When we left the Coq d'Or she'd just tried to get in touch with you. We assumed that's why you are here," he looked mystified. "Isn't it?"

Hubert looked from one to the other, then at Phillippe.

"Phillippe, do I understand correctly?" he asked in rapid French. "Did they say they think I am here because Kate Black has been to see me or told me something?"

Phillippe nodded. Hubert turned back to Joanne and John.

"I am afraid I have not heard from Madame Black. Perhaps you could tell me what she wanted to see me about."

Joanne and John looked at each other.

"Well," John began. "It was something that we had persuaded Kate she should go to the police about, but, for certain reasons, she was reluctant. If she hasn't yet spoken to you, I'm not sure we should say more, in case she's changed her mind."

"But she'd made up her mind! She phoned him!" Joanne broke in. "The police need to know!"

Hubert sighed. What was it with anything to do with this château? Bloody English, sticking together! Even shielding criminals? He held up his hands.

"Very well," he said. "The reason for me wishing to speak to you is this. Madame Carslow, I understand from Phillippe here that you were to visit your château today?"

"Yes, that's right," agreed Joanne.

"And did you?"

"Yes and no," replied Joanne. "I went yesterday, but I didn't leave until today?"

"I see. You decided to stay the night there?"

"Me, decide to stay! No, I did not!" Joanne spoke crossly.

"Look," she said to John. "This is silly. I'm going to tell him what I know. Even if Kate's changed her mind, I can't see I'll be doing anybody any favours by keeping quiet."

She turned back to Hubert.

"I'll tell you what happened to me. I went to the château yesterday, in the early evening. I just wanted to have a look at the place. Phillippe had suggested I wait until today before seeing Kate, but I couldn't resist just stopping by to see it again. So I parked out of sight up the track and then I walked down to the château."

****

When she had finished, Hubert sat back in his chair.

"Thank you, Madame," he said. "I am grateful to you. You have just saved us a lot of time. You are sure that Madame Black said they had removed all the drugs from the château?"

"Yes. That's what they told her, and she knew where they'd been hidden when they brought them over months ago. They weren't coming back. They'd chained her up in the cellar before they even found me. But you knew about all this?" Joanne asked. "I mean, about the drugs at the château?"

"Not until this evening when Phillippe phoned me," Hubert replied. "You may remember he told you he'd seen a furniture van leaving your château a couple of weeks ago?"

"Of course!" Joanne cried. "But how did he connect it with drugs?"

"You haven't seen the TV news today?"

They shook their heads.

"The same furniture van, the one you saw being loaded in your coach house, crashed on its way north last night. The driver was killed outright and his companion died this afternoon. We discovered the drugs hidden as you have described. Phillippe, by chance, saw it on the TV news. And remembered about the other van. Now we must go and visit Madame Black. It is important that she identifies our two smugglers. And of course, now we know that there is a third person involved. The boss. And he, it seems, has got away. Did you recognise any of the men, Madame? Did any of them look familiar? Someone you might have seen around here, or," he paused. "Someone who might have known or been known to Madame Black?"

Joanne shook her head.

"No. But I was quite a distance away, and it was dark. But Kate will be able to give you a good description. The one who was in charge stayed at the château with her when the others made the first delivery."

"But you said there were definitely only two people in the van?" Dan interrupted suddenly.

All eyes turned on him.

"What colour hair did they have?" he asked breathlessly.

Hubert looked puzzled. What was the kid getting at? He looked round the table. Apart from Phillippe, they all seemed to be holding their breath.

"The driver's hair was dark brown. The one we took to hospital was blond, with dark roots."

"You were right, Dad!" Dan cried. "They must have dumped Richard."

"Unless the other one's got him," Susie interrupted. "The boss might have taken him."

Hubert covered his eyes. Richard. He might have guessed. The missing Englishman had turned up. Maybe his guess hadn't been that far out. Maybe Alastair Black was the boss after all. He needed to talk to Kate Black.

"Capitaine," Joanne said. "That's the bit I've left out of my story. Kate wouldn't go to the police because this gang had found Richard after he'd disappeared in the storm in August and brought him back to the château with the drugs. They blackmailed Kate into keeping quiet by threatening to kill him. When they left with the drugs, they took him with them to make sure she didn't go to you. She really wasn't involved, you know. And this evening we'd persuaded her to tell you what had been going on so that you would have a chance of finding him. He was pretty ill, and we all felt that they would just dump him somewhere. She's at the Coq d'Or in Fromac. Why don't we go there now?"

13

Kate stood in the brightly-lit hospital morgue. An attendant in pale green overalls pulled on two handles in the bank of drawers. The slabs slid out silently. He flicked back the sheets that covered the faces of the two bodies and stepped aside. She moved closer, the smell of formalin catching the back of her throat. She looked down. Vin and Jimmy looked – what? Peaceful? No. They looked – nothing. Just dead. She nodded.

"That's them. This one was called Jimmy. The other is Vin. They're both English. That's all I know about them. They brought the drugs to the château. They stayed there all the time, keeping watch on Richard and me, and on anyone who came to the château. They weren't in charge. It was the other one, Frank. They did what he told them."

"Thank you," Hubert held the door open for her. "Please, wait for me outside. I will be a few minutes."

Kate walked down the corridor as if in a trance. Richard hadn't been in the van, thank goodness. But where was he? What if Frank had him? She sat down on a bench at the end of the corridor. It was very quiet in the hospital. She glanced at her watch. It was nearly midnight. That meant it must be about thirty hours since Jimmy and Vin had left the château. Probably Frank had left soon after them. She hadn't heard any vehicles after she'd come round in the cellar. That meant Richard had been without food or water or any medication since then, maybe dumped out in the open, in November. She buried her face in her hands. How were they going to find him? In time?

Hubert's voice broke into her thoughts.

"Thank you, Madame," he said. "I know it is late, but if we are to find this Frank, and Richard Talbot, time is of the essence. I need you to come to the station with me now and give a description of Frank. Then I would like you to see if you can think of anything, anything at all that might give us a clue to where the rest of the drugs might be hidden."

Kate nodded.

"Yes, I'll come."

****

An hour later, Hubert stubbed out his last cigarette. The ashtray on his office desk was over-flowing. Jean Joubert yawned loudly.

"Yes, we'll call it a day," he said. "Jean, please make sure Madame Black gets back to the Coq d'Or safely and I'll see you tomorrow at nine. In the Coq d'Or. I've asked the other English witnesses to be there. So I need you," he added to the gendarme.

Jean smiled wanly.

"Glad to be of service, Sir," he said.

He was beginning to think perhaps it hadn't been such a brilliant idea to perfect his English. He hadn't bargained for all-night sessions.

After they had left, Hubert sat down at his desk and looked at the photofit of Frank. It could be anyone. No distinguishing features. This guy would just blend into a crowd anywhere. He had that sort of face. And you couldn't stop everyone just because their name was Frank. Anyway, he had well over twenty-four hours start on them. Hubert shrugged. No, they'd never catch him now. This guy was smart. Unless, he pondered, unless Madame Black was up to her old tricks. Had she deliberately given a description of someone so ordinary-looking that no one would ever be able to pick him out? To shield the real boss? Possibly her husband Alastair? Very clever, in fact, to go for the ordinary, when the temptation would be to go for some striking feature, possibly opposite to the real boss. Hubert went over the story again. No, she couldn't be shielding her husband. Not if he'd left her chained in a cellar where no one would find her. And if it hadn't been for Madame Carslow, and Jim Munro and his dog, no one would have found her. No, he had to concentrate on finding the rest of the drugs that Vin had mumbled about as he lay dying. At least that would salvage some pride for his team. But more important, they'd keep it off the streets. That was what mattered to Hubert.

He got to his feet and tipped the contents of the ashtray into the waste bin. Perhaps he shouldn't have done that. Might set the office alight. He shrugged and set off down the corridor.

****

On his way home, he went over the case again and again in his mind. He believed Kate Black's story. She just wasn't the sort to be involved with drug smugglers. Her anxiety to find Richard Talbot was genuine. He'd have to talk to Jules about the Englishman in the estate agent's that Kate had mentioned and the French woman who she thought had followed her. Maybe he'd get a lead on Frank if he could track them down. Or maybe they'd just been two innocent bystanders. Kate Black seemed pretty unstable to him. Not surprising, he reflected. She'd had quite a year since she'd come to France. He wondered idly what had really happened to Richard Talbot on the night of the storm. It didn't matter much now. But, he thought ruefully, he was back where he'd started, in August: looking for the cache of drugs and looking for this missing Englishman. The irony was that Jules had known the château was the key, and he'd been right. They'd both turned up at the château but he'd been too – what? Unimaginative, not tenacious enough? Too unwilling to accept that the local gendarmes might be right? Whatever. Now he'd lost them both again. From somewhere in the depths of his memory, he had a clear vision of his old English mistress at the *lycée*. That stupid English play they'd had to perform. Something about losing one parent being a misfortune, losing two being carelessness. Bloody English. He was sick of them. His head ached from concentrating on the foreign tongue. And there was more to come tomorrow. Just as well he'd got Joubert to help.

****

Kate sat silent in the back of the squad car as Jean Joubert drove them quickly along the deserted roads back to Fromac. She'd felt nothing when she'd looked down at the still faces of Jimmy and Vin. Now she was starting to shake. Nick, the notaire's wife, the baby, Jimmy, Vin. Maybe Richard. Death seemed to surround her. Ever since she'd come to the château, everything had gone wrong. Her hopes and dreams of a new life with Nick, shattered. The pain and anguish she'd inflicted on Alastair. Her poor baby. Richard's nightmare, all caused by her. Her own deceitful and treacherous attempt to steal the château from Joanne. Herself and Joanne, left to die in the wine cellar, but for fortune and a Pyrenean mountain dog. She stared out of the car window at the unrelieved blackness. The car's headlights picked out the small, familiar white sign: *Château de St Geniès-Lafontaine*.

Kate flinched, remembering the first time she'd seen that sign. How it had seemed to glow with the promise of a fresh start. She thought about Joanne. Would she, Kate, have been so generous? Joanne could have kicked her and the baby out onto the street ages ago. She could ruin her now, have her sent to prison. But she wasn't suing her. Ever since they'd been rescued, she'd been urging her to get the police to find Richard, persistently asking her to remember all Richard had said to see if they could guess where the drugs might have been. Joanne's theory was that Richard must have stumbled on wherever the drugs were hidden originally, and the chances were that was where the remainder of the stash was still. Kate remembered John Nicholson agreeing and saying he thought that Vin and Jimmy would have dumped Richard where they'd first found him. It must be somewhere isolated since the police couldn't find him back in August. And so when he was eventually found, if he ever was, Frank would have figured that everyone would assume he'd been there since August and no one would suspect his death had any connection with them.

Kate suddenly sat up straight. All these people were trying to help her and Richard. She had to pull herself together. She had to try and remember everything Richard had said to her when they'd first brought him back to the château. He'd been delirious, but he'd kept repeating certain words. She remembered them quite clearly, but they made no sense. But perhaps if she told the others, they'd be able to make something of it. There might be some sort of clue. Perhaps they'd be able to work out how far from the château he might have got. She thought hard. If Joanne and John were right and he'd stumbled on where Jimmy and Vin had hidden the drugs, it must be somewhere down river from the château, but quite near to the river. He could have been swept quite a long way, but she judged the injuries to his legs and back must have happened when he was swept over the weir. So he might have travelled some distance in the water, but wouldn't have been able to move far on land. If Joanne and John were right, all they'd have to do was search the river banks, looking for barns or some sort of place where the drugs could have been hidden. Kate looked at her watch. It was nearly two am. Everyone would be in bed now. But first thing in the morning, she could tell them what Richard had said, and they could start looking. They might still find him in time.

14

"When he was delirious, he kept talking about stones, a big heap of stones, going round and round. Then something about a giant, and balancing stones. Afterwards, when he was feeling better, he tried to describe the place he'd been locked in," Kate said. "He told me he couldn't remember what had happened after the boat overturned. He remembered coming to in some sort of building, but he couldn't remember much about it. He said he was locked in, and it was cold and very dark. There weren't any windows. The only other thing he could remember was a big pile of fertiliser sacks. That was the drugs. I know that because when they brought him back to the château, they brought sacks like that. Blue plastic. They hid them in the cellar under the scullery. But he said he thought he was in a farm outbuilding. In fact, he thought he was in your barn, John. When he was delirious, he kept calling out, 'John, I'm over here'."

"He couldn't have been at our place, could he? And us not know?" Susie asked anxiously.

"And that is all?" Hubert asked Kate, ignoring Susie.

Joanne put her hand on Susie's and smiled.

"I don't think he could have been there," she whispered.

Hubert looked enquiringly at Kate.

"Is there anything else?"

"I don't think so," Kate replied. "Oh, but there is one other thing. His arms and hands were very scratched and covered in dried blood. You know how wet it was that night? It was very muddy and there was a lot of long, wet grass all along by the river, but he seemed to have a lot of small fragments of sharp chalk stuck in the flesh of his hands and forearms, as if he'd been crawling on a path or a track."

"Sounds as if he could have crawled quite a distance from the river then?" asked Jim. "There must be several tracks he could have reached if he'd been determined enough."

Hubert looked at Jules Espinet, who nodded. Hubert stood up.

"Thank you, Madame. It looks as if we are going to have to search quite an area. I'll try and get some more men. Jules, take Jean and make a start. Look at any tracks leading down to the river first. Start up by the weir. At this time of year, you should be able to see any buildings. Monsieur Nicholson, I suppose it is not possible that he was in fact on your property?"

John shook his head.

"I don't think so. We've just got the barn, and the only place he could possibly have been was the cellar. That's dark and the walls are stone. But it's choc-a-bloc with junk. I doubt there would have been room for one sack of fertiliser, let alone a whole stack. Anyway, we're in and out of there all the time. And our track is pure mud, I'm afraid. I haven't quite got round to putting any gravel down. But of course we'll have a really good look around."

"Thank you. We'll put out all the search notices again. Of course, it is only conjecture that Monsieur Talbot has been put back where he was first found. But," he shrugged. "We must start somewhere. If any of you, and you in particular, Madame Black, remember anything else, any detail, however small, please phone my office immediately."

When he had gone, Jim got up and called to Ferdie.

"I'm going to take a walk along the river bank from the weir. See if I can see anything."

"Let's do it together," said John. "We'll go to my place, check it out with Ferdie. Then me and the kids will do one bank, you do the other."

"I'll come too!" Kate was half out of her chair.

Jim and John glanced at each other.

"No," John shook his head. "You stay here. The Capitaine will want to know where to find you if he needs to. And try and think if there is anything else, any other clues in what Richard might have told you."

"Alright," Kate agreed reluctantly. "But I feel so useless."

****

"I've looked everywhere, Dad," Susie said. "There's no sign he's been here."

"No, I'm not surprised," replied John. "But we had to look. Now where is Dan? We should start."

"He's up at the new tree house with the binoculars."

"Well, go and get him. Tell him we're going without him. He can catch us up."

Susie set off up their track towards the road. As she branched off into the woods, Dan came crashing through the undergrowth towards her.

"Hey, where's Dad? Dad! Dad! Come here!" shouted Dan, slithering helter-skelter down the steep bank.

John was walking quickly and was almost at the river bank where Jim and Ferdie stood waiting on the other side by the time he heard Dan's shouts.

"What is it?"

"Dad, I think I know where he was!" Dan yelled, gasping for breath.

"Steady on, son."

John stopped and waited for Dan to catch up with him.

"Dad, you know what Kate said Richard had said when he was delirious? About piles of stones going round and round? Well, I've been thinking about it, and I know what he was talking about!"

"Go on," John said.

"*Gariottes*! You know, those circular shelters the shepherds have. They are round, and they're made of piles of stones. And they are dark. And," Dan paused for breath. " Because they're shepherd's huts, they are surrounded by sheep!"

John looked at him curiously. It had made sense so far.

"Sheep?"

"Yes, Dad!" Dan cried in exasperation. "Sheep eat grass! Anywhere round here where there have been sheep, the grass is really short and nibbled right down to the chalk. So that's how he'd have got the scratches. He might not have crawled up a track at all. He'd have got scratches like that if he'd crawled over a field where sheep had been!"

John nodded slowly. It still made sense.

"But there aren't any sheep around here anymore, are there?" he asked. "I don't remember seeing any."

"Not down in the valley," said Dan. "But up there," he pointed to the top of the steep field on the opposite bank. "There was a flock up there when we were down last Easter. I can see the field from my new tree house. And I've just been up there with the binoculars. And Dad, I was right! I thought there was a *gariotte* up there. You can see it quite clearly now the leaves are off the trees!"

John stared at him.

"Dan, you're a star! Quick, let's go and tell Jim. How far downstream do we need to go?"

"I was thinking about that too," replied Dan. "You know where there was that tree down in the storm, the big one that fell across the river near the bend?"

"Oh yes," said John. "We can cross the river there."

"Yeah," Dan nodded. "But that's not the point, Dad. That tree came down early on in the storm, right? So if you'd been in the river after it came down, you'd have crashed straight into it, wouldn't you? You probably wouldn't have been swept past. So Richard would be somewhere between the weir and that tree. And the *gariotte* is sort of straight up the hill from the tree, just a bit further on. So that's the first building he'd have come to. There's nothing else between the château and that next bridge on that side. So it must be where he ended up!"

"Come on, then," John grinned at his son.

It all made sense.

"Let's hope you're right and he's there!"

It wasn't long before they'd climbed the hill and the *gariotte* came into view. It was the perfect place to stash anything you didn't want found, thought John. It was virtually invisible from his own barn, and there were no other buildings around. It was in the middle of a large, sloping field. There was no sign of a track, although Jim Munro was pretty sure he knew where the nearest one was, and it would have been no problem driving across the sheep field, even in the storm.

The *gariotte* was about two metres high at it apex and constructed entirely from smallish, similar-sized stones, with no mortar. There was virtually no break between the short, vertical walls and the spiralling, cone-like roof. No wonder Richard had raved about piles of stones going round and round. That was exactly what it was. Dan was in the lead as they climbed the last few metres. The wooden door hung open. There was no sign of a lock or chain. It creaked slightly on its hinges in the wind. Dan came to an abrupt halt a couple of paces from the doorway.

"Wait there, Dan," John said quietly, but needlessly.

Dan certainly didn't want to be the first to go in. Jim grasped Ferdie's collar and slipped his lead off.

"OK, Ferdie," he whispered. "Let's see what we can find."

He took a small torch from his pocket and ducked in through the low doorway after Ferdie. John and his children stood together in silence, waiting.

A few minutes passed. Then Jim and Ferdie emerged. Jim shook his head.

"He's not here. There's nothing in there."

Dan's shoulders slumped. He'd been so sure.

"But look," Susie said. "Ferdie's got something in his mouth."

Ferdie dropped a small piece of thin cloth at Jim's feet and barked.

"Well," Jim said slowly. "I gave Ferdie that jacket of Richard's to sniff. Usually he barks when he matches the scent. Let's take it back to the Coq d'Or and see if Kate recognises it. It looks as if it's been torn from something, maybe caught on one of these nails in the door. Could be from Richard's shirt, or shorts or something. If he really was here."

****

"Yes," Kate nodded. "It looks like the trousers he was wearing on the night of the storm. But not what he was wearing the other day. He had on thick cord trousers and a tartan shirt. It was cold….," her voice wavered.

"Shit," said John under his breath.

It looked as if their theories were just that. Theories. OK, they'd been right, or rather Dan had guessed right, about where Richard had ended up after the storm. And presumably that's where the drugs had been hidden. But there was no sign of him or the rest of the drugs now. The trail had gone cold.

15

"According to Capitaine Lolmède, what the one who survived the crash actually said was: 'floor', 'got to get the rest', 'we'll share it, Jimmy', 'get the rest, it's underneath', 'we'll share, get it', 'floor', 'under', 'got to get the rest', 'go back afterwards and get it, we'll share it', 'get the rest, Jimmy, it's underneath', 'we'll share, get it, go back.' " Phillippe looked up from his notebook and shrugged. "It was taped and then translated for the Capitaine by the gendarme from Fromac, the one who speaks very good English."

"So it must be in a cellar somewhere?" John suggested. "But where?"

Jim shook his head.

"Could be anywhere. Maybe even in the château."

"No," John shook his head. "I don't think so. We looked everywhere, and the police have been over it again today, with the dogs. There was no sign of any more sacks, or drugs. No sign of Richard either. And it's him we've got to find. Let the police look for the drugs. They must have taken him with them. Perhaps we should search the route from the château to where they crashed. They might have just dumped him."

"Dad, that's miles. We haven't time. I still think they probably took him to where the other drugs were stashed. The one in hospital kept saying "go back", didn't he? Like there was more still somewhere? And they wouldn't want to stop more than once, would they? If the other drugs were, like, really well-hidden, that'd be the ideal place to dump Richard so he wouldn't be found."

"Yes, Dan," replied John. "But where? That's our problem. All we know is 'underneath'."

"Dad, the Capitaine said they thought that the drugs were kept at Lalbenque, didn't he? You know, at first. Then they raided the house there and only found a few kilos? So they must have moved them to the *gariotte* where Richard was before the police raid? But what if they didn't move it all there? What if they split it up for safety? Then if the police had found one stash they might have stopped looking. And Joanne said the secret compartments in the van floor weren't full when they hit her over the head. So what if they'd gone to where the other stash was and stopped there to dump Richard and load more on, and there was too much? That might have been what he was mumbling about – where they had to go back to. They'd go back later and collect what was left, double-cross their boss. He said they'd split it, didn't he?"

John and Jim looked at each other. It sounded plausible, but was Dan's imagination running away with him? They didn't have anything better to go on. But it didn't get them much nearer to finding out where Richard was.

"OK," said Jim. "Let's assume Dan's right. They moved the drugs out of the house at Lalbenque and split it into two lots. One they hid in the *gariotte* near your place and the other they hid – somewhere else. They had to collect the second lot on their way up to the Channel port, and that's where they dumped Richard. Maybe there was too much to fit in the van, so they left it behind –'underneath' and planned to go back later for it. So, where would they have hidden the second lot? Somewhere not far away, I'd guess. Once they knew the police were onto them at Lalbenque, they had to move quickly. It seems as if they know the area well. And they'd only got as far as Souillac when they crashed. So I'd guess it's somewhere not far away. Maybe another *gariotte*?"

"Jim!" Phillippe threw up his hands. "Do you know how many there are in this region? It would be like looking for the needle in the haystack!"

"And anyway," John interjected. "He said 'underneath'. That must mean a cellar or something. *Gariottes* are built straight onto the earth, aren't they? They don't have a proper floor so you couldn't hide anything underneath."

They fell silent. Through the café windows they all watched as Kate Black opened the door of the Coq d'Or and peered out. She looked anxiously across the square, hesitating on the doorstep. Pat appeared in the doorway behind her and after a couple of minutes, they turned back indoors, then stopped again as a car drew up outside the hotel. Kate's expression changed from hope back to desperation. It was Chloe. Pat pointed to the café and led Kate back inside the hotel. A few minutes later, the café door opened and Chloe came in. Phillippe leapt up to meet her. She looked radiant. Joanne smiled wryly. At least she could understand what Nick had seen in Chloe.

"So," Phillippe concluded. "That's what we think we are looking for, Chloe. Probably a small stone barn with a cellar underneath, somewhere near here, or near Lalbenque. But we don't have any other clues and time is passing. I fear we may be too late already."

"Just a minute," Chloe broke in. "You said you thought it was probably another *gariotte*, Dan? But it had to have some sort of cellar? I think I might know where there is a *gariotte* like that."

All eyes turned to Chloe.

"Yes," she went on. "A while ago I went on a horse ride over on the Causse, near Lalbenque. We followed a route from that little book I've got, you know the one, Phillippe – *'Les marches du Sud Quercy'*. There are lots of *gariottes* around there, but we only ever saw one that was sort of two storeys. I don't know how common they are, but I've never seen another one. And it might be what you are looking for. I think it was quite near Lalbenque and certainly tucked away. Although as I recall, it wasn't on its own. I think there was a house nearby. So perhaps it isn't what you're looking for."

Jim and John looked at each other.

"What do you think, Phillippe?" asked Jim. "Are there likely to be many of these two storey *gariottes* around? I've never seen one, but then I've hardly been over that way at all."

"I don't know," replied Phillippe. "I've never seen one either. But then, I'm as much a stranger round here as you are."

"Dad," Dan was tugging at John's sleeve. "Dad, can't we go and see anyway? It might be the place. And it'd be better than sitting around here."

"Yes, Dad," Susie put in. "We need to find him as soon as we can. Please let's go and look."

"Can you remember how to find it again, Chloe?" John asked.

"Well, no," Chloe said.

Dan's face fell.

"But I've still got the book at home," she added.

"Right." Jim spoke with authority. "We'll follow you home and borrow the book and then we'll go on and find this *gariotte*. Then we'll know, one way or the other."

"What about the police?" asked Phillippe.

"You come over to Chloe's with us, then once we see where it is, you phone Capitaine Lolmède. Tell him where we've gone and we'll call him if we find anything. We don't want to have to wait for them before we go and have a look. Dan's right. Every minute counts."

****

"I know it's here somewhere."

Chloe rummaged in the stack of magazines.

"Yes, here it is," she said, pulling a small, cream-coloured booklet out of the heap and handing it to Jim.

Jim ran his eye down the index.

"Lalbenque," he read. "Page 22."

They all clustered around, peering at the line drawing of a route.

348

"Look!" Dan cried. "There are three *gariottes* marked! It must be one of those!"

"Let me have a look."

Chloe peered over his shoulder and looked at the page, shaking her head.

"No, I don't think so. I don't think this was the ride we went on. Let me have the book for a minute."

John and Jim exchanged glances. Perhaps this was a wild goose chase. Chloe flicked through the booklet. A minute or two later, she pointed to a page.

"Here! This is it. Look at that drawing!"

In the top corner of the page was a small sketch of a *gariotte*, showing a flight of steps leading up to the doorway. Underneath and to the left, the drawing showed another doorway.

"Yes!" shouted Dan. "This has got to be it!"

****

John pulled the Land Rover onto the verge and stopped the engine. Jim was already out of his van, Joanne beside him, holding Ferdie by his lead. On the opposite side of the narrow track was a low stone wall, behind that an overgrown garden and a ruined house. Another stone wall ran from the house along the edge of a field. Where it intersected with the boundary wall of the garden stood the round stone shelter with its pointed roof. A flight of uneven stone steps up the side of the wall led to an open doorway in the shelter, facing away from the road. Alongside the steps, at ground level, was another doorway, leading underneath the *gariotte*. There was no sign of life. No tracks showed in the long grass leading across the field to the *gariotte*. It didn't look as if anyone had been there for a long time. Jim and Joanne cautiously approached the *gariotte*.

Epilogue

Kent, December.

Alastair looked across at Kate, her face half-obscured in the fading light. A few moments later she resumed her story.

"He was in there, but he was dead when they found him."

She stopped again, staring into the fire.

"Dan had guessed right about everything. There was a sack underneath the *gariotte* full of hashish. But they were too late for Richard."

Alastair reached across and took her hand. They sat in silence for a long time. The story replayed itself in his mind. Poor, poor Kate. What she had been through. Richard's loyalty to him had had terrible results. Alastair felt the tears pricking his eyes. And Nick. He didn't know why Kate had fallen for Nick. Nor did she. He'd betrayed her but he didn't deserve his fate. And then there was their poor baby. And Joanne. He looked across at Kate.

"Kate," he spoke quietly. "Promise me you'll never leave me again."

****

Joanne hesitated at the end of the drive before she turned into the lane. She glanced at her watch. She was early. Should she call in on Alastair and Kate? No, better leave them to it. Give them a bit more time. She turned the Porsche right and headed towards the motorway. She made herself drive slowly. There was plenty of time to get to the Channel Tunnel and anyway the wedding wasn't until the next morning. Phillippe had arranged for them all to stay the night with Chloe at his uncle's estate just outside Paris. He would stay at his parents' apartment near the Louvre. Joanne smiled to herself. How proper!

The check-in for Eurotunnel was quiet. As she pulled into the parking area at the terminal, she spotted the Land Rover straight away. She flashed her lights and Dan and Susie came tumbling out, running over to her. Behind them, John stood by the driver's door, smiling. Joanne felt her heart turn over.

The End